Also by Leonard Schonberg

Deadly Indian Summer

Fish Heads

LEGACY

LEGACY

a novel by

Leonard
Schonberg

SUNSTONE
PRESS

SANTA FE

Sunstone books may be purchased for educational, business, or sales promotional use. For information please write: Special Markets Department, Sunstone Press, P.O. Box 2321, Santa Fe, New Mexico 87504-2321.

Library of Congress Cataloging-in-Publication Data:

Schonberg, Leonard, 1935–
    Legacy : a novel / by Leonard Schonberg.
        p. cm.
    ISBN: 0-86534-357-8
    1. Jews—United States—Fiction. 2. Jews—Austria—Fiction. 3. Jewish families—Fiction. 4. Jewish women—Fiction. 5. Austria—Fiction. I. Title.

    PS3569.C5258 L44 2002
    813'.54—dc   2002070533

Published in SUNSTONE PRESS
                  Post Office Box 2321
                  Santa Fe, NM 87504-2321 / USA
                  (505) 988-4418 / *orders only* (800) 243-5644
                  FAX (505) 988-1025
                  www.sunstonepress.com

In memory of Isedor and Annette

Think, oh, *think*, of being happy for a year—for a day!
How brilliantly blue the sky would be;
how swiftly and joyously would the green rivers run;
how madly, merrily triumphant the four winds of
heaven would sweep round the corners of the fair earth!
What would I not give for one day, one hour,
of that charmed thing Happiness!
What would I not give up? . . .

Mary MacLane
The Story of Mary MacLane

1

Isaac Schneider's long fingers deftly fed a swathe of silk fabric over the steel plate of his sewing machine, the needle rising and falling so rapidly its movement was a blur. He was one of three tailors employed by Julius Kaltbrenner, whose drygoods store was well-known in Lemberg and the surrounding towns for the quality of its fabrics and the fine workmanship of its tailors. Situated on one of the narrow streets radiating from Market Square, the store's location was ideal. It was only one block from the Rathaus, the tallest building on the square, making it easy to find even for visitors to the city. One had only to turn away from the heraldic lions over the Rathaus's main entrance and follow the street directly ahead.

Every customer entering the store was greeted personally by the owner, a short, corpulent man whose completely bald head contrasted strikingly with his full black moustache. Julius Kaltbrenner sat behind the counter, a potentate presiding over bolts of silk, wool and cotton fabrics and stacks of pattern books. To Julius, the aroma of the material was sweeter than the fragrance of lilies on the flower sellers' pushcarts in early summer.

The Kaltbrenners were natives of Lemberg, but Julius was the only member of his family who remained there. He had refused to follow his brothers to

Vienna. Even his two sons had moved there to seek their fortune. Julius had never regretted his decision to remain in Lemberg. The capital of Galicia, Lemberg was not only a great commercial and rail center, but its location in the northern foothills of the Carpathian Mountains made it possible for Julius to indulge his passion for hiking whenever time permitted. His business, now thirty years old, was thriving. The sewing machines at the rear of the store hummed continuously.

Isaac hunched over his machine, concentrating on the delicate seam he stitched. His light brown hair was cut short, revealing a slight tendency to baldness that would assert itself with the years. It was Isaac to whom Julius Kaltbrenner entrusted the most complicated work, especially when it involved his best customers. Isaac had been with Kaltbrenner for almost fifteen years, more than twice as long as the other two tailors, and his skill and reliability were recognized not only by the owner and customers, but also by his fellow tailors.

On this particular November afternoon in 1913 most Austrians worried about the troubles in the Balkans. Europe hovered on the brink of war. Isaac, however, thought of the dinner his wife, Rachel, was preparing to celebrate his thirty-eighth birthday. Lost in the rhythmic whirring of the foot treadles and pounding needles, he was unaware that the door to the rear of the shop had opened. His twelve-year-old daughter, Hannah, a small dark-haired child who looked younger than her age, peered into the room, then ran to him and threw her arms around his neck.

"Happy birthday, poppa!" she cried, her dark brown eyes shining with happiness.

Much to the amusement of his co-workers, the startled Isaac almost fell off his chair. Although he discouraged her visits when he was working, Isaac was never able to hide his pleasure at seeing her. Fortunately, Mr. Kaltbrenner was equally charmed by the girl and, without her father knowing, invariably gave her a coin to buy candy when she visited the shop.

"Go home and help your mother with dinner," Isaac said, trying to muster a serious expression.

Hannah planted a kiss on his cheek and disappeared into the store. She picked up the schoolbooks she had left on the counter and tucked them under her arm. Mr. Kaltbrenner interrogated her with mock severity: "You are studying hard, Hannah? Being a good girl?" Before she could answer he whisked a shiny coin from his vest pocket and held it out to her. "Hannah, for being a good girl, buy yourself a candy." She thanked him delightedly, her hand just closing around the coin as the front door of the store opened. Two fashionably dressed women engaged in animated conversation entered.

"Good afternoon, ladies," said Kaltbrenner, patting Hannah on the head in a gesture of dismissal.

"Oh, Mr. Kaltbrenner, so much excitement with the fire," said one of the women.

"Fire?"

"On Bergstrasse. Five houses already burned to the ground."

"Bergstrasse!" exclaimed Hannah. "I live on Bergstrasse."

The women looked at her.

"I'm sure it's not your house," said Mr. Kaltbrenner, irritated by Hannah's interrupting his conversation with potential customers.

"On the block where Rosenberg's pastry shop is," the second woman said, watching Hannah.

The child's eyes opened wide. "That's the block where I live."

Seeing her on the verge of tears, Kaltbrenner excused himself and opened the rear door to call for Isaac.

"You had better go home with your daughter. These ladies inform me there is a fire in your neighborhood and the news has upset Hannah."

Isaac, surprised by the interruption of his work, stepped from the work-shop into the store. He looked in confusion at his daughter and Kaltbrenner, then at the customers. "I—I don't understand," he said.

"Poppa, there's a fire where we live," Hannah whimpered.

"A fire? What fire?"

The woman who had reported the news approached him and gently touched his arm. "I'm afraid I unintentionally upset your daughter. There's a fire on the Bergstrasse."

"It's on our block," cried Hannah. "She said it was the block with Rosenberg's pastry shop."

Isaac looked at the woman for confirmation. "Is it the block with the pastry shop?"

Before she could answer, Isaac grabbed Hannah's hand and raced from the

13

store. The other two tailors, curious about the commotion, poked their heads through the rear door and watched in amazement as the owner rushed to the front door of the store.

"Your jacket!" Kaltbrenner yelled. "You don't have your jacket!"

But Isaac and Hannah were already far down the block, hurrying past startled shoppers. Isaac, in his shirtsleeves, was oblivious to the late autumn chill. Hannah, too, paid no heed to the wind stinging her tear-moistened cheeks. They raced through Market Square, past the eighteenth-century fountains and the much older Renaissance-style Black House, former home of the secretary to the Polish king. The smell of smoke was heavy in the air as they emerged onto the narrow Bergstrasse. Here they became part of a crowd running toward billowing clouds of smoke and flames shooting from the tops of ancient four-storey buildings.

The fire brigade wagon, iron bells clanging, forced its way through the dense throng. Isaac and Hannah reached the block on which they lived but a line of policemen blocked their way. The building occupied at street level by Rosenberg's pastry shop, and the adjoining apartment building, in which the Schneiders lived, had been reduced to smoking rubble. Two nearby residential buildings were enveloped in flames and the crowd watched in horror as several occupants leaped to their deaths from the upper floor windows to the cobbled streets below. Sweating, shouting men, their faces soot-blackened, uncoiled loops of heavy canvas hoses and carried bucketfuls of water in a vain attempt to contain the blaze.

In spite of the searing heat, Hannah was aware that her father's hand, in which her own was still tightly held, had become cold. Isaac, his gaze fixed upon the blackened, smoking timbers of the building next to the pastry shop, pushed through the bystanders, dragging Hannah behind him. A policeman suddenly stepped in front of him, pushing him back roughly.

"You must not go any closer," he said gruffly.

"Where are the people from that house?" Isaac asked, his trembling finger pointing to it.

The policeman turned for an instant, then looked back at him. "All dead, I'm afraid. The fire that started in the bakery burned too quickly for anyone to get out."

"I lived there." Isaac mouthed the words, his throat choking the sounds as his face twisted in a futile effort to control the suffocating panic in his chest. "My wife was at home," he cried.

For the first time since leaving Kaltbrenner's store, Isaac was aware of the cold. Shaking, he dropped Hannah's hand. She began to wail. The policeman called to a nurse standing next to a horse-drawn ambulance to help him. Isaac was dimly aware of a blanket being placed around his shoulders as the policeman and nurse led him and Hannah toward the ambulance. He stumbled forward, his face turned toward the smoldering building. He felt himself losing consciousness, the smoke and flames fusing into a wall of blackness before his eyes. Hannah's sobbing sounded faint and far away. Only the hands of the policeman, gripping Isaac under his arms, prevented him from falling.

Another policeman approached them, leading a grey-haired woman still wearing her patched and faded kitchen apron tied high above her ample bosom. Isaac recognized the widow Herzel, an old friend of Rachel's parents who lived in the house directly opposite his own. She placed her hands on Hannah's shoulders and gazed at Isaac, her eyes brimming with tears.

"Mr. Schneider, it happened so fast. Believe me, your Rachel didn't suffer. I looked out of my window and saw the smoke coming from the pastry shop. Then there were flames everywhere. No one had time to get out. I'm so sorry. Please, you and Hannah come with me."

She wrapped one arm around Hannah's shoulders and eased her toward her building. Isaac followed numbly behind. They soon sat huddled together on the sofa in the Herzel apartment, Isaac shivering and Hannah crying softly, while the widow, who had known unhappiness in her lifetime, too, prepared tea for them. For the rest of that afternoon they sat in the darkened living room, the tea in their cups untouched.

"Poppa, what are we going to do?" Hannah asked.

"For now, you stay with me," said the kindly widow. "I have an extra bed and your father can sleep on the sofa."

Their conversation was interrupted by a knock on the door. The widow crossed the room and cautiously opened the heavy wooden door. A policeman stood in the dark hall. He bowed formally to her and she led him into the apartment. Staring uncomfortably at Isaac and Hannah, he sat down opposite them and cleared his throat.

"I'm sorry to trouble you, sir. We're trying to identify the victims of the fire. I understand you lived in one of the buildings."

"Number seventeen," said Isaac, his voice hollow. "We lived in an apartment on the second floor. Only my wife was at home."

The policeman pulled a small notebook from his jacket pocket. "May I please have your wife's full name and date of birth."

"Rachel Friedman Schneider. She was born April 4th, 1879 here in Lemberg."

"And your name?"

"Isaac Schneider."

"I cannot ask you to identify the body, Mr. Schneider. The fire—you understand?"

Isaac nodded dully.

The policeman reached again into his pocket. "We found this on the body. Do you recognize it?"

Isaac stared at the soot-covered wedding ring resting on the man's palm. His hand trembled as he picked it up. He wiped the inside of the ring with his finger. Rachel had insisted that the jeweler engrave Isaac's initials and hers in the metal. Sobbing, Isaac buried his face in his hands.

"We will need to know the funeral plans, but you can inform us tomorrow," said the policeman, putting away his pad. "We'll hold . . ." He hesitated. ". . . the body . . . until then."

He stood up and was led to the door by the widow Herzel. As if with an afterthought, he paused and turned toward Isaac. "Please accept my condolences on your loss."

Isaac spent that night next to the stove in the Herzel kitchen. He sat rigidly in a hard wooden chair, staring at the wall in front of him. The widow had suggested calling for the rabbi, but Isaac, who was not a religious man, shook his head in a forceful refusal.

Early the following morning, while the widow and Hannah slept, he wrapped himself in the blanket he'd been given and quietly left the apartment, stepping out into a cold grey dawn. The last vestiges of smoke curled from the charred remains of the burnt buildings. Standing in front of the rubble of his own building, he poked at the blackened wood, first with his shoe, then with a stick he had picked up, as if by some miracle his wife would appear from the debris.

A solitary water wagon remained parked near the burned-out area. Two firemen, one lugging a length of hose, prodded through the blackened beams and rubble, searching for live embers, directing a stream of water at any smoldering ashes.

Not since the death of his parents during a typhoid epidemic twenty years earlier had Isaac thought of the possibility of tragedy befalling anyone dear to him. Never once had he lit a memorial candle for his mother and father or prayed for God's intercession to protect those he loved. Now, in a city known for its churches and synagogues, he envied those who believed in a divine purpose. Only last Sunday he had strolled with his wife and daughter past the Church of the Assumption, the three of them stopping to examine the sculptured frieze of Biblical scenes on the outer walls of the church. Watching the worshippers emerge from the basilica after the mass, he had placed his lips next to Rachel's ear, commenting on the primitive foolishness of these people. If only there were a God, he thought now, who could return my Rachel to me.

As the sun's rays penetrated the smoky haze that hung over the Bergstrasse, a few pedestrians, casting saddened and curious glances in his direction, hurried by. Isaac knew he should return to the apartment before Hannah awakened but what comfort could he offer her, he wondered, when he himself did not know what to do.

The rumble of traffic on the street put an end to Isaac's reverie. People were heading to work. He wondered if Mr. Kaltbrenner would be expecting him at the store.

He was suddenly startled by a voice behind him. "I'm so sorry."

Isaac turned to see Tarnov, the postman, standing stiff and formal in his blue uniform.

"It's terrible, the fire. I was late making my mail deliveries yesterday. When I arrived, the buildings were burning and the police would not let anyone through. I saw you and your daughter but . . ." He spread his hands in a helpless gesture. "I have a letter for you from abroad. I was hoping I would be able to find you today."

Isaac stared at him, barely comprehending what he was saying. Tarnov, searching through the contents of the leather pouch he carried over his shoulder, extracted a letter and handed it to Isaac.

"Herr Schneider, my condolences," he murmured. Then he turned away to continue his rounds.

Isaac stared at the letter. The stamps were foreign. He recognized the handwriting of his older brother, Morris, his only living relative, who had left for America six months before. This was the first letter Isaac had received from him. He opened the envelope carefully, as if afraid he would damage its contents. From within the tissue-thin folds, a green banknote fluttered to the ground, coming to rest on a charred piece of wood. Isaac picked it up and stared at the numeral 100 emblazoned on its corners. Although he had no idea of the value of American money, he guessed that he held a bill of great value in his hand.

Morris' letter, written in a mixture of German and Yiddish, told of his work in a factory, where he had been taught to operate a lathe. America, he wrote, was truly a land of opportunity. Isaac, he said, should bring his wife and daughter and join him in New York. He warned his brother not to delay since he had read in the Jewish Daily Forward that war in Europe was imminent. The money he had enclosed would cover their passage from Bremen.

Had the letter arrived two days earlier, Isaac would have laughed at his brother's alarm. Isaac liked living in Lemberg and enjoyed his work at Kaltbrenner's. There would have been no reason for him to leave. Yes, war might come. But then again, it might not. Some people always looked on the dark side of things.

Now everything had changed. He and Hannah were alone, depending on a neighbor for the roof over their heads. Even if he were to find a new apartment, how would he be able to endure the sight each day of Bergstrasse, the street that had become the funeral pyre of his beloved wife? At least in America he would be with his brother and Hannah would have an uncle.

Still hugging the blanket to his shoulders, he climbed the steps to the widow's apartment and pushed open the door. Hannah, standing by the window, turned to face him. Seeing the deep shadows under his daughter's tear-swollen eyes, Isaac struggled not to cry.

"Hannah was worried about you. I'll prepare some breakfast now," the widow Herzel said, handing him a cup of tea and going into the kitchen.

Isaac went to his daughter's side. "I have a letter from your Uncle Morris," he said softly. "He wants us to join him in America."

Hannah looked at him with a vacant expression. If only I could suffer her grief as well as my own, Isaac thought. "I must make the funeral arrangements this morning," he said to her, trying to keep his voice under control. "After we say goodbye to your mother, I'll go to the steamship office to book our passage to America. There's nothing for us here now, Hannah."

"Mr. Schneider, let me help you," the widow Herzel said. "I know the rabbi. He was so good to me when my Mordechai died."

The following afternoon, Isaac and Hannah stood in silence at an open gravesite in the Jewish cemetery near the outer walls of the town. Isaac wore a dark suit that had belonged to the widow Herzel's late husband. She had even given him her husband's yarmulke for the funeral, one she had embroidered herself.

Although Isaac had rejected the tenets of Judaism in his adolescence, he reluctantly permitted the rabbi to intone the prayers for the dead. Rachel's parents, buried in the adjoining plot, had been orthodox Jews. Rachel herself, after her marriage, had abandoned many of the orthodox restrictions on women, such as shaving her head and wearing a wig, but she had continued to honor the sabbath, setting the table with the good German china she had inherited from her mother and lighting the sabbath candles. And each year she lovingly prepared Passover delicacies, Purim pastries, and Chanukah treats. Nonetheless, Isaac had always been uncertain about her true beliefs. For that reason, and out of respect for her family, he allowed the rabbi to chant the Kaddish.

Among the small group of mourners, most of them friends of Rachel, were the widow Herzel, her mouth set grimly against the painful memories of her own loved ones' funerals, and Mr. Kaltbrenner, whose genuine affection for Isaac caused him to grieve as if he were a family member.

Hannah, whose tears were exhausted, kept her head lowered as the unadorned pine box with her mother's remains was lowered. Isaac knelt to scoop a handful of cold, damp earth, hesitated, then tossed it onto the coffin. The splatter of the soil dropping on the wooden box struck Isaac like physical blows. Hannah followed her father's lead. Each mourner completed the same ritual and stepped aside. Hannah and Isaac silently accepted their embraces as they left the graveside.

Isaac, pausing before the tombstones of Rachel's parents, was unable to dispel a pang of guilt. Rachel's stone, in accordance with the Jewish religion, would not be unveiled for a year. He knew it would be impossible for him to be present.

As the service ended, Isaac approached Mr. Kaltbrenner and informed him of his decision to join his brother in America. Kaltbrenner nodded, as if he had expected the news, and placed his arm around Isaac's shoulders. "I will come in your stead for the unveiling," he said, as if reading Isaac's thoughts. He handed Isaac an envelope. "Please accept this for your years of service. It will help you and Hannah in America."

One week later, Isaac and Hannah were ready to begin their journey. In a final act of kindness, the widow Herzel presented Isaac with all of the clothes belonging to her deceased husband and, even more important, took Hannah shopping to replace the clothes and shoes she had lost in the fire. Now their two small valises stood at the door of the widow's apartment. Ignoring the woman's protests, Isaac placed some of the money given to him by Mr. Kaltbrenner in her hand and thanked her for all she had done for them.

2

It was the last day of November. A gray sky pressed down on the city as their taxi rattled over the cobblestone streets of Lemberg. The city, named centuries earlier by Prince Daniel of Galich for his son Lev, was still the major link between Kiev and Vienna. Isaac stared at the lions embossed on the decorative metal and chiselled stone-work of the imperial buildings as if seeing them for the first time. Hannah sat rigidly, looking straight ahead through the cab's windscreen. She thought only of the gaping hole in the cemetery that had received her mother's coffin. It had begun to sleet. Strangely, it comforted her to think of her mother mantled under a protective shroud of snow.

The train station was crowded with passengers and their friends and relatives who had come to wish them farewell. Women in traditional peasant costumes, men in three-piece suits, and Orthodox Jews wearing black caftans and long sidelocks jostled with soldiers in braided uniforms and food vendors hawking breads, bottled water and fruit. The babble of Emperor Franz Joseph's Austro-Hungarian Empire—German, Russian, Yiddish, Ukrainian and Hungarian—rose around them. Pushing their way past the luggage carts and peddlers, Isaac and Hannah made their way to the ticket window. Isaac held his daughter's hand with a firm grip. Slipping the money under the worn iron grillwork, Isaac requested two second-class tickets to Bremen. The ticket agent, a wizened man who appeared to have shrunk inside his uniform, shook his head. "America, America. They all want to go to America," he mumbled to himself.

"Platform three. Departure in thirty minutes," he said, brusquely shoving the tickets beneath the grill.

Neither Isaac nor Hannah had ever been on a train. Uncertain as to the procedure, they followed other passengers into one of the second-class cars. Seeing that people selected seats at random, they quickly chose theirs and Isaac placed their valises in the overhead rack before taking his seat next to Hannah. They huddled close to one another on the hard wooden bench, each oppressed with sadness at leaving their home and by the knowledge that they would never again see Rachel's grave.

An old woman wearing a tattered overcoat and an embroidered kerchief sat down next to Isaac and placed the covered straw basket she carried in her lap. Their section of the car was soon filled with the sour smell of cheese.

Isaac jumped as the train shuddered into motion. A blast from its whistle pierced the air. Slowly the station disappeared from view and soon Lemberg itself receded into the distance. As the train rounded its first curve, they caught a glimpse of the Carpathians, but the mountains were soon erased from view by snow, falling heavier now and settling on the rolling farmland. Isaac placed his hand on Hannah's, as much to comfort himself as her.

The train made slow progress through the snow-covered landscape. Isaac patted the inside pocket of his jacket many times to reassure himself that their North Bremen Line boat tickets were there. When they arrived in Cracow almost nine hours later, night had fallen. Isaac bought rolls, hard-boiled eggs and tea from a vendor on the platform. After they had eaten, he and Hannah dozed fitfully as they rocked in their hard wooden seats with the motion of the train.

Just before dawn the train pulled into Prague. Hannah and Isaac, their eyes dazed with sleep, were awakened by the conductor, who announced that they would be in the station for one hour while the train changed crews. Isaac heaved their valises from the overhead rack onto the wood bench. Grasping them tightly, they stepped out onto the platform. The one-hour stop gave them time to breakfast in the station restaurant, Isaac anxiously watching the wall clock while they ate.

They reboarded, only to find their seats filled. Moving through the crowded car, they found two seats on opposite sides of the aisle. Isaac stored their baggage, sat down and leaned forward to look at Hannah. She had rested her head against the window, her face pale and tired. He smiled reassuringly to her and she closed her eyes, her lips smiling in reply. As the train pulled out, Isaac got up to use the lavatory at the end of the car, taking his place behind a passenger who waited his turn.

The man in front of him, an elderly, ruddy-faced Austrian with a thick white moustache, turned to face him.

"Are you travelling to Germany?" he asked.

When Isaac nodded, the man asked if the young lady with him was his daughter. Isaac, made uncomfortable by the questioning, replied curtly.

Undeterred, the old man continued softly. "I have some advice for you. The Austrian officials are making it difficult for young, able-bodied men to leave the country. Having your daughter with you will not help. There is a war coming, you know."

"But I am not so young," protested Isaac, suddenly frightened.

"Young enough to serve in the emperor's army. I suggest you get off at the border and then reboard the train when it starts to move. Otherwise, they will see your documents and send you back where you came from."

"What if I tell them I will only be in Germany for a short visit?"

The lavatory's occupant had left and the old man, before entering, looked over his shoulder. "Take my advice," he said, closing the door behind him.

When Isaac returned to his seat, he was too worried to close his eyes. Hannah, thoroughly exhausted, slept with her chin on her chest. Being sent back to Lemberg was something Isaac had never considered. Perhaps he should have paid closer attention to politics. Even his brother, Morris, thousands of miles away in America, had warned him that war was imminent.

Isaac had no idea how far they were from the German border. As the wintry morning light filtered through the windows, Hannah awoke. She noticed his agitation and stood up, squirming past the passengers seated beside her.

"What is it, poppa?" she whispered, bending toward him.

Trying not to alarm her, Isaac replied that they would have to leave the train for a short time before entering Germany. "Just stay close to me," he said.

As they neared the demarcation line, the train suddenly slowed. Empty snow-covered fields spread out on both sides of the track. The train came to a halt opposite a solitary stone and stucco structure, built in the ponderous style of the Austrian capital. A squat cupola topped the massive squareness of the customs building. Uniformed Austrian officials stood on the platform, waiting to board. Isaac stood up as disembarking passengers began to gather their luggage from the overhead racks. He placed their valises in the aisle and motioned to Hannah to come with him.

As they moved down the aisle Isaac spotted the old man who had warned him. Their eyes met and the old man nodded.

"Follow me," Isaac said. "This is where we get off for a little while."

They stepped down the iron steps into the frigid morning air. A dirt road paralleling the railroad track was blocked by two gates that were manually raised and lowered by German and Austrian guards who inspected the documents of travellers crossing the border on foot or by vehicle. A small truck and two horse-drawn carts awaited inspection.

Isaac stood on the platform with Hannah at his side as the Austrian officials boarded the train. A few passengers were still disembarking, struggling to raise their heavy bags over the railing of the steps. Isaac stood on tiptoe, looking up and down the platform, as if he expected someone. At the same time he watched the progress of the uniformed officials through the windows of the train, trying to make certain they were no longer in the car he and Hannah had been in.

"Who are you looking for, poppa?" asked Hannah.

Isaac didn't answer as he drew her toward the steps of their car. The train's whistle had already sounded. Their car lurched as the engine began to pull the long string of cars forward. A uniformed figure stepped down from the last car and Isaac pushed Hannah up the steps, following behind her. He opened the lavatory door and pulled her in with him, their valises in the cramped space making it almost impossible for him to lock the door behind him. There was no window in the stall and he could not be certain if all the officials had left the train, which was moving slowly.

Hannah began to protest, but Isaac hushed her. "Don't speak," he whispered, his heart pounding. It was only when the train had picked up speed that

Isaac opened the stall door and peered out cautiously. The only person he saw was the old Austrian, still standing in the aisle. He nodded reassuringly to Isaac.

"We can take our seats now," Isaac said, leading Hannah through the swaying car. "It's safe."

It was early evening when they arrived in Bremen. Tired and hungry, Isaac and Hannah walked through a cold, soot-laden ground fog searching for a cafe they could afford. The one Isaac chose was crowded with workers lining up for their dinner. Each time the door to the kitchen opened, clouds of steam enveloped the servers as they ladled portions onto plates. Isaac and Hannah had eaten very little during their train journey. Now they stuffed themselves with bread, soup, meat and potatoes. Isaac, sated, pushed his chair back and waited for Hannah to finish. She gave her father a wan smile as she placed her knife and fork on the table, the fatigue on her face making her look older than her twelve years. Isaac berated himself for putting her through the rigors of this journey, wondering if he had been too impetuous. Driven by his own need to escape from Lemberg, so crowded with memories for him, he had given Hannah no time to cope with the death of her mother. Perhaps he should have found a new apartment in Lemberg. Then they could have gone on with their lives. Well, it was too late now, he thought bitterly. He paid for their meal and asked the proprietor where they might find an inexpensive hotel near the docks. She directed him to the Leuchtturm, situated two blocks from the pier where North Bremen Line ships were moored. It was only a short walk from the cafe and the proprietor assured Isaac that it was respectable in spite of its appearance.

The diffuse glow from the street lights, obscured by the fog, was as somber as Isaac's mood as they walked along the narrow cobblestone streets. Hannah threw furtive glances at the women standing suggestively in darkened doorways, soliciting the sailors who wandered down the street in search of a companion for the night.

Isaac sniffed at the air, his spirits faintly revived by the salt smell of the sea. "Do you smell the ocean, Hannah? We must be very close to the water."

Moments later, they arrived at their hotel, a run-down three-storey establishment built of the same coarse-grained grey stone as the nearby docks and harbor breaks. Inside, the walls were peeling and mildewed. Two tattered leather sofas and dark wooden chairs cluttered the lobby, where a pasty-faced, bald man dozed in a chair behind the clerk's desk. Isaac awakened him with a loud "good evening." He rose, grumbling. "One room? One night?" Isaac signed the ledger and paid for the night in advance. The clerk pushed the key across the desk and slumped into his chair to resume his slumber.

"He must be as tired as we are," Isaac whispered to Hannah, as they carried their valises up to the second floor. Their room was surprisingly clean given the appearance of the lobby. Too exhausted to change into night clothes, they collapsed onto their beds. Isaac was soon snoring. Hannah got up to cover him with a blanket, then went back to her bed. She lay there listening to the fog horns, an eerie sound that somehow reminded her of the Hebrew prayers chanted by the rabbi at her mother's grave. Her last thought before drifting off to sleep was how far away from home she was.

Hours later Isaac sat up abruptly, the blanket tangled about his legs. Watery morning light filtered into their room. He blinked in confusion, trying to remember where he was. Looking at his pocketwatch, he saw it was almost seven. Their ship was scheduled to sail at eleven.

Hannah groaned and rolled reluctantly into a sitting position as Isaac shook her gently to awaken her.

"Come," he said, "it's time to get up. We'll get some breakfast and walk over to the ship."

The desk clerk sat sleeping in the same chair where they had found him the night before, his mouth open. A thin line of drool ran down his chin. Isaac left the key on the desk and he and Hannah stepped out into a morning fog so thick they could not see more than a half-block ahead of them.

Isaac looked with concern at Hannah, who shivered in the damp air as she stumbled along sleepily at his side. Each carried a valise, but neither he nor Hannah had opened them since leaving Lemberg. Isaac steered Hannah across the street towards a basement tavern, advertised by a small sign swaying in the grey mist. They descended the broad stone steps, slick in the morning's dampness, and entered. Men who appeared to be dock workers stood at the bar and filled the benches and tables crowded together in the stone-vaulted room. The smell of their unwashed bodies and the beer they drank, although it was early morning, was heavy in the air. Hannah and Isaac meekly ordered their breakfast, rolls and tea, and carried it to a table in the corner. They ate quickly, listening to the men's coarse German dialect, then left, relieved to be out again in the salt-laden air.

Fully awake now, they walked briskly behind groups of sailors heading to the waterfront. Isaac hoped the men would lead them to their ship. Gulls swooped down suddenly like white kites falling out of the fog, which grew denser as they approached the water. It wasn't until they were almost at the dock that they saw the hull of their ship looming above them, its top deck and slanting smokestacks hidden in the thick mist. Passengers were boarding, crossing narrow ramps extending from both the midportion and stern of the ship to the dock. Noticing how well-dressed the passengers on the front ramp were, Isaac guided Hannah toward the stern, where they fell in behind a crowd of people who reminded Hannah of home and Lemberg—women in kerchiefs wearing thick wool peasant skirts and carrying small children in their arms; men dressed in cheap suits or caftans, trying to keep an eye on their children while struggling with bulging suitcases, wicker baskets and cloth-wrapped parcels. All around them, people laughed, cried, and called out, panic-stricken, to children who momentarily disappeared from their parents' sight.

Isaac presented their tickets to the white-uniformed official at the head of the ramp. He barked at them in coarse German to follow those in front of them down to steerage. His heart sank as they descended into the cavernous, dimly-lit bowels of the ship. The vast steerage hold was filled with rows of iron cots, each covered with a thin, stained mattress. Following the example of the others, Isaac chose two adjoining cots, and he and Hannah deposited their valises on the grimy mattresses. In spite of the vastness of the room, the air was musty, filled already with the odors of their fellow passengers. No curtains separated the beds and Isaac knew there would be no way to be alone and away from the gaze of hundreds of fellow passengers during the trip. Worse than the assorted smells was the deafening throb of the engines, the cries of babies, and the hundreds of simultaneous conversations conducted in many languages, some of which Isaac had never heard before. He wondered how they would endure this bedlam for the week and a half-long crossing.

On the cot next to theirs a haggard woman sat nursing an infant at her flattened breast. Her other child, barely out of infancy, slept on the filthy mattress, oblivious to the commotion that swirled around him. Isaac, already longing to breathe fresh air, spoke to the woman in German and asked if she would guard their bags. The woman looked at him apathetically, not understanding what he had said. Isaac asked again, first in Russian and then in Polish. This time there was a spark of comprehension in the woman's lustreless eyes and she nodded.

Isaac threaded his way through the hold with Hannah in tow, stepping over piles of luggage that filled the aisles between the cots, until they reached the stairs leading to the deck. They stood at the railing, breathing deeply and watching the remaining passengers board. Isaac was amazed that the ship, in spite of its size, could hold so many people, enough to make up the population of a fair-sized Galician town. He could not understand how it remained afloat with such a dense human cargo.

Finally, more than an hour after their scheduled departure time, the ramps were lowered from the ship and the hawsers released to be hauled on board. Two tugs nudged the ship from its berth, while crowds of people on shore waved and cried their last farewells. A misty rain replaced the fog, which had lifted earlier, and obscured their view of the coast. Isaac stood with his arm around Hannah's shoulder, watching the receding coastline and the gulls hovering above the ship as it sliced its way through harbor waters, flat and calm before them.

It was only when they left the protection of Bremen's gulf and entered the open expanse of the North Sea that Isaac had his first intimation of what they could expect on their voyage. A stiff wind blew from the north and the misty rain changed quickly to driving gusts of sleet and snow. The temperature dropped and Isaac and Hannah huddled against each other shivering. The grey-green water swirled and frothed, hurling waves against the rocking hull of the ship and covering them with clouds of spray.

"We'd better go inside," Isaac sighed, reluctant to return to the fetid atmosphere below deck.

For the next four days the ship, battered by North Atlantic storms, rolled and creaked, sinking into the troughs of the ocean and rising on the crest of towering waves. It seemed impossible that the steel plates of the hull could resist the battering force of the roiling waters. At first the steerage passengers feared imminent death, but after the second day of storms they groaned in their seasick misery, many of them praying for a rapid end to their suffering, even if it meant going to a watery grave. Isaac, sprawled on his cot, sporadically vomited rancid-tasting bile into a bucket shared by a dozen passengers. He fervently wished that he and Hannah, who fared no better, had been at home with Rachel when the fire struck. Surely death was better than enduring this sickness day after day.

And then, suddenly, the storms abated. The steerage passengers staggered out onto the decks and breathed the cold ocean air. Scattered whitecaps were all that remained of the ocean's spent fury. Inhaling the sea air and stretching their legs on walks around the open deck made it even more difficult to re-enter the thick atmosphere of the cramped steerage hold. Isaac and Hannah had tasted nothing but water and tea for days and held down almost none of it. They leaned weakly against the cold metallic railing, ignoring the icy winds that penetrated their clothes. For the first time in almost a week, they were aware of being hungry. They waited impatiently for the dry bread, watery cabbage soup, and potatoes that would be served for lunch.

As their strength returned, they gradually found it possible to tolerate the spells of bad weather, which were less severe as they approached the east coast of America. Finally, on a day neither of them would ever forget, land was sighted. Excitement swept through the steerage quarters as women began frantically to repack their hampers and baskets. By late morning the ship was easing its way into New York's harbor past the Statue of Liberty, which hovered, a colossus of tarnished green metal, above them. Many of the passengers lining the decks wept unashamedly, Isaac among them, while others cheered and the more religious among them prayed aloud, giving thanks for their deliverance from the sea and from the lives they had left behind.

3

Hannah and Isaac joined the crush of passengers streaming onto Ellis Island. Cordoned into long rows by rope barriers, the lines inched forward as the immigrants filed past immigration officials and white-coated doctors who peered down their throats and listened to their chests. Isaac scanned the faces in the crowd awaiting the new arrivals, wondering how he would ever find his brother in that multitude, when he suddenly heard his name called. Moments later he was gripped in Morris' embrace, both of them laughing and crying at the same time. Morris hugged and kissed Hannah, too, before looking around in confusion.

"Where's Rachel?" he asked.

He listened silently, his face drawn and pale, as Isaac told him about the fire. Isaac noticed with concern that Morris was no longer the ruggedly healthy brother he had known in Europe. His face had a sickly yellow pallor that spread into the whites of his eyes.

"You don't look well," Isaac said. "What's wrong?"

"I'm fine," said Morris, dismissing his brother's concern. "It's just so awful what you've told me. May Rachel rest in peace, brother." He scanned Isaac's face. "Come, let's go home."

Morris led them to the departure docks where the Immigration Service ferried new immigrants from the safety of the island to the bustle of Manhattan's south port. The grim brick infirmary buildings and barracks opposite the main hall reminded them that there were immigrants unlucky enough to be denied entry to America. Finally it was their turn to board the ferry. Morris stood quietly beside Isaac, his hand on Hannah's shoulder as the craft backed away from the dock. He surveyed the city's skyline as if he, too, were seeing it through their astonished eyes.

Once on land, Morris, with the practiced skill of a real New Yorker, hailed a cab and loaded the valises onto the luggage rack as Isaac and Hannah clambered into the rear seat. As the taxi crept slowly through the dense traffic of lower Manhattan, Hannah stared wide-eyed at the towering buildings and congested streets. But not even the excitement of this bustling metropolis prevented Isaac from casting furtive, worried glances at his brother.

They stopped on Houston Street in front of a four-storey red-brick tenement building girded with metal fire-escapes. Isaac and Hannah followed Morris up the steps to his third-floor apartment. Odors of cabbage and pickled herring filling the hallway made Isaac feel at home. Morris, breathing heavily, trudged slowly up the steps, his brother and niece exchanging worried looks each time he paused to catch his breath.

Isaac and Hannah were shocked by both the size and condition of Morris' apartment. It was not what they'd expected to find in America. The kitchen, living room and bedroom would have fit into the living room alone of the apartment they had lived in in Lemberg. The walls were grime-covered and the ceiling peeling and flaking, exposing wide strips of bare lathe and plaster. A long time had passed since any repairs had been made to the rooms. What passed as furniture—tattered chairs and sofa, a stained wooden kitchen table, and a small chest of drawers tilting forward due to the mismatched wooden blocks that replaced its missing legs—made it difficult to move about. Two beds filled the small bedroom, while a cot, reminiscent of the ones they'd had in steerage, took up a good part of the living room. The kitchen was just a corner of the living room. Roaches scrambled freely over the dirty dishes stacked in the sink and on the blackened, food-encrusted surface of the two-burner cast-iron stove.

"I apologize for the condition of the place," Morris said, sitting down heavily in an upholstered chair. "My work leaves me little time to clean."

"Don't worry, uncle," Hannah said quickly, "I'll do that for you."

Morris looked affectionately at the two of them. "She just crossed an ocean and already she's thinking of cleaning," he said. "First, you catch up on your rest. One of my neighbors was kind enough to lend me the cot." He pointed to the bedroom as he looked at his brother. "I thought you and Rachel . . ." His hand dropped and he shook his head sadly. "I'm so sorry, Isaac," he murmured. "What can I say?" He sighed deeply.

"Your work goes well?" Isaac asked.

"Yes. Long hours, but I'm saving some money. I hope that soon I'll have enough to get a nicer apartment, one without such junk." He made a sweeping gesture with his hand.

"And your health?" Isaac asked, still discomfited by his brother's sickly appearance.

"I've been a little run-down these past few weeks. But now that I have family here, I feel better already."

"You didn't have to work today?"

"I told my boss my family was arriving from Europe. He's a *landsman*, a fellow Galician, so he understands. But now, we have to celebrate your arrival." He pushed himself to his feet and retrieved a dark green bottle and three short, thick glasses from a small cabinet in the kitchen. "I got some schnapps for the occasion. I have seltzer, too, Hannah, but it's not cold," he said apologetically. "Someday, when I've saved enough, I'll buy an icebox."

"Water will be fine for me, uncle."

"Just water?" Morris raised his eyebrows in mock surprise. "Well, all right, you'll have an appetite for dinner. We're going to have a real Jewish meal. A delicatessen on the next block has wonderful food, blinis and stuffed cabbage just like in Lemberg."

"But the expense," Isaac protested. "You don't have to go to that bother."

"For my brother and niece he calls it a bother," he said, shaking his head.

For the rest of that afternoon, they talked of Lemberg and Rachel, of Mr. Kaltbrenner and the widow Herzel's kindness to Isaac and Hannah, and about Morris' life in New York since his arrival from Europe. He was more animated now, more like the Morris Isaac remembered. Perhaps their arrival would, as Morris said, have a salutory effect on his health.

Dinner that evening was a festive affair. In the same way that Hannah and Isaac brought life back to Morris, Morris' quiet humor was a balm for Isaac's sorrow. For the first time since Rachel's death, Isaac heard the sound of his own laughter. They feasted on stuffed cabbage and blinis, as delicious as Morris had promised. The delicatessen owner hovered around their table, going out of his way to see that their every need was satisfied. It was late when Hannah and Isaac stumbled exhausted up the stairs to the apartment behind Morris.

"I think New York is going to be good for us," said Isaac, wishing his brother goodnight and embracing him.

It was still dark when Isaac was awakened by the sound of Morris retching. A faint light was visible from the kitchen. Isaac got up quietly so as not to awaken Hannah, who was sleeping soundly in the other bed. He opened the bedroom door and stepped into the kitchen. Morris stood at the sink, his back to Isaac. Dim yellow light spread from the bare bulb dangling from a cord in the middle of the ceiling, casting long shadows on the walls and floor. Morris turned to face his brother. Isaac, seeing his brother's sickly yellow complexion intensified by the artificial light, was frightened.

"Morris, what is it?"

Morris made a dismissive gesture with his hand. "It's nothing. The food was a little rich for me."

"Have you seen a doctor?"

"Never mind doctors. I don't need a doctor to tell me what he doesn't know. I have to get ready for work. It's six o'clock. You go back to bed."

Isaac hesitated and Morris forced a laugh. "Stop worrying. I'm fine."

Isaac shrugged. "Morris, I can't tell you what to do, but you're not well, I know that." He reluctantly left the room. Closing the bedroom door softly, he crawled back into his bed. He lay awake listening to his brother moving about in the living room, sitting heavily to tie his shoes and scraping the chair on the wood floor as he lifted his jacket from its back. Finally, he heard Morris leave. Isaac closed his eyes but it was impossible for him to sleep.

As soon as the morning light illuminated the tattered window shade, Isaac got up and dressed. He peered around the edge of the shade at the street below, already bustling with traffic. Hannah sat up in bed and rubbed her eyes. "What time is it, poppa?"

Isaac looked at his pocket watch. "It's only seven. Don't you want to sleep some more?"

"No, I'm awake. Is Uncle Morris still here?"

Isaac shook his head. "He left for work. We'll see him at dinner time."

For most of that day, he and Hannah cleaned the apartment. The kitchen was the greatest challenge. While Hannah scoured the dishes and stove, Isaac battled the vermin, crushing the roaches with his thick-soled shoe as they scurried for shelter in the dark cracks and corners of the kitchen.

"There's not much food in the house. Do you have any money, poppa?" asked Hannah, standing in front of a narrow pantry, its shelves empty except for some tins of soup and tea.

"Yes, I have a bit left from what Morris sent to us in Lemberg."

"We could go shopping, poppa. Do we have enough? Do you think the storekeepers will understand us?"

"Well, we have no choice. Get your coat. We should go now before Morris returns."

The stairwell seemed even darker than it did before, the stench of cabbage stronger. They stepped out into pale December sunshine that provided no warmth. Discarded sheets of newspaper blew past them in the wind. Standing in front of the building, they looked up and down Houston, trying to decide which way to go. Cars and trucks rumbled by in both directions, their progress slowed by horse-drawn wagons, some loaded with blocks of ice, others with piles of junk. On one of the wagons, pulled by an ancient nag whose ribs and hips protruded, sat an old man dressed in black. He kept the wagon as close to the curb as possible while his voice, surprisingly powerful given his age, boomed out as he called in a singsong chant: "I cash clothes." Next to their building, a knife and scissors sharpener had set up his stand. His hands thrust deeply into the pockets of his threadbare jacket, he called out "Knives sharpened, scissors sharpened," first in English, then in Yiddish.

Isaac and Hannah wandered in the direction from which shoppers, laden with sacks, appeared. The sidestreets that led into Houston Street were filled with small shops and pushcarts, advertising their wares on signs printed with large black English and Hebrew letters. Merchants argued with their customers in English and Yiddish, and one particularly irate shopper shouted in Russian at a hapless peddler as Isaac and Hannah passed.

"We crossed the ocean to find ourselves in a stetl," said Isaac, shaking his head in wonder.

For a few pennies, Isaac purchased a used burlap sack with handles cleverly sewn on the sides. Hannah went up to a pushcart piled with potatoes and greens and Isaac watched with delight as his daughter bargained with the vendor, just as if she were on a street in Lemberg. She bought parsnips and kale, potatoes and onions, and oranges and apples, too. Her eyes widened with amazement as she weighed the fruit in her hand. "Look, poppa," she cried. "Look how big they are!" The meat market was strictly kosher, the butcher a beefy Galician who looked at home surrounded by dangling haunches of lamb, cow's briskets, and boneless cuts of meat. Hannah was more fascinated by the tufts of hair that grew out of his ears and nose than by the variety of meat. "You drive a hard bargain, young lady," the butcher said in Yiddish when after several minutes of haggling they agreed on a fair price for stringy beef shanks and stew meat. Finally, their sack bulging, Isaac stopped in front of a bakery displaying freshly-baked bread and strudel in the window.

"Hannah, remember momma's sabbath strudel—poppy seeds and hazelnuts together. Let's buy a little piece to share with Morris."

Hannah added a rye bread to their purchase.

"You have enough for a feast," Isaac said. "Come, let's head back."

As dusk fell, Isaac sat contentedly watching Hannah prepare dinner. The rich smells of simmering beef, onions and garlic filled the apartment. "This will be a nice surprise for your uncle," Isaac said.

"Momma was a good teacher," Hannah responded, a sad smile momentarily gracing her face.

It was the first time Hannah had spoken about her mother since her death and Isaac did not know how to reply. "You were a good pupil. You learned a lot from momma," he said finally.

It was almost seven when Morris' plodding steps sounded outside the door. Isaac immediately stood up, feeling guilty for relaxing while his brother put in a long day at the factory. If anything, Morris looked worse than he had that morning. The jaundiced cast of his skin was more pronounced and his brown eyes floated in a sea of yellow.

"Ach! How good it smells in here!" Morris exclaimed, affecting a joviality his physical appearance belied. "What have you done?" he asked with mock severity, looking around the apartment. "Is that what I brought you to America for, to spend your days cleaning and cooking? Are you trying to shame me?"

"Let me help you with your coat," said Isaac. "Here, sit down and rest. Dinner is almost ready."

Morris shoved Isaac playfully. "Just because I'm older than you doesn't mean I'm an invalid."

Throughout dinner, Morris complimented Hannah on her cooking but they could see he had no appetite. "What a fine cook you are, Hannah. If you weren't my niece, I'd ask you to marry me," he joked.

Hannah blushed.

"I'm surprised you haven't fallen into the clutches of an American woman," Isaac said, trying to mask his concern for his brother.

"Who has time to look for a wife? Here there is only time to work."

While Hannah cleared the table, Morris rose suddenly, the color drained from his face.

"Aren't you going to have tea and strudel, uncle?" asked Hannah.

"You'll have to excuse me," he said, "but I'm so tired tonight, I think I'll lie down."

"Please, you take one of the beds," said Isaac. "I'll take the other one. Hannah doesn't mind sleeping on the cot in here."

"But I'll wake you when I get up for work."

"I'm an early riser," said Isaac, "and Hannah can sleep through anything."

Too weak to argue, Morris disappeared into the bedroom and closed the door. Hannah looked at her father, perplexed and worried. "Uncle doesn't look well, poppa."

"He's just tired," Isaac answered unconvincingly. "He works too hard. Let me help you with the dishes. I'll dry, just like at home."

Hannah's face saddened at this memory of Lemberg, her mother washing the dishes after dinner while her father dried them, the two of them talking and laughing, never seeming to tire of each other's company. She wished now she had watched them more closely, so close that every detail of her mother's life would have been imprinted on her mind. She was already forgetting what her mother looked like. At night, before falling asleep, she tried to recall her face, every feature and gesture, and with each passing day it became more difficult to remember. Hannah was frightened, afraid she would forget completely. But loving her mother so much, missing her every day, she vowed to make herself remember.

Early the following morning, Isaac awakened with a start. He had been dreaming that he was back in the steerage hold, the ship rolling and groaning in the North Atlantic's stormy swells. The walls of the cabin creaked and moaned as the wind and waves battered the ship's side. He struggled in his dream to rise from his cot, frantically reaching out to Hannah. When he did awaken, his limbs felt limp. He was drained of energy, as if he had been truly battling the elements all night. Then he realized the groans he heard in his dream were coming from Morris, whose labored breathing rose from the bed across from him.

"Morris," he whispered loudly, "are you all right?"

He received no answer. Isaac swung his legs to the floor and stood between the beds, hovering over Morris. He wished there were a lamp in the room but the only light was from an unshaded overhead bulb. Isaac pulled the knotted string dangling from the fixture and blinked in the painfully bright light. Morris writhed in his bed, mumbling incoherently. Isaac shook him gently by the shoulder.

"Wake up, Morris! You're dreaming!"

But Morris did not awaken. Again Isaac touched his shoulder and this time, even through his brother's nightshirt, he felt the unnatural heat of his body. He placed his hand on Morris' forehead. My God, he thought, he's burning with fever. Isaac stumbled into the kitchen.

He ran cold water onto the dish towel he had left on the sink, wrung it out and carried it back into the bedroom. Morris quieted momentarily as Isaac placed the towel on his forehead, then he flailed his arms and cried out again.

"It's all right, Morris, it's all right," Isaac said helplessly.

"What is it, poppa?" called Hannah from the next room. "What's wrong?"

"Morris is sick," he said.

Hannah appeared in the doorway in her nightgown, blinking against the light. "Oh, poppa," she cried, "what are we going to do?"

"I've got to get his fever down," said Isaac. "Put some water in a bowl and find a cloth or towel. Quickly, Hannah."

Hannah raced to the sink, her bare feet striking the worn floorboards with a hollow slapping sound. Isaac pulled his watch from his pants pocket. It was only five o'clock, too early, he thought, to seek help.

For the next hour he and Hannah applied compresses to Morris' burning forehead. Suddenly, Morris rolled his eyes, blinked, and pushed himself onto his elbow. He grasped the wet cloth from his forehead.

"What time is it?" he asked.

"Lie down, Morris, you're sick," said Isaac, pushing gently on his brother's shoulders to settle him back onto the mattress.

Brusquely, Morris pushed Isaac's hands aside. "I've got to get up. I'll be late for work."

"No, you're too sick."

Morris leaned forward and feebly lunged into a standing position. Just as quickly he fell back onto the bed and began to shiver. "I'm so cold," he cried, his yellow eyes darting feverishly. Isaac, watching helplessly, felt his heart constrict. He was certain his brother was dying. In Lemberg, as children, he and Morris watched over their younger brothers and sisters when they were ill, nursing them helplessly as they died, the two youngest during an influenza epidemic and their favorite older sister from tuberculosis. Isaac had also witnessed his parents' untimely deaths. He was frightened, certain that Morris, too, was leaving him. Hannah pulled Morris' blanket over him, then stripped the blanket from Isaac's bed and piled it on top.

"Stay with him," Isaac ordered, pulling on his clothes over his nightshirt. "I'm going for help."

Not knowing where to find a doctor, Isaac rapped on the door opposite Morris' apartment. An elderly bald man in rumpled gray pajamas opened the door and peered out warily in response to Isaac's knocking. In rapid Yiddish, Isaac explained to the neighbor that his brother was sick and needed a doctor.

"Come in," the man said. "Let me get dressed. I know a doctor. We can bring him here."

Isaac followed him into the apartment. A short, stocky woman clumsily adjusted her robe and touched her hand to the wig that married Orthodox Jewish women wore in front of men other than family members. She obviously had just awakened. Her wig, slightly askew, was no impediment to her curiosity.

"He's a good doctor," said the man in a mixture of English and Yiddish that Isaac found difficult to understand. "He treats my Leah's sugar problem. What's wrong with your brother?"

"He has a high fever and is delirious. My daughter is with him."

"Leah, go help the girl," he said to his wife. "I'll be right back."

He dressed quickly and hurried out with Isaac. The sky was cloudless and it was cold enough for them to see their breath. They followed a sidestreet for three or four blocks to a more established-looking neighborhood of solid brick buildings. As they walked, the man introduced himself as Moishe Solomon. "But in this country," he said, "they call me Murray." They stopped before an imposing yellow brick building. Moishe swung open the ornate door to the lobby and they climbed to the second floor. He stopped at the first door and knocked softly.

The doctor, a thin, almost emaciated man wearing wire-rim glasses opened the door. Although it was early, he was already dressed in a suit. Moishe spoke to him in English, apologizing for disturbing him, and explained the emergency. The doctor gathered his coat and gloves and picked up his black leather bag. The three of them descended the stairs and stepped out into the street. Horse carts clattered by as they made their way back to Houston Street.

Hannah was waiting at the open door to the apartment where she had been listening for their footsteps on the stairs, a worried-looking Mrs. Solomon standing behind her. "Poppa," she cried, "I'm frightened."

Isaac hurried past her into the bedroom. Morris lay quietly in the bed and for one terrible moment Isaac thought he was not breathing. Then Morris groaned and murmured. Isaac sat down on the edge of the bed and held his brother's hand. "The doctor is here," he said softly, but Morris gave no indication he heard him.

"Please wait in the next room," the doctor said to Isaac and Hannah in halting Yiddish.

Isaac reluctantly left his brother's side. He sat morosely at the kitchen table while the Solomons stood uncomfortably in the living room, uncertain whether to stay or go.

"I'll make some tea, poppa," Hannah said.

Isaac stared into space and said nothing. He did not move until the doctor entered the room.

"Where can I wash my hands?" the doctor asked as he placed his bag on the table.

Hannah motioned toward the sink and ran to get a clean towel. The doctor dried his hands and sat down next to Isaac.

"You don't speak English?"

Isaac shook his head.

"Perhaps you understand German?" he queried in broken Yiddish. "I don't speak Yiddish, you see. I practiced in Berlin before coming to this country. There were not many Eastern European Jews in my practice."

Isaac looked at him directly and spoke in unaccented German. "Please tell me, doctor. What's wrong with my brother?"

"It's an infection in his liver," he replied, surprised at Isaac's fluency.

"Will he be all right?" Isaac asked.

"There's nothing to be done," the doctor said softly. "There is no cure for hepatitis. He's obviously been sick for some time, and now . . ." He studied his hands and then raised his eyes to Isaac's. "He's dying."

Hannah, standing at the sink, began to cry. Isaac covered his face with his hands. His shoulders slumped forward, unable to bear the weight of this new defeat.

The doctor stood up and rested his hands on his bag. "I'm sorry. I'll look in on him after my office hours this morning." He left the apartment, followed by the Solomons.

For the remainder of that morning, Isaac and Hannah sat at Morris' bedside in the room's gloomy half-light. Neither of them bothered to raise the window shade. Morris slept fitfully. In lucid moments he tried to tell Isaac that he'd been sick for many weeks. "I didn't say anything in my letter. I only hoped I would live long enough to bring you and your family to America."

The doctor returned shortly before noon and Isaac spoke briefly with him in the kitchen, then led him to Morris' bedside. Morris lay on his back, his sightless eyes staring at the ceiling. Hannah fled from the room as the doctor placed his fingers on Morris' lids, closing them forever.

Only days after their arrival in America and little more than a month after

Rachel's death, Isaac buried his brother. He had never felt so helpless. If it hadn't been for the Solomons' kindness in helping him to arrange the burial, he would not have known what to do. A small black Ford truck used by the burial society for funerals, and for odd jobs and deliveries at other times, carried Morris' body to the Jewish cemetery on the far side of the East River in Queens. Isaac and Hannah rode with the driver.

As Isaac stood in the cold rain at the cemetery, Hannah at his side and the rabbi intoning the prayers for the dead, he felt he was caught up in an unending nightmare. What terrible sins had he committed to warrant the wrath of a God in whom he professed not to believe? He cursed Him silently for taking his wife and brother.

That evening, he and Hannah sat across from each other in the darkened kitchen. They were too exhausted and too worried by the situation in which they found themselves to cry. They were in Morris' apartment, one to which they had no claim, alone and unemployed in a strange country whose language they didn't speak, with no relations to depend on. Isaac struggled to think what he could do to extricate them from their predicament.

"I have to find work, Hannah. We have very little money left. Tomorrow, I'll go see Morris' boss. Maybe he can help me find something. And you have to go to school."

"But poppa, wouldn't it be better for me to work? How can I go to school? I don't speak English."

"We have to learn English. For you, what better place to learn than school?"

The following morning they left the apartment early. Isaac carried a slip of paper with the address of Morris' employer written clearly in block print. Stopping passersby hurrying to their own jobs, he showed them the paper and asked in Yiddish, in German, and in Russian, how to find the address.

They wandered deep into the lowest, most cramped section of the city. The river flowed grey and cold against the solid stone and cobble embankments of the port. On Warren Street, Isaac found the factory in which Morris had worked. It was more modest than he had expected, a narrow two-storey brick warehouse wedged between taller buildings. He pushed open the heavy metal entrance door and they stepped into a small anteroom. Through the iron-framed glass walls they saw the entire length of the factory, filled with workers, all of the men standing before heavy cast-iron machines whose function Isaac could not begin to guess. The glass dividers provided no barrier to the noise of the factory, the hum reverberating in the small space. A dark-haired woman sat at a typewriter in a cubicle partitioned off from the anteroom. Isaac, staring at the workers, was unaware the woman was speaking to him until Hannah nudged him.

"Poppa, she's asking you something," Hannah whispered to her father.

"No English, please," Isaac said apologetically.

The woman lifted a phone on her desk and moments later a heavy, red-headed man with a receding hairline appeared. He wore an oil-stained smock hanging below his knees, but beneath it he wore a clean shirt and tie.

He glanced quizzically at Isaac and Hannah. "*Sprechen Sie deutsch?*" he asked.

"*Ja, ich spreche deutsch,*" Isaac replied, relieved.

"I am Herr Englehardt, the owner of the factory. Is there something I can help you with?"

"I am Morris Schneider's brother, Isaac."

"Where is he?" said Englehardt, his face clouding. "He hasn't been to work in two days."

Isaac related the news of his brother's illness and death. Englehardt's features softened. "I'm so sorry. He was a good worker." He turned to the woman at the typewriter and spoke to her in English. The only word Isaac understood was his own name, Schneider. The woman opened a ledger and began to write. "We owe your brother some wages. He had no other family, did he?" Isaac shook his head. Englehardt handed him a check. "Take this to the bank on the next corner. They will cash it for you."

"I'm looking for work," Isaac said. "My daughter and I arrived in America only four days ago."

"What kind of work do you do?"

"In Europe I was a tailor. But I will do anything."

Englehardt scratched his chin. "I need someone to fill your brother's job. Can you do it?"

"I don't know how to operate a machine."

"Neither did Morris when he first came to us. But he learned quickly."

"I will do my best," Isaac said, shaking hands with Englehardt.

"Be here by seven tomorrow morning."

"Poppa," said Hannah, as they walked out to the street, "you didn't even ask how much he will pay you."

Isaac looked at the check in his hand and saw it was for twenty dollars. "Hannah, if the man was honest enough to give me the money that Morris earned, I'm sure he'll be fair with me. At least now we know we can live."

That same day, in spite of Hannah's misgivings, Isaac enrolled her in the local grammar school. He felt intimidated as they walked up the steps of the red sandstone building. Fortunately, the first person they encountered was a Yiddish-speaking woman, Mrs. Diamond, who worked in the principal's office. She immediately put Isaac at ease and assisted him with the paperwork needed to register Hannah as a student. "Now, we must give Hannah some examinations to see where she's to be placed," Mrs. Diamond said.

She gestured to Hannah to sit at the desk in her office and handed her several papers and a pencil. Hannah's consternation flickered across her face as she scanned the first sheet. She looked up at her father with a worried expression, placed the first sheet aside, and picked up the second. This time she began to write.

"She's very good in arithmetic," Mrs. Diamond told Isaac. "Much better than we expect from students her age. But without English we have to put her with children in the younger grades." The woman smiled kindly at Hannah. "I know that will be difficult for you at first. The older children may tease you. But I'm sure you'll learn English very quickly and then we'll move you up to your age group."

Hannah, crestfallen, looked at her father in hopes of a reprieve, but Isaac was not to be dissuaded.

"When will she begin?" he asked.

"Well," Mrs. Diamond said, "we have a saying in this country: there's no time like the present. Come with me, Hannah, and I'll introduce you to your teacher and class. School will be out at three o'clock. You can meet Hannah outside, Mr. Schneider."

"I can find my way home by myself," Hannah said, hoping to show Mrs. Diamond she was capable of taking care of herself even if she didn't speak English yet.

"That's fine. And in case you're interested, Mr. Schneider, the Hebrew Immigrant Aid Society uses our school to teach a special class for adults to learn English. Three nights a week—Monday, Wednesday and Friday—from eight to nine. You should attend. That way you and Hannah will be able to practice your English with one another."

She took Hannah's arm and led her from the office. Isaac, watching them go, wished it were possible to make things easier for his daughter. She had endured the loss of her mother and uncle and now faced a new school in a strange country whose language she didn't speak. But at the same time, Isaac felt a surge of pride: they were on their way to becoming Americans.

4

Mornings had always been a difficult time for
Isaac. He arose before six, dressed quickly, prepared breakfast, and made their
lunches—a thick slab of bread, a slice of cheese, a small tomato, and an apple.
"Hannah," he'd yell for the third time, "breakfast is ready. You'll be late for
school." Exasperated, he'd lapse into Yiddish.

"English, poppa, English," Hannah would yell back. "I'm coming."

Some days Hannah was up before him and that was even worse. It meant
that she would get to the bathroom first, making it impossible for Isaac to wash or
shave, let alone empty his bladder. "What are you doing in there? Did you fall
asleep?" Isaac yelled.

In spite of their hectic mornings, they were now living well by immigrant
standards. During their first two years in New York they had kept Morris' apartment, bumping into one another in the clutter, fighting a losing battle against the
roaches, and worst of all, living with no central heating and with the stench of the
communal toilet. During the winter they huddled around their small kerosene
heater, while in the summer, even with every window open, they slept drenched
in perspiration. Finally, Isaac decided he had had enough. With his position at the

factory seemingly secure, Isaac began his search for a better apartment, one removed from the crowded tenements and squalid streets of the Lower East Side.

The apartment he found was on Thompson Street in the area New Yorkers called the West Village. It was on the fourth floor of a five-storey, brown brick building and had a separate kitchen and two bedrooms. What made the apartment seem luxurious to Hannah and Isaac were the central steam heat, provided by a radiator in each room, and the fact that it had its own bathroom with toilet, sink and tub. The rooms were small, especially Hannah's bedroom which could barely hold her bed and dresser, but she was happy to have more privacy.

At first, Isaac had had some concerns about the cost of the move. The rent was seven dollars more a month than they had been paying and the furniture, even though it was second-hand, had cost him half of the savings he had accumulated during his time working at Englehardt's factory. We'll manage, he reassured himself. After all, he was now a skilled machine operator, adept enough for Englehardt to entrust with the task of teaching new employees. And he was earning fifteen dollars more a month than Morris was making at the time of his death.

The war Morris had predicted arrived in 1914, but Isaac paid little attention to the headlines in the American and Jewish newspapers. When he thought of Austria and Lemberg, which was seldom, he visualized only Rachel's grave. The fire on the Bergstrasse had not only taken his wife from him, it had obliterated all memories of Europe.

With the advent of the war, America, although neutral, began modernizing its army and navy. Englehardt's factory, which until then had manufactured small engine parts for automobiles and trucks, now filled military contracts. Machines were retooled for manufacturing tank and military truck parts. The volume of work quickly outstripped the ability of the workers to cope with it. Not even the hiring of additional men helped ease the strain. As a result, the workers' hours were increased. Isaac's day at the factory still began at seven, but instead of working until five, he, along with the others, now worked twelve-hour shifts. All around him men grumbled, especially those who had been with Englehardt the longest. Their workdays were longer, but their pay had not gone up. And if they complained, they knew there were others anxious to take their place.

Isaac fretted about how little time he had to spend with Hannah, but she appeared to thrive in her new environment. She had begun her first year of high school, making an apparently effortless transition to both a new school and a higher grade level. Over dinner, she talked excitedly about her new teachers and the subjects she was studying. Now fifteen, she had matured into a young woman, a transformation that seemed miraculous to Isaac. Not only was she almost as tall as her father, but her resemblance to Rachel was striking. She had the same flashing black eyes and sensuous full lips. Even her body movements, the determined stride and slight sway of her hips, reminded him of his wife. Whenever he caught himself noticing the swelling of her breasts beneath her blouse, he turned away in embarrassment. He was aware, too, of the eyes of the young men they passed in the street during their Sunday strolls, their gaze fixed upon Hannah.

America, to Hannah, was no longer a new country. It was simply her country. Europe had receded into the past and it was hard for her to believe, when she thought about it, that America had not always been her home. She laughed now when she remembered the trepidation she felt when her father enrolled her in grammar school. Within a year her English had become virtually fluent and she was promoted to her own grade level. Once the hurdle of language was crossed, Hannah's confidence in her abilities knew no limits. The lines of A's on her report cards made her as proud as it did Isaac, but she knew her capabilities extended beyond those of a student. She ran a home as capably as any married woman and with that responsibility had come a subtle reversal in her relationship with Isaac. It was her father who was now more dependent upon her than she upon him.

Like Isaac, she found there were scarcely enough hours in the day to accomplish all she had to do. As soon as classes were over, she hurried to Salvatore's Barber Shop, only a block from the school. The owner, an affable, white-haired Italian immigrant, had hired Hannah for three hours a day, ostensibly to sweep the floor after haircuts. His canny intuition, however, had told him it wouldn't hurt his business to have a lovely young woman in the barbershop. His intuition proved correct. The busiest time of the day was now from three to six in the afternoon, the very hours when Hannah worked. Every seat lining the wall behind the two barber chairs was filled with customers. While waiting their turn, they bantered with Hannah in heavily-accented English, Italian words liberally thrown in. At first she blushed form the attention, but as the weeks went by and she got to know the customers, she became more comfortable. Most of them were older men, retired pensioners, many widowed and living alone.

The presence of the beautiful Jewish girl who greeted them with a smiling "bongiorno" made them forget their age and their loneliness.

Hannah didn't extend the same familiarity to the younger customers. The lascivious stares and suggestive remarks of the young Italian men made her uncomfortable. Turning her back to them, she concentrated on her sweeping.

When her work was finished, Hannah raced to the markets to do her shopping. Ordinarily, she would have enjoyed her daily trips to the greengrocer, butchershop or bakery. Nothing gave her more pleasure than choosing the freshest vegetables and ripest fruits or smelling the aroma of fresh-baked bread. But there was no time for dawdling during the school year. By the time she finished sweeping the last bits of shorn hair at the barbershop she barely had time to make her purchases and prepare dinner before Isaac came home.

"Smells good," he invariably said as he entered. "So how's school, Hannah?"

"Good, poppa."

"Well, I'll just wash up."

Standing at the stove, she watched him walk wearily toward the bathroom. The twelve-hour workdays were taking their toll and Hannah worried about him. She knew she was doing everything in her power to make her father's life comfortable, but what they had once shared as a family was gone forever. No matter how well she ran the household, there was nothing she could do about his long hours at work and his loneliness. And even though she considered herself an American, she had to admit that life in Lemberg had in many ways been easier— and for her father certainly, better.

After dinner, Hannah always tried to do the dishes but Isaac shooed her away. "I have to get my hands clean from the factory. Go do your homework."

Hannah would then disappear into her room, piling her books and papers on the bed. Some of her friends, she knew, had desks, but for Hannah that seemed an unattainable luxury. Besides, she thought, where could I put it?

Isaac, too, brought work home with him. As soon as the kitchen table had been cleaned, he spread his papers, ruler and pencils on the wooden surface and computed the measurements he needed for whatever parts he was working on at the factory. Arithmetic did not come easily for him. Having had little formal education, he had learned these skills under the tutelage of Mr. Englehardt during his first months at the factory. As competent as he now was in his work, Isaac always intercepted Hannah when she came into the kitchen.

"Hannah, can I ask you a question? Could you maybe help me with this little problem I'm having?"

Hannah leaned over the table and patiently checked his long division or demonstrated how to multiply and divide fractions. Her own assignments, enough to keep her busy for hours, awaited her but it was impossible to refuse his pleas for help. On many nights, Hannah would still be working when Isaac called out "Good night, Hannah. Don't stay up too late." Often she didn't get to bed until midnight. On the mornings that followed, Isaac, driven to distraction, pounded on her door again and again to wake her.

Hannah had always spent Sundays with Isaac. They would travel by subway and on foot, exploring the city, becoming familiar with its museums, zoos and parks. But recently she had become friendly with two girls in her class and preferred to spend Sundays with them. At first, this made her feel guilty. Her father had no friends and leaving him to spend the day by himself seemed to her an act of desertion.

"Poppa, Ruth and Jessica want me to go with them to Coney Island this Sunday," she said the first time they asked her to join them.

"Good. You go and have a good time."

"Yes, but what will you do?"

"What am I, a child who needs to be amused? I'll relax, go for a walk, read the newspaper—don't worry about me."

It was a day of firsts for Hannah—the first time at a beach, the first time she stepped into the waters of the ocean, the first time she visited an amusement park, and above all, the first time she had spent a day with friends since arriving in America. It was Jessica, a shy, quiet girl, with whom Hannah felt closest, but Ruth was the one who drew both of them out their shell. "Come on," she called as they stood on the boardwalk surveying the mob on the beach, "follow me." They threaded their way through the sand, around the beach blankets and multicolored umbrellas, until they reached the water's edge. Ruth took off her shoes and the other two girls followed her example. "Catch me," Ruth said, running through the shallow water. They splashed their way down the beach until they were out of breath.

"We're soaked," Hannah called, exhilirated by the cold, gravelly give of the sand beneath her feet.

'You'll dry in the sun," said Ruth, shrugging her shoulders. "Hey, look, those boys are watching us."

Hannah and Jessica turned to find a group of boys who looked seventeen or eighteen watching them and laughing. Hannah blushed.

"Should we go meet them?" Ruth asked.

"No!" Hannah and Jessica exclaimed.

"You're right," Ruth said in mock seriousness. "They're just kids. Let's go to the amusement park."

Hannah stared wide-eyed at the roller coaster as cars of screaming riders hurtled down. "I'm going on that," Ruth said. "Who's coming with me?" In spite of her pleading with them to join her, Hannah and Jessica stood their ground. They watched the car with Ruth in it make its slow ascent to the high point of the track. "It's scary," Jessica said, and Hannah agreed. "I'm glad we didn't go." Again the screams as the cars thundered down. Hannah closed her eyes, unable to imagine what Ruth was experiencing. They waited for her at the entrance to the ride and she stumbled toward them ashen-faced. "Never again," Ruth said. "I feel like my head is down here." She pointed to her stomach. "You were brave," Hannah said. "You were," Jessica agreed.

From then on, with one exception, Hannah spent every Sunday of her summer vacation with her two friends. When Isaac asked if she would join him for an outing on the Sunday of Labor Day weekend, Hannah found it impossible to refuse. She no longer felt guilty about leaving him to his own devices, but she knew he wouldn't have asked if it wasn't important.

"Where are we going?" Hannah asked as they rode the subway to lower Manhattan.

"It's a suprise," Isaac said.

They soon stood on the tip of Manhattan Island, staring out at the Statue of Liberty, less imposing as a monument from that distance but still poignant as a reminder of what they had felt when they saw it as new immigrants. It was their first trip back since they timidly followed Morris off the ferry from Ellis Island. Now they watched the disembarkation of passengers from the ferry dispassionately, not with total detachment but more with the secure knowledge of people who had made the transition from immigrants to Americans. With war raging in Europe and the young men of both sides slaughtering one another on the battle-fields, the number of new arrivals had diminished. Most of the passengers leaving the ferry were old people, or women and children coming to join family members who had preceded them.

Isaac suggested they sit on one of the benches overlooking the water. "Do you remember the day we arrived, Hannah?" he asked.

"Of course, poppa."

"Do you ever think of momma? And of Uncle Morris?"

Hannah turned to him, surprised by his question. After Morris' funeral, Isaac seldom mentioned his brother and he rarely spoke of Rachel. She suspected that, in spite of his reticence, they were often in his thoughts. There were times when they did the dishes together that she caught him looking at her in an odd, remote way. She knew that at those moments he was remembering. And whenever they happened to pass the old tenement where they had lived, he glanced at it with that same distant expression, then looked quickly away as if the sight of it was too painful.

His question confirmed her suspicions. Isaac sat staring now at the sunshine glinting off the water in the harbor. He seemed moody and preoccupied.

"Sometimes, poppa," she said softly.

He reached into the inner pocket of his jacket and removed a small photograph. "I thought I'd lost this picture," he said, showing Hannah a faded sepia photograph of her mother. "But I found it in the envelope with our immigration papers. I thought we could take it to a photography studio. Maybe they can make copies. It's the only picture of momma that I have."

Hannah stared at the face in the picture, a face caught in one brief instant of time so long ago. Somehow that face was incompatible with the image Hannah carried within her. It had been so long since she had seen her mother's smile that the face in the photograph might as well have been that of a stranger. She knew at that moment that while remembering, she was also forgetting, that try as she might to clutch the memory of her mother to her, it was receding into the mists of time.

Hannah turned toward Isaac and studied his profile as he looked at the photograph. For the first time she began to think of him in a different way. He was not simply her father. He was also a man, no longer young but not old either, a man who had lost the woman he loved and who was as alone as the Italian widowers who came to the barbershop to assuage their loneliness by joking with her. She knew how much her father loved her, how important her presence was to him. But she could never provide the love her father needed. She had never considered the possibility of another woman in Isaac's life, but now she wondered if that wasn't selfishness on her part.

Hannah's perception had not been entirely wrong. Isaac, holding Rachel's picture in his hand and looking out at the harbor that signified for him not only the beginning of a new life, but also the ending of the life he had shared with his wife, was caught up in memories of this lost love. There had been so many times during the past few years when he had struggled under the burden of loneliness, times when immersing himself in his work and devoting himself to his daughter didn't assuage his pain. It was not only a matter of Isaac missing his wife in the way that a man misses the woman he loves. Rachel had also been his confidante, the person he could go to when he needed help with problems outside the home. Whether it involved dealing with the tax collector or approaching Kaltbrenner for a raise in his salary, he was always amazed that his wife, whose life revolved around domestic matters, had the ability to cope so well with matters outside her experience. Rachel was able to simplify everything and demonstrate to him that his worries were unfounded. It was her innate wisdom and sage advice he needed now.

There were serious problems at work. The workers' simmering anger at their long hours had led to talk of unionizing the factory. Many evenings the men gathered in small groups on the street or headed off to a local bar to air their grievances. Isaac was the only one of Englehardt's thirty employees who kept himself apart. When they asked him to accompany them, he excused himself by saying he had to get home to his daughter, who was alone and waiting for him. In reality, Isaac, who had shied away from confrontation all his life, was frightened by the dissension that swirled around him.

The idea of a labor union was a new concept to him. In Lemberg, his working life had been simple. It was understood that Mr. Kaltbrenner and his tailors were working together for their mutual benefit. As owner of the business, Kaltbrenner was entitled to the lion's share of the profits. But at the same time, he was meticulously fair with Isaac and the other tailors. If, for some reason, there was a sudden influx of work that had to be completed by a certain time, Mr. Kaltbrenner would discuss it with them and the men themselves would decide how to apportion the work and the extra hours needed to complete it. They were also compensated for those hours.

In America, Isaac discovered, things were different. The men in the factory were not consulted. If overtime work was required, Mr. Englehardt simply issued the order and the men were expected to comply. Isaac personally had no complaints about the factory owner. If anything, he was grateful to him. Over the years the owner had increased Isaac's responsibilities, but he had also increased his salary.

Isaac did feel they should be compensated for the additional hours. But he knew, too, that the factory owner was threatening to fire workers who complained. Englehardt had made that clear on the Friday afternoon when he first appeared on the shop floor to announce that until further notice they would work until seven. Perhaps, Isaac thought, that was the way things were done in this country. At first, he thought it odd no one was willing to approach Englehardt to discuss it with him. When he suggested to some of the men they should meet with the owner, they laughed at him.

One of them, Henry Sperling, a young German Jew, took Isaac aside one day during their lunch break. "Isaac," he said, "anyone who goes to the boss to complain will be branded a troublemaker. That means Englehardt will find some excuse to fire him. The only way to stand up to a boss is to have all of us do it. We need a union. Then, if he still won't come to terms, we can go on strike. The way things are now we have no say in the matter. If he wants us to work twenty-hour days, we do it or he fires us. Dog eat dog, Isaac. That's the way things are here unless we learn to stand together."

Isaac wasn't convinced. He persisted in his belief that Englehardt was a reasonable man. The others continued to meet after work, but Isaac didn't join them. When Henry rented a local theatre for a Sunday morning so that a representative from the American Federation of Labor could address the workers, Isaac contributed his share to the rental but declined to attend. The men, noting his absence, gave him unfriendly looks at work. Even when he passed them in the street, they glared at him in silence. Only Henry, who by the unspoken consent of the workers appeared to have taken over their leadership, continued to join him at lunch. "He'll come around," he assured the other workers. "Isaac's a good man, just a little naive."

These concerns preoccupied Isaac as he sat with Hannah on the bench that Sunday, the photograph of Rachel in his hand. Caught between the sympathy he felt for the men he worked with and his loyalty to Mr. Englehardt, he couldn't help but wonder what advice Rachel would have given him.

On the first day back at work after the Labor Day holiday, Isaac removed his smock when the lunch whistle sounded. Sitting on the bench next to his lathe, he spread the waxed paper holding his sandwich on his lap.

"Can I join you, Isaac?" Henry asked.

"Of course. Sit down."

"We're having another meeting at the theatre next Sunday morning," said Henry, unwrapping his sandwich. "We'll be forming a union."

Isaac took a bite of his sandwich and said nothing.

"We'd like you to be there, Isaac."

Isaac shook his head. "Henry, I'm trying to raise a child alone. I don't want to get mixed up in this union business. If I were to lose my job . . ."

"Don't you think the other men worry about the same thing? But Englehardt is taking advantage of us. If we stick together, we can win."

"Henry, he was good to me. When my brother died, he gave me the money owed to Morris. And he gave me the chance to learn a new trade. I had just arrived in America. If it wasn't for Mr. Englehardt, Hannah and I could not have survived."

"Isaac, I know your heart is in the right place. But that's not the issue. I'm talking about exploitation of workers." Exasperated, he put the rest of his sandwich back in its bag. "Let me tell you a little about my own family. Do you know about the Triangle Shirtwaist Company fire?" Seeing Isaac's blank look, he continued. "That was about six years ago here in New York. My sister, Ruth, who was twenty years old, worked in that factory. The bosses kept all the doors locked to make sure no one could leave during the workday. There was a fire and all the workers were trapped. More than a hundred-twenty women died. My sister was one of them. Her life in this promised land of America was a short one. But there are changes coming, Isaac—big changes, here in America, even in Russia. Only one thing can make those changes happen—solidarity of the workers. We have to stick together.

"Oh, and one other thing," he said. "Let me tell you about my cousin, Arthur. He's the son of my mother's sister. When my family and his left our village in Germany, I was an infant and Arthur was about two years old. We came to America on the same ship and lived in the same tenement in New York. He and I grew up together and went to the same schools. Then, when Arthur was seventeen, my aunt and uncle moved to Newark, New Jersey. Arthur had just started a job in a factory here so he moved in with us. I don't remember what he did exactly, working some kind of machine press. The fellow working next to him, who'd been there for about twelve years, somehow got his hand pinned by the machine. He was screaming and my cousin tried to get his hand out but the press wouldn't budge. Finally, he got some kind of tool, a crowbar or something, and lifted the press just enough to get the man's crushed hand out. Every bone in the hand was broken. And by prying the machine off the fellow's hand, Arthur had managed to break the press. So what do you think happened? The worker whose hand was crushed was fired. The boss said he'd been careless. And Arthur, he said, would have to pay for the damaged press. Each week they would take the money out of his pay. Arthur told me they'd have to catch him first. So he got on a train and headed west, to a place called Montana." He laughed at the memory, then turned serious again. "That's one way to handle exploitation, I guess. Just move on. But I wonder if it's any better out there."

Isaac had listened patiently. He looked up now at the wall clock. "The whistle will sound in a minute," he said.

"We need you, Isaac. We're counting on you to be with us."

Isaac kept his eyes on the clock, waiting for the whistle.

5

Sunday came and went. Hannah spent the day with her girlfriends while Isaac remained at home, the newspaper spread out in front of him on the kitchen table. Ordinarily it would have given him pleasure to read through one section, then put it aside to pick up another. But on this day he was unable to concentrate. He stared at the clock, thinking of his co-workers at their meeting. No matter how many excuses he made to himself for not attending, he could not dispel a gnawing sense of shame.

On Monday morning the men ignored him when he came to work. For several days no one said anything to him. It was toward the end of the week that Henry approached him at the end of a work day. Isaac, not knowing what had transpired at the previous Sunday's meeting, assumed Henry was going to berate him for his absence.

"Isaac," he said, "do you remember the cousin I spoke to you about? Arthur, the one who moved to Montana?"

Surprised by the question, Isaac nodded, wondering what that had to do with the meeting he had not attended.

"I got a letter from him on Monday. He's coming to New York for a visit. I'll be meeting him at the train station Sunday. Why don't you come along with me? We can have lunch together and you and I can learn about the life of workers out west."

"But I was planning to spend Sunday with my daughter," said Isaac, questioning the young man's motives in asking him and searching for an excuse not to go. He'll try to convince me to join the union he always talks about, Isaac thought.

"Bring her along."

Isaac hesitated. "Can I ask my daughter tonight and let you know tomorrow?"

"Of course. Tell her I insist she join us."

Isaac, upset with himself for his suspicions, thought about Henry's invitation as he headed home that evening. If he wanted to talk about the union why would he have his cousin and Hannah there? Henry was the first person he'd known in America who had offered him friendship. Even in Lemberg, Isaac had been so involved with work and his family that friendship eluded him. Rachel had had her circle of friends, women in the neighborhood with whom she shopped or gossiped. Hannah had her own friends from school. Maybe it was time for him to stop closing himself off.

During dinner, Isaac mentioned the invitation from Henry and asked Hannah if she would like to join them.

"I wouldn't be in the way?"

"Henry says to tell you he insists you come."

"Why then I'll come," she said, secretly pleased her father had made a friend.

Henry Sperling was not what Hannah had expected. Henry, she thought, would be someone fortyish, serious like her father. Instead, a thin, young man in his late twenties greeted her. Beneath his easy affability and ready smile, there was an intensity best revealed in his dark blue eyes, their gaze penetrating deeply into the person he addressed. Hannah found him charming and quite handsome.

They stood on the corner of Seventh Avenue and 34th Street exchanging pleasantries until Henry looked at his watch. "Well, Arthur's train should be arriving in a little while. Let's go meet him."

Isaac and Hannah were awed by the vast size and modern splendor of Pennsylvania Station, its marble, glass, and concrete construction completed only six years earlier.

"It's so big," Hannah said to her father.

Big enough, thought Isaac, to engulf Lemberg's train station, and even that of Cracow and Prague.

As they stood on the platform, Henry talked to them about his cousin. "I haven't seen Arthur in seven or eight years, not since he headed west. I don't even know what he does out there. The letter from him was the first in a long time. I remember him as being a very funny fellow."

"This place, Montana, is it far away?" Isaac asked.

"About two thousand miles, I'd guess."

"How did your cousin choose such a place?"

"You'll have to ask him. Just before he left, he asked me to go with him." Henry's eyes met Hannah's and she blushed. "You're very quiet," he said.

"Why didn't you go?" she asked.

"I beg your pardon."

"To Montana. Why didn't you go with your cousin?"

"Oh," he laughed. "I was tempted but I didn't want to leave my family. And I had a job in a factory, not the same one I have now." He shrugged. "Arthur was more adventuresome, I guess."

They heard the rumble of the arriving train and Henry leaned over the edge of the platform to watch its approach, the beam of light from the engine penetrating the darkness of the tunnel as it came nearer.

Isaac and Hannah stood open-mouthed at the train inching its way down the platform. The sleek lines of the cars and the luxurious interior, replete with curtains and plush seats easily visible through the windows, were as far removed from the train that had carried them to Bremen as a modern automobile was from a peasant's donkey cart. When it had come to a complete stop, black porters wearing uniforms and caps assisted the passengers with their luggage. Isaac stared in fascination at these Negroes, their white teeth resplendent in the smiles on their black faces as they received their gratuities.

"There he is!" said Henry, waving to a stocky, well-dressed man stepping down from one of the cars. The two men shook hands warmly and Henry introduced his cousin to Isaac and Hannah. Henry had told them earlier that his cousin was two years older, but to Hannah Arthur Herbst's solid appearance accentuated Henry's youthfulness, making him appear a boy in comparison.

Arthur was taller than Henry and wore a large moustache. Dressed in a pale blue suit and vest and wearing a dark necktie and grey fedora, he was a picture of good health and affluence. A gold watch chain was visible on his vest and he carried an ivory-handled walking stick.

After shaking hands with Isaac, Arthur reached out to Hannah, surprising her by pressing his lips to her hand. "I'm always pleased to meet a lovely young woman," he said. He exuded charm and self-confidence and within moments had captivated Isaac and Hannah.

"Shall we take your bags to my apartment and then get lunch?" Henry asked.

"No need to do that," said Arthur. "I'll check the bags here and we can pick them up later."

Arthur passed his luggage to the clerk at the baggage counter and tucked the receipt in his jacket pocket.

"It's almost noon," said Henry. "Are you hungry?"

"I'm famished."

"I know a good restaurant not far from here."

Isaac and Hannah followed behind as Henry, walking next to his cousin, led them to a small German restaurant, the Heidelberg, on 31st Street.

"He's taking us to meet some *landsmen*," Arthur said over his shoulder.

The Heidelberg was a modest establishment, its walls covered with prints of the Bavarian Alps and a large poster of a smiling German girl in peasant costume, her blond braids prominently displayed. Only a few of the restaurant's twenty tables were occupied.

"*Guten tag*," said the proprietor, shaking hands with Henry, whom he obviously knew, and bowing to them. "I have your table ready."

"This cousin of mine had it all planned," said Arthur, slapping Henry on the back.

"Well, actually I stopped by last night and told Emil that we might be coming for lunch today," said Henry, blushing in response to his cousin's praise.

"See, what did I tell you?" Arthur said, winking at Isaac.

As soon as they were seated, the waiter brought their menus and opened a bottle of white wine.

"You think of everything," Arthur said to Henry, throwing back his head and laughing as if at some joke.

Hannah wondered why Henry's cousin laughed at everything. She had never known anyone who did that and it made her uneasy.

Isaac, too, was suddenly uncomfortable but for a different reason. Opening the Sunday menu, he was surprised at how expensive everything was. He tried to remember how much money he had with him. Instinctively, he reached for his pocket, then, embarrassed, let his hand fall into his lap. Henry noticed Isaac's gesture. "Before we order," he said, "I want it understood that this lunch is my treat."

Isaac started to protest, but Arthur interrupted. "Nonsense," he said, turning to Henry. "When you come to Montana, then you'll pay. I'll take care of this."

"The wienerschnitzel and sauerbraten here are both very good," said Henry to Isaac, leading the conversation away from the bill. He then turned back to his cousin. "So, Arthur, what brings you back east?"

"Oh, I just wanted a little change of scenery for a while. And I wanted to see the family and some old friends. I'm not a very good correspondent. My mother starts off every one of her letters with 'why don't you write?' But why am I telling you how bad I am about writing letters? You already know that."

The waiter hovered over the table to take their orders. Isaac and Hannah ordered wurst and sauerkraut, the least expensive item on the menu. Henry exchanged glances with his cousin, then berated Isaac. "Those aren't good choices, Isaac."

"Bring them both the wienerschnitzel," Arthur said to the waiter, ignoring Isaac's protest.

"So what is this place like where you live?" Isaac asked.

"You mean Butte? Or the whole state of Montana?" Arthur laughed.

Flustered, Isaac held up his hands helplessly.

"Well, Montana is very big. It's got everything—the Rocky Mountains, rivers and plains, big ranches, grizzly bears, Indians—"

"Indians!" Hannah exclaimed. "Do you really have Indians?"

"Not right where I live, but there are big reservations with lots of Indians."

"And where you live," Isaac asked, "what kind of place is it?"

"Butte's a mining town. First it had gold, then silver, and now, copper. The mines are so big a man can walk two miles underground from one part of town to another. It's called the richest hill on earth."

"So it's a big city like New York," Isaac said, trying to picture it in his mind.

"No," Arthur laughed, "not as big as New York. No place is that big. But it's growing every day. There are plenty of jobs."

"What do you do there, may I ask?"

"I'm in business for myself," he said, turning to look at the waiter who at that moment arrived with his cart. He set their entrees on the table—breaded veal, boiled potatoes, sweet peas, and small dishes of sweet and sour cucumbers. "And another bottle of wine," said Arthur.

"Please excuse my ignorance," said Isaac, "but what is copper? I mean, what is it used for?"

Arthur sat back in his chair and pointed at the light bulbs on the walls. "That's what it's used for," he said. "Electricity. If you have electricity, you need copper. And with the war in Europe, the mines are busier than ever. They operate twenty-four hours a day."

"But how?" Isaac asked.

"There are three shifts of workers. And since the miners work around the clock, the saloons stay open, too. They never close." Isaac stared at him wide-eyed. "But don't get the wrong idea," Arthur reassured him. "There are plenty of respectable people in the town. In fact, Butte has the biggest synagogue in the state of Montana."

Hannah, since Arthur's mention of Indians, hung on his every word. She listened to his descriptions of Butte and Montana, no longer wary about his easy laughter.

"This is delicious," said Isaac, tasting the veal. Arthur, his mouth full, nodded his agreement. The proprietor himself brought the new bottle of wine. As he opened it, Henry looked around the restaurant, surprised to see most of the tables still empty.

"Not many customers today, Emil."

A gloomy expression crossed the owner's face. "It's been like this for some time. All because of that British ship that was sunk."

"You mean the Lusitania?" Henry asked.

Emil nodded. "The regulars still come, but others stay away. Americans blame Germans for everything, even though Germany warned the British it would happen."

"That's the ship that was torpedoed?" Arthur asked, when Emil walked away.

"Yes," said Henry. "They're both to blame, of course. The British kept the German fleet bottled up in Jutland so a German submarine sank the Lusitania. More than a thousand people dead, including Americans on the ship."

"I think war is stupid," Hannah said suddenly.

They all turned to her in surprise. Arthur laughed but Henry's expression was serious. "I agree with you, Hannah. It's not the workers who want war, it's the rich people. But they use the workers to fight it for them."

"What do you think, Henry?" asked Arthur. "Do you think America will get into it?"

"I hope not."

"A lot of people in Butte think we'll be in it by next year."

"Everywhere people angry, fighting," said Isaac. "Like at the factory."

"That's different, Isaac," said Henry. "The workers just want to be treated fairly. The capitalists are too greedy. They don't want to share the wealth."

Isaac was upset with himself for bringing up the problems at the factory, but now he couldn't let it go. "Mr. Englehardt is a capitalist? I don't think he is so rich."

Henry smiled. "Not rich like Mr. Rockefeller or Mr. Carnegie. But he is a boss and he doesn't want to pay his men fairly for the hours they work."

Hannah didn't know what her father and Henry were talking about, but she knew when Isaac was upset. He had placed his knife and fork on the table and stared at his plate. She was about to say something when Henry spoke.

"Hannah, when was the last time you had a torte?"

"A torte?" She looked at Isaac questioningly.

"I've never had one," Isaac said, relieved to have the conversation take this new tack.

"Then you both have a nice surprise coming."

The waiter brought dessert and coffee. Hannah's eyes closed dreamily when she tasted the dense chocolate. The three men laughed, dispelling the tension provoked by the discussion earlier. Arthur excused himself from the table after they had their coffee. Henry chatted with Hannah about her studies in school until Arthur returned, then beckoned to the waiter.

"It's all taken care of," Arthur said.

"I'll have to watch you more closely," said Henry with mock severity.

They clustered together outside the restaurant to say their goodbyes. Isaac thanked both men and shook their hands.

"It's been especially nice to meet you, Hannah," Henry said. "I hope we can get together again."

As Henry and Arthur walked back toward the train station to get Arthur's luggage, Arthur hummed to himself, then laughed.

"What's so funny?" Henry asked.

"I think my cousin is falling in love."

"Oh, come on, she's very nice but a little too young for me."

"Not that young. And in a couple of years, not too young at all."

Henry laughed and gave his cousin a playful shove. "What did you mean about being in business for yourself?"

"Well, one of the first things I discovered about Butte, Montana is that there are a lot of single men with money in their pockets. They were looking to spend it and I decided to help them. The two fastest ways I could think of were with a deck of cards and with women. I was always pretty good at cards and I had no desire to be a pimp. Don't you remember when we were kids and I used to win all your pennies playing cards?"

Henry smiled at the recollection. "I never thought you'd make a living at it."

"I make quite a good living at the three establishments I frequent. I didn't want to tell Isaac that. He's such a serious fellow and I wanted him to think well of me. Of course, there are some risks to my occupation. Recently I cleaned out some miners from Cornwall. They were rough fellows and didn't take their losses gracefully. Somehow they got the notion I'd been cheating. Next thing I knew, word came to me that they were planning a necktie party."

"A necktie party?"

"A hanging. Mine. Don't look so skeptical. In Montana, those things are done."

"Aren't you exaggerating?"

"I didn't want to stick around to find out. I decided it would be better for my health to make a trip back east and give these men a chance to calm down. By the time I get back, they'll have lost money to someone else and be mad at him instead of at me."

6

Isaac and Hannah, after parting from Henry and Arthur, decided to walk home along Broadway. It was a warm day with just enough of a breeze to make the late summer humidity bearable.

"That was a good lunch," said Isaac. "Did you enjoy it?"

"What did you mean, poppa, about people fighting at the factory?"

"Oh, it's nothing, Hannah. Just some people complaining about the hours."

"Like your friend?"

"Henry? Yes, he thinks the boss is taking advantage of us by not paying us for the extra hours we work. But if we do complain, Mr. Englehardt might replace us. Anyway, it's too nice a day to talk about it."

'How old is he, poppa? He looks very young."

Isaac gave his daughter a surprised look. "I don't know. Would you like me to ask him for you?"

"No, poppa," said Hannah, blushing.

"He is a nice fellow," said Isaac. "We argue sometimes but he remains a friend."

"Wasn't it interesting, what his cousin told us about Montana?" said Hannah, still trying to overcome her embarrassment and steer the conversation away from

65

Henry. "Can you imagine being able to walk underground for two miles? And having saloons that never close? And Indians on reservations?"

"It was interesting," Isaac concurred. "It sounds like a good place for a young man with ambition."

"You're young, poppa."

"I'm going to be forty-one this year and you're telling me I'm young? Henry and Arthur, they're young. Are you telling me you want to move to this Montana?"

"Oh, poppa, stop teasing me. I would like to see it someday, that's all."

At work the following day, Henry came up to Isaac after the lunch whistle sounded. "I enjoyed our outing," he said. "You have a lovely daughter."

"Thank you. We had a nice time, too. Is your cousin still with you?"

"No, he left this morning for Newark to see his family. I expect I'll see him again before he goes back."

"Hannah was certainly interested in his stories. It was hard for her to imagine such a place."

"Well, maybe we can get together again before he leaves. Tell Hannah I said hello."

During the next few weeks Isaac and Henry seldom spoke, acknowledging each other only with a brief "good morning" or a nod of the head. The atmosphere in the factory had worsened. Isaac concentrated on his work but it was difficult to ignore the tension around him. When the noon whistle sounded, the men shut down their lathes and tossed their aprons aside. They sat on benches with their metal lunch pails open on their laps, their voices hushed but their expressions betraying their fury. At the end of the work day, their anger poured out in the heated discussions that took place on the sidewalk outside the factory. Henry was always surrounded by a group of workers. An abrupt silence occurred when Isaac walked past. It was obvious that the men didn't trust him. He was always aware, too, of Henry's eyes following him, a condemnatory gaze that upset Isaac more than the aloofness of the others. What does he want from me? Isaac thought angrily.

On the morning of October 17th, when Isaac was still a block away, he saw a crowd of men gathered in front of the factory. Shielding his eyes against a chill wind that blew swirls of dust into his face, he glanced in confusion at his pocket watch. It was almost seven. Why were the men still outside? Two policemen stood at the edge of the group, one of them speaking to a man who, from Isaac's distance, looked like Henry Sperling. Isaac wondered if there had been an accident or if Mr. Englehardt was ill. It was only when he approached his fellow workers that he saw the signs held by some of them against their chests. "On Strike" their placards proclaimed in bold, black letters.

Isaac walked around them to get to the factory door. At that moment, Henry responded to a call from one of the men. He pushed his way through the throng and stationed himself in front of Isaac. "You can't go in there, Isaac."

"But it's seven. We'll be late for work."

"There won't be any work today. The men voted unanimously Sunday to go on strike. You should have been at the meeting."

Isaac, who never paid attention to the times and dates of the men's meetings, looked around him helplessly. A few of the workers standing near him sneered and gestured in his direction. "You better not try to go in there!" one of the men yelled. "Yeah, we'll teach you a lesson if you do," cried another. Henry held up his hand to calm them.

"If we don't work," Isaac said, looking imploringly at Henry, "we won't get paid."

"Isaac, I've told you before, Englehardt is taking advantage of you—of all of us. We have to stick together."

"But, Henry, Mr. Englehardt was so good to me . . ."

The mob of restless men grew silent as Henry and Isaac confronted one another. "Give the bastard a good whack!" yelled one man. One of the policemen shouldered his way through and spoke softly to the man.

"Isaac," Henry said, his lips tight and his voice angry, "if you go in there I won't be able to protect you. These men are angry. Please, Isaac . . ."

Isaac looked at the men surrounding him as if seeing them for the first time. These were men he had worked with for almost three years. Until recently he had thought of them in the same way he had thought of the two tailors who worked with him in Lemberg, fellow laborers struggling together to make a business succeed. But their faces now were grim, hostile. He knew he couldn't enter the factory without betraying them. He nodded to Henry. The men cheered as Isaac walked into their midst, receiving a pat on the back from a few of them.

For most of that day, the men carrying placards paced back and forth, calling to passersby. "This factory is unfair to its workers!" they shouted, pointing at the Englehardt Manufacturing sign. The rest of the men huddled together against the stiff breeze from the waterfront and talked quietly to one another. Every now and then they cast glances at the building's entrance, wondering if Englehardt dared show his face. Isaac moved from one group of men to the next, listening to what they had to say. "Englehardt won't be happy until he's made slaves of all of us!" "The man has no conscience!" "He doesn't care if our children starve!" Isaac dared not refute them.

As the afternoon light faded, the men drifted off, pledging to return to the picket line the next day and for as many days as it took for them to receive fair treatment from the factory owner. Henry approached Isaac, who stood motionless in front of the building. He put his arm around the older man's shoulder. "Are you all right?" he asked.

"What's it for?" said Isaac. "We've been standing here in the street all day when we could have been working. What did we accomplish?"

"What we've accomplished is standing together—fighting for something we believe in. How else can we make the bosses understand?"

Isaac raised his hands in a helpless gesture. "Henry, I know you mean well. But I just don't understand. I know I have to support these men. I work with them. But still, I don't understand. So what if we have to work a few hours more right now? Mr. Englehardt makes it possible for us to earn our bread. Without him, what? We find another job? And maybe a boss who's far worse. And then what?" He made a dismissive gesture. "I must go home."

"Isaac," Henry called as his friend walked away. Isaac stopped and turned around. "Soon we're going to have a union. I want you to know that I advised the men to wait until then to see if Englehardt would be willing to negotiate with the union leadership. But the men refused to wait. They'd had enough. Their grievances are legitimate, Isaac. It's Englehardt who has refused to compromise in any way. At a time like this none of us can stand apart as individuals. We have to remain united. It's the only way to attain what we've been struggling for. And just to remind you, what we've been fighting for is nothing more than fair treatment."

Isaac turned away and again Henry called to him. "Isaac, you're a good man. Don't forget to tell Hannah I said hello."

When Hannah arrived home from her job at the barbershop she was surprised to find Isaac sitting at the kitchen table, a cup of tea in front of him.

"Poppa, what are you doing home so early?"

"There was no work today."

Hannah stared at him, not comprehending. "No work? How can that be? You've been so busy at the factory."

"What I mean is that there is work if we wanted to work, but the workers have decided to go on strike. Now no one can go in."

"So that's what you meant about people fighting at the factory. Why didn't you tell me?"

Isaac shrugged. "I didn't want to worry you. And who knew it would come to this?"

"How long do you think the strike will last, poppa?"

"Maybe it will be over tomorrow. The men have to work if they're going to eat and Mr. Englehardt has a business to run." Sighing, Isaac pushed himself up from his chair. "Let's not worry now. We'll see what the morning brings."

But in the morning nothing had changed. The men holding signs paraded back and forth, calling out to onlookers. "Englehardt steals the bread from our children's mouths," one shouted. "He exploits his workers," yelled another.

A few of the men chatted idly with the two policemen, the same ones who had been there the day before. They watched the strikers impassively, idly twirling their nightsticks.

Isaac spotted Henry in the crowd and approached him.

"Good morning, Isaac," said Henry.

"I would like to ask you a question, Henry. How long will this go on?"

"That's up to Mr. Englehardt."

"But why don't we sit down and talk to him? He seems like a reasonable man. I'm sure he doesn't like seeing his machines idle."

"Don't you think we've tried, Isaac? Even though I was sure we wouldn't get anywhere, we met with him last Friday. Most of the men were already talking strike so I knew there was nothing to lose. We told him how we felt. We also told him the men were getting impatient and a strike was certain if he wouldn't compensate us for the extra hours we worked."

"What did he say?"

"What he said was 'it's my factory. I make the rules and I give the orders.' He left us no choice."

"But how am I to pay my rent and buy food if I don't work?"

Henry's eyes narrowed, displaying sparks of anger. "Isaac, everyone is in the same boat. There are men here with wives and children. Don't you think they're worried about the same thing? But if we give in now, what have we accomplished? Nothing. Perhaps if Englehardt sees his machines 'sitting idle,' as you say, for a few days, he'll change his mind."

By the end of the week it was obvious to everyone that Englehardt had no intention of backing down. Isaac was sick with worry. He had lost a full week's pay. The rest of the men, too, were sullen and angry. They no longer bantered with the two policmen who, aware of the men's growing tension, kept their distance.

"If this isn't over by Monday," Isaac told Hannah that evening, "I'll have to look for another job. We won't even be able to buy groceries unless I take some money from the bank."

Hannah, who had been spending most of what she earned at the barbershop on groceries, decided not to meet her girlfriends that weekend. She was unwilling to spend money for subway fare. Instead she accompanied Isaac on a stroll through their own neighborhood. "At least the air is free," Isaac said gloomily.

On Monday morning, Isaac felt uneasy as he approached the factory. Even from a distance he heard the men's angry voices. "The bastard must be in there," someone said. "He probably arrives when it's still dark and sits in there laughing at us." "We ought to drag him out and teach him a lesson," another shouted. "I say we burn the damn building down!" someone yelled. Isaac saw Henry moving from one small group of men to another, trying to calm their anger. Suddenly, Henry shouted for quiet and a hush descended on the gathering. They all turned to look as a mob of men, at least thirty of them, approached from the east end of the block, men none of them recognized. They carried clubs and bats. For the first time Isaac realized that the two policemen were absent that morning. Pedestrians crossing on the sidewalk opposite turned abruptly, quickening their pace as they left the factory area.

The mob was only a short distance from the strikers when they stopped. A few of them menacingly slapped their clubs against the palms of their hands.

Henry stepped forward and confronted them. "We don't want any trouble," he said.

"Then get the hell away from the factory," said a burly man holding a bat.

"We have a right to strike. Our fight isn't with you."

"Like hell it ain't," said the man. "Are you going to move?"

The workers looked at one another uncertainly. "Where are the policemen?" one of them asked the crowd. Henry turned to say something. At that moment the burly man, apparently the mob's leader, nodded his head almost imperceptibly and they charged the strikers. Henry raised his hands, urging the men to remain calm as some turned to run. Others held their ground and fought back as the hooligans waded into them, swinging their bats and fists. Above the shouts and oaths of the men, Isaac heard police whistles sounding in the distance. He stumbled back away from the mob, covering his head and trying to keep low as he ducked the blows of the strikebreakers. He caught a glimpse of Henry struggling to wrest the bat from a goon's hands. Suddenly a huge thug rose up behind his friend and smashed his club onto Henry's head and shoulders, again and again. Isaac forced his way through the struggling men, making his way toward the spot where Henry had collapsed. He knelt beside him and that moment felt a blow to the side of the head.

Crumpling across Henry's body, he fought against the pain and blackness that threatened to engulf him. Men tripped over him as they wrestled and struck one another. The whistles were louder now, drowning out the grunts and curses of the attackers. Isaac faintly heard a new sound, the thudding of hooves and the whinnying of horses. He lifted his head, his vision blurred by the blow he had received, and saw a mounted policeman, a baton in his upraised hand, forcing his way through the men. The club-wielding strikebreakers scattered in all directions as more police officers arrived, some dismounting and swinging their billysticks indiscriminately. Still dazed, Isaac struggled to his knees and looked around him. At least a dozen men lay sprawled on the ground, blood pooling beneath them. His head throbbed and he pressed his hand to his scalp, where the blood was sticky and congealed. He stared in horror at the blood covering his fingers and palm. Henry, lying in front of him, had not stirred. The hair on the back of his head was matted with blood. Isaac reached for his friend and struggled to turn him over. His hands recoiled when he saw Henry's open, staring eyes and ashen skin. "No, no, no!" he screamed, pulling Henry's shoulders off the ground. "Don't die, don't die!" he yelled, hanging on to the lapels of his friend's jacket and shaking him. Henry's head lolled from side to side, the unseeing eyes still staring grotesquely. "Help me!" Isaac cried. "Somebody help me!" He staggered to his feet, his head throbbing worse than ever, then hurtled forward, the side of his face slamming against the rough grain of the sidewalk.

7

As she walked to school, Hannah had a foreboding. Her father had not been his usual self, barely speaking to her as he prepared their breakfasts. She knew how much he dreaded arriving at the factory to find nothing changed. If that were the case their situation would indeed be desperate. Even if Isaac could find another job, he couldn't hope to earn the same wages he made at Englehardt's. And what Hannah earned could barely buy some groceries. Isaac would have to use their savings to pay rent and bills.

Her friends, Ruth and Jessica, noticed how preoccupied she was and tried to cheer her up as they ate their lunch together in the cafeteria. "You're going to get wrinkles if you don't smile," Ruth said, "and then you'll look like this." She held up a piece of dried salami from her sandwich. Hannah, needing someone to talk to, told them about the strike at the factory.

"That's terrible," said Ruth. "What do you think will happen?"

"I don't know, but I have a bad feeling about it."

"Something like that happened to my father," said Jessica. "He asked his boss for a raise. He'd worked for him for three years, never missing a day. The boss told him to quit if he wanted to, that there was always someone who'd want his job. It's not fair."

"What did your father do?"

"What could he do? He just kept working. But I know how much it upsets him. He gets terrible pains in his stomach and the doctor told him he has an ulcer."

Hannah appreciated the sympathy of her friends but nothing could dispel the gloom that had settled upon her. She arrived at the barber shop after school to find the usual assortment of old men sitting along the wall awaiting their turn with Salvatore. Each time Salvatore finished with a customer, Hannah swept up the hair from around the chair, stepping out of the way as the next man sat down. "Hannah," called one of the old Neapolitans, "everything you sweep is white. Maybe you should use a snow shovel." The old men laughed, but Hannah responded with a half-hearted smile. Several times that afternoon, she caught Salvatore looking at her in a strange way as he rhythmically stropped his straight-edge razor or made his final scissors-snips on a customer. She knew she wasn't being her usual self but she was too worried about Isaac and the factory.

When the last customer had gone, Salvatore disappeared into the small back room used as a storage area for his pomades and lotions. He usually paid her each day for the few hours she worked and she waited for him to come out.

"Hannah," he called from the back, "lock up, then come in here for a minute."

Expecting him to give her the money, she parted the striped curtain separating the room from the work area. The room was dimly lit, its only light provided by a weak bulb dangling from the ceiling. Salvatore stood against the back wall of shelves and studied her as she held the curtain open.

"You don't feel well, Hannah?" he asked. "Something is wrong today?"

"No, Mr. Salvatore. Nothing is wrong."

"Come closer," he said. "I want to see your face."

Hannah released the curtain and approached. She stood directly in front of him. The old man cocked his head, his white hair taking on a yellowish cast from the overhead light.

"I don't like to see you sad, Hannah. You are too pretty to be sad. *Tu sei bella, capisce?*"

Hannah nodded, forcing a smile. "I really have to get home and make dinner for my father, Mr. Salvatore." She was about to turn and leave when Salvatore placed his hands on her shoulders. In the confines of the closet-like room, the faint smell of garlic on his breath mingled with the after-shave lotion he wore. Suddenly he pulled her toward him and tried to kiss her. "No, Mr. Salvatore!" Hannah cried. He continued to hold her tightly with his left arm while he groped at her breasts with his other hand. She struggled to free herself, slapping his hand from her breasts. He seized her flailing wrist and shoved her hand down to the firm bulge of his crotch. Unable to break away, Hannah threw herself against him, forcing him against the shelves. Salvatore grunted in pain as the sharp edge of a shelf caught him in the back. Hannah broke free. Dashing from the room she fumbled with the lock, jerked the front door open, and fled.

Tears streamed down her face. Head down, she walked quickly home, repeatedly glancing back over her shoulder to make certain Salvatore wasn't following. How could this have happened? she asked herself. How could such a nice man become like an animal? She would never set foot in his store again even though Salvatore hadn't paid her for the day. She didn't know how she could ever walk past his shop again. Now she had no job. What would she do? The money she earned each day wasn't much but it provided for some of their food. She trudged slowly up the dim stairway of her building. She didn't even have money to buy anything for their dinner. What can I cook? she wondered as she twisted her key in the apartment door's lock. But the door was already unlocked. She pushed it open.

Isaac was sitting at the table, his head swathed in a bandage, a red stain oozing through the white dressing.

"Poppa!" she cried, running toward him. "What happened?"

He raised his eyes, glazed with pain, and shook his head. "A mob of hooligans attacked us. They beat us with clubs."

"How could they have done that? Where were the police?"

"The police," he repeated softly. "The police weren't there. Not until it was too late."

"Poppa, who sent these men to do such a terrible thing?"

Not since the deaths of her mother and uncle had Hannah seen such a mournful expression on her father's face. "There was only one man who could have sent them. Mr. Englehardt."

"Oh, poppa, that's terrible. No, he couldn't have. I can't believe that of him. Remember when we first went to him after—"

"That's not the worst, Hannah. Sit down."

"Can I make you some tea first, poppa?"

"The tea can wait. I have some very bad news."

"You'll have to find another job, right, poppa?"

"Yes, I will never go back to that factory. But it's worse than that. These men—these hoodlums—they killed two of the workers."

Hannah's face blanched. "Killed?" Her mouth was open, as if she was about to say something else, but no words came.

"They killed Henry."

Hannah began to cry, sobbing until she could barely breathe. Henry's death, her father's injury, Mr. Englehardt's treachery, and the indignity she had suffered at the hands of Mr. Salvatore—it was all too much to bear. How little control they had over their own lives, she thought. There seemed no way to bring an end to the losses inflicted upon them since that terrible day in Lemberg.

8

Isaac ladled small amounts of dye from one vat to another trying to match the color on the swatch of cloth handed to him by his supervisor. His hands were discolored by the vivid colors of the substances he worked with. Lemnitz Enterprises, Isaac's employer, manufactured curtains and drapes. The work was tedious and not particularly interesting, but Isaac considered himself fortunate to have found a job so soon after their arrival in Butte. After a month in the city, he still found it hard to believe he and Hannah were actually in Montana.

■■■

"Poppa," Hannah had said after learning of Henry's death, "I don't want to live here any more."

Isaac, still seated at the table, his head throbbing, had looked up. "You mean in this apartment?"

"No. I want us to leave New York. There's nothing to keep us here."

"But where can we go? And what about school?"

"There are schools everywhere. Henry's cousin said there were lots of jobs in Butte, Montana. We can go there."

"But we know nothing of Montana. I don't even know Arthur's last name or how to find him."

"What did we know of New York when we came. Weren't we on our own after Uncle Morris died?"

She's right, Isaac thought. Morris is dead, Henry is dead. And Arthur did say Butte was growing and jobs were plentiful.

Isaac soon sold their furniture to the second-hand store, emptied their bank account, and only a week later they boarded a train for the first leg of their journey west. There was even less in their valises than when they had fled Lemberg.

Isaac gazed thoughtfully out the window as the train lurched to a start and the platform slowly receded. It seemed like only yesterday when he and Hannah had stood on the platform with Henry to meet Arthur. What a nice day it had been. How hard it was to believe that a young man of such promise should meet his death at the hands of hoodlums. And even worse, hoodlums ordered to do what they had done by a man Isaac had respected and defended.

Hannah pressed the leather seat with her hand and smiled.

"What?" Isaac asked.

"I was just thinking of the difference between this train and the one in Europe. These seats are so nice. And there's no smell of cheese."

"So you remember," Isaac said. "It's something we never talk about."

Hannah shrugged. "It seems so long ago. And it makes me sad to think of momma."

Isaac nodded. "Maybe better things will await us in your Montana."

"It's not my Montana, poppa. It will be ours."

Day and night their train had rumbled across the country, the towns and cities blurring in Isaac's mind. It was only when they began to cross the prairies, the fields of recently harvested wheat and corn stretching for mile after mile, that Isaac truly appreciated the size and grandeur of America. For both of them it had begun to feel as though they would spend the rest of their lives on this train, watching the sun rise and set on fields of gold. At night they slept fitfully in their seats, Hannah's head resting against her father's shoulder.

One afternoon they had stared in awe at buttes and mesas, which were then replaced by islands of mountains that jutted skyward from rolling meadows and flat prairie. They were crossing eastern Montana, stopping at stations in the middle of nowhere. "Look, look!" Hannah pointed excitedly at three men on horseback herding cattle into a corral. A dog snapped at the heels of the steers. "Do you think they're cowboys?"

"Well," said Isaac, smiling at his daughter's excitement, "they're young men, they're riding horses, and they're working with cows. I guess that makes them cowboys."

"Oh, poppa, don't tease me."

As night fell they seemed no nearer their destination. The sparsely-populated land stretched out on all sides.

"Do you think people really live in this Montana?" Isaac asked almost to himself.

Hannah had dozed off and didn't hear him.

The train's whistle suddenly awakened them. Isaac looked at his pocket watch. It was early morning, not yet six-thirty, and streaks of light slashed their way across the night sky, gradually extinguishing the glow of the few bright stars still visible. Hannah's face was pressed to the glass as they entered Butte's valley. Isaac, as intrigued as Hannah by their surroundings, half-stood from his seat and leaned across his daughter to peer out the window.

With morning upon them, they stared out at a panorama of mountains on the horizon, many with a dusting of snow. But it was the town itself that had them wide-eyed. Massive chimneys belched columns of smoke into the sky. The skyline was dominated by black derricks of steel, from which elevators carrying miners descended into the bowels of the earth. Interspersed between these "gallows frames" were the small wooden houses where miners and their families lived, and above it all hovered a mountain of granite, the richest hill on earth. Butte's downtown streets were steep, lined by red-brick commercial buildings and stores. Isaac and Hannah were amazed by the crowds that filled the streets at this early hour. Miners hurried to work carrying their lunch pails, shoppers entered and left stores and bars. The bars, often as many as three on the same block, were the busiest establishments. A constant stream of patrons filed in and out of each one.

"Remember what Henry's cousin told us, poppa?" Hannah said, turning her head to him. "The saloons never close."

"Amazing," was all Isaac could utter.

They stepped from the train into the mountain chill. Neither was dressed for the weather. They quickly placed their valises on an empty bench and fished out wool sweaters to put on underneath their jackets. After leaving the station, they paused and turned toward one another as if to ask 'now what?'

"I have an idea," Isaac said, "but first let's get some breakfast."

They walked up the hilly streets until they spotted the blinking lights of a saloon-restaurant called the M&M. They pushed through the door into a large smoke-filled room. Men lined the bar on the left, some hefting steins of beer, while others threw back whiskey served in shot glasses. On the opposite side of the room, diners sat on stools at a counter. Signs tacked on the wall announced the breakfast specials. There were a few empty stools but none next to each other. A bearded man seated next to a vacant stool glanced at them and without a word, picked up his plate and cup, gesturing with his head. Isaac thanked the man. Surprised, he nodded and mumbled something Isaac couldn't make out.

"What's your idea, poppa?" Hannah asked, while they enjoyed toast and eggs.

"Well, we don't know anybody and finding Arthur in a town this big would take a miracle. But he did say there was a synagogue. Why don't we go there? I can describe him and maybe they'll know him. Even if they don't, I'm sure they'd be willing to help some *landsmen*. At least they could suggest a place where we could stay and maybe someone there would know of a job. Then as soon as we're settled, we can get you into school."

"Poppa, I've been thinking, too. I know you want me to finish school, but it would be better if I went to work." Anticipating his protest, Hannah spoke quickly. "I know what you're going to say, that I'm only fifteen. But soon I'll be sixteen and I do look older than my age. I'm not saying I won't go back to school. But I've missed part of this term already and it would help us if I went to work for the rest of this school year."

Isaac stopped eating and thought for a moment. "I'm not saying yes or no right now," he said. "Let's see what kind of work I can find and how much they'll pay. Then we can decide."

As they were leaving the M&M, Isaac spotted a policeman walking his beat and asked for directions to the synagogue.

"It's too bad we have to carry these valises," Isaac said, as they trudged the long blocks in the direction the policeman had indicated. The sun had come up and even though the morning was as chilly as when they stepped off the train, seeing the sun made them feel warmer.

The synagogue, an imposing building of sandstone and granite, was impossible to miss. "That's it," said Isaac, pointing when they were still a block away. As they approached, a well-dressed man wearing a dark suit and a yarmulke came out of a door to the right of the entrance. Isaac asked him if the rabbi was in the synagogue.

"I'm Rabbi Gersohn," he said.

Isaac, introducing himself and Hannah, explained their situation. He then described Henry's cousin.

The rabbi shrugged. "I don't recognize the man from your description." He took a pad and fountain pen from his jacket pocket. "A nice widow, Mrs. Kovsky, has an apartment to rent in her home. This is the address. It's only two blocks from here. Just tell her I sent you. Once you're settled, go see Herman Lemnitz, a member of our congregation. I believe he's looking for help at his factory. I'll write his address for you and Mrs. Kovsky will tell you how to get there."

Isaac thanked the rabbi and turned to go. "Oh, Mr. Schneider," the rabbi called. "I'll be looking forward to seeing you and Hannah on *shabbus.*"

Isaac nodded, but said nothing.

"Are you really going to go to synagogue, poppa?"

"No, but how could I tell the rabbi that after he tried to help us."

■■■

Isaac, bent over his vats of dye, smiled to himself as he remembered that day. Hannah had been pleased when Mrs. Kovsky, a plump grey-haired woman, readily agreed to rent the upstairs floor to them. Each had their own room and would share the kitchen with Mrs. Kovsky. The rent, Isaac thought, was very reasonable, less than what they had paid in New York for an apartment not half as nice.

But Hannah's happiness turned to disappointment when her father told her that he had been hired by Mr. Lemnitz.

"The pay will be plenty for us to live on," he said to Hannah. "Now you can go to school."

Hannah knew it was pointless to argue. Isaac accompanied her to the high school that very afternoon and Hannah registered. In a matter of days, Hannah was her old self, busy with her homework and telling him about her teachers and her new friend, Maude.

9

In spite of his tedious work, Isaac was happy to be occupied and especially pleased that the transition for Hannah had been so easy. He lifted a ladle of blue stain from the vat in front of him. At that moment a worker passing behind stumbled against him. Isaac always wore a work apron and although his hands were discolored by the vivid colors of the substances he worked with, he was careful not to let the dyes stain his clothing. This time he was unlucky. Indigo droplets spattered his partially rolled-up sleeves.

The worker apologized profusely but the damage was done. This particular shirt was one he had made himself when he worked for Kaltbrenner and it had held up well over the years. Isaac had only one other shirt, a sorry affair that had been mended so many times it embarrassed him when, of necessity, he had to wear it. Although reluctant to spend money to have his hand-made shirt cleaned, he knew the stains probably wouldn't come out with a simple washing. He then remembered passing a Chinese laundry while walking to and from work each day. It's worth a try, he thought.

On his way home that evening, he stopped in. A Chinese man of indeterminate age, wearing a dark silk robe and black skullcap, was eating with chopsticks from a small bowl in his hand. He placed the bowl and chopsticks on the counter and stood up, smiling and bowing to Isaac.

Isaac removed his jacket and pointed at the stains. "I got dye on my shirt. Do you think you can get it out?"

The man came out from behind the counter and ran the fabric of Isaac's shirtsleeve between his fingers.

"This is good quality," he said. "We don't often see shirts like this."

"I made this shirt years ago," Isaac said. "I was a tailor then."

"Why aren't you a tailor now? You do good work."

Isaac explained that he had only arrived a month earlier and now worked at Lemnitz's factory.

"So that's where you got this," the laundryman said, pointing at the blue spatters. "But for a man who can make a shirt like this to work at Lemnitz . . ." He shook his head. "Maybe I can get these marks out. I can't promise. But I still think you should go into business as a tailor."

"I'm a poor man," said Isaac. "I don't have the money for a shop or a sewing machine."

The Chinaman ran the few wisps of hair growing from his chin between his fingers. "My name is Ah Yeh," he said. "What is yours?"

"Isaac Schneider."

Ah Yeh studied Isaac for several seconds, then nodded. "I make you a proposition," he said. "I will rent a Singer machine for you and you can set up your business in the front of the store. I will charge you very little rent until you get enough customers. Then you can take over the payments for the machine, or maybe even buy it, and we can decide on a rent that's fair. I think this arrangement will be good for both of us."

Isaac stared at the laundryman in astonishment. A perfect stranger was making it possible for him to have his own business. "You are very kind," he said.

Ah Yeh smiled. "Like I said, it will be good for both of us. Laundry and mending all in one place. So you accept my offer?"

"When would you like me to start?"

"I will rent the machine tomorrow. You can begin the next day."

Isaac couldn't wait to get home and tell Hannah. Perhaps this was the beginning of a change in their fortunes.

"Oh, poppa, I'm so happy for you," Hannah squealed excitedly. "It's so generous of him. And we've never known a Chinaman."

"Well," said Isaac, his eyes twinkling, "maybe he's never known two immigrants from Lemberg."

Isaac resigned his position at the factory the following morning. "What's the matter, you're too good to do this kind of work?" Lemnitz growled as he begrudgingly paid Isaac the money he owed him.

When Isaac arrived at the laundry that afternoon, there was a Singer sewing machine sitting in a corner at the front of the shop. A small hand-printed sign, 'I. Schneider, Tailor' was taped to the door.

"This is Li, my oldest son," Ah Yeh said, introducing a young man of about thirty who was at least a head taller than his father. "Li will watch the store and I will go with you to buy all the supplies you need for your work."

They returned two hours later with a large assortment of different color threads, needles, shears, in fact everything Isaac once had at his disposal in Lemberg. Only this time the supplies and the business belonged to him. "I will pay you back for everything," he said to Ah Yeh. "And I'll never forget your generosity."

What Ah Yeh had not told Isaac was the scene that had transpired the previous evening at his home. When he had informed his three sons about the arrangement he'd made with the white tailor, they looked at him as if he'd lost his senses.

"You must remember," Ah Yeh said in his defence, "any customer for the tailor is a potential customer for the laundry. Mending clothes and cleaning clothes are sister tasks."

"But you don't even know if he'll have any customers," Li, the oldest, argued.

"I've seen the quality of his work. When word gets around, the customers will come."

"In the meantime," Li persisted, "he stands to lose nothing, while you with your generosity are responsible for the payments on the sewing machine."

My oldest son, Ah Yeh thought, when he gets his teeth into anything he's like a dog with a bone. But Ah Yeh had to admit to himself that his son had a point. The workmanship on the shirt was indeed excellent, but Schneider himself had admitted that he hadn't worked as a tailor for years. There was no guarantee he could reproduce such fine work. Sill, it wasn't only because of the potential benefit to the laundry that Ah Yeh had come to this business arrangement with the tailor. And this was something he could never explain to his sons. During the short time he had talked to Isaac, he had the feeling he was dealing with an honest man. It was obvious that life for Isaac as an immigrant had been difficult. And he was raising a child, a daughter, by himself. How blessed I am to have three sons, Ah Yeh thought. Sons are the best security a man can have. They'll care for him when he's ill or old, whereas a daughter must care for her husband and his family. And there was more Ah Yeh could never tell his sons. This tailor, Isaac Schneider, a white man, reminded him of his own father.

Some day, perhaps, if he and Isaac became friends, they would sit and talk. Ah Yeh would then tell him about how difficult life had been for him and for his father as immigrants in America. My father was about your age when he brought me to America from Canton province, Ah Yeh would say. We were desperately poor in China and my father always talked about America, the land he called "the gold mountain." My parents used to argue about this. My father wanted to emigrate but my mother refused to leave the land of her ancestors. "There will be no one to tend my parents' graves," she always said.

Finally, my father left, taking me with him. My mother and two sisters remained behind. I was already a young man, strong and eager to work, and my father thought the two of us would make enough money to send back to China, not only to take care of my mother and sisters, but to buy land. After a few years, we'd go back to Canton and be respectable landowners.

We came to Montana where we knew many Chinese were being hired to work on building the railroads. The work was hard, more difficult than we'd imagined. And nothing had prepared us for the winters. We sent what money we were able to my mother but our expenses were high. We had to pay for our room, our food, and our clothes, and since we never earned as much as we thought we would, there was little left over to put in the remittances to China. The dream of being landowners, we now knew, would always remain just that—a dream.

After three years of following the railroad, my father had become an old man. It was obvious he could no longer do the labor that was required. To make matters worse, he was now ill, often coughing up blood. Fortunately I was strong and by working even longer hours and keeping our expenses to a bare minimum, I managed to send something back to my mother each month.

It soon became apparent that my father wouldn't live much longer. A doctor from a small town almost twenty miles away came to see him. He was a kind old man but could offer no hope. My father, he said, had consumption and would not live to see the spring come. By giving him the medicines he prescribed, we could at least keep him more comfortable. I told the doctor we sent our money to my mother and sisters in China and had none to buy medicine. The doctor then did something I will never forget. He gave me the money for the medicine and didn't charge us for the visit. No one in America had ever been that kind.

My father died that winter. It was so cold in our room the morning I found him dead in his bed that there was frost on his eyelids. Not long after that I received a letter from a scribe in our village in China. The neighbor who paid the scribe to write to us said that famine had come to the entire province and my mother and sisters were all dead. Not even the money we sent them had been able to keep them alive.

I was now twenty-two and alone in the world. With my mother and sisters gone, there was no longer an obligation to send money back to China. I was tired of the grueling work on the railroad and had heard about the jobs available in Butte. The gold and silver booms were over but the mines of "the copper mountain" offered work for everyone. I knew mining was hard work but at least it would be a change. Most of the miners were immigrants like myself, but they were from Cornwall and Ireland and Bohemia. The men were hostile to me because I was Chinese and the foreman gave me the most difficult and most dangerous jobs.

My work as a miner came to an end after only three months when a supporting beam fell on my leg, breaking the bone. I suspected the beam had been intentionally loosened, but who would believe a Chinaman? The company paid for a doctor to set my leg and gave me the money I had earned for the days worked that week. If it wasn't for the Cantonese who ran the Chinese restaurant in town I don't know how I would have survived while the bone mended. They permitted me to sleep in a room in back of the restaurant and fed me. When I was able to bear weight on my leg again, I paid them back by working as a waiter and dishwasher.

Mr. Chou, the owner of the restaurant, saw that I was a hard worker and took a liking to me. He had two daughters and no sons. The older daughter, Mei, did most of the cooking in the restaurant. She was a homely girl, short and squat, but worked as hard as any man. She also angered easily and the other waiters feared her sharp tongue. Her sister, SuYin, still attended school and worked in the restaurant on weekends. In every way she was the opposite of her older sister. A gentle, soft-spoken girl, she had a lovely face and a body as slender as a reed. I knew by the furtive glances in my direction that she was as attracted to me as I was to her. But Mr. Chou had other ideas.

One evening as I was cleaning up, Mr. Chou took me aside. "I'd like to talk to you after everyone leaves," he said.

Mei followed the waiters from the restaurant, exchanging a glance with her father as he locked the door behind her. Mr. Chou took out a bottle of whiskey from a cabinet and motioned for me to sit down. Joining me at the table with two glasses, he poured us each a drink.

"I want you to know I've been very happy with your work," he said, raising his glass to me.

"Thank you, sir," I replied, still wondering where the conversation was heading.

"I'm not getting any younger, you know. I'd like to take a little time off now and then. And I'd like to see my daughters settled. What would you say to my making you manager of the restaurant?"

"I'd be honored," I said.

He nodded. "Have you given any thought to getting married?"

I took my first swallow of the whiskey, wincing at the burning sensation as it went down. "No, I haven't."

"Well, I think it's good for a young man to be married. Since you have no family of your own, I'd like to be a father to you. How would you feel about marrying my daughter?"

I visualized SuYin's lovely face and felt intense happiness. "I would like that very much," I said.

Mr. Chou smiled and poured himself a second drink. "Then I have gained a son, the son I always wanted, and soon many grandchildren will follow."

His second drink disappeared with one swallow. "I will go home and tell Mei at once."

"But, sir," I stammered, "it is SuYin I would like to marry."

The smile disappeared from his face. "The oldest must marry first. Besides, SuYin is still in school. She is too young."

"I would be willing to wait until you feel she is of age."

He shook his head forcefully. "No, you must marry Mei."

"You've been very good to me and I don't want to disappoint you, but—"

"If you are grateful, as you say, then you will make me happy and marry Mei."

I felt I had no choice but to swallow my disappointment. And that is how I became both a restaurant manager and a husband. SuYin, I believed, was as disappointed as I was, but of course she would never go against her father's wishes.

Marriage didn't cure Mei's sharp tongue, but in her defence she continued to be a hard worker and provided me with three fine sons. When some years later SuYin was married to a young man from Szechuan province, I cried at her wedding as I toasted the bride. Everyone, except Mr. Chou who knew the truth, thought they were tears of joy.

It wasn't long after SuYin's wedding that Mr. Chou became ill. The doctor informed us he had cancer and only a few months later, he died. I was the last one to see him alive when he was on his death bed. His body had shed its robustness as the cancer ate away at him and he was almost too weak to raise his arms. He motioned for me to come closer and spoke softly into my ear.

"I have done my duty to my daughters and die at peace. Thank you, Ah Yeh, for being a good son."

In spite of the unhappiness that never left me because of having lost SuYin, I was glad I'd been able to repay him for his kindness to me. As it turned out, his death saved him from much unhappiness. Within a few years, two more Chinese noodle parlors opened in our area and the competition did great harm to our business. This only increased the bickering between Mei and myself, but even that came to an end when an epidemic of influenza swept through Butte. Mei and SuYin were among its victims, both dying within a week of each other.

I no longer had any enthusiasm for running the restaurant and sold it to a recent immigrant from Canton. With the modest sum I received, I opened a laundry, and as each son became old enough, he joined me in the business. The younger ones will someday go their own way but Li, I believe, will keep the laundry going when I am gone.

These are the things I would tell Isaac if we become friends. In the meantime, Ah Yeh thought, it will be good to have him working in the store. When Li and the other boys are here, they're always in back doing the washing and ironing while I work in front doing packaging and seeing customers. Now when I'm at the counter, Isaac will be here working at his machine and we can talk. I find I am more lonely in the store than at home. The two older boys have given me four grandchildren and their presence in the house in the evening helps to dispel the loneliness I sometimes feel.

For the first few days of his proprietorship, Isaac sat behind his sewing machine, watching with anticipation each time the door of the shop opened. The customers, all of whom were delivering or picking up their laundry from Ah Yeh, reacted with surprise when they saw the tailor sitting in his corner.

"This is Mr. Schneider, a very good tailor," the Chinaman said, introducing everyone who entered.

One morning, as gusty winds blew swirling clouds of dust through the streets of Butte, Isaac received his first customer. From then on at least a few of the people who entered the store each day came to see the tailor. Isaac, hunched over his Singer, was happy to be working again. The staccato noise of the treadle as he mended, patched, and hemmed drowned out the sing-song speech of Ah Yeh and his sons. Isaac's work area allowed him a view of the street through windows covered with grime. Above him, a dim light bulb was suspended from the ceiling, providing barely enough light for him to work by. Every few minutes he raised his watery blue eyes and glanced at the muddy tableau of cars and pedestrians, their outlines blurred by the dirt-encrusted glass.

A bell hanging over the door jangled each time a customer entered. Ah Yeh, if he wasn't already at the counter, immediately materialized form the rear of the store, only to vanish just as quickly if the customer had come to see the tailor. For many weeks that was not usually the case. Most people entered the shop with armloads of laundry and were greeted by a smiling Ah Yeh as if they were long-lost friends or family. He bowed repeatedly as he spoke and Isaac couldn't help but notice the look of amusement on each customer's face at the Chinaman's deferential behavior and numerous mispronunciations of English. Isaac readily sympathized with Ah Yeh. His own command of English, while better than Ah Yeh's when it came to pronunciation, was far from fluent. Even though he had grown up speaking a hodgepodge of Polish, Russian, German, and Yiddish, Isaac found English to be the most difficult language of all. Americans, he saw, had a tendency to look with barely concealed derision at people who spoke English with an accent or dressed differently. Perhaps because he had lived among the diverse groups of people in Emperor Franz Joseph's Austro-Hungarian Empire, Isaac found nothing strange about sharing a shop with a Chinaman and his sons. Ah Yeh's garb seemed no more odd to Isaac than the black caftans and long sidelocks of the Hassidic Jews in Lemberg. Watching Ah Yeh carry the laundry to the rear of the shop, his silk robe rustling and pigtail bobbing as he walked, Isaac knew how mistaken the customers were if they thought they were dealing with a fool.

Hannah took to stopping at the store each day on her way home from school. Seeing her father bent over his machine brought back memories of Kaltbrenner's shop and she was filled with a bittersweet sadness remembering their life in Lemberg.

Ah Yeh was as charmed by Hannah as Mr. Kaltbrenner had been and looked forward to the girl's visit each day. The faces of Ah Yeh and Isaac broke into smiles when the door opened and Hannah, her cheeks flushed by the cold weather that had settled in, appeared.

"How is little missy today?" Ah Yeh invariably asked. "Will you have some tea with us?"

Hannah, amused at first by his appearance and speech, began to look forward to her cup of Chinese tea as much as she had looked forward to the coin Mr. Kaltbrenner gave her for sweets when she was a young girl in Lemberg. Some days she even brought her friend, Maude, along. The freckle-faced Butte girl, her hair worn in two long braids, was shy initially, but her reserve melted away after her first few visits. She and Hannah giggled and chattered gaily when leaving the shop.

"So nice to see young people happy," Ah Yeh said to Isaac.

Isaac agreed. How fortunate I am, he thought, to have a child like Hannah. His daughter had lost her mother when young, been uprooted from her home, lived a hand-to-mouth existence in a new country, and faced all that adversity with no complaint and no self-pity. Were it not for Hannah, Isaac knew, he would have had no desire to go on living after Rachel's death.

By the end of their first winter in Butte, Isaac was busy enough to have taken over the rental payments for his Singer from Ah Yeh and to pay a few dollars more for his rent at the store. He was already thinking of making arrangements to purchase the sewing machine.

As Hannah's birthday approached, Isaac decided to surprise his daughter with a dress he himself would make. He studied his pattern books, finally selecting a simple pattern that he felt would appeal to Hannah. He purchased a fabric of soft wool, deep blue in color, and worked on the dress when not busy attending to customers' orders. Anticipating changes still a few years away, Isaac raised the hemline to a few inches above the six inches from the ground that fashion dictated. Ah Yeh watched admiringly as the dress took form.

"Hannah will be very happy to receive your dress," he said. "Will you give her the gift in the store so I can see her face when she opens it?"

Surprised, Isaac chuckled softly. "Yes, I can do that."

On the sixth of April, Hannah entered the store looking subdued. Isaac knew she was thinking he had forgotten her birthday since he had said nothing that morning. Ah Yeh, standing behind the counter, rubbed his hands. "Chilly today, yes, missy?"

"I suppose," Hannah replied.

Ah Yeh caught Isaac's eye and Isaac stood up from his chair. "I have something to tell you," he said to his daughter.

Hannah looked at him questioningly.

"Happy birthday, Hannah," he said, handing her a box gift-wrapped with white paper and a red bow.

"Oh, poppa," she said, "you did remember."

"Did you think I'd forget?" he laughed. "So don't just look at the box. Open it."

"Here?"

"Why not?"

Hannah carefully unwrapped the package and removed the cover. She stared transfixed at the folded dress, then quickly held it up in front of her. "It's so beautiful," she said. "Poppa, did you make this?"

"He did. I watched him," Ah Yeh said.

"Thank you, poppa, thank you." As she kissed his cheek, the bell over the door jingled and a tall, stylishly-dressed woman entered, her blond hair cascading over the fur collar of her coat. A cloth bag dangled from one hand. Behind her they could hear the sound of drums and loud voices in the street.

Ah Yeh came out from behind the counter, bowing and smiling. "Madame Claire, what a pleasure to see you."

Isaac was aware that he was staring but he couldn't help himself. Madame Claire was the most beautiful woman he had ever seen.

"You must be Mr. Schneider, the tailor," she said, her mellifluous voice rolling over Isaac as she turned to him.

Isaac was speechless and Ah Yeh interceded. "Yes, this is Mr. Schneider and his daughter, Hannah."

Hannah, still holding the dress, lowered her eyes as the woman's gaze lingered.

"How old are you, dear?" she asked.

"Sixteen today," Ah Yeh said. "Her father just gave her a dress he made for her."

"Would you show it to me?" Madame Claire asked.

Hannah shyly held the dress up and Madame Claire touched the fabric lightly with her hand.

"It's a lovely dress. A lovely dress for a lovely girl. I daresay the men of Butte will be driven out of their minds."

Hannah blushed and smiled as she put the dress away.

"A friend told me you did very nice work," Madame Claire said, turning to Isaac. "Now I know she was telling the truth." She then removed a bolt of burgundy-colored satin and a rotogravure picture from the bag she carried. "Would you be able to make this gown for me?" she asked, handing the picture to Isaac.

"Of course, madam," said Isaac, struggling to find his speech. "We would need some measurements—"

"You can take those today. But before you agree, I'd like you to know that time is of the essence. I'll need the gown by early next week."

Isaac stared at the smooth-textured fabric, then studied the picture.

"I'll do my best, madam." I'll work twenty-four hours a day if I have to, thought Isaac.

"Well, you might as well take your measurements, Mr. Schneider," she said, removing her coat.

"Right here?"

"Of course."

Hannah watched wide-eyed while Isaac, intoxicated by Madame Claire's perfume, stretched the tape between the woman's shoulders, then, with trembling hands, around her bosom, trying not to let his hands touch her. He circled her waist with the tape and finally, asking Hannah to hold one end of the tape at Madame Claire's shoulder, stretched the other end to the floor. His tongue licking his dry lips, Isaac jotted the measurements onto a pad with the stub of a pencil. "I think I have what I need," he said.

"If I'm pleased, Mr. Schneider, you'll have more work than you ever dreamed of. Easter is coming, you know, and when women see a gown that strikes their fancy, they always want to know where they can get one like it."

She looked over at Hannah, then back to Isaac. "Why don't you have your daughter deliver the gown to me on Tuesday along with the bill. My house is close by. Ah Yeh can tell you where it is. Hannah can give me her opinion after I try it on."

Hannah, as captivated by the woman's beauty as her father, felt a tingle of excitement.

"If any alterations are necessary, I'll come back with it. Agreed?"

"Agreed," Isaac said.

"Do you go to school?" Madame Claire asked Hannah.

"I go to high school," Hannah replied softly.

"You can bring the gown after school. I'll be waiting for you."

Ah Yeh followed her to the door. "Hannah," she called, smiling, "happy birthday."

"Thank you." Hannah's shy reply was inaudible.

As Ah Yeh opened the door, they were assailed by the racket in the street. "What is all the noise?" Ah Yeh asked.

"Congress just declared war on Germany," Madame Claire said disdainfully, "and suddenly everyone is a patriot. The poor fools. They don't know what's in store for them. I'm proud of Jeannette Rankin, our representative in Congress. She voted against the declaration. Well, it's been a pleasure to meet you and Hannah, Mr. Schneider," she said to Isaac. "Until Tuesday."

10

Hannah clutched the package her father had given her to her chest as she hurried down the street. The bitter wind and snow flurries caused her eyes to water. Easter Sunday was only days away but it felt more like winter than spring. In spite of the cold, which penetrated her old wool coat and sweater as if they were summer cotton, her excitement overcame her discomfort.

She soon turned into Mercury Street, the hub of Butte's entertainment district. Her father had reacted with surprise when Ah Yeh told him where Madame Claire lived. "How can that be?" he asked. "She's such a lady."

"Oh yes," said the Chinaman, no hint of sarcasm in his voice. "Only the best people go to Madame Claire's."

Like everyone else in town, Hannah knew what transpired behind the walls of the houses lining this street for more than a mile. No matter how imposing the appearance of a house, the women, some strolling along the sidewalks, others peering from the windows, dispelled any illusion of respectability. Attired as if they were oblivious to the cold, their decolletages and their exposed legs shocked Hannah.

Any man passing by was approached, and for every woman he turned down there was another to make an offer. If he chose one, she immediately took hold of his arm as if to say, "he's mine, now get away."

There were other sections of Mercury Street with meaner-appearing houses, no better than hovels. Their inhabitants, mostly older women, sat by small windows in the rooms, or 'cribs,' where they entertained their customers. They called obscenely to the men passing by. With so many men volunteering for the Army, Hannah thought, times must be particularly difficult for these women. Most of the men she saw, in fact, were older and she was aware, too, of the glances they cast in her direction. She worried one might approach her and, at the same time, experienced a thrill at the thought.

There were many nights now when Hannah, tossing restlessly in her bed, thought of Mercury Street and the women who lived there. Her adolescent body had filled out in the past year and as she gently ran her hands over her erect breasts in the darkness, or into the softness between her thighs, she imagined herself in one of those little rooms, a handsome young man gazing down on her. These thoughts and the touch of her own hands made her shudder with pleasure. Clutching her mouth, she stifled the cry that would have awakened her father in the next room.

Hannah paid more attention now to the houses. Ah Yeh had described a three-storey sandstone building with elongated windows. "Impossible to miss," he said. "Nicest house on the block." Hannah, watching transactions between women and potential customers, thought of Madame Claire. She found it difficult to reconcile her image of this elegant woman with the fact that she was part of this life on Mercury Street. That was apparently what had troubled her father, too, when Ah Yeh told him where Madame Claire lived. Hannah had noticed the way Isaac looked at Madame Claire when she came into the shop and when he was taking her measurements. Not since her mother's death had she seen him look at any woman, and certainly not in that way.

Madame Claire's profession appeared not to trouble Ah Yeh at all. He spoke of her only with respect. Hannah was pleased that neither he nor her father had cautioned her about entering the district she had heard an itinerant preacher refer to as Sodom and Gomorrah the previous summer. It indicated, she thought, a recognition of her maturity. And then it dawned on her that perhaps it was just the opposite. Perhaps they thought of her as a child. That might be the case with her father, she decided, but if she had to judge by the way Ah Yeh looked at her when she entered the store, she knew she was not a child in his eyes.

Lost in her thoughts, Hannah almost missed her destination. She stopped abruptly and stared at the smooth sandstone facade, one that wouldn't have been out of place on Butte's finer streets. She walked up the stone steps and peered through the glass panels in the front door. Flame-shaped bulbs burning in wall-sconces illuminated a wide stairway leading to the upper floors. Hesitantly, she pressed the button at the side of the door and jumped at the sound of the buzzer.

Madame Claire herself came out of a room that led off the hallway and opened the door.

"Come in, my dear," she said, her gleaming white teeth visible as she smiled at Hannah. "Let's go upstairs and see what your father has made for me."

Hannah quickly followed her up into a large room with floors covered in oriental rugs. Thick maroon drapes hung on each side of the windows and a chandelier dangled from the ceiling. A large flower-patterned sofa sat against one wall faced by a mahogany coffee table. Large, soft chairs were everywhere. Madame Claire turned on the light switch and pulled the drapes. The small bulbs and glass pendants in the chandelier glistened like diamonds. Hannah, staring at the chandelier, stood frozen in place until she heard Madame Claire laughing. Her cheeks flushed with embarrassment.

"Forgive me, Hannah, I wasn't laughing at you. It's just that you look so serious."

"I was thinking how beautiful this room is."

"It is lovely, isn't it? May I see what your father sent?"

Hannah handed her the package.

"Please sit down. I'll just go slip this on. Then I want to hear your opinion."

She disappeared through the door and Hannah sat down on the sofa, gradually allowing herself to sink into the cushions. Resting her head against the back she thought how easy it would be to close her eyes and fall asleep. The heavy drapes blocked out the street noise and she became immersed in the profound silence of the house, wondering where the women were who worked for Madame Claire.

Suddenly a rustling sound caused her to start and she realized she had drifted off. Before her was a vision so startlingly beautiful that she wondered if she was dreaming. Madame Claire, wearing the burgundy-colored satin gown her father had made, stood before her. The tops of her breasts swelled from the low-cut bodice. Hannah followed the lines of the gown, noticing how perfectly it enveloped the woman's thin waist before descending almost to her ankles.

"It's lovely," Hannah said, her voice a whisper.

"Your father does beautiful work. I'm going to be the envy of all my friends. When they find out where I had this made, there'll be a line outside his door."

"I'd forgotten what a good tailor my father is. It's been so long since we left—" She hesitated and Madame Claire looked at her questioningly.

"Since we left our home in Europe after my mother died. My father was a tailor there in a fashionable shop." She lowered her eyes, surprised and embarrassed to have divulged her memories to a woman she barely knew.

"He's lost none of his skill," said Madame Claire. She sat down on the sofa next to Hannah and took her hand. "Do you miss your mother?"

Hannah nodded. "It's been four years. I don't think of her now as much as I used to." Transported to the past, she stared unseeing at Madame Claire. "It was my father's birthday and my mother was preparing a special dinner for him. I had stopped at my father's shop after school and a woman told us there was a big fire on our street. When we got there our house was gone."

The first tears Hannah had shed for her mother since that terrible day in Lemberg rolled down her cheeks. Madame Claire took Hannah in her arms and held her.

'I'm sorry," Hannah sputtered. "I don't know what came over me."

Madame Claire's delicate fingers wiped the tears from Hannah's cheeks and her grey eyes looked into Hannah's. "Never be sorry about showing your feelings to people who care about you. I think we're going to be good friends, Hannah. I felt that from the first moment I saw you."

"What made you feel that?" Hannah asked, smiling through her tears.

Madame Claire laughed. "Who knows? It was just my intuition and my intuition is seldom wrong. Let me bring you something nice to drink and we can have a pleasant chat. That way we'll get to know one another better."

Madame Claire soon returned carrying two long-stemmed glasses.

Hannah sipped at the dark liquid. "I didn't know whiskey tasted so good," she said.

"It doesn't," smiled Madame Claire. "This is a sweet liqueur. Now, tell me all about yourself."

Hannah then spoke about her family's life in Lemberg, her voyage to New York, her uncle's death, and the strike that led to their coming west. She was surprised at how easy the words tumbled out, words she had never spoken to anyone before.

"You must think I do nothing but chatter," Hannah said at last. "You haven't had a chance to say anything."

"That's all right. I feel I know you much better. Next time I'll tell you about me, but I'd better let you get back to the store or your father will worry. It's almost six. She took Hannah's hand. "I'm so glad we're friends, Hannah. And now, before I forget, did your father tell you how much I owe him?"

"My father said since this is the first gown he's made in America, you can pay him what you think it's worth."

Madame Claire laughed. "How can I put a price on the envy of my friends?" She removed two twenty-dollar bills from her purse. "Tell your father if this isn't enough, he can tell me the next time I come in."

Hannah's eyes opened wide as Madame Claire handed her the money. "That's too much!" she exclaimed.

"Beautiful work should be rewarded. Will you come to see me again?"

"Oh yes," Hannah nodded, "I would love to."

"Afternoons between twelve and six are always a good time. The women aren't working then. One more thing, Hannah. Do you know what kind of business I run?"

"Yes."

"Does it bother you?"

Hannah shook her head.

"Good. Come, I'll walk you to the door."

Hannah hurried down the street, her hands thrust into her coat pockets. One of them still clutched the money Madame Claire had given her. I don't care what Madame Claire does for a living, she said to herself. She knew the love she felt for her father had now expanded to include Madame Claire in its orbit.

11

After Hannah left, Madame Claire stretched out on her bed and closed her eyes, allowing her thoughts to float through the stillness of the house. With the drapes drawn, her bedroom became a sanctuary, and she surrendered herself to the silence, to the fragrance of the perfume on her skin, to the remembrance of a young girl held in her arms and to Hannah's tears.

Charlotte, her cook, would arrive at six, her other employees an hour later. But until seven, Madame Claire had the luxury of solitude, a time given up to her memories, to the joys and sorrows of her life. Charlotte was the most recent embodiment of those feelings. Listening to her in the downstairs kitchen for the past few weeks, making more noise than was warranted as she selected her pots and pans and pounded away on the chopping board, Madame Claire was aware of how angry the girl was, of how desperately she wanted her employer to know what she was thinking.

Until recently she and Charlotte had been lovers, but like all the others before her, Charlotte was unable to satisfy Madame Claire's craving. If anyone had asked her what that craving was, she would not have been able to give an answer. She sighed deeply. It was frustrating not to know the object of one's yearning. Of course I'm still fond of her, she said to herself, but Charlotte will have to learn, as I did long ago, that there's an impermanence to all things.

Her thoughts drifted back to the early years of her childhood in Minneapolis, a time she considered idyllic. The Stewarts, her father's people, were among the most prominent in the city. Her father was a respected attorney, his brother the former mayor, and her grandfather a member of the bench, first in Minneapolis, later in Butte. Her mother, a beautiful and well-educated woman, divided her time between her three children and her civic duties.

Summers were spent at the family cabin overlooking Pelican Like in the north woods. During those perfect months there were canoe trips and campfire dinners, ducks circling above and the haunting calls of loons and owls as daylight faded. Young Claire Stewart thought her happiness would never end.

On a July morning in her tenth year, Claire watched from the window as her father, an avid fisherman, put out from shore by himself in the family canoe. The sun was just making its appearance above the horizon and everyone in the cabin was still asleep. She was tempted to run outside and call to him to take her along but in less than a minute his strong strokes had propelled the canoe far out onto the lake.

The day, which had begun so beautifully with sunshine and blue skies, changed suddenly in the early afternoon. Thunder rumbled in the distance, then gradually came nearer. Gusting winds swept across the lake, lashing the water into a roiling confusion of waves and currents. From the cabin Claire's mother, with the children clustered next to her, apprehensively watched the darkening sky. The storm soon swirled around them, the air rent by bolts of lightning and deafening cracks of thunder. As quickly as it had arrived, the storm moved on to the south. The sun reappeared, vaporizing puddles and suffusing the air with the smell of damp earth.

Mrs. Stewart scanned the lake every few minutes for the rest of the afternoon. When her husband had still not returned by dinnertime, she asked Claire to keep the two younger boys in the house while she drove the team to Cormorant to notify the authorities. It wasn't until the following morning that the overturned canoe was found. Two days later the sheriff summoned Mrs. Stewart to identify the body that had floated to shore a few miles from their cabin.

Daunted by the prospect of raising three children by herself, Mrs. Stewart, still a young woman, accepted a proposal of marriage one year later from a man she had known only a short time. Her neighbors, the Lees, had invited her to dinner while their cousin, Everett, was visiting from Montana. After that first meeting, the cousin prolonged his stay in Minneapolis. Mrs. Stewart's brother-in-law, the former mayor, tried to dissuade her from rushing into marriage with a man she barely knew, but Claire's mother, craving the security of marriage and knowing how desperately her children missed having a father, refused to heed his advice. Besides, Everett Lee was a paragon of kindness. Claire and her two brothers doted on their "Uncle Ev," convincing their mother that she'd made the right decision.

Everett Lee, who had grown up on a ranch in Montana until his family fell on hard times and was forced to sell, persuaded his wife to use the insurance money she'd received after her husband's death to purchase a ranch in Choteau. Claire and her brothers, capivated by Uncle Ev's stories of cowboy life, eagerly awaited the move. Soon they would have their own horses and learn to ride and rope cattle.

Back in the world he knew, Everett Lee changed rapidly, a transformation his new family at first tried to deny. He began to drink heavily, verbally abusing the Stewarts no matter how apologetic they were about not giving him the help he needed. Ranching was not the romantic way of life the children had envisioned. It was hard work and they were novices. The weather was unpredictable with summers of drought and winters of cruel blizzards. Worst of all, the family was at the mercy of unseen forces setting the price of beef cattle. Mrs. Stewart and the children now knew that they had deluded themselves, that blinders were not worn only by horses. As their financial situation worsened, Everett sought his solace in bottles of whiskey. His black moods led to outbreaks of violence in which he beat Claire's brothers with his belt or struck his wife. The first time Claire saw him use his fists on her mother, she became ill, vomiting on the kitchen floor. Mrs. Stewart, her face bruised and her nose bleeding, pushed Claire out of the kitchen. "He doesn't mean it," she said, "he's under a lot of stress."

But they could no longer find excuses for Everett Lee or pretend that everything would get better. They knew they were trapped in an intolerable situation. Claire saw by the stony expression on her mother's face that she no longer put any faith in Everett's tearful apologies which followed his violent outbursts.

The culmination of their nightmare occurred just before Claire's twelfth birthday. Although Mrs. Stewart had purchased the ranch outright, their desperate situation led Everett to borrow money. The bank was now threatening to foreclose and take the ranch. After one particularly terrible row with his wife, Everett disappeared for two days. He returned during the night when the family was asleep. Claire awoke to find him hovering above her, his breathing harsh like an animal's and the smell of alcohol on his breath. Before she could scream, he was on top of her, his large hand clamped over her mouth. Claire struggled but couldn't free herself. She screamed silently, feeling as if she were being torn apart. Then, satisfied, Everett rolled over onto his back and slept.

Sobbing, Claire ran to her mother's room. Mrs. Stewart was horrified when she saw the blood on her daughter's nightgown. Clasping her to her breast, she tried to comfort her. "Stay here," she commanded once Claire was quiet. She got out of bed and went into the living room. Then Claire saw her mother move past the open door, a poker from the fireplace in her hand. She heard the door of her own room open and close softly. There was a soft thud accompanied by a grunt. Minutes later, her mother reappeared, her face flushed and her breathing rapid. She carried an armful of Claire's clothing.

"Wash yourself off in the bathroom, then get dressed while I wake your brothers. We're leaving here tonight."

Groggy with sleep, they packed their valises. While Mrs. Stewart and the boys carried the bags out to the wagon, Claire remembered the music box her mother had given her for her eleventh birthday. It was still in her bedroom. She tiptoed rapidly through the living room and down the hallway. The first grey light of dawn was just coming through the window as she entered her room. Everett still lay on his back in her bed, the features of his battered face no longer recognizable. The poker lay on the floor next to the bed. Terrified, Claire grabbed the music box and ran from the room.

As they rode past fields of wheat, the horses snorted, the August sun rose as it did every morning, cattle lowed, hawks circled, and it was as if nothing had happened to change their lives forever. While her mother flicked the whip over the team, Claire and her brothers slept, and when they stopped for breakfast, Claire wondered if it had all been a dream.

"We'll be visiting your grandparents in Butte," her mother said matter-of-factly.

Claire had a vision of a tall, unsmiling, white-haired man and a silent mouse of a woman she had last seen at her father's funeral.

"Will we be going back to the ranch after that?" one of her brothers asked.

"No, the bank is taking the ranch."

As if by an unspoken understanding, no one asked about Everett Lee. During those first months in Butte, Claire often wondered if the police would come looking for them. She knew her mother must have taken the elderly Stewarts into her confidence since she overheard her grandmother reassuring her that no one in the family would admit to knowing her whereabouts. When meeting anyone, Claire's mother introduced herself as Mrs. Stewart, not Mrs. Lee. As time passed and they settled into their new life, images of the ranch and of her stepfather's battered face receded for Claire. The music box, however, was a constant reminder. In spite of it being a gift from her mother that she treasured, she discarded it during their first year in Butte.

As the years passed Claire's mother struggled to support the family by working as a clerk in a dress shop. Unwilling to depend on her former in-laws indefinitely, she had rented a small apartment. Claire, tired of having every necessity, even shoes, thought of as a luxury, informed her mother she was leaving school. "I'm sixteen and old enough to help out," she asserted.

"It's important to get an education," her mother said. "Having a diploma can get you a better job." Claire was about to remind her mother that she had a diploma and what had it gotten her but a job in a dress shop. "But . . ." her mother continued and Claire bit her tongue, waiting to hear what she would say. "But if that's what you really want to do, I would be grateful for your help. And maybe when the boys finish school and are able to work, you can resume your studies."

Claire knew there was little likelihood of her ever returning to school, but was relieved to have been spared an argument. She dreaded making her mother unhappy in any way. Mrs. Stewart had aged drastically during her short marriage to Everett Lee and her daughter feared for her health. She knew, too, that if her mother became ill, they would need far more money than she could earn by working in a shop like her mother.

The entertainment district in turn-of-the-century Butte was a wild place.

Like the mines, the saloons and brothels operated twenty-four hours a day. Claire found it impossible to push what her stepfather had done to her out of her mind. Thinking of herself as already soiled and aware of the way men looked at her ripening beauty as she walked down the street, Claire took it upon herself to boldly approach Helen Donnelly, madam of Butte's best known brothel. Always looking for new talent and appreciative of Claire's obvious charms, she hired her on the spot. Claire quickly became the girl most in demand and Madame Helen charged her clients far more than the going rate for the privilege of being with her.

Claire, aware of the extra income she was bringing in, insisted on her share.

"But you've only been here a week and I pay you exactly what I pay the other girls," Madame Helen argued.

"I bring in more than they do."

The madam crossed her arms across her ample bosom and shook her head. "You'll get what the others get, no more, no less."

"Then I'll have to go elsewhere. I'll pack my things now."

Madame Helen's mouth fell open. She wasn't accustomed to being spoken to in this way by one of her girls. Still, she had to admire Claire's spunk. And she also had to admit the girl was her most valuable commodity. She drew Claire aside and agreed to pay her what she asked. "But you're not to tell the others," she cautioned.

What set Claire apart from other girls was her parsimony. She never squandered money on baubles, opium or liquor. Half of what she earned went to her mother and the rest she saved, spending only what was absolutely necessary for clothes to entice the customers.

Madame Claire, lying on her comfortable bed and thinking back to those early days at Madame Helen's, suddenly remembered her mother's expression when she first gave her money she had earned. Mrs. Stewart looked at the money in her hand with an uncomprehending expression. Although it was only half of what Claire had earned in a week, it was more than her mother made in a month. "But how . . ." she stammered, looking her daughter in the eye. Claire returned her mother's gaze stolidly, betraying no emotion. As the realization dawned, tears welled in Mrs. Stewart's eyes. "You didn't have to do this," she said in a barely audible voice, shaking her head.

"We have to keep the boys in school," was all Claire said.

Madame Claire sighed deeply. In spite of her mother's misgivings she had accomplished what she set out to do. Her brothers remained in school, both eventually choosing their father's profession and becoming attorneys. Until the day of Mrs. Stewart's death, three years earlier, they never spoke of Claire's profession. Her mother had lived long enough to see her sons graduate from law school. Without her daughter's assistance that never would have happened and for Madame Claire, that was a source of pride. If her brothers suspected anything, they never let on.

Mrs. Stewart meanwhile, had managed to put aside more money than Claire believed possible. Claire had been named her sole heir and when her inheritance was combined with the money Claire had saved over the years, she had enough to go into business for herself and *Madame Claire's* was born. It was ironic, Claire knew, that she took no pleasure from her profession, even if her customer of the moment happened to be handsome and treated her with tenderness. There were many men, wealthy and well-placed, who wanted to make her their mistress. Others fell in love with her and dreamed of reforming her. But Claire Stewart had realized early on that whatever physical yearnings she had were not directed toward men. She wondered at times if that had anything to do with her rape as a child. Whatever the cause, she came to accept herself as she was and enjoyed her intimate encounters with other women, even though none were long-lasting.

Becoming the proprietor of her own business eliminated the distasteful need to sleep with clients. Men still desired her but Madame Claire brushed aside their solicitations and diverted them to other attractive women in her house. The girls working for Madame Claire knew she was a fair employer who looked out for their interests. A number of them knew her in a more intimate way.

Madame Claire's had now been in business three years, long enough for her house to be known by everyone in Butte. Her clientele included many from the pinnacle of society and it wasn't unusual for her to be invited into their homes for social functions. Some of the wives were not pleased to see her. Although they believed the existence of Mercury Street and places like *Madame Claire's* protected good girls in a town with thousands of single miners, they preferred to draw the line when it came to socializing with a "notorious" woman. Others, however, for whom marital passion had faded or been directed elsewhere, welcomed her with open arms.

Suddenly, the telltale clanging of pots and pans in the kitchen let her know Charlotte had arrived. Poor girl, Madame Claire thought. She would never believe I'm still very fond of her even though I no longer want to take her into my bed. In less than an hour the girls would arrive and they would all have dinner together. It may have been a custom unique to her brothel, but Madame Claire believed it created a camaraderie that made them feel like a family. When she chose a girl to work for her, Madame Claire was very selective. There was a surplus of girls on the sidewalks of Mercury Street, some of them professionals, others working girls who wanted to make enough money to buy the pretty things they saw in shop windows. For Madame Claire, it was not enough for a girl to simply be pretty. There had to be an allure, a graceful charm to entice men. Those attributes permitted her to charge more than the other houses. The men, knowing that what they got at *Madame Claire's* was more desirable than elsewhere, were more than willing to pay what she asked.

Claire stretched and thought of Hannah. It was obvious to her the girl had attributes that could make her the most desired girl in the house. Perhaps it was her innocence that made her so appealing. During her visit she had cried when talking about her mother's death.

It was not with a mercenary eye that she looked at Hannah. She was attracted to the girl's soft, vulnerable beauty and fantasized taking her into her bed. Proceed with caution, she said to herself. She's young and you don't want to frighten her. Be patient.

12

Madame Claire's words to Isaac had been prophetic. She had worn the satin gown to the mayor's Easter Ball, where she was surrounded by wives of political appointees, drawn to her by both her beautiful physical presence and her notoriety. Within a month Isaac had more work than he had ever dreamed of, so much in fact that it was difficult to find the time to do the simpler repairs and alterations many customers needed. Ah Yeh laughed delightedly each time the front door bell tinkled. He knew that he, too, would be the eventual beneficiary of this increased business.

For Isaac, gowns and fancy dresses became the order of the day as Butte's wealthiest women streamed into the shop. How can one woman have so many friends? Isaac wondered. "I'd like this in time for the party I'm giving in June, Mr. Schneider." "I'd like to wear this dress for our Fourth of July celebration, Mr. Schneider." "I'll be wearing this for our anniversary dinner so it will have to be ready in two weeks, Mr. Schneider." "These three gowns will have to be ready by the end of November, Mr. Schneider, in case any alterations are needed. I couldn't possibly wear the same gown to every Christmas party."

Request followed request. While trying to oblige everyone, promising them their dresses and gowns by the date specified, Isaac inwardly fretted, not knowing how he could accomplish the impossible task he had set for himself. He now owned his Singer but even that was little consolation.

By the time Hannah awoke each morning, her father was already gone. Often he worked until late in the evening and Hannah carried his dinner to the store. She delighted in his success, even more so because it had been Madame Claire who had publicized his abilities. At the same time Hannah worried, seeing her father always bent over his sewing machine. "Poppa, I brought your dinner," she'd say. Isaac would look up, give her a grateful smile, then rub his tired eyes. After yawning and stretching, he would eat hurriedly, then return to his work.

When he did finally come home, he barely had the energy to drag himself off to bed.

"You're working too hard, poppa," Hannah told him.

"I'm sure things will slow down by the end of the year," he said. "Schneider the tailor won't be such a novelty by then."

"I wouldn't be so sure of that," she said, smiling in spite of her concern. She knew how important it was for him to practice his trade and enjoy the success he had once known. "I just don't like to see you exhausting yourself," she said.

When Hannah brought his dinner between six and seven in the evening, she noticed that Ah Yeh was usually still behind the counter. His sons would already have left for the day, but he remained behind. Peering through the grimy glass window one evening before entering the shop, she noticed Ah Yeh standing behind the counter staring at the door. She knew he was waiting for her. Young as she was, Hannah was perceptive enough to know that the Chinaman looked at her with more than normal interest. Although this made her somewhat uncomfortable, especially after her experience with Mr. Salvatore in New York, she couldn't forget that it was Ah Yeh's kindness that had given her father the opportunity to work as a tailor.

With that in mind, one evening she prepared extra portions. Ah Yeh, after all, was a widower, like her father, and any generous gesture she made was a way to reciprocate his kindness. "I made some for you, too," she said to Ah Yeh, as she served her father. The expression on the Chinaman's face almost made her blush. One would have thought she had offered him some precious gift.

Hannah's preoccupations with school, her father, and managing the household had precluded any visits to Madame Claire. But they didn't prevent her from thinking about the woman and longing to see her again. On the day before Christmas students were dismissed early from school. Hannah took some of the money she had saved and raced to the florist. Shielding the bouquet in her arms, she walked rapidly down Mercury Street, oblivious to the wind burning her face. Her heart raced as she ran up the steps and rang the bell.

"How wonderful to see you," said Madame Claire. "But look at you, you're frozen. Come in."

"I brought you something," said Hannah, handing her the flowers.

"They're lovely," she said, peeling off the paper covering. She inhaled their aroma, then placed them on the hall table and hugged her visitor. Hannah, bathed in the warmth of the house and the heady scent of the woman's perfume, was aware of an intense happiness as Madame Claire embraced her.

"Let me help you with your coat, then we'll find a vase for these beautiful flowers. I've thought of you often and wondered why you hadn't come to visit. I've been to the store a few times and asked your father how you were. He says you're very busy with school and taking care of the house."

"I wanted to come sooner, but besides school and the house I have to prepare dinner for my father and take it to the store almost every day. He's been so busy."

Madame Claire laughed. "I'm not surprised."

"I worry about him because he works such long hours, but I know he's happy to be doing the work he likes. Thank you."

"Don't thank me, Hannah. It's his skill that's responsible for his success. Come, let's not just stand in the hallway." She took Hannah's hand and led her up the stairs to the reception room, where logs were blazing in the fireplace. "You're just in time for tea, but first let's have some of that liqueur you liked so much."

Hannah's eyes followed Madame Claire's graceful movements as she came into the room with their drinks. She wore a pale blue robe that fell away from her breasts as she leaned over the coffee table.

"I hope I'm not disturbing you by just dropping by," she said.

"Oh, my robe," she laughed. "No, I was just relaxing. I don't have to dress until dinner. You mustn't think me lazy, Hannah. Our busiest time is from nine in the evening until three in the morning. I usually don't get to bed until five." She noticed a flush of color on Hannah's cheeks. "And now, I have something for you. I was going to take it to the store and ask your father to give it to you, but I'm so happy I can give it to you personally." She left the room, returning with a small gift-wrapped package. "Merry Christmas, Hannah."

"You don't have to give me anything," Hannah said. "You've done so much for my father and me already."

Madame Claire made a dismissive gesture. "Now open it so I can see if you like it as much as I like your flowers."

Hannah slowly removed the gift wrap and lifted a small gold locket from its velvet-covered case. Her name was engraved on the front. She stared in disbelief at the first piece of jewelry she'd ever owned, then looked over at her hostess. "It's so beautiful. Thank you, oh, thank you."

"Let me help you put it on."

Madame Claire snapped the clasp, then brushed her neck with her lips. Hannah's skin tingled at the touch.

"Now, let me bring some tea while you go see how lovely you look. There's a mirror hanging there."

Hannah's eyes wandered from its gilt frame to her own face and finally to the shining gold heart resting above the bodice of her blouse. She thought of how her own heart was filled with love for Madame Claire.

"Come sit next to me," Madame Claire said, setting the tea service and cookies on the table.

Hannah basked in the warm silence as they sipped their tea. "Do you mind if I ask you something?" said Madame Claire. "I was wondering if the thought of the work here makes you uncomfortable."

Hannah shook her head a little too quickly.

"You and I share more than you know," Madame Claire said. "During your last visit you told me about your life in Europe and the death of your mother when you were still very young. I was about the same age when my father died. He was a wonderful man and I loved him as much as you loved your mother. Things were very difficult for us after his death. My mother had three children to raise. She remarried but unfortunately made a very bad choice. It still pains me deeply to think of the cruel man who was my stepfather. Finally, my mother left him. We were very poor when we came to Butte. My mother barely earned enough to support us. I also had two younger brothers to think about. That's how I got into this line of work. It made it possible for my brothers to stay in school and they're both lawyers now. When my mother died I had the satisfaction of knowing that I had done all I could to make her life easier."

"But wasn't it difficult for you to do this work?" Hannah asked, a slightly pained expression on her face.

Madame Claire hesitated for a moment. "Perhaps at first, Hannah, but you see, from the very beginning I thought of it as work. I realize that it's not what most people have in mind when they think of an occupation, but really, that's exactly what it is. And I knew what I was working for. Most of the girls who get into this life are poor and once they have money, they spend it frivolously. Then, when they're older and they no longer have their youthful charms, they're even worse off than when they started. I was determined that wouldn't happen to me. Even while helping to support my family, I saved what I could from my earnings. And the result is—" She made a sweeping gesture with her arm. "*Madame Claire's*. Does what I've said shock you?"

"No, I understand," she said earnestly, "but . . ."

"But?"

"I know I have very little experience, but I don't understand why men find it necessary to buy love."

"There's no simple answer to that question. For some men it's because they're lonely, like widowers, for example. For others it's because they can have sex with no responsibility." She shrugged her shoulders. "There are probably reasons even I haven't thought of."

"Well, take my father, for example. I'm sure he never—or would never . . ." She blushed and stared at the teacup in her lap. "There hasn't been another woman since my mother died."

"Not all men are the same, Hannah. Have you ever wished your father would marry again?"

Hannah looked directly at Madame Claire. "Not until now."

"What do you mean?"

"I wish you were my mother."

Madame Claire looked away and placed her cup on the table.

"Have I made you angry?" Hannah asked.

Madame Claire patted the girl's hand. "Of course not. It's just that I've never thought of myself as your mother. How old do you think I am, Hannah?"

"I know you're not old enough to be my mother, it's just that I wish you were. Please don't be mad at me."

"I'm not mad at you. I'm flattered that you think so highly of me." She laughed and took Hannah's hand in hers. "You know, from the first time we met I've felt close to you. It's just that I've never felt maternal. I'm thirty-two years old, Hannah. That might seem ancient to you since I'm twice your age." Hannah shook her head, bringing a smile to Madame Claire's face. "And now I have a confession to make. I've debated telling you this and it may be difficult for you to understand, especially because of my profession. I hope it won't make you think any the less of me."

"I can't think of anything that would make me think less of you," Hannah said softly.

"I hope that's true, Hannah. To put it bluntly, I've never been attracted to men. Do you find that strange?"

Hannah felt a tingling feeling in her groin and was aware of her heart beating more rapidly as she shook her head.

"Do you like boys, Hannah?"

Her eyes were held by Madame Claire's and she found it difficult to speak. "I—I don't know," she stammered.

"You've never been with anyone?"

"No."

"Have you ever felt—desire?"

"Yes." Hannah looked down at her lap. "At night when I'm in bed," she mumbled. She felt Madame Claire's lips against her scalp.

"Would you like me to hold you in my bed, Hannah?"

Hannah's heart beat too strongly for her to speak. Madame Claire stood and took both of Hannah's hands in her own. Feeling as if she had no will of her own, Hannah rose to her feet. Madame Claire then led her out of the room to another door down the hall. She paused and smiled at Hannah, then pushed the door open.

The floors were covered with Persian carpets and the drapes, pulled shut, blocked the outside light. The orange glow of the flames in the fireplace cast shadows of the two women onto the wall. Hannah could not take her eyes off the double bed dominating the room.

Madame Claire removed her robe, letting it fall to the floor at her feet. She wore nothing underneath. Hannah, enchanted by the woman's beauty, found it difficult to breathe. Madame Claire walked slowly toward her and began unbuttoning Hannah's sweater and blouse. She soon stood naked, not knowing where to put her hands, and shivered in spite of the heat in the room.

"Don't be afraid. I'm not going to hurt you," Madame Claire said.

She pulled back the embroidered quilt and gently eased Hannah into the bed. Hannah closed her eyes as Madame Claire's lips found hers. She instantly found herself returning the older woman's kisses and as Claire's hands moved over her body, Hannah did likewise.

Claire's lips moved from Hannah's erect nipples down to the warmth between her legs and Hannah felt the muscles in her thighs tighten, then relax as she moaned with pleasure. For the next hour their bodies floated on a sea of passion.

As they finally relaxed, Madame Claire propped her head on her arm and looked down at Hannah. "I hope you don't regret what we've done."

Hannah shook her head, embarrassed not because of their intimacy but because she craved more.

"I don't think your father would approve."

"I love you," Hannah said. "I'm not going to tell him."

"I'm afraid time's gotten away from us. It's almost five. I'd better let you go."

She slipped on her robe as Hannah dressed, then put her arm around the girl as they went downstairs.

"Hannah," she said as she helped her into her coat, "do you think you might like to work for me someday?"

"You mean—here?"

Madame Claire nodded.

"I don't know. My father wouldn't—"

"I know. It would be difficult to tell him. I had the same problem with my mother. But you're not a little girl anymore. You could earn a great deal of money, enough so your father wouldn't have to work so hard. Give it some thought." She embraced the girl. "You will come back to see me, won't you?" she whispered in her ear.

"Yes," she said, tightening her embrace. "Thank you again for my beautiful locket."

"Thank you for my flowers. And for being my lovely Hannah."

13

Isaac was daydreaming as the fabric of the dress he was making flowed beneath the pounding needle of his Singer. One moment he was stepping off the train in Butte, a town he had found uglier than most with its gouged-out earth, its mine tailings, and the miners' hovels. I've been duped by stories of riches, he thought, we'll have to move on. But because of Hannah, whose education had already been interrupted twice by their moves, he decided to make the best of it, at least for a year.

How could he ever have imagined that a simple soiled shirt would turn his dream of having his own business into reality? Even now Isaac wondered if he'd suddenly wake up to find he had been dreaming all along.

There were still times when he felt Rachel's presence, her warm breath on his ear as she whispered "I always believed in you." He was overcome by happiness at those moments, until the jangle of the bell above the door and the entrance of a customer interrupted his reverie. Jolted into reality, Isaac would try to mask his confusion, at the same time fearing for his sanity. While walking home from the shop at night, he often imagined that Rachel was waiting for him. It gave the lie to what people in Lemberg had told him after the fire, that time would heal the wound of his wife's death. Instead, he grieved for her just as deeply with the passage of the years. If it wasn't for Hannah, he thought, I'd have no desire to go on living.

Then the image of Hannah's face drifted across his mind. I'm blessed to have a child like her, he said to himself. Surrounded by the sordid ugliness of Butte, Hannah had developed into a lovely young woman.

Isaac suddenly paused and looked up, his brow furrowed with worry. Madame Claire's face had suddenly intruded upon his thoughts. In spite of the debt of gratitude he owed her for all the business she had sent his way, Isaac was troubled. He had seen the reverence in Hannah's face whenever her name was mentioned. And then there was the matter of the locket.

He could understand the woman taking a liking to Hannah. Even Ah Yeh, who ordinarily kept his emotions hidden, fawned on her. But a gold locket was such a generous gift. Hannah had never had a possession of value and obviously it meant a great deal to her. But in youth, Isaac believed, there is always vulnerability and as gracious as Madame Claire was, Isaac could not ignore the fact that she was the madam of a house of prostitution.

This tawdry business was accepted as a fact of life in Butte and there was certainly no way he could shield Hannah from the fact of its existence. Nevertheless, Hannah was young and impressionable. For a while Isaac thought his daughter nursed hopes of a relationship developing between him and Madame Claire. He felt that was no longer the case but Hannah remained infatuated with the woman. Even though Madame Claire herself did not solicit men on the streets, she employed others who did. And while Isaac couldn't conceive of Hannah's being seduced by the life Madame Claire led, it didn't stop him from worrying.

Although Isaac never discussed his fears with Hannah, one comment he had made led to a rare show of peevishness by his daughter. "I don't understand why she gave you such an expensive gift," he said after Hannah showed him the locket.

"It was her Christmas present to me," she replied defensively.

Isaac, realizing he had upset her, tried to change the subject. "I'll be glad when the holidays are over. All these women wanting their fancy dresses and gowns for New Year's parties."

"Don't you like Madame Claire?" Hannah persisted.

Isaac sighed, berating himself for having started the conversation. "What reason would I have not to like her? She's a charming women and you know what she did for my business."

"Then why are you so upset by her gift?"

"I'm not upset. It's just that she hardly knows you and—and . . ." He looked at her sheepishly. "Maybe I'm jealous because you like her so much."

Hannah stared at him, a surprised look on her face, then laughed. She leaned across the sewing machine and gave her father a peck on the cheek. "You can be silly, poppa. I've got to go shopping so I'll see you later. Remember, you promised to be home for dinner. By six-thirty."

That night, lying in her bed, Hannah thought about what her father couldn't bring himself to say. His inane comment about jealousy had not fooled her. In spite of the fact that he trusted her, she had to wonder if he feared Madame Claire's influence. But perhaps that wasn't it at all. Perhaps he looked upon her affection for the woman as a betrayal of the memory of her mother.

It was obvious to Hannah how much her father missed his wife. Often, when he wasn't aware she was watching him, he would study the faded photograph, the only one that had survived the fire. As Hannah got older she often found herself wishing her father would meet a nice woman, someone who could dispel the loneliness he must feel.

Ah Yeh, too, was a widower, but he had his sons working with him and when he wasn't at the laundry he was surrounded by his grandchildren. If the day should come when Hannah had to leave, it worried her to think of her father going home each evening to an empty apartment.

Her concerns didn't prevent Hannah from admitting to herself that she was happier in Butte than she'd been in any of the other places. She wasn't blind to the ugliness of "the richest hill in the world" or to the poverty of the miners, their ramshackle homes clinging to the hillsides or obscured by the dark shadows of the gulches. When she walked through those neighborhoods, her heart went out to the women she saw, haggard creatures with drawn faces, and to their sickly, ragged children, but not even the evidence of such misery could dispel her happiness.

All of it, the poor shacks and the mansions of the copper kings, Chinatown and the fancy stores uptown, the mines and the red light district, were a part of the town she'd come to love. And much of what she felt, she knew, was due to the presence of the three people she cherished: her father, who adored her and was now content with his work; Ah Yeh, whose kindness had made everything possible and whom she looked upon as a favorite uncle; and Madame Claire, whom she loved without reservation.

Hannah had also developed a circle of friends in school, girls with whom she spent the weekends window-shopping in the uptown district or picnicking in the park during the summer. Boys, too, now took notice of Hannah. Attracted by her good looks, they invited her to dances promoted by the American Legion and Butte's social clubs. A few of the more daring girls bobbed their hair, put rouge on their lips, and wore dresses with low-cut waists. "You've got to be more stylish, Hannah," said Mary Flaherty, the girl with whom Hannah felt closest, but Hannah's only concession to Mary's freewheeling spirit was to put on lipstick and powder, both of which she wiped off before going home. Whether or not her father would have complained about her using cosmetics Hannah, in truth, had no idea. It might give him the wrong idea about me and my friends, she thought.

Before she began dating, Hannah had wondered what her father's reaction would be. To her pleasant surprise, Isaac extended his hand and graciously welcomed her young men. "Have a nice time," he always said, "and don't come home too late."

Hannah enjoyed silent movies and the melodramatic riffs of the bald-headed man who pounded away on the piano near the front of the theatre. But she preferred parties at the homes of her friends, especially at Mary's where no parents were present. Mary's father spent his nights in the saloons and her mother, who was a nurse, worked the evening shift at the hospital. Dixieland jazz records had found their way to Butte's music stores and the young people, swept along by the vibrant rhythms from the old phonograph, danced themselves into exhaustion. They also disappeared for short periods into Mary's bedroom where ardent kisses and embraces were exchanged. Each time a couple came out they found another waiting their turn outside the door. The girls, when they were alone, talked about their 'conquests,' but Hannah doubted any of them went beyond kissing. None of them, she was sure, wanted to risk being unwed mothers.

Hannah received her first kiss in the darkened hallway outside her apartment. After walking her home, the tall, dark-haired Welsh boy took her in his arms. With her body pressed aginst his, Hannah felt the familiar tingle of arousal.

What was different was the thrusting firmness against her pelvis. As his hand encircled her breast, Hannah quickly pushed him away and disappeared into her apartment.

What Isaac didn't know was that Hannah continued to visit Madame Claire. Her friend always welcomed her warmly and listened attentively to Hannah's stories about school and her social life. In spite of their intimate relationship, Hannah didn't hesitate to speak of her growing interest in boys, a fact that didn't seem to bother Claire. "It's entirely normal, Hannah," she said. The times in Madame Claire's bed came less often, but when they did the passion was as intense as it had always been.

Oddly enough, it was a visit to Madame Claire's on an afternoon in October that provoked the only unhappiness Hannah was to know during her seventeenth year. Butte's brief autumn was already being eclipsed by the first chilly weather of the impending winter when Hannah arrived at the house that was now as familiar to her as her own. She reacted with surprise when instead of Madame Claire, a young woman wearing an apron opened the door. Hannah knew Madame Claire had a cook named Charlotte, but she was never there this early.

Flustered, Hannah was informed that Madame Claire had gone out on an errand. The woman, pretty in a coarse way, had a thick brogue. She pouted as she studied Hannah.

"So yer the new one, are ye?" she finally said, her manner surly.

"I beg your pardon."

"Is yer name Hannah?"

"Yes, it is."

The woman snorted. "Yer pretty enough, but ye won't last. She'll tire of ye just the same as the others."

Hannah was aware that she was blushing and turned abruptly and ran down the stairs, the woman's harsh laughter following her. "I'll tell her ye called, dearie."

The woman's hideous laugh rang in Hannah's ears on the way home. She threw herself onto her bed and sobbed into the pillow. It took weeks before Hannah could gather up the courage to return. She rang the bell hesitantly and was relieved when she was greeted by her friend.

"Come in, Hannah. How good it is to see you."

Hannah silently followed her upstairs where Madame Claire took her hand

and led her to the sofa. The serious expression on the older woman's face was one Hannah was not accustomed to.

"I heard you were here a few weeks ago while I was out."

Hannah lowered her eyes and nodded.

Madame Claire placed her hands on Hannah's shoulders. "You must be honest with me. Was Charlotte rude to you?"

Hannah looked up, eyes welling with tears. "She said you would tire of me like you did of all the others."

"That awful girl. I had her come early that day to prepare the dinner I was giving that evening. Before going to the market to get some items I'd forgotten, I told her that if you came by, she should have you wait. When she told me you had come but had left immediately, I suspected something was wrong. That same evening I told her she would no longer be working for me.

"Oh, Hannah, Hannah. Don't you see? She just wanted to hurt you. I love you, Hannah. We'll always be friends."

She opened her arms, taking Hannah's face to her breast. Hannah's tears soaked her blouse, bringing tears to her own eyes. Without speaking, the two women walked hand in hand to the bedroom. Later, as dusk fell, a chill breeze blowing through the partially opened window swept across their nakedness, making them shiver. Exhausted, they remained locked in an embrace, neither one wanting to let go.

Hannah dressed in silence. As they stood by the front door, Madame Claire kissed her lips. "I'll always love you, Hannah," she said.

Hannah nodded slowly. "I love you, too."

Walking slowly down the steps, Hannah took a deep breath. She kept her eyes focused on the last vestiges of sunset, orange and violet streaks lacerating the otherwise intact sky. A feeling of lassitude came over her as she walked home. Her father would be wondering why Hannah had not come by with dinner, but she felt no sense of urgency. It wasn't fatigue she was experiencing, she realized, but peace. She knew she loved Madame Claire. She also knew she had been in Madame Claire's bed for the last time.

Less than a month later, Butte's streets resounded with the noise of celebration. Cars sounded their horns and people waving American flags followed a brass band into the downtown area. In Hannah's classroom the students looked at one another in puzzlement as the din penetrated the closed windows. The teacher, Miss Winslow, left the room, only to return moments later with the news that an armistice had been declared in Europe. The war was over. To the applause of the students, she informed them that they were free to join the celebration and that school was cancelled for the next day.

As Hannah joined the excited students gathering up their coats and books, she heard her name called. "Hannah, let's chat for a moment," Miss Winslow said, placing a chair at the side of the desk. "It's wonderful to have this terrible war end at last. I know you want to join your friends, but I'd like to discuss something with you. I read your composition last night. It was so well written and so poignant it brought tears to my eyes. Have you done much writing?"

"No. When you said to write about one of our parents, I really didn't know where to begin. I tried to remember everything I could about my mother and suddenly the words just came. I had to write quickly just to keep up with my memories."

"You have a gift, Hannah, and it's one that should be nurtured. Have you given any thought to college?"

"Not really."

"It's something you should be thinking about. This is your senior year and you should be applying."

"But I can't afford to go to college, Miss Winslow. My father doesn't have the money."

"There are scholarships available for deserving students. They're difficult to get but that's how I was able to attend. Give it some thought and we can meet again after school next week. I want you to know that I'd be willing to recommend you when you apply."

"Thank you," Hannah said, flattered by her remarks but doubtful that college was in her future.

"In the meantime, you must make sure to continue getting good grades. And above all, keep writing. Write about anything that comes to mind. I'd consider it a privilege to read anything you write, so don't hesitate to bring it to me." Her wrinkled face broke into a smile. "And now, I suppose we should join the festivities."

Hannah's friends were already gone when she came out. Butte's streets were filled with revelers. Trying to avoid the drunks staggering out of saloons, she pushed her way through the crowds and headed toward the shop.

Isaac was in his customary place when Hannah entered. He raised his head and smiled and it was as if she was seeing him for the first time. Although still relatively young, his hair was now thinning, exposing a bald spot on the top of his head. Deep wrinkles had formed at the corners of his lips, and his eyes had a milky blue consistency that she associated with old people. How can I ever leave him? she thought.

"Well, Hannah, it's over. Millions dead and maimed and they're all celebrating out there." He shook his head. "Stupidity," he said softly, then, as if reminding himself of something, he blinked. "How come you're not in school?"

"Classes were dismissed early. They gave us tomorrow off, too."

At that moment, Ah Yeh appeared behind the counter. Hannah couldn't understand why she had never noticed the transformation that was occurring in the two men. Ah Yeh appeared to have grown even shorter and his hair, which had been black the first time she'd seen him, was now streaked with gray. How could this have happened without her being aware? And if Ah Yeh and her father were changing before her very eyes, what was happening to her?

"A happy day, eh, young missy?" he said. "We should have celebration, too."

Disappearing into the back of the store, he returned with his three sons. In his hands, Ah Yeh held a tray with a bottle of whiskey and six glasses. He poured whiskey into five of them, hesitated with the mouth of the bottle over the sixth and looked at Isaac. "Is all right for missy?"

"Yes," said Isaac, and Hannah raised her glass to Ah Yeh's toast to peace. She grimaced at the taste of whiskey, to everyone's amusement.

Li and Chiang, the two older sons, disappeared almost immediately to resume their work. Only Wong, the youngest, remained behind, which surprised Hannah. Always shy in her presence, he had never done more than nod a greeting when they met. Perhaps it was the whiskey but he actually smiled at her and raised his glass a second time. Ah Yeh said something to him in Cantonese and the young man placed his glass on the tray, then reluctantly joined his brothers.

Li and Chiang, Hannah knew, were both married and had four children between them. Wong was the only single son now. "Twenty-five, still no wife," she had heard Ah Yeh complaining to Isaac one day. "He is too American. Always wants to speak English and asks everybody to call him Will. How will I find him good wife if he keeps forgetting he is Chinese?" Hannah had thought it funny that Ah Yeh was searching for a wife for his son. "It's their custom," Isaac had said when she mentioned it to him.

"My teacher, Miss Winslow, spoke to me today," Hannah said to her father as Ah Yeh carried the tray away. "She likes my writing and thinks I should go to college. She said she'd recommend me for a scholarship."

Isaac, again behind his Singer, sat back in his chair. "That's wonderful. I'm proud of you."

"But—"

"But?"

"She said scholarships are hard to get, and besides—I don't want to leave you."

Isaac shook his head and smiled sadly. "Have I become so old and infirm, Hannah, that you feel you have to take care of me? I'll be fine. It's your future you have to think about. If a scholarship is offered, you must take it. And even if it isn't, I'll do whatever I can to help you."

"Well," she sighed, "I'll think about it."

Butte's holiday season was the most festive in the town's history. Not even the returning wounded staring from sightless eyes or hobbling on crutches put a damper on the joy of the celebrants. With the almost certain coming of prohibition in the new year that was now only days away, drunkenness was rampant. It was as if people hoped that by consuming extraordinary quantities of whiskey, they could store it for the dry periods.

The town brothels were busier than ever, much to the relief of Butte's matrons, who feared for their daughters now that the streets were filled with veterans home from the war. Their mothers may have been apprehensive but many of Butte's young women were excited by the appraising looks of men they considered mature by dint of their overseas experience; for those who succumbed, tears of shame often followed as these same men, made restless by their years at the front, moved on to other towns and other states. The unwanted babies they left behind were often deposited by their despondent mothers at the Catholic orphanage in Helena.

Hannah, too, received her share of leers and propositions whenever she walked down the street, but she never acknowledged them. Because of all the unwanted attention, it made her more uncomfortable now to enter Mercury Street. Nevertheless, as Christmas approached she paid a visit to Madame Claire, bringing with her a gift of chocolates. Since she hadn't seen her friend in more than two months, she feared what her newly discovered awareness would reveal. Would Madame Claire, like her father and Ah Yeh, suddenly appear older?

Hannah saw immediately that she needn't have worried. Madame Claire's loveliness was unchanged, and her reception was as gracious as it had always been. The relationship between them had undergone a subtle change, however. Madame Claire, recognizing Hannah's growing maturity, no longer condescended to her as if she were a child. The physical attraction between them remained, but neither acted on it except for embraces and kisses when greeting or taking leave.

Hannah told her about the talks she had had with her teacher. "I've applied to three schools as a scholarship student, one in Montana, one in Nebraska, and one in Minnesota. Miss Winslow wrote letters of recommendation."

"What wonderful news. Which college in Minnesota did you apply to?"

"Carleton College."

"That's in Northfield, not too far from where my brothers live. It's supposed to be a fine school."

"Miss Winslow says it's a difficult school to get into. What really bothers me is I'm still not sure if I'm doing the right thing."

"A year ago, Hannah, I asked you if you'd like to work for me, but that was before I got to know you better. I'm convinced far better things await you. You must go to college. And if money is a problem, you must tell me."

"That's part of it, but I worry, too, about leaving my father."

"I think it would make him feel terrible to know you passed up a wonderful opportunity because of him. You're a caring girl, but in this matter you must think of yourself. And now, before you go, I have something for you. I'll be right back."

Lulled by the warmth in the room and the silence, Hannah rested her head on the back of the sofa. It was difficult for her to believe that more than a year had passed since her first visit, a year in which she had become as comfortable in this house as she was in her own. If the day comes when I fall in love with a man, she thought dreamily, I hope my love is as strong as it is for Madame Claire.

She opened her eyes to find Madame Claire standing in front of her. "I didn't hear you come back," Hannah laughed.

"You must promise not to open this until you're alone," Madame Claire said, handing Hannah a thick envelope. "And I think it would be best if you didn't say anything to your father about it. He might not understand."

She then led Hannah to the door and embraced her. Hannah breathed deeply of the familiar fragrance of Madame Claire's perfume. "Have a wonderful holiday, Hannah. And let me know just as soon as you receive an acceptance."

As soon as Hannah arrived home, she sat down on her bed and opened the envelope, staring in disbelief. Inside was three hundred dollars and a letter: *Dearest Hannah, I'm so proud of you. This is for college. I suggest you open an account at the bank. Love, C.*

Hannah's second surprise came a week later at the shop. As her father hunched over his sewing machine, Ah Yeh beckoned to her while holding an index finger to his lips, cautioning silence. He quickly handed her an envelope and motioned for her to put it in her pocket.

"So, little missy, what will you do for New Year's?"

"My friends and I will be going to a dance at the Hibernia Hall."

Isaac looked up from his machine. "That's good, Hannah. So much better than spending the evening with old people, right, Ah Yeh? We'll probably be asleep long before midnight."

A wistful expression crossed Ah Yeh's face as he looked at Hannah. "Yes, much better to be young. I go help sons now," he said, disappearing into the back of the shop.

"Is Ah Yeh all right?" Hannah asked.

"Of course," said Isaac.

Walking home, Hannah remembered the way Ah Yeh had looked at her. His expression was one she had seen before in men's faces and it held more than plain affection. How sad it is, she thought, to lose a spouse and grow old alone. If I could have one wish granted it would be for Ah Yeh and for my father to remarry. Lost in these thoughts as she took off her coat back in the apartment, she had almost forgotten the envelope Ah Yeh had given her.

Hannah felt her legs go weak as she looked inside. Sinking into a chair by the kitchen table, she held two hundred dollars in her hand. The note, written in Ah Yeh's almost illegible handwriting, said simply: *Save for college.*

She stared down at the table, overwhelmed by her gifts and wondering what she had done to deserve so much love from Ah Yeh and Madame Claire. Opening her school notebook, she began composing a piece about two men, both widowers, who work together but must confront their loneliness alone. She was still writing when Isaac came home.

"Oh, my goodness!" Hannah exclaimed, jumping up from the table. She had forgotten to take his dinner. "I didn't realize it was so late. I'll make dinner right now, poppa."

"Don't rush. It's nice to see you working at your writing."

Hannah quickly cleared her papers and tucked Ah Yeh's gift into her bureau.

"Before you begin cooking, Hannah, I'd like to give you something," said Isaac. "It's so you can start saving for college."

As Hannah took the two fifty-dollar bills she threw her arms around her father. "Thank you so much, poppa."

"It's not much," Isaac said, "but we'll have time to save more."

Hannah thanked him again before she went to bed that night, saying nothing about the gifts from Ah Yeh and Madame Claire.

14

Mary Flaherty was standing on the steps outside Hibernia Hall when Hannah arrived.

"I thought you weren't coming."

"I had to take my father his dinner."

"On New Year's Eve?"

Hannah shrugged. "He doesn't pay much attention to holidays. Are the other girls here?"

"They're inside. Hey, mister, watch it!" she called as a drunk leaving the hall stumbled against her.

"I thought this dance was just for our school," Hannah said.

"The Hibernia Club is having their party across the hall. It's early and half of them can barely stay on their feet. We're not allowed in there."

"It's cold out here. Shall we go in?"

"Wait. I want to show you something."

Mary grabbed her friend's arm and led her into an alley at the side of the building. "Look what I have," she said, removing a flask from her coat pocket.

"What is it?" Hannah asked as Mary unscrewed the top.

"Something to make us feel good."

"Whiskey?" Hannah asked, making a face.

"It's not as bad as all that. I've mixed it with soda pop." She held the flask out to Hannah. "Come on, try it."

"I don't—"

"Oh, for Chrissake, Hannah, it's New Year's Eve." As if to emphasize how special a time it was Mary pulled a pack of cigarettes out of her pocket. "Want one?"

Hannah shook her head as Mary put a cigarette between her lips and lit it. Her face took on an orange glow for an instant as the match flared.

"Go ahead then, take a swallow and pass it to me."

Hannah lifted the flask slowly. "Jasus!" Mary exclaimed, pushing Hannah's arm up higher. Hannah tried not to choke on the bitter fizz. "That's more like it," Mary said, taking the flask from her. She took a long swallow, then passed it back.

"I think I've had enough," Hannah said.

"Let's finish it. We'll have more fun that way."

Beginning to experience a warm sensation in the pit of her stomach, Hannah raised the flask. "It's not too bad mixed with the pop."

"You're right," Mary laughed. "Now, drink up."

Hannah drank, shook the flask and giggled. "I don't think I left you much."

"Now," Mary said, after draining the remnants and replacing the flask in her coat pocket, "let's go show those boys how to dance." She took Hannah's arm and they walked unsteadily to the party. "Oops," Mary said, tripping on the steps. Hannah laughed as if her friend had done something terribly funny. Still laughing, both girls pushed their way through the crowd in the dance hall. The band hadn't started when they entered, but boys and girls milled about while others, seated at tables around the room's perimeter, had launched into a spontaneous chorus of "K-K-K-Katy," a song that had become popular in recent weeks.

Just then the band began to play and Hannah threw her coat over a chair at an empty table. She turned to see a boy leading Mary onto the dance floor. Her friend waved before disappearing among the dancers and moments later, a boy Hannah recognized from school asked her to dance. Knowing she wasn't a very good dancer, Hannah would have normally refused but the whiskey gave her confidence.

She tripped over her own feet more than once while dancing but instead of feeling embarrassed, she only laughed. The boy soon led her back to the table and said something, but Hannah couldn't hear him. The room was now spinning and she felt nauseated. Ignoring the boy, who was asking her if she felt all right, she jerked her coat from the chair. "I've got to get some air," she said, staggering past him.

Hannah lurched down the front steps and stumbled blindly past other revelers. The smells of beer and urine coming from the saloons intensified her nausea. Remaining on her feet with difficulty, she tripped over drunks lying on the sidewalk and finally, too dizzy to walk, she leaned against a slatted fence plastered with posters. She closed her eyes and swallowed repeatedly, trying not to be sick. Moments later she retched uncontrollably. She had been too excited that evening to eat dinner and had almost nothing to bring up. Doubled over by spasms, she slid slowly to the ground, too miserable to feel ashamed.

Sprawled on the sidewalk, she was just one of many who found themselves in the same position that evening. People who staggered past, laughing, talking, drinking from open whiskey bottles, ignored her. Hannah's head lolled back against the fence. She closed her eyes in a futile attempt to control her dizziness, while the noise of the crowd rose and fell around her. She had no idea how long she had lain there when she heard someone calling her name.

She opened her eyes with difficulty and a face she vaguely recognized swam in and out of her consciousness.

"Hannah, it's me, Will. Ah Yeh's son. Are you all right?"

Her reply was a groan. "I'm so sick," she mumbled.

"Let me help you," he said, reaching down. "I'll take you home."

"No, I can't let my father see me like this." She fell limply against him as he struggled to keep her on her feet. Midnight was only minutes away and the streets were now mobbed. Drunken cries of "Happy New Year" and slurred renditions of Auld Lang Syne floated on the whiskey-laden air. But Hannah heard none of it. She was only vaguely aware of being held up on her feet, of being half-dragged, half-carried.

"You can rest here," a voice said.

She was now out of the cold and in a room that seemed familiar, but she thought it might only be only a dream. She smelled cloth, starch, clean scents.

When she opened her eyes she saw only darkness but it swirled around her. Unable to control herself, she collapsed. An arm beneath her shoulders supported her body as she slowly sank into a pleasant softness. Someone was helping her out of her coat and then fingers played with the buttons of her blouse. For a moment soft hands cupped her breasts, then those same hands were lifting her dress and removing her underclothes. I'm dreaming, I'm dreaming, she thought, as a weight descended upon her. She felt lips upon her face, kissing her and murmuring in a language she didn't understand, and then a pain between her legs, a stabbing, penetrating pain that made her cry out. Panting breaths and moans accompanied every thrust into her body. Her own cries were smothered by a strange, animal sound, half-roar, half-scream, and then the weight on top of her grew heavier, forcing her deeper into the soft cushions.

Just as suddenly the weight disappeared and she became aware of the soft pressure of hands holding a cloth on her thighs, hands wiping away the moist stickiness. Someone was dressing her, slipping on her underclothes, pulling down her dress, buttoning her blouse. Far away she heard the soft click of a lock as a door closed.

"Hannah, wake up!" Someone was shaking her and she swatted at the unseen hand. "You have to get up. Your father will be worried. Maybe he'll call the police."

She opened her eyes and blinked in confusion. Her mouth was so dry she couldn't swallow. "Where am I?" she said in a voice she didn't recognize as her own.

"You're in the shop. I brought you here last night and you've been asleep."

Hannah stared at the worried face of Wong and she struggled to remember. She looked around and recognized the laundry. Through the open door she saw the front counter where Ah Yeh always stood and beyond that her father's sewing machine. "How did I get here?"

"I found you in the street last night. You were sick from drinking too much. I wanted to take you to your house but you didn't want your father to see you, so I brought you here. But now it's morning, Hannah, past six. Your father must be frantic."

"Oh, God," Hannah wailed, pressing her fists to her throbbing brow. "My head hurts."

"Here, take my hand," Will said, pulling her to her feet. "Can you walk?"

"I've got to go home," Hannah whimpered, walking unsteadily toward the front of the shop.

"Let me help you with your coat."

Hannah rushed outside, her coat unbuttoned, into the frigid morning. She struggled against the icy winds that assailed her like knife thrusts and headed home. Panting, and blinded by a headache, she trudged heavily up the stairs, dreading the encounter with her father. Before she could put her key in the lock, Isaac had wrenched the door open.

His eyes were bloodshot, his thin hair unkempt, as if he had been pulling at it. Hannah, seeing his frantic appearance, broke into tears. "I'm sorry, poppa, I'm sorry."

"Hannah, my God, Hannah, I was so worried. I imagined so many terrible things." His words spewed out, his thoughts outpacing them. "I didn't know whether to go out looking for you or wait here. Where have you been? Are you all right?"

"Poppa, poppa, I'm fine. I didn't feel well so I slept at a friend's house. I didn't mean to worry you."

Hannah's headache worsened and her nausea returned. Lying to her father only intensified her misery. "It's just an upset stomach. I'll be all right."

She darted past him to the bathroom.

"Should we find a doctor?" Isaac asked when she finally came out.

"I just need to get some sleep. You look like you could use some, too, poppa."

"You're right," he said, forcing a smile. "If I go to work now I'll only fall asleep on my machine."

Hannah slowly undressed in her room, wincing at the morning light creeping through the window. She held her underclothes in her hand and stared at the crusting of blood and white stains. Her hand went down to her genitals and she frowned at the soreness. What had happened? she asked herself again and again as she tried to remember. Her memories came as fragments, images like those that flashed across the screen of the movie house. She had been drinking with Mary, then she was at the dance. After that she remembered nothing until Wong woke her at the shop. He had taken her there, he said, but she had no memory of it. Had he—? She paused at the thought. He was Ah Yeh's son, he would never do such a thing. But then how, why . . . ?

She fell into a troubled, dream-haunted sleep in which there were recurring images of her mother's grave and another next to it, this one open and waiting to receive a wooden coffin, a coffin just like her mother's in Lemberg. It had no lid and the body inside was her own. She saw her father standing there, his head bowed, his hair so white it was blinding. "Hannah, Hannah," he said, over and over.

Hannah sat up abruptly, her eyes wide, staring with fright. She was covered in sweat, her hair stuck to her face. Her father, dressed in his pajamas, stood next to the bed. "Hannah, you were having a nightmare."

"Oh, poppa," she said, covering her eyes with her hands as if she could obliterate the images. "It was terrible. I dreamed I died and was being buried next to momma."

Isaac placed his hand on her shoulder. "It's all right, it was just a dream. Is your stomach feeling better?"

Hannah nodded. She was no longer nauseated and her headache was now no more than a dull ache over one eye. But the dream, she thought, the dream was worse than any headache, worse than her retching.

■■■

"Where did you disappear to the other night?" Mary asked her in school. "I came back to the table and you were gone. The boy you were dancing with said you ran out."

"I felt sick," Hannah replied.

Mary laughed. "That was a potent concoction I made up, wasn't it? I didn't feel so good myself. And the next day . . . I don't even want to think about it."

Immersed again in her schoolwork, Hannah pushed the events of New Year's Eve from her mind, her terrible dream secreted in some deep recess of her consciousness.

January and February were bitterly cold months in Butte, the temperatures not rising above zero for days at a time. Hanah, shivering in spite of her layers of clothes, thought at times she would never be warm again. She was also aware of an occasional queasy feeling. It came upon her in the morning and disappeared quickly after she had eaten breakfast. She thought no more about it until the end of February when it suddenly dawned on her that she had not had a period for two months. She occasionally skipped a month, but never two. No, it's impossible, she thought, unwilling to entertain the idea.

One thing she couldn't deny was that she was hungry all the time. If you don't stop eating, she told herself, you'll get fat. Many nights, while undressing for bed, she looked at herself in the mirror to see if she was putting on weight. No, she decided, she looked the same as always. In March she noticed spots of blood on her underwear for several days, which reassured her. It was a strange period, she thought, but at least it was a period.

During the last week of March Hannah received word from the colleges. She had been accepted to all three but only Carleton in Minnesota, the college she thought she had no chance to get into, had granted her a full scholarship. She read the letter over and over, unable to believe her good fortune.

"What wonderful news!" her father said.

"But I'll be so far away," Hannah replied.

"Nothing is far when you go by train."

"Are you forgetting our train ride here from New York, poppa? That took forever."

"But that was from New York," he laughed. "From Minnesota it's nothing."

■■■

Spring, as it always happened in Butte, came in fits and starts, warm one day, cold the next. A storm dropped eight inches of snow in the middle of April and it melted away quickly in the warm week that followed. In May, Hannah and her classmates began rehearsing for their graduation ceremony. But graduation was not what concerned Hannah. Again, she was preoccupied with her periods, having had no bleeding in April. When she looked in the mirror she couldn't deny what her own eyes were telling her. Her breasts, fuller than she'd ever seen them, were tender. Her abdomen, too, appeared swollen, and she couldn't pretend that the butterfly sensations in her belly weren't there.

Each time she asked herself how it was possible, her thoughts returned to the night of the dance. She struggled unsuccessfully to remember what had happened and became more desperate with each passing week. If she was pregnant, she must be five months gone. She had to talk to someone.

The previous weekend she and Mary had gone to the movies to see Theda Bara in "When a Woman Sins." As they walked home, Hannah had been tempted to confide in her friend, but she hesitated. Mary would be of no help. She would just gossip to the other girls.

Hannah knew, too, she couldn't inflict her fears on her father no matter how much he loved her. Madame Claire was the only one to whom she could turn.

"Hannah, come in," her friend said cheerfully on the afternoon Hannah rang her bell. "Do you have some good news?"

"If you mean college, yes. Carlton offered me a full scholarship."

Madame Claire embraced her. "I'm so proud of you, Hannah."

"But that's not what I want to talk to you about."

"Let's not stand in the hall," Madame Claire said, noticing the worried expression on Hannah's face. When they were seated on the sofa in the familiar upstairs parlor, Hannah reached for Madame Claire's hand.

"Tell me what's wrong," she said.

"I think I'm pregnant," she blurted out.

Madame Claire stared in disbelief. For the first time in her life she found herself speechless.

"I'm not even sure who did this to me."

"You're not sure? I don't understand."

"It happened New Year's Eve. I went to the dance at Hibernia Hall and one of my girlfriends shared her flask of whiskey with me. I remember feeling sick and going outside to get some air." She paused, concentrating.

"Then what happened?" Madame Claire asked gently.

"I don't remember anything else from that night. I woke up in the laundry early next morning. Actually it was Wong, Ah Yeh's youngest son, who woke me. He told me he'd found me in the street and brought me there because I refused to go home." She looked helplessly at Madame Claire. "If only I could remember what happened . . ."

"Do you think Wong—?"

"I don't know. I just can't remember. When I got home my father was very upset. You can imagine how worried he was. I told him I hadn't felt well and had spent the night at a friend's house. When I got undressed to go to bed I saw blood and—something else—on my underwear. What am I going to do? How will I go to college if I'm pregnant? And the shame for my father! I can't bear it!"

Madame Claire patted her hand. "The first thing we have to do is see if you really are pregnant, and if you are, how many months along. Let's go see Doctor Halliday right now. He takes care of my girls.

"And don't worry," she added, "I'll explain the situation to him. He'll know you're not working for me."

Doctor Halliday was a paunchy man, well past middle-age. His bald crown resembled a tonsure and his appearance was more that of a gnomish monk than a physician. As soon as he spotted Madame Claire among the patients in his waiting room, he led her back to his office while Hannah waited. A few minutes later, Madame Claire motioned for Hannah.

"So, young lady, Madame Claire informs me you might be in somewhat of a predicament." Hannah, fascinated and repelled by the tufts of white hair protruding from his ears, nodded without saying anything. "When did you have your last period?" he asked.

"In December. Then I had some light bleeding in March." Hannah couldn't believe she was revealing these intimate details to a man, a complete stranger.

"I'll examine you. If you'd like, Madame Claire can be in the room with you."

"Yes, please," Hannah said, looking over at her friend.

Hannah's face burned with shame as she lay on the examining table and she bit her lip as the doctor inserted his fingers while his other hand pressed down on her lower abdomen.

"All right. That wasn't so bad, was it? After you're dressed come talk to me in my office."

Hannah, dreading to hear what he had to say, followed Madame Claire back to the office. Doctor Halliday sat behind his desk, writing in a chart.

"Well, Hannah, I'm afraid it's as you suspected. You are pregnant, almost five months along in fact. I understand that someone took advantage of you. It might be best to go to the police—"

"Is there anything we can do?" Hannah asked softly.

"You mean an abortion? I'm afraid not. You're too far along. It would be very dangerous for you."

Hannah looked over at her friend.

"When do you think this baby will be born?" Madame Claire asked.

"Sometime in September."

Hannah clutched the wooden arms of her chair. She felt numb, too drained to cry. Madame Claire abruptly stood up. "We'll take care of everything from here on, doctor. Just put the visit on my account. Come, Hannah."

The two women walked back to Madame Claire's house in silence.

"Are you angry with me?"Hannah asked, when they were upstairs.

"I'm angry, Hannah, but not with you. With Ah Yeh's son. He raped you. There's no other word for it."

"I don't want to go to the police."

"No, I don't think you should. It will only make things worse for everyone. Leave Ah Yeh's son to me. It's you we have to think about."

"It's all my fault for letting Mary persuade me to drink that whiskey. I should have known better."

"Don't blame yourself for having drinks on New Year's Eve. Nothing that happened is your fault. Tell me, when do your classes begin?"

"On September 6th."

"That's not too bad then. If Doctor Halliday is right, you may only miss a week or two of school at most."

"But what do I do in the meantime?"

"When school starts you'll tell them you have a family emergency, that your father is ill and you have to take care of him. What you tell them doesn't matter. You're a bright girl and you'll make up whatever work you miss."

"What about the baby?"

"You'll put the baby up for adoption, of course."

"Yes," Hannah said softly, "I suppose so."

"Suppose so! Hannah, you didn't ask to be pregnant."

"I know. It's just that this baby is growing inside me and the idea of giving it away is difficult."

"Difficult or not, it's what you have to do. You have a life of promise ahead of you."

Hannah nodded. "What I'm most worried about is my father. He's bound to notice in another few weeks. What can I possibly tell him?"

"I may have a solution for you. I mentioned to you that my brothers are lawyers in Minnesota. They're in Saint Paul, not too far from where you'll be going to school. I'm going to write to Jeffrey, the oldest, about your living with him and his family during the final months of your pregnancy. You can go out there after graduation. Then, after the baby is born, you'll be ready to start school."

"But what will I tell my father? And how will I pay your brother?"

"You can tell your father you have to be at the college early to make up some classes the high school here didn't offer. You'll be close enough to the college so he won't suspect anything. As for paying my brother, don't concern yourself with that. He and his wife have two young children and I'm sure they'd appreciate your help while you're there.

"Now," said Madame Claire, "do you feel better? Life no longer looks so bleak, does it?"

"Thank you," Hannah said, trying to hold back her tears.

"You can thank me with a smile. I'm not accustomed to seeing you with such a long face. And while you're summoning up that smile, I'll go make us some tea."

15

Hannah adjusted quickly to life with Jeffrey and Elisabeth Stewart in Saint Paul. The Stewarts were sympathetic people, going out of their way to make certain she was comfortable in their home. The Stewart children, Robert and Claudia, who were eight and six, doted on Hannah, and she returned their affection. Hannah knew no one except the Stewarts and she felt no embarrassment about her pregnancy. Visitors to the house asked her no personal questions.

A month had passed since Hannah's graduation and departure for Saint Paul, but it had taken almost that full month for her to stop grieving over the events of her final weeks in Butte. Until ten days before graduation everything had gone so smoothly for her she was able to laugh at herself for having doubted Madame Claire. No one had noticed anything different about her. By choosing carefully what she wore she had been able to hide the slight swelling of her abdomen. And Jeffrey Stewart had responded enthusiastically to his sister's request to have Hannah stay with him. Madame Claire had even shown Hannah his letter, in which he wrote that he and his wife were looking forward to Hannah's arrival. The children, too, they said, pestered them daily about how many more days until Hannah came.

Hannah, looking forward to her graduation, had been able to push the pregnancy from her mind and enjoy the days spent with her girlfriends. Mary Flaherty never failed to make them all laugh when she talked about the Hibernia Club dance on New Year's Eve and how drunk she and Hannah had gotten. It's almost as if she's talking about someone who's not me, Hannah had thought. Plenty of time to concern myself with the pregnancy and with college when I'm in Minnesota, she had said to herself.

Isaac and Ah Yeh seemed in good spirits, truly happy for her good fortune and the bright future that lay ahead of her. But everything changed after Madame Claire's visit to Ah Yeh. When Madame Claire had told Hannah she would attend to Ah Yeh's son, Hannah never dreamed she would involve Ah Yeh. Hannah's first preminition that something terrible was about to happen occurred when her father came home early from work one evening.

"It's nice to have you home for dinner," Hannah said.

"I'm glad I got here before you carried the food to the store."

"So how is work, poppa? It must be slower if you're here this early."

"No, I'm busy like I always am. But something strange happened today. It bothered me and I couldn't concentrate on what I was doing."

"What happened?"

"Madame Claire came by the shop this afternoon. She didn't seem herself."

"What do you mean?" Hannah said, worried about her friend.

"Well, you know how charming she always is, a smile for everyone. Today she was very serious. Oh, she greeted me, of course, but it was Ah Yeh she wanted to see. She spoke to him at the counter, very softly so I couldn't hear anything, and then Ah Yeh left with her. He told me to call Li to the counter if customers came."

"Did they say where they were going?"

"No. It's very peculiar."

Hannah found herself trembling at her father's words.

Her mind kept wandering during the next day's graduation rehearsal. Afterward, Hannah raced to the laundry to assure herself that everything was all right. As soon as she entered, she knew it was not. Her father was working at his

Singer but Ah Yeh was not behind the counter. Li, his oldest son, was writing up a slip for a customer.

Hannah leaned across the sewing machine. "Where's Ah Yeh?" she whispered.

Isaac's eyes darted toward the counter, then back to Hannah. "His son says he's not feeling well today," Isaac said softly. "The younger son, Wong, didn't come to work either. I think something's wrong, but how can I ask—?" He gestured with his chin toward Li.

Li, finished with his customer, looked up at Hannah. Normally, he greeted her warmly. On this day, he nodded, then looked quickly away.

"I'll bring dinner down if you're not home in time," Hannah said, anxious to leave the store.

Once outside, she debated whether to visit Madame Claire, then decided against it. She would wait to see what her father learned.

Ah Yeh returned to work the following day, but he was almost unrecognizable to Isaac. Isaac had heard stories when he lived in Lemberg of people aging overnight, of hair turning all white and vigor being replaced by decrepitude. He had put little credence in those tales until he saw his friend. It was an old man who entered the store that morning. His steps were halting, unsure, and he walked as if he bore a huge weight on his shoulders. His hair hadn't turned completely white but it had changed along with the rest of his appearance. To make matters worse, he said nothing, treating Isaac as if he wasn't there. Whenever the tailor tried to catch his eye, Ah Yeh looked away. Gone, too, was his usual friendliness with customers. By the end of the day, Isaac could stand it no longer.

"Ah Yeh, what is it? Is there anything I can do to help?"

Ah Yeh looked at him strangely. He had developed a tic near his eye and for a moment Isaac thought his friend would burst into tears. Instead, he shook his head and shuffled off to the rear of the store.

What Isaac didn't know was that his daughter's unspoken fears had come to pass. Madame Claire had not minced words when she spoke to Ah Yeh. After leading him down a deserted sidestreet, she stopped and turned to him.

"Your son, Wong, has done something terrible, Ah Yeh. It pains me to tell you this, but you have to know."

As she related what Hannah had told her, his face twitched and he kept shaking his head, mumbling in Chinese, repeating the same words over and over again. Madame Claire feared he was about to suffer a stroke. "I'm sorry to have to be the bearer of such unpleasant news."

"I thank you for telling me," he said, trying to regain control. "As Wong's father, it is only right I should be told." He turned away from her and headed home.

His daughters-in-law looked at him warily as he sat in stony silence in the living room. Not even his grandchildren, whom Ah Yeh loved dearly, could elicit a response when they spoke to him. Their mothers, aware of how upset Ah Yeh was, called the children away and told them to go into the yard to play. The two women whispered to one another in the kitchen, trying to figure out what had happened. Whatever it was, they knew something bad was about to happen.

As soon as his sons got home from work, the Chinaman stood up from his chair. The boys had been puzzled by their father's absence from the store that afternoon. Li and Chiang saw the alarm on their wives' faces and backed away from Ah Yeh as he approached.

But Ah Yeh's attention was directed toward Wong. Without saying a word he grabbed the broom resting against the wall in the kitchen, raised it in the air, and brought it down on Wong's head. Wong tried to shield himself with his arms but was unable to ward off the blows. A trickle of blood ran down from his scalp to his eyebrow. The children screamed, the women cried, and his two older sons tried to restrain him.

"You miserable, wretched boy!" he screamed in Chinese. "To do this to a sweet and innocent girl, the daughter of my friend. How will I ever be able to face Isaac and Hannah again? You are no longer my son. Take your clothes and leave this house."

The two older boys pleaded with their father while Wong ran to his room, but Ah Yeh turned a deaf ear to them. "Send the children outside," he told his daughters-in-law. When they were gone he told his sons and their wives what Wong had done. Li and Chiang lowered their faces in shame and the two women wept. No one looked at Wong when he came into the room carrying a small valise. He took one last imploring look at his father, then at his brothers, but they refused to look at him. He left the house as if he were departing a funeral, closing the door softly behind him so as not to disturb the mourners.

Since Isaac had no idea what had happened, the behavior of Ah Yeh and his sons was incomprehensible. Hannah, although she surmised what had transpired, kept her silence. She understood the suffering of Ah Yeh and his sons. To spare them additional pain, she decided to stay away from the store. In another week she would leave for Minnesota and perhaps things would get better.

"Poppa," she said to Isaac, "please don't work late this week. You know I'm leaving next Thursday. It would be nicer for us to have dinner together at home every night in the short time I have left."

As if the disgrace brought to his family wasn't bad enough, more misfortune was in store for Ah Yeh. Two days before Madame Claire had spoken to him about his youngest son, a woman had walked into the Butte police station and set in motion a train of events that was to have unforseen repercussions. The agitated woman sat at the sergeant's desk wringing her hands. She reported that her adolescent daughter had left home a month earlier and moved into a rooming house uptown. She had visited the girl there several times, but was unable to find her this morning. The landlady said the girl had moved out a few days before.

The police located the girl that same week in a rooming house near Chinatown. She was registered as the wife of a Chinaman. Their investigation revealed that she was the mistress of the man, who provided her with money for her drug habit. The girl apparently belonged to a group of young women who frequented Chinatown and purchased their cocaine in a cafe that was a front for the drug trade.

The story was featured in the headlines of Butte's newspaper, whose editors railed against the heathen influences in a godfearing town. They succeeded in provoking outrage among the citizenry and one afternoon, as a light drizzle fell, an angry crowd of men poured out of one of the town's roughest saloons. They headed for Chinatown, some wielding bats and shovels which they used against the windows of Chinese-owned shops.

Hannah had heard the noise and the shattering of glass as she walked home from graduation rehearsal. Most of the din appeared to be coming from the street where Ah Yeh's laundry was located. Hannah raced in that direction, arriving just in time to see two men smashing the plate glass window of the laundry while the mob roared its approval. Her father and Ah Yeh stood helplessly behind the counter.

"Cowards!" Hannah screamed, running up to the two drunk men. "You ought to be ashamed of yourselves. What did these people ever do to you?"

"Let the chinks get out of Butte!" yelled a voice from the crowd.

"Butte would be better off without the likes of you," Hannah shouted, tears of rage running down her cheeks.

Some of the men, uncomfortable at the sight of the young woman crying, drifted away.

"Come on," called one of the others, "let's get out of here before the police come."

Hannah stared at the shattered window, then stepped through the shards of glass and entered the store.

"Are you all right?" she asked.

"We're fine," said Isaac, "but you shouldn't have argued with them, Hannah. They were all drunk."

"That's no excuse for what they did."

Ah Yeh leaned heavily against the counter as if his legs could no longer support him. His appearance reminded Isaac of the time a group of Russian Jews, survivors of a pogrom, had straggled into Lemberg. Ah Yeh's face had the same beaten expression. It was, Isaac thought, an expected response to the crowd's hateful act, but in reality it was because of Hannah. Having this young woman whom he was so fond of and whom his son had disgraced standing before him, still solicitious for his well-being, was more than Ah Yeh could bear.

Isaac placed his hand on Ah Yeh's shoulder. "Think of it this way, my friend. That window was so dirty and the lettering so faded, it needed to be cleaned or replaced. Now we'll be able to get a bright new glass."

Ah Yeh smiled weakly, appreciative of his friend's attempt to console him.

After a few days, Butte returned to normal. The town's newspaper, on the day after the disturbances, sheepishly reported that "some excesses" had occurred, which they blamed on the "inebriated state of some of the citizens."

For Hannah, Ah Yeh's suffering cast a pall of gloom over her graduation. Isaac had told her that Wong no longer came to the store. Gathering up his courage, Isaac had asked Li where his younger brother was. "He is gone," Li said. "Not work here any more." But he would not elaborate.

Watching from the side of the auditorium, where the graduates were lined up for their entrance onto the stage, Hannah saw Madame Claire discreetly choose a seat in the rear of the room. Ah Yeh appeared, too, entering just before the parade of the graduates. People's heads turned as the Chinaman, looking straight ahead, walked down the aisle and sat down next to Hannah's father, who greeted him warmly and shook his hand.

As Hannah watched the two men, her hand unconsciously moved across her abdomen. A few days earlier she had become more aware of the baby. It chose this moment to deliver a few strong kicks. In spite of this reminder of her circumstances, Hannah's heart went out to Ah Yeh. None of what had happened was his fault and he was the one who suffered the most.

On the day before her departure Hannah paid a farewell visit to Madame Claire. She wondered if she was sitting on the plush sofa for the last time. The two women held hands and Hannah was surprised to see her friend's eyes filled with tears.

"I'm glad you're not angry with me," Madame Claire said. "You know that I spoke to Ah Yeh about his son. The news hurt him terribly, which wasn't my intention. I still don't know if I did the right thing but Ah Yeh had to know. Otherwise, Wong may have felt he got away with it once so why not do it again if the opportunity presented itself? But then this business with the drunken rabble at the store occurred and I felt even worse. Poor Ah Yeh, so much to bear."

"I feel bad for him, too," Hannah said. "I don't know what he did about Wong, but he's not working at the laundry anymore. My father heard a rumor that Ah Yeh had thrown him out of the house. It's terrible, but if I stop to think about it, you're right. I wouldn't want another girl to be put in this position."

"It makes me feel better if you believe that. But now, let's think of more pleasant things. Jeffrey will be waiting for you at the train station in Saint Paul. He's so afraid of missing you that he wrote to tell me he'll be holding up a sign with your name on it. I know Jeffrey will send a telegram or write when—when the child arrives, but I hope you'll write to me, too."

"You know I will."

"I'm sure you'll like living with Jeffrey and his family, but if there's any problem, please let me know."

"I'll be fine. My father doesn't suspect anything. You know how grateful I am to you."

"Once this is over and you're at Carleton, we'll both be relieved. I expect great things from you, Hannah, and I'll miss you," she said as they embraced. "Perhaps one day I'll surprise you with a visit to Northfield. I'm sure you'll forgive me if I don't see you off tomorrow."

The following day at the station, Isaac stood at the train's steps with Hannah. Ah Yeh had sent a small present.

"He said this is for luck," her father said.

"Tell him I said thank you and that I'll miss him," Hannah replied.

Sitting at her coach window, Hannah held the open box in her lap. It contained a small jade brooch. She waved to her father as the train moved slowly along the platform. Then she noticed Madame Claire, hidden in the shadows near the ticket booth. Blowing a kiss, she hoped Madame Claire would understand it was for her.

The hills of the town glowed orange in the early morning sun as they receded in the distance. But the image of Butte that Hannah took with her was the devastated expression on Ah Yeh's face on that June day when he realized he did not belong.

16

As Isaac watched the train pull away he felt as if his heart was being wrenched from his body.

How strange life is, he thought. Seven years ago I sat at my sewing machine in Kaltbrenner's shop in Lemberg thinking I had a clear view of the future. Rachel and I would grow old together. Hannah would finish school and marry, and maybe someday I would have grandchildren and my own shop.

To me, it's stranger than any fairy tale I ever heard. I crossed an ocean with my child and settled in a new country, in a town I never heard of, where I now share a store with a Chinaman. And my daughter, who spoke no English when she came to America, is now going off to a fine college with a full scholarship. If only Rachel could have lived to see our daughter's accomplishments. As happy as I am for Hannah, I dread going home every night to our empty apartment.

Madame Claire, back at home, sat in front of the mirror in her bedroom. She saw herself as unchanged over the years—the same eyes, the same mouth, a few more fine wrinkles perhaps. Only one thing made her aware of the passage of time and that was Hannah.

She remembered vividly the first time she had seen Hannah in her father's shop, no longer a child but not quite a woman. How strange, she thought, smiling inwardly. The first time in my life when it wasn't I who ended a physical relationship and I didn't mind. It was only today, as the train pulled out of the station, that I experienced the most painful sense of loss since my father died.

She ran a brush through her hair with slow, deliberate strokes and thought of Hannah's emergence into adulthood. Someday, Madame Claire was convinced, she would see Hannah again. For now, though, she worried. She knew Hannah would be taken care of in Jeffrey's home, but still . . . Her concern showed in the face staring back at her in the mirror. "I won't be at ease until she's past all this and at school," she said aloud.

Of the three people who loved Hannah, Ah Yeh probably suffered the most when she left. Sitting behind the counter in his laundry, his mind was far away from the customers. A new plate glass window had been installed and Isaac had arranged for a sign painter to prominently display Ah Yeh's name and his own. "It's very nice, Isaac," he had said, but he felt no real enthusiasm. He was no longer concerned with the business or with the world he could now see so clearly through the new glass. He would have been happy with the old, soot-covered window he had known for so many years if only things could be as they were before Madame Claire delivered her terrible news.

The gods must be very angry with me, Ah Yeh thought. He stared unseeing at Isaac hunched over his Singer. His tea, brought to him silently by Li, sat on the counter growing cold. First my own son, Wong, brings disgrace upon my family and then my business is attacked by a white mob. Not even the loss of Mei and SuYin caused me so much unhappiness. Death, after all, is something that people have no control over. But to have my son, a boy I cherished, ravage an innocent girl, the daughter of my friend, and then to be victimized by a mob while Hannah, who should hate me as Wong's father, stands up to them and drives them away, is more than I can bear.

I've always known that certain people in this country couldn't accept the color of my skin. But what man has control over who his parents are and where he is born? Am I to be ashamed of China, whose civilization existed when this country was inhabited only by roaming bands of Indians?

I thought I was accepted like any other immigrant. What a fool I was. The men who came to my shop may have been drunk, but I looked into their eyes and saw their hatred. Foolish old man, feeling sorry for yourself. I can no longer go back to China. This is now my country. It's where my father is buried and where my sons live.

■■■

Hannah stared out the window for hours. She dozed fitfully, only to awaken to the same river of wheat. She had no idea when the train left Montana and entered North Dakota. The scenery was unchanged.

As night fell, Hannah could only see her own reflection in the window. The people in her car kept changing, some getting off at platforms in the middle of nowhere, others stepping on in stations that looked no different from those they'd passed hours earlier.

Unbidden, an image from childhood flashed through Hannah's mind. She was walking past the ancient buildings of the university in Lemberg. The foundation stone had the date 1661 chiseled into it. During its hundreds of years thousands of students had passed through its gates, but for Hannah Schneider, the daughter of a poor tailor, staring at the building from the outside was the most she could hope for. And yet here in America, her adopted country, she was now off to college.

The baby's kicking brought her back to the present. She tried to dismiss this new life within her and think instead of what her life would be like once she was in Northfield. But the baby was persistent, kicking harder than it ever had. Gradually, thoughts of the future faded, replaced by images of what she had left behind: the town she had come to love until its violent face made her feel deceived; her father, united as one with his Singer but lost without his beloved wife; Ah Yeh, a good man whose sufferings were undeserved; and Madame Claire, who introduced her to passion and became her dearest friend.

As the train pulled into Saint Paul's station her attention was drawn to a tall, well-dressed man on the platform. His finely sculpted features and sensuous mouth looked familiar to her. She had no doubt he was Madame Claire's brother.

17

"Are you sure you won't come with us, Hannah?" Elisabeth Stewart asked.

"Please, Hannah, please come to the lake with us," the children pleaded.

"I'm not feeling very well today," Hannah said as she leaned back against the cushions on the sofa.

"Perhaps it would be better if we all stayed home," Elisabeth said, catching her husband's eye.

"No, please go," Hannah said. "I'll be fine. It's just that it's so hot and it's making me feel a little out of sorts."

"Well, if you're sure, I'll ask Mrs. Olsen, our neighbor, to look in on you. And we'll be back by dinnertime."

Hannah closed her eyes as soon as the Stewarts left, relief flooding over her. As much as she loved the two children and delighted in their antics, they had become too much for her to handle in the past week. The pregnancy had drained her energy and all she wanted was for the baby to be born so she could resume her normal life.

Late August in Saint Paul seemed much warmer than in Butte. Hannah's skin was covered with a film of sweat and she struggled to sit up, then awkwardly got to her feet. After drinking a glass of water, she walked over to the living room windows and closed the curtains to block the sun. Even with the windows wide open the room was sultry, the air heavy and oppressive.

Suddenly Hannah felt her abdomen tighten. For the past two weeks she had been having more frequent contractions. The obstetrician said they were false labor pains, that she probably wouldn't go into real labor until September. The news hadn't pleased Hannah. She knew she couldn't wait any longer to advise Carleton and resolved to write her letter to the school that morning. As much as she hated to lie, she had no recourse but to resort to the plan Madame Claire had suggested and use her father's illness as an excuse for her late arrival. The tightness in her abdomen intensified and Hannah doubled over, feeling dizzy and nauseated. This is the worst yet, she thought. Can labor be worse than this?

Meanwhile, her father was experiencing his own discomfort. He was sitting behind the Singer, but he hadn't started his work. Since awakening that morning, Isaac had felt pain down the inside of his left arm. He just sat, opening and closing his hand.

Ah Yeh looked up. "What are you doing?" he asked.

"I must have strained my arm," Isaac said. "It's been hurting me all morning."

The Chinaman came out from behind the counter. "I have some linament."

"If it's no bother," said Isaac.

Ah Yeh disappeared and returned with a small jar with a dragon on the label. "Just rub it in with your hand," he said.

Isaac felt the heat on his skin, but his pain only seemed worse as he broke into a sweat.

Ah Yeh noticed his pale face and suddenly feared for his friend. "I'll get a doctor," he said.

"I'm sure it will go away," Isaac objected. "Let's give the linament a chance to work. I received a letter from Hannah yesterday," he said quickly, trying to take his mind off the pain.

Ah Yeh smiled sadly. Hearing Hannah's name always made him think of Wong. He missed the boy and wondered where he was. But he would never relent and allow him to return. "How is she?" Ah Yeh asked.

"She says she's doing well. Anxious to finish her makeup classes and begin the school year in September. She says it's very hot in Minnesota. And she asked that I send you her best wishes."

Ah Yeh nodded. He knew Hannah was with Madame Claire's brother waiting for the baby to be born. Twice since Hannah left he had gone to see Madame Claire, each time taking money to send to Hannah.

"That's not necessary," Madame Claire had told him.

"For my sake," he had said.

At that moment, Isaac's groan caught Ah Yeh's attention. "What is it, my friend?"

"The pain is very bad. I feel sick."

"Don't move," Ah Yeh said. "Doctor O'Neill is just down the street."

The doctor was just about to leave for the hospital when an excited Ah Yeh ran up. "Slow down," he said, "I can't understand you."

"Let me get my bag," he said once Ah Yeh's words had registered. As they raced up to the store, Ah Yeh's son, Chiang, waved frantically. "Isaac sick," he yelled.

Isaac was lying on the floor, the older son, Li, kneeling next to him. He looked up at his father with fear in his eyes. Dr. O'Neill quickly reached into his bag for a stethoscope and squatted down next to Isaac. Contemplating Isaac's open, unseeing eyes and the bluish discoloration of his skin, he knew there was nothing he could do.

Curious pedestrians were poking their heads into the store but Chiang motioned to them to leave. Dr. O'Neill slowly closed Isaac's eyelids, then opened them several times, looking for any reflex to light. Finally, he stood up. "He's gone, I'm afraid," he said, turning to Ah Yeh.

If Li hadn't caught him, Ah Yeh would have fallen to the floor. "My friend, my friend," he sobbed. "Poor Hannah. Who will tell her? Enough, enough."

He buried his face against Li's chest as he cried, wondering why the gods inflicted one misfortune after another upon him.

■■■

Hannah was curled up on the Stewarts' sofa, gritting her teeth against the pain in her pelvis. Unaware that Mrs. Olsen had come to check on her, she screamed as another knifethrust of pain coursed through her body. Mrs. Olsen hastened to her side, horrified at the sight of all the blood on the sofa. She ran to the telephone to call for help.

In the emergency room, Hannah writhed on the examining table, oblivious as needles were inserted into her arms to draw blood and connect an intravenous drip. While the surgeons and anesthesiologist hastily changed into scrub clothes, nurses readied the operating room.

Two orderlies then lifted Hannah onto the operating table. The anesthesiologist, placing a mask over Hannah's face, said "This is just oxygen. Take some deep breaths. I'm going to start your anesthetic now."

But Hannah didn't hear him. She was floating above the table looking down at the body of a young girl covered with blue drapes. A bright light illuminated the girl's exposed abdomen. While a nurse hung a bottle of blood on the intravenous stand the operating surgeon's arm swept across the girl's swollen abdomen. A line of red appeared on the stretched white skin. To Hannah, floating higher and higher above the table, the tiny creature drawn from the girl's blood-filled abdomen was no bigger than an insect.

■■■

The front door was open when the Stewarts returned.

"Thank goodness you're back," Mrs. Olsen cried, running toward them.

"What's wrong?" asked Elisabeth. "Has Hannah's time come?"

"They took her to the hospital this morning. I found her covered in blood and screaming in pain. I tried to clean the sofa as best—"

"Mrs. Olsen, would you please take the children to your house while Jeffrey and I go to the hospital?"

"Of course. Is there anything else I can—"

"Robert, Claudia, you have to go with Mrs. Olsen. Daddy and I have an errand to run."

"But, mother, can't we stay with Hannah?" Robert asked.

"Hannah isn't home right now. Do as I say."

"Visiting hours aren't until seven," the young nurse at the desk informed them.

"We just found out that Hannah Schneider was brought in this morning. She's been living with us and—"

"Oh. Please wait a moment. I'll call my supervisor."

Minutes later, a short, grey-haired woman walked briskly up to them. "I'm Mrs. Higgins," she said. "I understand you've come about Hannah Schneider?"

"Yes, I'm Mrs. Stewart and this is my husband. She's been living with us for the past few months."

"Do you know how we can contact her parents?"

"I don't understand. What's wrong?"

Mrs. Higgins, seeing the alarmed look on Elisabeth's face, asked them to her office down the corridor. "Please, sit down," she said.

"You're frightening me," said Elisabeth.

"Hannah was in a bad way when she arrived. She had suffered a premature separation of the placenta and was bleeding heavily. Dr. Edwards did an immediate Cesarean section. The baby was still alive. A little girl."

"But what about Hannah?"

"She had uncontrollable bleeding," Mrs. Higgins said. "That sometimes happens in these cases. In spite of five transfusions, Dr. Edwards was unable to save her."

"Oh, my God," said Jeffrey.

"She never regained consciousness."

"Jeffrey . . ." Elisabeth burst into tears and collapsed in his arms.

"I know how terrible this is for you," Mrs. Higgins said. "Do you know how we can contact her parents?"

"I'll send a telegram to my sister," Jeffrey replied, his voice subdued.

18

Madame Claire tore open the telegram as soon as she had closed the door behind her. Jeffrey's words brought her close to fainting. She sat down and read the telegram again, then let it fall to the floor.

The first of her clients were already sitting in the salon and she tried to compose herself before entering. "The girls will be down in a moment, gentlemen," she said. "I'll send Alice up with your drinks." She then walked quickly down the hall, knocked on a door and entered. Emily, who had been with her the longest, was dressing in front of a mirror.

"Emily, I have a family emergency and have to catch the evening train to Saint Paul. Would you tell all the girls and take charge until I return?"

"Of course," Emily said, looking at her with concern.

Madame Claire arrived at the station with only moments to spare. After purchasing her ticket, she sent Jeffrey a telegram giving her arrival time.

She sat as if in a trance as the train rumbled its way through the night. Jeffrey's telegram would not leave her mind. What could have happened? she kept asking herself. So much promise, she thought, and now it would never be realized. Her face clouded as she suddenly thought of Wong. He was the one responsible for this. She tried to remember what he looked like but the only face that came to her was that of Everett Lee, her stepfather.

Jeffrey was waiting when the train pulled into Saint Paul. Claire's eyes felt swollen, her face puffy, and she had forgotten her hair brush. Her brother, she saw, was having a difficult time. His eyes were swollen and reddened. The last time she had seen him cry was when he was a small child.

"Thank you for coming," he said, embracing her. "I'm so sorry this happened, Claire." He brushed away tears with his hand. "It's been a nightmare for all of us. We didn't even know what to tell the children."

"What happened?" Claire asked, her face a stony mask.

"They told us her placenta had separated and she hemorrhaged. The doctor performed a Cesarean. He couldn't stop the bleeding but he did save the baby."

"Hannah is dead and that baby lived? Oh, God."

Jeffrey hung his head.

"Can I see Hannah?" she asked.

"The nurse said they won't release her for burial until they speak to her parents. Perhaps you can say . . ."

Claire nodded.

"Elisabeth wanted to come," Jeffrey said as they headed for the hospital, "but she had to stay with the children. We told them Hannah had to leave suddenly to go home and they couldn't understand why she hadn't said goodbye to them." His voice broke and he pounded his hand against the steering wheel, then shook his head angrily.

The day supervisor, Mrs. Wheeler, a tall woman with black hair drawn back into a bun, looked sympathetically at Claire. "I'm so sorry about your daughter," she said. "The doctors did everything they could. Would you like to see the baby?"

"I'd like to see my daughter first," Claire said.

"Of course. Please come with me."

"I'll wait out here," Jeffrey said. "I can't . . ."

His sister patted his arm and followed the nurse into a room with white-tiled walls, the formalin smell in the air stinging her nose.

"Hannah is here, Mrs. Schneider." The nurse pulled back the sheet and

Claire stared at Hannah's alabaster face, as beautiful as it had been in life. She bent over and touched her lips to the cold skin of her forehead.

How ironic, she thought, remembering the time she'd asked Hannah if she wished her father would marry again. Hannah said she wished I could be her mother, and now she has her wish.

"I'd like Hannah sent back to Montana for burial," Madame Claire said. "Can you suggest a funeral home here that can make the arrangements for me?"

"We can go to my office and I'll give you the information. Shall we go see the baby now?"

In the nursery, five basinettes held infants and the nurse pointed through the window. "There's your granddaughter," she said. "I don't think I've ever seen a baby with such a head of black hair. She's lovely."

How can I resent this child? Claire thought. She didn't ask to be born. Still, she cost my lovely Hannah her life.

"You'll be taking the baby with you now?" Mrs. Wheeler asked.

The question caught her by surprise and she thought of asking the nurse to make arrangements to put the infant up for adoption, but she swallowed the words. "Yes," she said, "I'll take her back to Montana."

On the way home in her brother's car, Hannah's daughter wrapped in a blanket in her arms, Claire opened the small parcel of Hannah's things given to her by Mrs. Wheeler. Looking at the gold locket resting on her palm, she remembered Hannah's face when she had first seen it. "Oh, God," she murmured softly, trying not to cry. Without thinking, she placed the locket's delicate chain around the baby's neck, tucking the golden heart inside the blanket.

Jeffrey glanced over. "What are you going to do about telling her father?"

"I'm going to have to ask your help on that."

"I don't understand."

"I'd like you to write a letter. You can pretend you're a teacher or dean or something. You can say that Hannah became ill with—with pneumonia—and passed away. Then add that you've made arrangements to have her body returned to Butte. I'll have the funeral home in Butte contact her father so he can arrange the burial. I'm sure you'll know what to say."

"And the baby?"

"I'll take care of that."

"She doesn't even have a name," he said.

Claire looked down at the almond-shaped eyes that seemed to be looking directly into her own. Hannah's white face flashed through her mind.

"Her name is Pearl," she said.

19

Baby Pearl had slept in Claire's arms most of the trip but when she awakened just before dawn, she was hungry. Embarrassed by the infant's cries and the annoyed looks of passengers, she rummaged through her bag for a bottle of milk.

Claire, like almost everyone else in Montana, knew about Saint Joseph's in Helena. Founded by the Sisters of Charity and located in the northern part of town on grounds that covered a hundred acres, the orphanage was home to more than two hundred children, all living in a three-storey brick building. In the years since its founding, more buildings had been constructed and the complex now included a schoolhouse, laundry, bakery, barn for the dairy herd, vegetable garden, and an outdoor swimming pool.

Stepping out of the taxi from the station, Claire, with the driver's assistance, hefted her valise while pressing Pearl to her bosom. A smiling nun held the door open for her as she approached. "Good morning. I'm Sister Eucharia," she said. "May I help you?"

"I hope so," Claire said, suddenly shy in the presence of the nun.

"Please," said the nun, "let me hold the baby. You can leave your valise on the bench.

"What's your child's name?" Sister Eucharia's pale blue eyes were set in an ageless face and they directed a penetrating stare at Claire.

"She's not my child," Claire replied. "A dear friend of mine was visiting my brother and his family and . . ." The words came with difficulty. Saying them brought a finality to Hannah's life. Even as she had looked at Hannah's lifeless face in the hospital morgue, she had not accepted the reality of Hannah's death. "She died in childbirth. That's why I'm here."

"Where was the mother from?"

"From Butte. That's where I live."

"And the baby's father?"

"Unfortunately, the baby's father is unknown. It's a tragic case. My friend was—violated. She came to me for help and my brother was kind enough to take her in his home for the final months of her pregnancy." Claire's lips quivered.

"Is there no other family?"

"The baby's grandparents are dead. There's no one."

"And you yourself?"

"I couldn't possibly. I work, you see, and . . ." Madame Claire lowered her head. "I loved Hannah and I wish I could care for her child. But it's impossible."

The nun watched in silence while Claire struggled to compose herself. "Does the child have a name?" the nun asked.

"Her name is Pearl Schneider."

"Schneider. That's a German name."

"Hannah told me she was from a town called Lemberg. She left there before the outbreak of the war."

"When was the baby born? Do you know if she's Catholic or has been baptized?"

"She was born four days ago. August thirtieth. I don't believe she's been baptized."

Just then Pearl began to cry. "Oh my," the nun exclaimed. "She's quite wet. And hungry I would imagine."

"I have another bottle all prepared in my bag," Madame Claire said.

Sister Eucharia took the bottle. "Please, have a seat while I call Sister Margaret. She'll look after the baby. I'd like to get a little more information when I return."

"Oh, sister," Claire said. "The locket the baby is wearing belonged to her mother. Please save it for her until she's older."

Claire decided not to wait. She knew the sisters would try to find Pearl a good home. Picking up her bag, she quickly slipped out the front door and walked rapidly toward the heart of Helena.

After several long blocks she paused to catch her breath, then hailed a taxi and directed the driver to take her to the bus terminal. Service was frequent between Helena and Butte and a bus was preparing to depart as the taxi drove up. By early afternoon, Claire was home.

After a few days, feeling that Jeffrey's news must have arrived, Claire walked over to Ah Yeh's store. She dreaded the encounter with Isaac, knowing how devastated he would be. To her surprise, the laundry was closed, a handwritten notice on the door advising that the store would reopen the following week.

"Terrible, isn't it?" said a voice with a heavy brogue.

Startled, Madame Claire turned and found herself looking at the ruddy face of a policeman.

"Such a nice man. To be taken so suddenly. It's a pity."

"I don't understand," Claire said.

"Mr. Schneider, the tailor. It's going on four days since he passed away. His heart gave out, they say."

"Mr. Schneider is dead?" She stared wide-eyed at the officer as she tried to digest the news. "Four days ago?"

The policeman nodded. "I understand the poor Chinaman was so shaken, his sons had to carry him home. The store's been closed since."

Four days, Madame Claire thought. Isaac never knew about Hannah. Maybe it's better this way.

"Are you all right?" the policeman asked.

"Yes, thank you. Just shocked."

"Aye, it is shocking," he said.

As she walked away, still numb, Claire realized Hannah's body must still be at the funeral parlor. She walked hurriedly toward the mortuary, only five or six blocks away.

"Thank goodness you're here," the proprietor said. "The body arrived yesterday and we've been unable to locate Mr. Schneider. The only address we had was his business and the store is closed. We need him to make the funeral arrangements."

"I just learned that Mr. Schneider passed away four days ago."

"Oh, that's terrible. Does that mean he never knew about . . ."

"No, I don't believe he did."

"Well, it's a blessing, I suppose, that he never found out. It's very difficult to lose a child. Is there someone else in the family who can make the arrangements?"

"She has no other family, but I can make all the arrangements."

As much as she would have liked to bury Hannah next to Isaac, Claire knew that wasn't possible right now. Ah Yeh probably knew where Isaac was interred, but she couldn't bring herself to bother the poor man. He had enough to bear with Isaac's passing. If he were to learn Hannah had died in childbirth, she feared what the news might do to him.

The following morning, under a cloudless late summer sky, a veiled Madame Claire was the only mourner at Hannah's funeral in Mountain View cemetery. She stared at the mountains in the distance as Hannah's coffin was lowered into the ground. An eagle circled lazily above the ridge line and in spite of her own uncertainty about God's existence, at that moment Claire wanted to believe that He did exist and that He would welcome Hannah into his heaven. She found herself silently saying the Twenty-third Psalm, the only prayer she remembered from her childhood.

20

"Pearl, Sister Eucharia is calling for you," Sister Margaret said.

"How is she feeling today, sister?" Pearl asked.

"I don't think she'll be with us much longer," said the nun with a sigh.

During her sixteen years in Saint Joseph's Pearl had watched Sister Eucharia's gradual decline. As a young child, Pearl considered her ancient. Now, with the nun in her ninety-fourth year, she truly was. Crippled by arthritis and weakened by the after-effects of a stroke, Sister Eucharia was bedridden much of the time.

"Don't look so sad, Pearl," Sister Margaret said, lifting the girl's chin. "It's all in God's hands and if He wants Sister Eucharia at his side, that's the way it will be."

"I know, sister. It's just hard to imagine Saint Joseph's without her."

"And what about you, Pearl? I think that's what Sister Eucharia wants to talk to you about. Soon you'll have to make a decision."

Pearl nodded. Sister Eucharia often asked if Pearl had decided to take her vows. And Pearl always dreaded the disappointment in the old nun's eyes when she told her she hadn't.

164

"It's so difficult," Pearl said to Sister Margaret, "especially since I don't feel the calling." Pearl felt closest to Sister Margaret, the only nun to whom she could express her true feelings. She had always assumed that Sister Margaret was a young woman, but the wrinkles around her eyes and lips and the wisps of grey hair escaping from beneath her wimple made Pearl aware of the nun's passage into middle age.

"It is difficult," Sister Margaret said. "That's why you must be sure."

Pearl wondered if Sister Margaret was warning her away from becoming a novitiate. Sister Eucharia, on the other hand, did not allow for uncertainty.

"God is testing you, my child," Sister Eucharia always said. Her words came with difficulty, her mouth drooping on one side. "I believe that's why He has kept you with us for so long, so you can make the right decision."

Pearl knew Sister Eucharia was a wise woman, certainly closer to God than she was, but she felt there was a more basic reason why she had been at Saint Joseph's since infancy. She had seen hundreds of children come and go through the years. Whenever the nuns brought couples seeking to adopt a child to the dormitory or to the school, Pearl, like all the others, had looked at them with pleading eyes, hoping she would be the one. What would it be like, she'd wonder, to live in a real house, to have a mother and father to love me?

The couples always made a choice, but it was never Pearl. Why? she asked herself, why not me? If no one was around, she would study herself in the small mirror she kept in her room. She saw a face that she would have deemed pretty if she had seen it on anyone else. The cheekbones were high, the nose small, the lips not too thin and not too full, and her hair was lustrous and black, attractively worn at shoulder length. But there was one thing that set her apart from the other children, the shape of her eyes.

She had first become aware of their slanting, almond shape when she started school, but she was too embarrassed to discuss it with the sisters. Her unique appearance was brought home to her one day when she was about eight. As she walked out of the school building, two older boys came up to her laughing. "Your mother or father must have been a Chink," one said. "Yeah, or a Jap," said the other. "What do you mean?" she had asked. "Are you dumb?" one responded. "You've got slant eyes."

Pearl felt her face flush, not because of what they had said but because she knew it was meant to be malicious. "Do you know who your mother and father are?" she asked the freckle-faced, blond boy.

"No," he shot back, "but I know they weren't Chinks or Japs."

"Maybe they were stupid, like you," she said, turning her back on them and walking away.

As mean as the boys' words had been, they gave her cause to wonder if that was the reason she hadn't been adopted. By the time she was twelve she was sure of it. A mulatto infant had been brought to the orphanage a year earlier and not one couple had wanted to even look at the baby.

It was clear to Pearl that nobody wanted to adopt a child who was racially mixed. Or for that matter, one as old as Pearl now was. People wanted white infants or toddlers, babies whom they could claim were their own. At sixteen, Pearl was one of the few children at Saint Joseph's who had lived their entire lives with the nuns.

Pearl wondered and fantasized about who her mother and father were and why they had given her up for adoption. Until recently she had kept a small notebook in which she wrote her most private thoughts, ones that usually involved her origins. *My father was a sailor who loved a Japanese princess. He brought her to America, where I was born. He went to sea again and drowned and my mother died of a broken heart. My father was a nobleman from China. He came to this country to visit the president and fell in love with my mother, an American. I was born and they were very happy, but then a flu epidemic came and they both died.*

On her sixteenth birthday, just two months ago, Pearl had picked up her notebook and flipped through its pages. You're not a child anymore, she said to herself. Slowly and deliberately, she ripped each page from the book and tore it into little pieces.

"Come, I'll walk with you to Sister Eucharia," said Sister Margaret.

The old nun's room was, if anything, more austere than the dormitory rooms shared by the children. It contained only a narrow bed and a small dresser on which rested a Bible. A large crucifix hung above the bed. Sister Eucharia was propped on her pillows, her eyes closed.

"She won't be able to talk for long," Sister Margaret whispered. "She tires more quickly with each passing day. I'll wait for you outside."

As the door closed, Sister Eucharia opened her eyes, clouded with cataracts that made her virtually blind. "Is that you, Pearl?"

"Yes, sister."

"I was dreaming. I thought I felt the Savior's hand on my brow. 'It's time,' he said to me. Maybe it wasn't a dream."

"Have you decided, Pearl? Will you join us in doing the Lord's work?"

"I haven't decided, sister."

A hiss of air escaped the nun's lips. "You must decide. It's something I would like to know before God takes me. It's an evil world beyond these walls, Pearl. If you don't become a novitiate, we'll have to ask you to leave immediately after your graduation. That's less than a year away."

"I know, sister. I pray for guidance."

"Pray harder," said the nun, turning away.

Pearl knew this was the signal to leave and she closed the door quietly behind her. Sister Margaret, seeing Pearl's troubled expression, gave her a reassuring pat on the shoulder. "Don't let it get you down, Pearl. Our dear Sister Eucharia has been getting quite cranky in recent weeks—and she likes to get her way."

"Do you believe the outside world is as evil as Sister Eucharia says?" Pearl asked as they walked slowly back to the lobby.

"I don't look at it as good or evil, Pearl. Let's just say it has good people and bad people."

"Sister Margaret, does Saint Joseph's keep a record of who brings each child here?"

The nun gave her a quick glance. "I can't say for sure. Until she became ill it was Sister Eucharia who signed in every child, and now it's Sister Ursula." Anticipating Pearl's next question, she continued. "Even if the person bringing the child is named on the record, those files are kept in a locked cabinet. Why do you ask, Pearl?"

"Sometimes I wonder who my parents were. And why I was given up for adoption."

"All the children think about that. It's normal."

"Not knowing turns my life into a mystery. I don't even know where I was born, only the—"

Suddenly the floor began to heave and rock beneath Pearl's feet. She heard the screams of children coming from the dormitory rooms. Sister Margaret lost her balance, tried to brace herself against the wall, then fell. "It's an earthquake!" she yelled. "Run! Get out of the building!"

The earth beneath them rolled like a rough sea. Pearl clutched Sister Margaret's hand and, struggling to stay upright, pulled the nun to her feet. Thrown from one side of the corridor to the other, they stumbled to the lobby. Sisters holding the youngest children in their arms shepherded the older ones before them. "Don't block the door! Get out of the building!" they shouted.

Outside, the ground continued to heave. Large cracks appeared in the dormitory and school buildings, bricks and mortar dust cascading down.

"Get away from the building!" Sister Margaret yelled.

As suddenly as it had started, the tremors ended, followed by an eerie silence. The afternoon sun was obscured by the dust that hung over the town like a massive expanse of dirty gauze. In the distance flames and smoke were visible over downtown Helena. Sirens wailed in every direction, one of them approaching the orphanage. A police car roared through the entrance gate and pulled up in front of the main building.

"Is everyone all right?" the two officers called out.

"We don't know if all the children are out," said Sister Ursula.

"What about Sister Eucharia?" Sister Margaret asked.

"I'd better go see," Sister Ursula replied.

"No, stay here with the children," said one of the officers. "We'll look through the building."

Ten minutes later, the two policemen reappeared. One of them, a beefy older man approached the nuns. "All the children are out of this building. Were there any in the school?"

"No, it's Saturday," Sister Ursula reminded him. "That building is locked. Did you check on Sister Eucharia?"

"Is she the older nun in the room at the rear?"

"Yes."

"Maybe the earthquake frightened her. She doesn't appear to have any injury. We thought at first she was sleeping. I'm very sorry."

Sister Ursula nodded. "Sister Eucharia wasn't frightened by the earthquake,

I assure you. She knew her time had come, that's all. Last night she had me call Father Murphy to give her last rites."

Sister Margaret started looking for Pearl among the students when the ground began to heave again. The younger children screamed in panic as bricks and mortar dust showered down from the buildings. This time, however, the tremor was brief.

"It's just an aftershock," shouted the younger officer, trying to calm the children. "We'll probably be feeling a few of those for a while."

"What shall we do now?" Sister Ursula asked the older policeman. "It's freezing out here and the children don't have their jackets."

"Don't go back into the building. It's not safe. We'll arrange shelter for you and the children and in the meantime we'll have blankets, food and water sent out."

Sister Margaret then spotted Pearl with the older children and told her about Sister Eucharia.

"She was ready to die," Pearl said sadly, regretting she had been unable to say the words the old nun wanted to hear. "She told me the Savior had visited her."

"Yes, she was prepared," Sister Margaret agreed.

"Did the policeman say what we should do now?"

"They're going to arrange a place for us to stay."

Helena had been severely damaged and the civic authorities, led by the governor and his staff, struggled to coordinate relief efforts. Homeless citizens wandered the frigid streets in a daze, many of the dead and injured were still buried in the rubble of collapsed buildings, and fires blazed in the heart of downtown. Housing had to be found for the nearly three hundred children of Saint Joseph's and the women of the Catholic sodality came to their rescue. Many took children into their own homes, providing their charges with a life most had never known. For those not so fortunate, the Northern Pacific Railroad offered passenger cars that doubled as classrooms during the day and sleeping quarters at night.

Sister Margaret was as fond of Pearl as the girl was of her and arranged for her to stay with her sister, a widow. Mrs. Krantz lived alone in a spacious two-storey house on the west side of town. "It's much too big for me," she told Pearl, "but it's where Mr. Krantz and I spent our life together and I can't bear the thought of moving. I'm glad you're here. It will be nice to have someone to talk to."

As comfortable as the house was, Pearl soon realized the widow had been alone too long. Starved for company, she talked incessantly. Pearl heard every detail of the woman's life, which hadn't been exceptionally interesting, and to make matters worse, she soon began to repeat her stories. School was Pearl's only escape. Each morning she left the house earlier than was necessary for the walk to the railroad cars, where classes were held.

She dawdled on her way home, dreading the sound of Mrs. Krantz's voice. It's so ungrateful of me, she thought, but I don't know how much longer I can bear this. It was as if the old woman lay in wait to pounce upon her as soon as she opened the door. "I was just thinking, Pearl, about my aunt Felicia, I told you about her, I'm sure, the one who lived in Elliston. She's the one whose daughter, Emily, went . . ." By now Pearl no longer listened to anything the widow said. She nodded politely, murmured a few sounds, and plotted her escape. "I have so much homework today," she said, excusing herself. She heard the woman still talking as she raced up the steps to her bedroom.

Fortunately, all of Saint Joseph's children were soon moved to Boulder Hot Springs, where a resort complex was put at their disposal while repairs were made to the orphanage.

Winter passed uneventfully. The snows melted early and fed the streams around the resort, while the aspens awoke from their dormancy and sprouted new leaves of brilliant green. With startling suddeness, Pearl heard her first meadow-larks and realized it was springtime. After the long months of winter with its unchanging white landscape, Pearl always looked forward to spring, but in this year of 1936 her joy was tempered by the knowledge that her days as a ward of Saint Joseph's were coming to an end. Graduation was only weeks away. The future remained a questionmark and complicating everything was the depression the entire country was mired in. Jobs, she knew, were scarce. If she became a novitiate, she would at least have a roof over her head and food to eat, but that was not a good enough reason to become a nun. She couldn't live with the hypocrisy since she knew with certainty it wasn't what she wanted.

"I'd like to go up to Helena Saturday," she told Sister Margaret. "Perhaps I can find a job."

"You've definitely decided then?"

"Yes, sister. I'm sorry."

"It's nothing to be sorry about. It's better to find out now than suffer for the knowledge later. Mrs. Harper, the music teacher, goes to Helena every weekend to be with her family. I'll arrange for her to take you."

Walking down Helena's Main Street on Saturday morning, Pearl had a sense of expectancy. It was exciting to be in a town, the streets filled with people, streetcars rumbling past. Most of the rubble from the earthquake had been cleared. Renovations were still in progress on some buildings but the damage was far less than what Pearl had expected to find. She stopped suddenly outside the Gans Department Store, her eye caught by a small sign on the door. Salesgirl Wanted.

Pearl entered the store and looked around in wonder. Accustomed to wearing the donated clothes provided by the nuns, she had never bought any item of clothing for herself. Now she was surrounded by dresses and fabrics and shoes and suits. It was a wonderland. She walked slowly down the aisles as if in a trance, her eyes staring first in one direction, then another. It wasn't only the profusion of clothing that amazed her—it was the ability to reach out and stroke the cottons and silks and woolens, to inhale the aroma of the materials. Jostled by other shoppers, she took no notice. Only when she stumbled into a portly matron who glared irately at her did Pearl awake as if from a dream. "Excuse me," she murmured.

Walking past the open door of a storage room, she noticed a young man perched on top of a ladder. He held several boxes of shoes in his arms and was straining to stack them on the uppermost shelf. One box suddenly slipped from his grasp. Trying to catch it, he almost tumbled off the ladder. For a second Pearl stood transfixed, then she hurried in, knelt down, and retrieved a pair of men's shoes, replacing them in the carton.

"Thank you," said the young man, smiling down at her as she held out the box. He climbed down to take it from her and Pearl got a good look at a boy she guessed was about her age. He had a lean angular face with fine features and piercing blue eyes.

"Thanks again. My name is Nathan Rubin. What's yours?"

"Pearl Schneider."

He studied her face as if trying to place her. "Do you live in Helena? I've never seen you before."

Pearl hesitated. "I'm from Saint Joseph's," she said.

"It must have been scary for you when the earthquake hit. I saw the damage it did to the buildings." Suddenly, he laughed. "Did you have to go to school in the train cars?"

She smiled and nodded.

"That's sure different. I'm graduating from Helena High School next month, but we still have our classes in the same boring old building."

"Ours are in Boulder Hot Springs now. I'm graduating, too," Pearl said.

"What are you going to do after that?" he asked.

"I'm looking for a job. I saw the sign on the door"

"Oh, then you want to talk to Harvey, Mr. Gans' nephew. He interviews all the applicants. I'll take you to see him."

"I don't want to keep you from your work."

"That's him standing there," Nathan said, motioning toward a pot-bellied, balding man with glasses perched on the end of his bulbous nose. "Come tell me what he said after you talk to him. I'll still be here."

Pearl looked over her shoulder as he walked away, then approached the man Nathan had pointed to.

"I saw your sign on the door," she said.

He stared down at her. "Have you had any experience?"

"No. I'm graduating from high school in a few weeks. I'm a fast learner," she added.

"Good," he said. "What's your name?"

"Pearl Schneider."

"I don't recall meeting any Schneiders in Helena. I'll have you fill out an application in my office. Can you start work right after you graduate?"

"Yes, I can," Pearl said, already wondering where she might find a place to live.

"Where do you live?" Harvey asked.

"I'm at Saint Joseph's."

"Nothing wrong with that," he said, noticing the hesitancy in her voice. "You'll need a place to live then?"

"Yes, I will."

"There's a very nice lady named Mrs. Bascomb. Several of our girls rent rooms from her. She's very reasonable." He pulled out a pen and paper from his jacket pocket. "Here's her address. It's only a few blocks from here. Just walk to your left when you leave the store and you'll come to Sixth Avenue. Tell her Harvey Gans sent you."

"Does that mean I have the job?"

"I'm willing to give you a try." He suppressed a smile.

"Thank you. Thank you very much."

Pearl then filled out the application while Mr. Gans waited.

"Come back after you see Mrs. Bascomb," he said when she finished, "and we'll talk about your hours and wages."

"I'll come right back," she said excitedly.

She quickly headed for the front door, but suddenly remembered Nathan.

"Hello again," he called down from the ladder. "Come on in. Did you get the job?"

"I did. I'm on my way to see about a room."

"Mrs. Bascomb's?"

"Yes. How did you know?"

"Harvey sends all the girls to see her. It's a nice place."

"Have you worked here long?"

"I work here every summer and some days after school."

"What will you do after you graduate?"

"I'll be going to the university in Missoula in the fall. Are you going to be around this weekend?"

"I'm staying with the family of Mrs. Harper, our music teacher, for the weekend. We have to go back to Boulder tomorrow evening."

"But you're staying in town now?"

"Yes. I'm on Ewing."

"I finish work at three. Can I buy you an ice cream soda at the Parrot? Best ice cream in town."

Pearl hesitated. She had never been out with a boy before.

"Please say yes," Nathan persisted. "You can meet me right outside the store."

"All right. I'd better go see Mrs. Bascomb now. Then I have to come back to see . . ."

"Uncle Harvey?"

"Harvey is your uncle?"

He laughed. "Whenever you see a man working here, you know he's part of the family. See you later then."

Pearl felt very satisfied with herself as she left the store. On her first morning alone in town, she had found a job, been asked out on a date (although she wasn't sure if having an ice cream soda qualified as a date), and was on her way to see about renting a room. It made her feel like an adult.

Mrs. Bascomb, a cheerful elderly woman, welcomed her when she mentioned Harvey and Pearl followed her up two flights of stairs to the top level of the old Victorian house. "This is the only vacant room I have," Mrs. Bascomb said, opening one of the doors. The room was small but spotlessly clean. This will be the first time in my life I have a room to myself, Pearl thought, as she looked at the bed and dresser. "You'll share a bathroom with the other two girls on the floor. The rent is three dollars a week. Five dollars if you plan on having breakfast and dinner here."

Mrs. Bascomb saw the concern on Pearl's face. "Is that too much?"

"No, it's just that Mr. Gans didn't tell me what my salary is going to be. I have to see him again after I leave here."

The woman laughed. "If he starts you off like he does the others, you'll be making eighteen dollars a week."

"Oh, then I'll definitely take it," Pearl said. "But there's another problem. I won't graduate for two weeks. Can you hold it for me until then?"

"You have a nice, honest face. I'll hold it for you. What's your name?"

"Pearl Schneider."

"Well, Pearl, we'll expect you right after your graduation. Mr. Gans will advance you the money for your first week's room and board."

Pearl felt she was walking on air as she returned to the store. Everything was falling into place.

Harvey and Nathan were talking together outside the stockroom when Pearl returned. "Well, young lady," said Harvey, "how did you like Mrs. Bascomb's place?"

"It was very nice. She's going to hold a room for me until I graduate."

"I take it from the admiring look on my nephew's face that you two have met?"

Pearl blushed. "Yes."

Harvey looked at Nathan with mock severity. "You'll have to watch out for this boy, Pearl. He has an eye for a pretty face."

"Oh, Uncle Harvey, you'll make Pearl think badly of me."

"He's really a good lad," Harvey said, pinching the boy's cheek.

"That's better," Nathan said, winking at Pearl.

"Graduation is in . . . ?" asked Harvey.

"Two weeks. On a Friday."

"When can I expect to see you then?"

"If I can get a ride from my music teacher, I can be here on Saturday morning."

"Well, I'm here every Saturday so I'll look for you—or you look for me."

"Or for me," Nathan chimed in.

"An incorrigible boy," Harvey said.

As Harvey showed Pearl to the door, Nathan held up three fingers to remind her about their meeting.

It was a little past one when Pearl left the store. I'll just walk around town, she thought. Of the many nice things that had happened to her that morning, two in particular lodged in her mind. Mrs. Bascomb had said she had an honest face and Harvey had implied she was pretty. No one had ever said anything nice about the way she looked. It pleased her to know that while she might have parents of different races, that didn't prevent her from being pretty or looking honest.

"I'm not late, am I?" Pearl said when she met Nathan.

"No. I'm a few minutes early. What have you been up to?"

"Just strolling. When I was at Saint Joseph's we almost never got into town. And now that they moved us to Boulder Hot Springs, I might as well be a thousand miles away."

"Well, soon you'll be a free woman and can walk abround town any time you like. There's the Parrot."

Pearl's mouth watered as soon as they entered the ice cream parlor. The display cases were filled with an assortment of chocolates, all made on the premises, and the soda fountain stretched half the length of the store.

"My favorite is a chocolate ice cream soda," said Nathan. "What's yours?"

"I've never had one," she said shyly.

"Oh, then you have a treat in store. Shall I order for you?"

"Yes, please."

Pearl's eyes widened with pleasure when she tasted her soda. "This is delicious," she said.

"Next you can try the vanilla, then the strawberry."

"Oh, won't that be too much?"

"You'll have to see how hungry you are. And so, Miss Pearl Schneider, you know nothing about your origins?"

"Nothing. So you'll have to tell me about yourself."

"There's not much to tell. I was born in Helena. My father owns the stationary and cigar store in the Gold Block. My mother helps out at the store sometimes but mostly she's home."

"Do you have brothers and sisters?"

"I have an older sister. She's married and has a baby. They live in Iowa."

"Then you're an uncle."

'Yes," he laughed, "I suppose I am."

"Do you ever get to see her?"

"My sister? She visits at least once a year. I haven't seen the baby yet."

"Do you know what you're going to study at college?"

"Sciences mostly. I'd like to be a doctor someday."

"Oh, that's wonderful."

"What about you? Did you ever think about going to college?"

Pearl gave him a surprised look. "I have no money for college."

"Well, I see you did enjoy your soda," Nathan said, changing the subject. "Would you like another?"

She shook her head. "Mrs. Harper will scold me if I'm too full to eat the dinner her mother is cooking."

"Can I walk home with you?"

"I—I'd like that," Pearl said, "but I don't know what Mrs. Harper would think. We'd better not."

"Well, I'll see you when you come to work in two weeks then."

"Thank you, Nathan, for the soda."

"We'll have to do it again."

Pearl smiled and nodded.

"Promise?"

"Promise," she said.

Pearl could hardly wait to get back to Boulder to tell Sister Margaret all her news.

"I'm happy for you," the nun said, "but I am going to miss you, Pearl. Especially when we return to Saint Joseph's next year. Why, you've been there almost as long as I have." She smiled at the memory of Pearl as an infant. "You were such a good baby, I knew you'd be just as good when you were grown up. I'd like to give you something that might come in handy." She reached into the folds of her habit and removed a black purse, along with a small jewelry box. She fished out three one dollar bills from the purse. "I've been saving these for a good cause. And I believe I've found it."

"Oh, sister, I can't take your money."

"Please, Pearl. What do I need it for? The Sisters of Charity provide for all my needs. Maybe it will make things easier for you during your first week in Helena.

"I wasn't going to give you this," she said, showing Pearl the box, "until after graduation, but you might as well have it now. Go ahead, open it."

Pearl stared at the locket, surprised and perplexed by the gift. On the front of the locket she read the name Hannah. Sister Margaret smiled.

"Sister Eucharia gave me that many years ago for safekeeping. She was afraid if she put it away, she'd forget all about it. She told me to give it to you when I thought you were ready to have it. It belonged to your mother."

"My mother's name was Hannah?" Pearl placed the locket on her palm, staring at it as if it were a magical amulet. Closing her eyes, she stroked its shiny surface, willing it to reveal the secret of her past. Then, almost afraid to look, she slipped the clasp and opened it.

"There were no pictures," said Sister Margaret.

"Did my mother give Sister Eucharia the locket?"

Sister Margaret hesitated. "All I know is that whoever brought you to Saint Joseph's left the locket and told the sister it belonged to your mother."

Pearl held the two ends of the chain out to the nun. "Please, sister," she said, turning around.

"It looks lovely on you, Pearl."

Pearl kissed the nun's cheek. "Thank you, Sister Margaret. I'll never forget you."

21

Deep in conversation on a warm Sunday in late August, Nathan and Pearl paid little attention to where they were until they found themselves at the northern edge of town. The Helena valley spread out before them.

"Oh, there's Saint Joseph's," Pearl said, pointing. "I had no idea we'd come this far."

"They're still doing repairs," said Nathan. "Let's go see."

Wooden barricades had been set up on two sides of the dormitory building and men were perched on scaffolding that clung to the building's facade. Seemingly oblivious to the clouds of dust created by the construction machinery below them, the workers chipped away at remnants of old mortar in the damaged areas. Repairs had not begun on the school building.

"It looks worse than I remember," said Pearl.

Nathan's blue eyes were alert as he studied the buildings.

"What are you thinking?" Pearl asked.

"I was trying to imagine what it was like for you here."

"I just took it for granted," she said. "It was home for me. The nuns were nice enough, one especially, Sister Margaret. But now that I have my own place in town I realize how cloistered our lives were." She glanced over at Nathan and smiled. "It's appropriate, isn't it? Cloistered with the nuns? But that's what it was like, as if they were sheltering us from the world around us. Sister Eucharia was always trying to convince me to become a nun."

"I'm glad you weren't persuaded," said Nathan.

"It's wonderful to have privacy, to go out when I please and to be a part of the world around me. I don't believe it's necessary to have walls around us to keep temptation away. It's more a question of character, isn't it?"

"A funny thought just occurred to me. Maybe you're Jewish."

"Chinese is more like it," Pearl said.

"But if your name is really Schneider, then maybe your father was Jewish."

"I did find out one thing before leaving Saint Joseph's. My mother's name is Hannah. It's on my locket." She lifted it so he could read the name. "Sister Margaret told me this locket belonged to my mother."

"Maybe your mother was Jewish," said Nathan.

"Is your family Jewish?"

"Yes, but they don't practice the religion."

Pearl shrugged. "How will I ever know what I am? For years I made up identities for myself, but now I've resigned myself to never finding out the truth."

"All I know is you're a wonderful girl. Whoever your parents were, they made a beautiful daughter. And—and this has been the nicest summer of my life."

"It's been nice for me, too, Nathan," Pearl said, her words more than just a courtesy. She had looked forward to each of their meetings. After their first date at the ice cream parlor, Nathan had asked her out regularly. At least one evening a week he took her to the cinema, a special treat for Pearl who during her years at the orphanage had never seen a film. They also spent every Sunday together, strolling through the town's neighborhoods and parks.

"Two months ago," he said, "I was looking forward to being in college. Now I'm sorry I have to leave."

"You shouldn't think that. Think of all you'll learn."

"But that's just it. All I can think about is you."

Their eyes met for a moment, then Pearl looked away. "We'll see one another again. Some day."

"Will you write to me?"

"If you'd like me to."

"I would. Very much. Do you think about the future, Pearl?"

"Some. But I've always thought more about the past."

"You're a smart girl, Pearl. Can you see yourself years from now working as a clerk in a department store?"

"I haven't thought about it. I'm just glad I have this job. You know how difficult times are."

"Yes, I do know. And I know I'm lucky because my father has his own business. But I was thinking—now don't laugh at this—have you ever thought of becoming a nurse?"

Surprised, she looked at him. "A nurse? No, I hadn't thought about it," she laughed. "What made you think of that?"

"Well, if I'm going to be a doctor someday . . ."

"I wouldn't know where to begin. I'd have to go to a nursing school, wouldn't I? And that would cost money, wouldn't it?"

"There's a nursing school in Missoula. Saint Patrick's. A friend of my mother's went there. You could find out about it."

"Nathan, are you trying to get me to move to Missoula?"

"Well, unless you're stuck on Uncle Harvey." They both laughed, but Nathan soon turned serious. "I just don't want to lose you."

Pearl, at a loss for words, looked away as he took her hand. "As soon as I'm able," he said, "I'm going to ask you to marry me."

Slowly, Pearl turned to face him. "But you're still young. How do you know what you'll want by the time you finish college? You may meet someone in Missoula . . ."

He shook his head. "I'll be eighteen in January. And there is one thing I do know. I'll feel the same about you when I finish college as I do today. I just hope you'll wait for me."

"I'll wait," she said.

Nathan looked around to see if anyone was looking, then placed his lips on hers. Pearl closed her eyes, not wanting the kiss to end.

"When is your birthday?" Nathan asked as they headed back toward town. "I can't believe I never asked you that."

"In two days."

"Two days! The day I leave for Missoula! Oh, Pearl, I don't even have a gift for you."

"You just gave me a gift."

Mrs. Bascomb was just coming out as Nathan and Pearl arrived. They greeted her, and Nathan, shy in the presence of Pearl's landlady, mumbled his goodbyes and left.

"I like your young man," Mrs. Bascomb said. "I do believe he fancies you."

Pearl, pleased but embarrassed, smiled and excused herself. In her room, she closed the door and sat down on the bed. She knew she was fond of Nathan, perhaps even loved him although she was unsure of what love was. How can I know how to love someone, she asked herself, if no one has ever loved me? Even if she and Nathan were truly in love, could she realistically pin her hopes on a relationship that involved years of absence? Was it fair to either of them? And yet—he had seemed so certain of what the future would hold. She sighed and lay back, suddenly tired from the long walk. Closing her eyes, she tried to envision the future, but before any images came, a black curtain of sleep descended upon her.

22

"Pearl," Harvey Gans said, "I just want you to know how pleased I am with your work. You've been with us more than a year now and I've noticed how much the customers like you. When you're busy, some women would rather wait than have anyone else attend to them. I'm going to make you manager of the women's clothing department and give you a raise to twenty dollars. How does that sound?"

"I—I don't know what to say," Pearl sputtered.

"Since you have such a good eye for what the ladies want, you'll help me when I do the ordering. And I'd like you to think about the window displays, too."

Pearl nodded, speechless.

"So, tell me, Pearl, have you heard from Nathan?"

"Yes," she said, feeling her face grow warm. Would it surprise him to know that Nathan had written her at least once a week during the year he'd been gone?

"I was sorry he couldn't come back to work for us this summer. He told you about that job they offered him?"

Pearl nodded. When she'd received his letter in May telling her he couldn't come back for the summer, she had cried. His biology professor had offered him a position as his assistant in the laboratory and Nathan found it impossible to refuse. I miss you so much, he wrote in every letter. Please think about Saint Patrick's. She knew Nathan was unhappy about not being able to return to Helena and she believed he missed her as much as he said. But in her letters to him, she never made mention of Saint Patrick's, although it was very much on her mind. After the long summer Pearl realized she couldn't go through another year, let alone three, without seeing him. And Nathan had been right about the work. It was no longer satisfying at Gans' even though the customers liked her. If she did move to Missoula, she certainly didn't want to work in another department store. Nursing school was a good option, she thought, but how?

Preoccupied as she walked home from work, Pearl passed her usual corner by and soon found herself on the Gold Block. She was about to turn around when she noticed a cigar and stationary store on the opposite side of the street. She hurried across. Inside was a grey-haired man of about fifty behind the counter. The resemblance to Nathan was unmistakable. He looks like a nice man, she thought. I wish I had the nerve to walk in and tell him I'm a friend of his son. Just then, Mr. Rubin looked up from the newspaper spread out in front of him and saw Pearl. He smiled at her, but, embarrassed, Pearl turned and quickly walked away.

You could at least have said hello, she admonished herself. Arriving at Mrs. Bascomb's, she checked the hall table for mail. It had been only two days since she had received Nathan's last letter, a card for her eighteenth birthday, and she didn't expect another so soon. Mrs. Bascomb's newspaper was lying on the table and the headline caught Pearl's eye: Saint Joseph's to reopen. She quickly scanned the article, and at that moment an idea came to her. She would visit Sister Margaret and ask her advice.

On Sunday, Pearl put on her best dress and with a mixture of anticipation and reluctance set out for the orphanage. She hadn't been back since she and Nathan had walked there.

Sister Margaret embraced her warmly. "Pearl, just look at you, all grown up. Come to my room. We have a lot of catching up to do."

She's aged, Pearl thought. Her face was more deeply etched with wrinkles, her eyes weary with fatigue.

"I'm sorry I haven't written more often, sister. I've been working six days a week."

"I wouldn't have had time to answer," laughed Sister Margaret. "This move has all of us exhausted. I never want to go through another earthquake."

"It all seems like a dream now," Pearl said.

Pearl told the nun about her job, then brought up the nursing school. "I'd like to apply, but don't know where to begin or whether I can even afford to go." She decided not to mention Nathan.

"I think it's a wonderful idea," Sister Margaret said. She laughed suddenly. "As to where to begin, it's with Sister Adrian."

"Sister Adrian?"

"She's the administrator. She's not in my order, but we have something else in common. We grew up together in Kansas, went to the same schools, and we haven't seen each other since. I did write to her when I came to Montana and she wrote when she took over at Saint Patrick's, but then we lost touch. Won't she be surprised when I write to her about you?"

"Oh, sister, would you do that?"

"I'll have my letter out in tomorrow's mail. Can you come see me again next Sunday?" She laughed. "We might have a letter from her by then."

As soon as Pearl saw Sister Margaret's excited face the following Sunday, she knew she had been right.

"You better sit down, Pearl. Can you leave immediately for Missoula?"

"What?"

"All the positions for their new first year class were filled, but one of the girls withdrew. Sister Adrian says she'll let you take that place."

"But how can I afford it?"

"Sister Adrian said you shouldn't worry. They'll work it out with you."

"I can't believe this. How soon do I have to be there?"

"Classes begin in three days."

Pearl began thinking ahead. Telling Mrs. Bascomb posed no problem. Her room was paid up for the week and Pearl knew it wouldn't remain unrented for long. But she dreaded giving Harvey Gans such short notice, especially so soon after her promotion. Then Nathan's face came to mind.

"Well, Pearl, what shall I tell Sister Adrian?"

Pearl took the nun's hands. "Tell her yes. And thank you, sister, for everything."

"I'm sure you're making the right decision. I'll call Sister Adrian tomorrow."

Sister Margaret walked Pearl out and gave her a hug. "Please write," she said.

"I will. And sister . . ." Pearl took three one-dollar bills out of her purse. "I'd like to give this back to you. Maybe you can help someone else with it."

"You're sure you don't need it?"

"I have enough to get me to Missoula."

The nun smiled. "You're a good girl."

Harvey Gans stared at her in disbelief as she told him her plans. "I don't understand. The raise wasn't enough?"

"No, you've been very good to me. It's just that I want to become a nurse."

"Why didn't you tell me sooner? Then I could have trained someone to take your place."

"I didn't know I'd been accepted until yesterday. I'm sorry."

"And my nephew, he has nothing to do with this sudden move to Missoula?"

"He knows nothing about it," Pearl said.

"And so you're leaving tomorrow?"

"Yes. Classes begin next day."

Harvey shook his head. "Well, there's nothing more for me to say. You've been a good worker and I'm sorry to see you go."

"I can work today, Mr. Gans, and you don't even have to pay me," Pearl said.

"No, I'm sure you have a lot to do. Wait here a minute." He returned with an envelope in his hand.

"I was paid Friday," Pearl said.

"This is just a little extra from me. Just tell that nephew of mine that he's a scalawag. Tell him I won't forgive him for stealing you away from us."

23

The first half-hour of their initial meeting was devoted to Sister's Adrian's reminiscences of growing up in Kansas with Sister Margaret. And then, understanding Pearl's circumstances, she agreed to a half-scholarship. Pearl would pay off the balance of her tuition, room and board over a two-year period after she completed the curriculum. She would live in the student nurses' quarters adjoining the school.

It wasn't until the end of her first week that Pearl wrote to Nathan. Another week went by and Pearl still had no reply, but on a Saturday morning she was summoned to the administration office at the school. Nathan was standing by the receptionist's desk.

"Hello, Pearl," he said, as if he couldn't believe his eyes.

"Nathan," Pearl replied, smiling shyly.

"Can I take you out for tea—or a soda?"

"That's fine," the receptionist said, "just make sure you're back by dinner time."

They had walked an entire block before Nathan put his arm around her and gave her a quick kiss on the cheek. "Why didn't you let me know you were coming?"

"I didn't find out until three days before the semester started. I still can't believe I'm here."

"You're not the only one. God, Pearl, I'm so happy."

"But I have a message for you. Your Uncle Harvey blames you for my leaving Gans.' He says you're a scalawag."

Nathan laughed and clapped his hands. "That means he approves. Let's go over to the university," he said. "I'll show you around and then we can get lunch downtown."

"It's such a lovely day," Pearl said after they had toured the campus. "Can we have a picnic?"

"Great idea," said Nathan. "There's a market near here."

They carried their bread, cheese and fruit to an embankment overlooking the Clark Fork River.

"I used to imagine days like this when I'd think about your being here," Nathan said. "I still can't believe it's all come true."

"I saw your father," Pearl said.

A look of concern crossed Nathan's face. "You did? When? Where?"

"I passed the tobacco store on the Gold Block and saw a man behind the counter who looked just like you."

"That was my father all right."

"I was too embarrassed to go in."

He laughed, looking somewhat relieved.

"You don't want your parents to know about us, do you?" Pearl said.

"It's not that. It's just that my mother would get all concerned. She's so set on my finishing college, any girl would seem a threat. She'd think I was going to get married and drop out of school."

Pearl looked away, focusing her attention on two mallards drifting by.

"Don't be angry with me."

"I'm not angry. Anyway," she laughed, "your mother is worrying for no reason. We know you'll finish school and as for us . . . we're not thinking about marriage so the whole conversation is silly really."

"You should have added the words 'right away.'"

"What do you mean?"

"We're not thinking about marriage right away. I plan on our getting married when I can support us."

"We have plenty of time to think about it then."

"Will you see me tomorrow?"

"I can't. You wouldn't believe the amount of work I have. This is all so new to me and there's so much to learn. I'll be studying all day"

"Well," he said, "I'd be foolish to pout, especially after having gone an entire year without seeing you. We can meet every weekend, can't we?"

"You know I'll try."

Nathan took a bite of his apple. "I was just thinking," he said, "we're going to graduate at the same time."

"It seems so far away and the work is so hard, I can't even imagine it."

Nathan and Pearl tried to meet at least once during every weekend, but there were times when one or the other had to study for examinations. And then there were the occasions, at least once every three or four months, when Nathan's parents came to visit. "I'm sorry," Nathan would say, "I have to spend the day with them." "Of course," Pearl agreed, trying not to show her disappointment at not being invited.

Pearl's second year of school was even busier than her first, but somehow she found the work less taxing and her initial contacts with patients exhilirating. For the first time since her arrival at Saint Patrick's, she felt she had made the right career choice.

The days and months flew by. Nathan again spent the summer break working in the biology laboratory at the university and Pearl found employment during her vacation at a local home for elderly blind people. Her pay wasn't much but it allowed her to begin paying back the tuition.

In addition to helping the staff at the home, Pearl spent a few hours each day reading to the occupants. She chose her books from the public library and, for Pearl, it was an expansion of her own education, more pure enjoyment than work. Looking at the wrinkled faces of the blind men and women in the activities room, some in wheelchairs, all of them hanging on her every word, Pearl felt more contented than she had ever been. The nurses and attendants, freed from the demands of their charges while the young nursing student read to them, were content to let Pearl read for as long as she wanted.

It was only when meals were served that they interrupted her. "Let her keep reading," complained her listeners. "After lunch," said the supervisor, shaking her head in amazement. "They'd rather hear stories than eat," Pearl heard the woman tell an attendant.

"When will you begin applying to medical schools?" Pearl asked Nathan at the beginning of his senior year.

"I've decided to put it off," he replied.

"Why?"

"I just feel obliged to work and save some money toward tuition, at least for a year or two. My parents will fuss but I know what kind of burden it will put on them if I start school in the fall. The store isn't making my father wealthy by any means. My professor said he'll keep me on full time in the laboratory and I'd also be assisting him with students in the classroom."

"You haven't said anything to your parents?"

"I'll tell them next time they come to visit. I know it means waiting even longer before we can marry but . . ."

"You have to do what you feel is best," Pearl said, keeping her true feelings to herself. "We're still young," she reassured him, her words sounding hollow. She had witnessed Nathan's reluctance to cross his parents, his mother in particular, often enough to wonder if he would ever get up the nerve to tell them about her, let alone their plans to marry.

"Have you thought about where you'll work after graduation?" Nathan asked.

"Sister Adrian has asked me to stay on as a nurse in the hospital."

"That's wonderful. I was hoping that would happen."

"She's willing to let me stay in the student dorm. That will help me pay back the money I owe even faster."

"I'm planning to rent a room in town," Nathan said, a gloomy expression crossing his face. "I was hoping we might be in the same building."

The privacy, she thought, would be nice but it also posed a danger. What if some day they got carried away while . . .

"It's better this way," she said. "Where do you think you'll apply when you've saved some money?" she asked, changing the subject.

"The University of Washington for sure. Maybe a midwest school, too, but

190

I think my grades are good enough to get into Washington. I'm sure you'll like Seattle."

"Oh?"

"You didn't think I'd leave you here, did you?"

Nathan's mother wasn't pleased when he finally told her about his decision. "We'll come up with the money," she argued.

"It's already too late for this fall, mother. And I want to do it my way. It will make me feel better to know I'm contributing my share."

There was no way she could compel him, so she swallowed her disappointment.

And Pearl had to swallow hers when Nathan failed to introduce her to Mr. and Mrs. Rubin at his graduation. "It's just not the right time," he whispered.

Walking angrily back to the dorm, Pearl thought seriously of breaking off her relationship. She was as fond of him as ever, but she doubted his ability to stand up to his mother. And besides, what did she really know about love? The novels she read spoke of an overwhelming passion, of being swept away by desire. Pearl had felt herself getting aroused at times when she was with Nathan, but never had she felt what the stories said she should feel. Maybe, she thought, it would be better if they didn't see one another—at least for a while.

"I have a surprise for you," Sister Adrian said a week later shortly before the nursing school diplomas were awarded.

"Sister Margaret!" Pearl exclaimed. "You came all this way to see me?"

"You and my old friend, Sister Adrian. I'm proud of you, Pearl. And grateful to Sister Adrian."

"I'm grateful to you both," Pearl said.

"You've been a good student," Sister Adrian said. "And Pearl will be working for us at the hospital," she said, turning to Sister Margaret.

Pearl suddenly spotted Nathan. "I'd like you to meet a friend of mine, sisters," she said, motioning to Nathan. "This is Nathan Rubin. He's from Helena, too, and just graduated from the university."

"It's nice to meet you, Nathan," said Sister Adrian. "Sister Margaret and I have some catching up to do so we'll let you young people enjoy the day."

"They seem very nice," said Nathan. "They're the first nuns I ever talked to."

"They're just people who happen to dress differently."

"Do you have any plans for the afternoon?" Nathan asked.

"I'll probably head over to the hospital."

"You're mad at me, aren't you?" he said.

"Why should I be mad at you?"

"I should have introduced you to my parents last week."

"Well," she said, "I have to go. I'm sure we'll see one another around."

Her anger subsided as she walked toward Saint Patrick's. She knew she'd been hard on him. Maybe it's better this way, she decided. I'm not a child anymore and I can't create fantasies for myself. We'll just have to see what happens.

Pearl had little time to think about Nathan during the week that followed. The transition from student to working nurse took some getting used to, the added responsibilities leaving her exhausted. On Saturday, as her shift was nearing its end, she received a call from the admissions desk. "There's a young man here to see you."

Pearl couldn't lie to herself. She was glad he had come.

"You look great in your nurse's uniform," he said smiling.

"Is that what you came to tell me?"

"I was wondering if we could have dinner together tonight."

She paused for a moment, pretending to be thinking about it.

"Please, Pearl. I have to talk to you."

"Why don't you meet me in front of the hospital at six."

"I'll be there."

24

"Isn't this too extravagant?" Pearl asked, as she cut into her steak.

"Not when I'm with the girl who's going to be my wife."

"You're so sure of that then?"

"Oh, Pearl, don't torture me."

"Your food will get cold," she said.

"I wrote to my parents last week."

Pearl poked at her mashed potatoes, feigning disinterest.

"Don't you want to know what I told them?"

"I'm listening."

"I told them about you. I said I should have introduced you during the graduation. I told them you're the girl I want to marry."

"And if they say no?"

"It's my life."

They were soon back in their old routine, continuing to see each other regularly.

"I don't understand why you won't come up," Nathan said one Saturday when she met him in front of his building.

"It's just better this way."

"Don't you trust me?"

"Maybe I don't trust myself."

"I promise to control my lust and not ravage you," he said dramatically.

Pearl laughed. "I'm still going to resist temptation."

"You're not allowed to bring guests to your room at the nursing school dorm and you refuse to come to my room. We're having a public courtship."

"We'll survive."

"You're a hard woman, Pearl Schneider."

"That I'm not. Just a cautious one."

"I have a surprise for you. My parents are driving out next Sunday."

She shrugged. "So we won't see each other that day?"

"On the contrary. My mother said she hoped to meet you. We arranged to have lunch at Riverview."

"Well, that is a surprise."

"She's taken it into her head to have a new worry."

"What's that?"

"She's afraid we're going to get into that war in Europe and that I'll get drafted into the Army."

"You don't think that will happen, do you?"

"Reading our newspapers you wouldn't think so. Anyway, you'll join us, won't you?"

"You know I'll come."

■■■

"You look lovely," Nathan said, when he came to pick Pearl up at the hospital.

Pearl had chosen a simple blue dress from her limited wardrobe, the one she liked the most. She smiled at Nathan, grateful for his compliment.

"September's the nicest month of the year," he said. "Don't you think so?"

The sun's rays were shimmering on the river as they approached. The waters of the Clark Fork flowed lazily in keeping with the warmth of the late summer day.

"They're here already," said Nathan, motioning toward a couple sitting at an outdoor table on the Riverview's patio.

Nathan's parents stood up as they approached. Nathan embracd his mother and shook hands with his father.

"This is Pearl Schneider, whom I wrote to you about. Pearl, my parents."

"You look very familiar," said Mr. Rubin when they had taken their seats. "I can't forget a face as pretty as yours."

Pearl blushed, remembering how foolish she had felt when he caught her staring at him in the store.

"Pearl's from Helena so you've probably seen her there," said Nathan.

"My husband's not just being gallant, Pearl. You are pretty—and exotic."

"Thank you," said Pearl, uncomfortable at being the center of attention. "No one's ever called me exotic before."

Mr. Rubin laughed. "Nathan says you're a nurse."

"Yes, I graduated in June and work at Saint Patrick's."

They then placed their orders. Mrs. Rubin turned to her son, then to Pearl, as the waitress left. "How did you two meet?"

"We met in Helena," Nathan replied, smiling.

Surprised, the Rubins looked at each other. "When? How?"

Nathan laughed. "Pearl and I were both working at the store. She knows Uncle Harvey."

Nathan's mother sat back in her chair. "Well. My own brother, and he never said a word. But you haven't worked there in years, Nathan. That means you two have known one another for—"

"Years," Nathan said.

"How is Mr. Gans?" asked Pearl. "He's a very nice man."

"He's fine. I don't know how nice he is though when he won't even confide in his sister."

"Now, now," said Mr. Rubin, patting his wife on the arm and laughing.

"What do you think, Pearl, about Nathan's putting off his application to medical school? I think he's making a big mistake."

"Mother, you asked Pearl what she thinks."

"I'm used to that," said Mr. Rubin. "Roberta always asks me questions and then gives me her answer."

They all laughed.

"Well, I think it's really Nathan's decision. It makes him more comfortable to do it his way. Putting it off for a year isn't so bad."

"It's the war that makes me nervous. If we get into it, they'll be drafting the young men. But if Nathan was in medical school, they would let him finish."

"But we're not in the war, mother. President Roosevelt said we wouldn't get into it."

"None of us know what's going to happen. I just have an uncomfortable feeling about it."

"Your mother is a worrier, Nathan," said Mr. Rubin. "Ah, here comes lunch."

"Do your parents live in Helena?" Mrs. Rubin asked.

"I'm an orphan," said Pearl as matter-of-factly as she could.

"Oh, I'm sorry. But who raised y—"

"Roberta, that's prying," said Mr. Rubin.

"I don't mind," said Pearl. "I was raised in an orphanage."

"Then you have no family?"

"None that I know of."

Mr. Rubin gave his wife an unhappy look. "Roberta, no more questions."

"I hope you didn't mind my mother's prying," Nathan said after lunch.

"They're very nice people."

"I think they like you. In fact, I think my father is smitten. But I saw you first."

She gave him a playful poke in the ribs. "There is some truth in what your mother says, though. If you were in medical school, they probably wouldn't draft you if war comes."

"But we're not at war," he laughed, "so why worry?"

"Will you apply for next fall?"

"I'll decide in February. But I promise I'll write for applications before that."

"I don't have a good feeling about this. I'm inclined to agree with your mother. You know your parents will help you as much as they can. And I hardly spend anything. I can help you, too."

"Oh, Pearl, are you going to start on me, too? Everyone wants to help me. But I want to know I can do it on my own."

"There's nothing wrong in taking help when it's offered."

"Now what did you say back there in the restaurant?" Nathan said angrily, pointing his finger at her. "You said it's Nathan's decision. Why did you say it if you didn't mean it?"

"It's just that I've given it more thought and—"

"Stop," said Nathan, holding up his hands. "I don't want to fight with you. I just want you to understand what I feel. I don't want to be dependent on my parents."

"I understand that. I guess I'm just worried for you."

"Why don't we save the worrying until it's needed. Okay?"

Pearl forced a smile. "I won't say any more about it."

As the weeks and months passed, Pearl was true to her word. It was Nathan who brought the subject up as the year of 1940 came to an end.

"I'd like to tell you what I've decided," he said as they sat in a diner on a Saturday morning having coffee.

"About what?"

"About medical school. I have the applications. For Washington and for Iowa. But there's no way I can come up with the money. Not yet. If I work one more year I know I can save enough for the first two years. Then, working summers, I might be able to earn the rest."

He studied her face. "You're disappointed with me, aren't you?"

"A little disappointed, but not with you."

"I will make you a promise. Next February, a year from now, I'll send my applications in. There'll be no more excuses."

"You know what's happening in Europe."

'It's been happening for a while. There's too much opposition in America for us to get involved. By September of 1942 I'll be in medical school—if they accept me, that is—and then you can stop worrying.

"Oh, by the way, my mother wants to throw a birthday party for me in Helena. Just family and some friends from high school. I'm going to be twenty-two next month but she must think I'm still six. But if people want to throw a few dollars my way it'll go into the bank and come in handy for medical school tuition. She asked if I'd bring you."

25

It was Nathan's birthday, but Pearl was the center of attention. She was aware of the puzzled look on the faces of his relatives when they were introduced to her, as if they couldn't understand where she fit in. Nathan's friends, however, accepted her immediately. They clustered on the enclosed front porch, surrounding Pearl.

"You're a lucky fellow, Nathan," said his friend, Robert, as Nathan handed Pearl a glass of soda pop.

"That's what I tell him," said Pearl, eliciting laughter from the group.

"I know I am," Nathan said, meaning it.

"What's wrong?" Pearl asked softly when she managed to get him alone.

"It's just my mother."

"Is she still upset about your application?"

"That and other things. Let's not talk about it now."

Mrs. Rubin, Pearl had noticed, was drifting from one group to another. At first Pearl thought she was just being a good hostess, but she couldn't help noticing the furtive glances cast in her direction by Nathan's uncles and aunts. Only Mr. Rubin gave her a warm smile each time their eyes met.

Pearl felt a sense of relief when Mrs. Rubin finally brought in Nathan's birthday cake. Nathan obliged by blowing out the candles and enduring a chorus of the Happy Birthday song, then thanked everyone for coming.

"It's been good to see you all again," he said, directing his remarks more warmly to his old school friends than to his relatives.

"We should leave now if we're going to catch the six-fifteen bus," Nathan said to his father. "If we miss it, we won't get back to Missoula until very late."

"I'll get the car ready while you say your goodbyes," he told his son.

Nathan and Pearl then said their farewells to each of Nathan's relatives and friends. Pearl couldn't help but notice the tension between the two when he said goodbye to his mother. They barely spoke to one another and "Goodbye, Pearl" was all she said to Pearl.

The silence in the car on the way to the bus stop made Pearl uncomfortable. Finally, Mr. Rubin glanced past Pearl at his son. "Try not to be upset with your mother, Nathan. She means well."

"I wish she'd stop treating me like a child," he said.

"Mothers are like that sometimes. They see their children becoming adults and feel they're losing them. What do you think, Pearl?"

"I'm not the one to ask, Mr. Rubin."

His face reddened. "I meant in general, Pearl."

"Some mothers may be overprotective," she said, not wanting to antagonize the one person in Nathan's family who seemed genuinely fond of her. "But sometimes . . ."

Mr. Rubin glanced at her. "Sometimes what?"

"Some mothers want to control their sons."

He nodded. "You've got yourself a perceptive girl," he said to his son.

Mr. Rubin waited with them at the bus stop until the bus rolled in, about five minutes after they got there. He embraced them both and gave Pearl a slight kiss on the cheek. "Happy birthday again," he called, waving out the car window as he drove away.

"Your father is such a nice man," Pearl said when they were seated on the bus.

"It makes up for my mother," I guess.

"I still think she means well."

"She has a strange way of showing it sometimes."

"It was nice of them to give this party for you," Pearl said, trying to be cheerful.

"I'm sorry if my relatives made you feel uncomfortable, Pearl."

"I think they were just surprised by my appearance, that's all. They probably never expected you to have a girlfriend who looks Chinese."

"They could have had better manners even if they were surprised. I saw the looks they were giving you." Suddenly he smiled. "But they weren't blind. I overheard my Aunt Helen, the one with her glasses perched on the end of her nose, telling my mother how attractive you were. That was the word she used—attractive."

"It's nice to see you smiling again."

"There's something else to smile about. I got about three hundred dollars in gifts. That's really going to help toward my tuition."

"What did your mother say that got you so upset?"

His face clouded over and she immediately regretted having asked.

"She cornered me in the kitchen when you went out onto the porch and then she started on me about medical school. She was really angry I hadn't applied for this fall. She still has it in her head that we're going to get into the war."

"It's only because she cares about you."

"I probably shouldn't even tell you this because it'll make you really dislike her, if you don't already. She said I should break off with you, that I'm in no position to have a steady relationship, that I should be thinking only of school. And what really made me furious is she said we have no idea what kind of background you come out of. I asked her if she thought she was descended from British royalty."

"So that's why she seemed so angry."

"I guess so. Well, she started it."

Darkness fell about an hour after they left Helena and they rode in silence. A few times Pearl caught herself being lulled to sleep by the motion of the bus. They stepped out into a frigid evening in Missoula, clouds covering the stars.

"It almost feels like snow coming in," said Nathan.

"I can get back to the hospital by myself," said Pearl when they reached Nathan's building. "You must be tired."

"No, I'll walk you. Come up for a minute just so I can put this money away."

Pearl hesitated, then followed him up the two flights. There were three small apartments on each floor. Nathan took her hand and led her down the dark hallway to his door. Inside, he turned on the light and Pearl found herself in a room that would have fit in one corner of the Rubin dining room in Helena. A bed nestled against one wall and a sofa against the other. A doorway led into a kitchen barely large enough for one person.

"Where's your bathroom?" Pearl asked.

"In the hall. We have to share it. Would you like me to show you?"

"No. I was just curious. You keep the place pretty clean."

"I try," he said, heading for the kitchen, where he slipped the cash into a cannister on a shelf above the stove. "Would you like some tea?"

"No, thank you."

Returning, he took his jacket off and put his arms around Pearl and held her close. "It's so good to feel you next to me. Why don't you take your coat off and stay for a few minutes?"

"It's getting late, Nathan," she said as he helped her out of her coat.

He then took her in his arms again, kissing her on the lips. Pearl resisted slightly, then yielded, her lips parting. "Oh, Pearl," he whispered, running his hands down her back as she rested her head on his shoulder. "We never get to be alone like this."

Pearl knew she should leave but she couldn't find the will. Nathan's hands were all over her now, one moment cupping her breasts, the next pulling her tightly against him. She felt the bulge of his sex against her and knew she wanted him. Nathan was right. They had never been alone like this, and Pearl knew it was for this very reason. It was not that she didn't yearn to be loved, to be taken by him. Alone in her bed she had often run her hands over herself, pretending they were Nathan's, until she had her release, muffling her moans in her pillow.

Now she didn't have to pretend. She didn't want him to stop. Nathan gently unbuttoned her blouse and helped her out of her skirt. He then turned off the light and she heard him take off his clothes. She could barely make out his dark form as he drew closer. Their naked bodies came together and she felt the urgent pressure of his penis against her. On the bed, she lay on her back, breathing rapidly and watching his shadowy form above her.

"Gently," she said, as he forced against her. "Oh, it hurts, Nathan. Gentle. Gentle." She was wet now, more excited than she had ever been. He entered her with difficulty, then slowly, slowly, penetrated deeper and deeper. "Oh, Pearl, I love you so much," he said breathlessly.

Pearl was now floating on a rising sea, the waters carrying her into a red and yellow void flashing and enveloping her. She heard a moan of pleasure, not realizing it was her own voice merging with Nathan's cry.

"Did I hurt you?" he asked softly, his voice muffled against her neck as his body rested heavily on top of her.

She shook her head slowly.

He then eased himself up and slipped out of her, resting his head on her shoulder. "I love you so much, Pearl."

"What would your Uncle Harvey say if he could see us now?" she said.

Nathan laughed softly. "I didn't plan this, Pearl. I hope you won't think badly of me."

"If I didn't want this to happen, I wouldn't be here."

"I want you to marry me. As soon as possible."

"It's not the right time. Your mother isn't wrong about everything, Nathan."

"Oh, God, don't bring my mother into this."

"If we were to marry now and I got pregnant, what would we do? I wouldn't be able to work and you'd end up doing something you didn't want to do. It's better to wait."

"I can't wait until I finish medical school. That's years away. And what happens if you're pregnant now?"

"My monthly is due tomorrow so I'm sure we don't have to worry."

"But there are ways to prevent your getting pregnant. And you can work as a nurse while I'm in school."

"Nathan, I will marry you. I just want it to be at the right time."

"I'm not going to school unless we marry and you come with me."

She laughed and sat up. "You haven't even been accepted yet. We'll talk about it when the time comes. I'd better go. The nuns don't like us coming into the dorm later than eleven."

"I'll walk with you," he said, dressing rapidly.

"You don't have to."

"I want to."

They soon stood in the shadows outside the dormitory and Nathan kissed her goodnight. "I already feel married to you," he said.

"I love you, Nathan."

26

As Pearl cleaned off the crusted blood and semen, the entire evening seemed like a delicious dream. The taste of Nathan's kisses was still on her lips and she stared in fascination at the washcloth in her hand. Just like that, she thought, no longer a virgin.

In spite of the nuns' teachings, she felt no guilt. If anything, she felt exactly the opposite.

Lying in her bed that night her hands seemed to drift of their own volition to her genitals. She was still tender and touched herself gently. She remembered Nathan's face above her and writhed with pleasure. Again she climaxed, muffling a moan with her hand.

She wondered if it was normal for a woman to desire sex the way she did. At the orphanage it had been a taboo subject although some of the older girls spoke in whispers about it. While she had no misgivings about what she had done, she knew she would have to be careful. The slight cramping in her pelvis and tenderness in her breasts let her know she was on the verge of getting her period. She knew her ready giving in to Nathan was not only because of her desire for him, but also because pregancy was virtually impossible at this time of the month.

She thought about Nathan's telling her he loved her. It was the first time he had spoken those words and she wondered if it was only his passion expressing itself. He had told her more than once that he wanted to marry her. Could that have been driven by passion, too? No, she refused to believe that. She had expressed her love for him, too, and that was truly how she felt. They were not versed in the meaning of love, but how could what they seemed to feel for one another be described as anything else? Nevertheless, she could not simply jump into marriage. She had meant what she said. Nothing must interfere with his plans to go to medical school. As difficult as it would be for them, they had to wait until he finished his education. In the meantime, if they chose their times together very carefully . . . She felt a tingling again between her legs and rolled onto her stomach. Better go to sleep, she told herself. You have to be up early.

■■■

Spring gave way to summer and then, before they had a chance to adjust to autumn, the first snow fell in the beginning of October. Pearl and Nathan spent every moment they could together. They had made love a half dozen times since Nathan's birthday, but Pearl had chosen those times, always a day or two prior to her period. She was never late and was attuned enough to her body to know.

At the end of November Nathan asked her to meet him at his apartment.

"It's the wrong time of the month," she said when she came in.

"Not for that," he laughed. "I want to show you the admissions information and catalogues from the three medical schools I'm going to apply to. And I'll fill out the applications while you're here so you'll know I'm serious. I've saved enough to get me through the first two years and I'll have enough for the third year, too, if I work next summer."

They sat on Nathan's small sofa and flipped through brochures from University of Washington, University of Iowa, and Northwestern. "They're all good schools," Nathan said, "and I'd be happy no matter which one took me. I'm going to send my transcripts and applications right after New Year's. The only thing worrying me is if they don't accept me, will I still have time to apply elsewhere?"

"I'm sure you'll get in," Pearl said. "Your grades were so good."

"I hope you're right."

"We just have to hope America keeps out of the war—at least until after you're accepted."

"If it hasn't happened by now, I don't think it will," said Nathan. "Congress almost didn't renew the Selective Service Act this year. Most Americans don't want to fight in a war across the ocean."

"I don't follow it very much, but I know Hitler is evil. He stops at nothing to get what he wants. I feel so sorry for the British and for the people in the countries he's conquered."

"The British and French should have stopped him two years ago. Well, maybe the Russians will teach him a lesson, just the way they did Napoleon. Let's not talk about the war," he said pulling her to him.

"Behave yourself," she said. "You better get started on those applications."

He looked thoughtful for a moment. "Did you mean what you said about not marrying me before I started school?"

"At least get through the first year or two. Then, if you feel the same way, we can. At least I'll know you're close enough to getting your degree so it anything happens . . ."

"You mean like an unexpected event? One that wears diapers?"

"Exactly."

"But you will come with me if I end up in Chicago or Seattle or Iowa, won't you? There are plenty of hospitals where you can work."

"I don't worry about getting a job. I worry about distracting you. But if I stayed here I'd probably worry more about other nurses distracting you."

"No chance," he said, his face serious. "You're my girl and always will be."

27

On a Sunday morning in early December Nathan paced outside Pearl's dormitory, patting his gloved hands together to keep warm.

"I'm sorry I'm late," Pearl said as she rushed out.

"Watch those steps," Nathan said. "They're icy."

Pearl carefully picked her way around the slick spots, then clutched Nathan's arm. "Brrr, it's freezing."

"We'll both feel better after breakfast and hot coffee."

They walked quickly through the almost deserted streets, the vapor of their breath visible in the frigid air as they headed for Benton's, a diner popular with workers and students. A blast of steamy air enveloped them as they entered.

"Oh, that feels good," said Pearl.

The few patrons were all at one end of the counter. Along with the cook and waitresses, they were listening intently to the radio.

"I wonder what's going on," Pearl said.

They were about to take a table but no one was paying any attention to them. "Maybe we should go up to the counter," Nathan said.

An excited male voice was coming over the radio.

"What's happened?" Nathan asked.

A beefy man in a lumberman's jacket swung around. "The Japs bombed our naval base in Hawaii."

Nathan felt Pearl's fingers tighten around his arm. They quietly listened to the ghastly news. Most of the American fleet sunk, hundreds, maybe thousands, dead. "Yellow bastards," growled the lumberjack softly.

Breakfast was now forgotten. A waitress had placed cups of coffee in front of them but they sat untouched. Pearl was shivering in spite of the warmth in the diner.

"You should drink your coffee," Nathan said.

"Let's go to your place," Pearl replied. "I've lost my appetite."

"Try not to be upset," he said, as they quickly paid for the coffee and left.

Nathan turned up the steam heat as soon as they were in the apartment. Pearl sat huddled in her overcoat on the sofa while Nathan put a kettle of water on the stove and brought out cups, tea, and sugar from the cabinet.

"What are we going to do?" Pearl said.

"We'll have to see what Roosevelt is going to do," he said. "Shall I turn on the radio?"

"No. I keep thinking of all those sailors. Terrible, terrible," she muttered. She looked over at Nathan with tears in her eyes. "I knew something bad was going to happen. Ever since that German submarine sank our destroyer off Iceland, I've had the feeling that it was only a matter of time. That's why I've been so worried. I kept expecting you to get your draft notice and was thankful at the end of each day when you hadn't. I don't pray anymore but I kept wishing there was a God who could stop the madness from spreading to America. Now it's happened."

"I know you're right but I want to believe that there's some way to—"

"There's no way to stop it now," she said. "By tomorrow men will be lining up to enlist—and those who don't will be drafted. It's too late to apply to medical school. They'll probably defer only the students who are already enrolled."

"I don't know if I'd go to school now anyway."

"What do you mean?"

"This is my country and it's been attacked. I hate war as much as you do, but I'd feel like I was shirking my responsibility."

"What will you do?"

"I think I should enlist. Maybe I won't have to become part of the killing if I join the Navy. I'm a college graduate so they'll make me an officer. There's just one thing . . ."

Pearl looked at him as he paused.

"Will you marry me before I go, Pearl?"

She slowly shook her head. "I think we should look at all this as a temporary interruption of our plans. You know I'll wait for you."

Nathan took her in his arms.

"Your mother is going to be very unhappy when you tell her."

"I hadn't even thought about her," he said. "We've barely spoken since my birthday. They haven't even come out for a visit."

"Have you talked to your father?"

"I called him a couple of times at the store. Poor guy. He's caught in the middle. He makes excuses about why they haven't been able to make the drive. He always asks how you are."

"Maybe you should talk to him first."

Everything was just as Pearl had predicted. Long lines formed Monday morning outside the recruiters' offices and Nathan took his place in one of them. Four days after the Japanese attack Germany and Italy declared war on America. No more talk now of keeping out of a fight most Americans had looked upon as a European war. Nathan received his ensign's commission in the Navy, followed almost immediately by orders to leave for basic training at Great Lakes on December 18th. He called his father and the following weekend his parents drove to Missoula.

Nathan had arranged for them to come to his apartment. Pearl had arrived an hour earlier and helped him tidy up. She had never seen Nathan so fidgety and they both jumped when they heard the knock on the door.

Nathan shook hands with his father, and seconds later Roberta Rubin was tearfully embracing her son. Embarrassed, Nathan patted her back. "It's okay," he whispered.

Mr. Rubin turned to Pearl and smiled. "How are you, Pearl?" he said. "It's good to see you again."

"It's nice to see you, too."

Nathan's mother dried her eyes as she greeted Pearl. "I'm sorry for being so foolish," she said, taking Pearl's hands.

"I understand," Pearl said. "I love him, too."

Mrs. Rubin nodded and smiled.

"I'd hoped this day would never come," she said when they were seated on the sofa.

"We all hoped it wouldn't," said Nathan's father.

Pearl was between his parents and Nathan sat on a hard-backed chair facing them.

"Shall I make some tea or coffee?" he asked.

"No, Jerry and I want to take both of you to lunch," Mrs. Rubin said, turning to Pearl.

"That would be very nice," Pearl replied.

Talk during lunch focused on the war and Nathan's plans for the future. "Wonderful," Mr. Rubin said when Nathan told them about their marriage plans. "Then you have something to look forward to," Mrs. Rubin said, smiling at them both.

Back at the apartment after tearful goodbyes from the Rubins, Pearl sat on the sofa with her head on Nathan's shoulder.

"My mother was on her best behavior," he said.

"We all were," Pearl replied.

"You always are," he said, kissing her on the cheek.

"I remember your words from the other day, about shirking responsibility. I don't think there's much point in my remaining in Missoula. The sisters have enough help at the hospital." She laughed softly. "They might be glad to lose one of their nurses. One less person to pay."

"What do you mean?"

"There's going to be a big need for nurses at military and veterans' hospitals." She smiled sadly. "So, what I've decided for now is to go back to Helena and apply for a job at the veterans' hospital."

"Fort Harrison?"

She nodded. "They're probably going to be busier as time goes by."

"With your memories of Saint Joseph's, I never thought you'd want to go back to Helena."

"I can live with memories. Besides, I met you in Helena." Pearl shifted onto her knees and leaned her weight against him. He fell back on the sofa with Pearl on top of him.

"It's all right?" Nathan asked.

"Yes, it's all right."

28

Days now took on a monotonous sameness for Pearl. It reminded her of her years in the orphanage, being with the same people when she was at work, eating her meals with the same nurses and students, and having nothing to look forward to. The only difference was having her own room, where she was able to decide for herself when she wanted to go to sleep.

She had applied for a position at Fort Harrison but hadn't heard anything yet. Nathan's letters began to arrive and he filled pages telling her about his training and the pleasure he took in being out on the lake for his seamanship courses. And he wrote of how much he loved her.

Propped against her pillows at night, Pearl read them over and over. And she thought about love. Was it just an assumption that because they were together they were in love? She remembered the first time Nathan had told her he loved her, and how she had wondered whether his words were prompted by passion. Maybe that's what love between a man and a woman is all about, she told herself. At least at first. She had no doubt, now, that she truly loved Nathan and that her love was reciprocated.

For almost three weeks Pearl waited for a response from the veterans' hospital. And just as she was about to give up, it came. She was approved for a position and was to begin working on the first of February.

Sister Adrian listened quietly as Pearl gave her notice. "I knew you'd be leaving us, Pearl," she said, breaking into a smile. "The veterans' hospital contacted me for a recommendation. I even called Sister Margaret to let her know you'd probably be returning to Helena."

Pearl stayed on at Saint Patrick's for two more weeks. During that time she wrote to Fort Harrison asking if they could advise her about accomodations. She also wrote to Nathan, giving him her news.

Pearl's first year back in Helena went so quickly she could scarcely believe it when she saw 1943 instead of 1942 on calendars. Her responsibilities on the wards increased with the passage of time as more and more wounded were brought to Fort Harrison. Instead of the chronic care patients she had taken care of when she first arrived, those with emphysema and heart disease and urinary blockages, she now found herself attending to amputees and young men disfigured by burns and shell blasts. Many of them were no older than schoolboys.

How can people do this to one another? she wondered. To rob young men of their limbs, to scar their bodies and souls—it was almost more than she could bear. It was difficult to leave her patients at the end of each day. The images of their tortured bodies continued to haunt her and seeing the ravages of war made her worry even more about Nathan.

His letters were infrequent since he shipped out, often arriving in a cluster. Because of military censorship he was unable to tell her where his ship was and whether he had seen any action. All she knew was that he was ensign on a destroyer.

As Pearl became more resigned to Nathan's absence and more adapted to her work, she found herself enjoying her spare time. She had rented a small apartment less than a half-mile from the hospital and she relished her walks to and from work. In early morning, especially from spring to fall, she looked forward to the golden glow of the sun's rays on the scratchgravel hills beyond Fort Harrison. By the time she left work in mid-afternoon the sun was making its slow descent toward the continental divide to the west. Pearl often walked around the hospital grounds, then sat on a bench near the flower beds for an hour or two and read. But winter put an end to that. Bundled in her sweater and coat, she would head home, the wind at her back, looking forward to the warmth of her apartment.

One day merged imperceptibly into the next, the weeks flying by as she settled into a routine. Pearl paid more attention now to the news coming over the radio and read the local newspaper each day. During most of 1942 reports from the front, both in Europe and the Pacific, had been anything but hopeful. But with the new year she sensed a change. The tide had turned and the allies now appeared to have taken the offensive. Names she had never heard before became commonplace—Stalingrad, Midway, Guadalcanal and El Alamein—and she listened intently to stories told by the damaged young men on the wards. A few spoke openly of their fears for the future.

Pearl had few answers for their questions. Will a girl love me with these scars on my face? Who would marry a man with no legs? She could offer only kind assurances, which she herself often didn't believe.

In April of 1943 the first warmth of spring settled over Helena. Pearl and the other nurses, familiar with the vagaries of Montana weather, joked with one another, each choosing a date when the next snowstorm would probably arrive. But in the meantime they took comfort in the rapidly melting snow, a sure sign that a real spring was not far off.

Meanwhile, Nathan's last letters, a packet of them, had arrived all at once about a month earlier. Another packet will probably arrive any day, she thought. But as the month passed, Pearl became more apprehensive. By the first of May, she could no longer stand the strain.

When she had arrived in Helena, Pearl had thought more than once of dropping by Mr. Rubin's store. And she had also thought of visiting Nathan's Uncle Harvey, and Sister Margaret at the orphanage. In the end though, for one reason or the other, she had seen only Sister Margaret.

Now, she decided, was the time for a visit to Nathan's father. She chose a Saturday morning, putting on her best dress.

"Pearl!" said Mr. Rubin as she came through the door. "It's so good to see you again. I've been wondering about you. I told Roberta last night that you must be too busy at the hospital."

"I have been busy at work, but that's no excuse. I should have come sooner."

214

"As long as you're here now, that's what counts. Have you heard from Nathan recently?"

"Not since early March. Have you heard from him?"

He shook his head. "The last letter we got was in early March, too."

"I wonder if there's someone we can contact."

"If there was anything wrong, I'm sure we would have received some word," he said, trying to believe his own words.

"I'm really worried," Pearl said, almost in tears.

"I am, too, Pearl. At home I have to pretend I'm not. I don't want to upset Roberta more than she is. But I don't know what we can do. Do you have a telephone at home?"

Pearl shook her head and gave him her number at work.

"Whoever hears anything first will call the other. Agreed?"

Pearl nodded.

"And once we know Nathan is all right, then we'll have you over for dinner. No sense all of us sitting around the table with long faces."

Pearl left the store more troubled than when she had come and it was impossible for her to dispel the thought that something terrible had happened. Nathan would have written if he was able, she told herself. What if he's hurt, or . . . ? It was too horrible to contemplate. For the first time she regretted having lost her faith. She knew if she still believed, she would be saying prayers every day for Nathan's safe return. It would at least have given her the sense that she was doing something rather than waiting helplessly.

Two of the other nurses on Pearl's floor had husbands serving overseas, one stationed with the Air Force in England and the other with the Marines somewhere in the Pacific. Desperately needing comfort, Pearl talked to them about her fears. She quickly learned she wasn't the only one who was worried.

"Whenever we get a new admission," said Lori, a young blond who was already a mother, "I'm almost afraid to look at the name. Sometimes letters don't come for weeks. That's when I worry the most. I know how you feel."

Another ten days went by and there was still no news. She had to be brave, Pearl told herself, strong enough to face whatever happened.

On Saturday, the weather turned colder and angry clouds formed over the Elkhorns. It would probably snow by nightfall, but Pearl didn't care. She seemed not to care about anything. In desperation she stopped by Mr. Rubin's store. He was alone behind the counter, staring off into space.

Seeing her sad face, he shook his head.

"Nothing?" Pearl said softly.

"Nothing. I called the War Department but they were no help. I even tried the Red Cross but . . ." He made a gesture with his hands. "I don't even know the name of the ship Nathan is on."

It's not fair, Pearl thought, as she walked home. Her tears flowed so suddenly that Pearl was taken by surprise. She ran up the steps to her apartment and collapsed onto her bed. "Nathan, oh, Nathan, where are you?" she said aloud.

Pearl had deep circles under her eyes when she reported for work on Monday morning.

"Are you ill?" Mrs. Jennings, the daytime supervisor, asked.

"No, I'm fine."

"I hope so because you've got a busy day ahead of you. Five transfers arrived on the weekend and no one was discharged. That means every bed on the ward is filled."

"Don't worry about me," Pearl said, glad that she would be busy.

Mrs. Dawes, the night shift supervisor gave the report as Pearl joined Mrs. Jennings and the other nurses clustered around her in the lounge. After reviewing the patients Pearl knew, Mrs. Dawes detailed the new admissions. "We have Henry Porter, a twenty-two year old, transferred from Tripler. Corporal Porter has above the knee amputations, bilateral. Healing has been slow so keep watching for any sign of infection. Private First Class Anthony Pelosi is a twenty-one year old transferred in from Cleveland with second and third degree burns over the lower half of his body, mainly legs, genitals and lower abdomen. He's got a catheter in so watch for any sign of urinary tract infection. The doctors plan to begin skin grafting later this week. Nathan Rubin is twenty-four, he's a naval officer, an ensign, and was transferred in from Illinois."

Pearl instantly jumped up, her heart pounding. "What was that name?" she asked, barely able to speak.

"Nathan Rubin. Do you know him?"

"Where is he from?"

"We only have his military address," Mrs. Dawes replied. Next of kin are his parents and they're right here in Helena."

Pearl placed a hand over her mouth.

"Are you all right, Pearl?" Mrs. Dawes asked.

"What happened to him?"

"You'd better sit down."

Several of the other nurses helped Pearl to her chair.

"Ensign Rubin was blinded when his ship was torpedoed. He also suffered extensive burns on one side of his face. He's here for revison of his skin graft. The initial surgery was done at Great Lakes Hospital in Illinois."

"Pearl, do you want to take a break?"

"What?" Pearl was dazed, not even aware that Mrs. Jennings had addressed her.

"Maybe you should lie down for a while."

"What bed is he in?" Pearl asked, struggling for self-control.

"Bed two," said Mrs. Dawes.

Pearl excused herself and left the room. She stood in the doorway of the ward, her gaze sweeping across the room. Nathan was sitting with his head propped against two pillows, staring off into the distance. His right profile looked like the Nathan she remembered, but his hair was cut short and he seemed older.

Pearl bit her lip and tried to stay calm as she approached.

"Who's there?" Nathan asked, as he turned.

His right eye was opaque, a silvery film obscuring the pupil. The grafted skin in back of where his left eye should have been was still raw. The gauze dressing covering his left cheek was stained with dried blood and yellow serum.

Pearl leaned over him. "Nathan, it's me."

"Oh, Pearl," he gasped as he turned his face away. "Don't look, Pearl. Please." He brought his hands up to his face and began to sob.

"Nathan," Pearl said, her voice a whisper, "I'm so glad you're alive and back with me."

"My life is finished, Pearl."

She pulled up a chair and took Nathan's hand.

"For me nothing has changed. I'm here with you. I know your parents will be so relieved that you're safe."

"God, I don't know if I can bear for them to see me."

"You can't think this way. What's done is done. Now it's time to get healed. After that, think of the future, not the past."

"But you're the best part of my past. How can I not think of that, of what I once had?"

"I'm also part of your future."

Nathan again turned his face away.

"You'll see," she said, kissing his hand.

"Pearl?"

"I'm still here."

"Break it gently to my father."

Pearl called Mr. Rubin from the nurses' desk.

"My God, my God, how will I ever be able to tell his mother?" he said.

"Mr. Rubin, I love Nathan as much as you do and this isn't easy for me either. Nathan needs us to be strong. He's terribly depressed. He feels sorry for himself so we can't. You can understand that. You've got to explain all this to Mrs. Rubin."

Pearl heard him blowing his nose.

"I'm sorry, Pearl. It's just such a shock. But he's alive. At least he's alive."

"Visiting hours are at two. I'll see you then."

Lori came over just as Pearl hung up. "That's your fella?"

Pearl nodded.

"Is there anything I can do?"

"No, it's just going to take time. Especially for him."

Pearl stole glances at Nathan as she busied herself with patients. He sat there just the way she had left him. His lunch tray sat in front of him untouched. An aide tried unsuccessfully to get him to eat. Pearl heard her ask if he'd like a radio at the bedside. Nathan shook his head.

At two o'clock Pearl, who had just finished a dressing change on one of her amputees, met the Rubins at the door. Pearl looked from one to the other. "Are you ready?" she asked softly.

"I must look a sight," Mrs. Rubin said, brushing away a tear. "What am I saying? He won't be able to see me."

"Please, Roberta," her husband said, taking her hand.

Pearl quietly took them to their son and then left to attend to her other patients.

At three o'clock, Pearl joined them. "I'm going off duty after I give report. I'll be back in about a half hour, Nathan," she said, smiling at his parents.

Nathan made no response, but Mrs. Rubin stood up and motioned for Pearl to wait.

"I'll be back in a moment, too, dear," she said. "I just want to use the restroom."

She followed Pearl out of the ward.

"I feel so helpless. I don't know what to do for him," she said.

"We'll just have to be patient and do what we can to get him through these first weeks. Once the grafting is completed . . ."

"But how will he live? Who'll take care of him?"

"Do you remember the last time we were together with Nathan? Just before he left for the Navy?"

"Yes. At his apartment in Missoula."

"He told you then that we were planning to get married. Remember?"

"Yes, I remember."

"Those plans haven't changed. Not for me at least."

"Oh, Pearl."

"It's because I want to," Pearl said, as Mrs. Rubin took her hand. "I have to give report now. I'll see you inside before you leave."

After giving her report, Pearl waited until the other nurses had gone and she had the locker room to herself. She removed her uniform and dressed, then stood at the small window overlooking the parking lot. The events of the day were only now beginning to register. If she married Nathan, his burden would become hers. Was she up to it? she wondered. Nathan's appearance did not bother her. She had seen enough skin grafts to know she could live with that kind of scar. It was the blindness and its helplessness that concerned her, along with the deeper scars on his self-worth. What a wretched world this can be, she thought, as she headed back to the ward.

"I enjoyed being on the destroyer," Nathan was telling his parents as she came up. "There was a camaraderie among the officers and men, easygoing compared to what I'd seen on other ships. There was always some tension when we were accompanying convoys or the weather was bad. We knew the U-boats were out there. But most of the time it wasn't very stressful. In March we were escort for a big convoy and ran into a wolf pack off the Azores. Ships were blowing up all around us. We had just released our first depth charges when everything went black for me. When I came to I was in a lifeboat. I couldn't see anything and the pain was terrible. Then I must have passed out. When I woke up someone told me I was on another destroyer that had picked up survivors from my ship."

"Pearl is here," Mrs. Rubin said, but Nathan didn't reply.

"Visiting hours are over," said a nurse who had just appeared in the doorway.

"We'll be back tomorrow," said Nathan's father, patting him on the shoulder. "We're really glad to have you back, son."

Mrs. Rubin leaned across the bed and kissed Nathan's forehead. "We'll see you tomorrow," she said.

They said their goodbyes to Pearl, as she sat down by the bed.

"Are you still here?" he asked, turning in her direction.

"I'm here."

"I know you'll think it's my self-pity talking, but I wish they hadn't put me in that lifeboat. It would have been easier for everyone—you, my parents. You could have remembered me the way I was. I was unconscious anyway."

"The supervisor told me the plastic surgeon will see you tomorrow morning. He does good work."

"Can he make eyes see again?"

"I'll find out about Braille teachers. There must be one in Helena."

"Please don't sacrifice yourself for me, Pearl."

"Before you left for the Navy, we talked about how we'd wait to get married until you'd finished a few years of medical school. To me, that was a sacrifice. Now we don't have to wait."

"You haven't thought this through. Do you know what it means to live with a blind man? To have a man dependent on you? What about children?"

"I seem to recall you had no problems in bed. You weren't wounded there, were you?"

"You know what I mean."

"We'll manage."

"What if I tell you I don't want you? That I don't love you anymore?"

"I wouldn't believe you."

"Think about it at least. Don't just make rash decisions."

"There's nothing to think about. I love you."

29

During Nathan's first few months in the hospital, Pearl came to his bedside after her shift. While on duty, she intentionally kept her distance, however, letting Lori do all of his dressing changes.

"I don't want him thinking of me as his nurse," she told Lori.

Multiple skin grafts were performed during those early months, some of them partial-thickness grafts, others, for the more severely burned areas on the side of his face, full-thickness. The skin was always taken from Nathan's hips. The takes were better for some grafts than for others. Those that were less successful had to be repeated. But as week followed week, Nathan's face gradually healed. Pearl knew from experience with her other burn patients that scars became less noticeable, especially to the eyes of a person who looked at them regularly.

There were long periods of silence between them during their first weeks together. Pearl did not force him to speak to her, nor did she make smalltalk. She just sat at his bedside and waited for him to let her in on his thoughts.

When he did speak, he talked of his days on the destroyer. "The sea was so beautiful," he told her one evening. "All I knew about bodies of water while I was growing up was the Missouri River and some of the lakes around here. But to be out on the ocean, the blues and greens stretching as far as you can see, that was something. Did you know you could see the curve of the earth on the horizon? And the salt smell of the sea was always with you. God, it was beautiful." There was the faintest hint of a smile on his face. "Well, not always beautiful," he said. "Not when there was a storm. Remember how high Saint Joseph's was? Well, we had storms with waves higher than that. They'd come crashing over us and we were amazed the ship could stand up to their force."

"Did you ever get seasick?"

"Most of us did at first. But after a while we got our sea legs. That's what they call it when you don't get sick anymore."

Pearl welcomed these conversations, but the more intimate ones, the ones that would reveal his pain and fears, would come later, she thought.

"My left thigh is bothering me," he said one evening. "That's where they took the last graft. Would you take a look at it and make sure it's not getting infected?"

"I'll call the nurse," Pearl said.

"But you are a nurse."

"But I'm not your nurse. I'm the woman who loves you." She motioned to Arlene, one of the evening shift nurses, and stood aside as she inspected Nathan's thigh.

"It's still a little raw," Arlene said, "but there's no sign of infection. Would you like something for the pain?"

Nathan shook his head.

"You know," Pearl said, "they've taken so many patches your hips are beginning to look like a map of the United States."

"She's right," Arlene said. "Should we call him Mr. America?" she asked, winking at Pearl.

The first real smile Pearl had seen since his arrival crossed Nathan's face.

Pearl's next cause for optimism came many weeks later when Nathan ran his fingers across the left side of his face and into his empty left orbit. "It's all healed now, isn't it?" he asked.

"Yes, it is. The last grafts took very well."

"Do you think they'd give me an eye patch?"

It was the first indication that he cared about his appearance and Pearl took that as a good sign. "I'm sure they will if you want it. Just ask Doctor Wheeler when he visits you tomorrow."

The Rubins came every day. Mr. Rubin would close his store for an hour and a half each afternoon, pick up his wife and bring her to the hospital. Some visits went smoothly. Other times, Pearl noticed, Nathan seemed irritable after they'd left.

Passing near the bed one afternoon Pearl saw Nathan sliding his hand across his lunch tray, searching for his coffee cup. Mrs. Rubin picked up the cup to put it in his hand.

Pearl stepped to the bedside and placed her hand on top of Mrs. Rubin's arm, gently exerting downward pressure. Mrs. Rubin, surprised, looked up at her and Pearl shook her head. Nathan's mother placed the cup back on the tray, where his groping fingers found it.

The two women stared at one another for several seconds. Mr. Rubin gave Pearl an almost imperceptible nod of approval that was meant for her eyes alone.

"My mother's reverting to her old ways," Nathan said one evening.

"Oh?"

"Telling me what to do and not do."

■ ■ ■

"Your young man seems much improved," Mrs. Jennings, the supervisor, said to Pearl one day as they were about to begin their shift. "He seems more comfortable with himself since he got that eyepatch."

Pearl had noticed the same thing and was pleased that it wasn't just her perception. "I've been thinking of asking Doctor Wheeler what we can do to help Nathan confront his blindness. He refuses to talk about it."

"I've been meaning to speak to you about that. I have a friend, Jane Gardner. She teaches at the elementary school here in Helena. Jane knows Braille."

"I've been wondering where I could find someone."

"Jane's mother went blind when she was in her thirties. Retinitis pigmentosa. Jane was a child at the time and while her mother was learning Braille, Jane learned it with her. I know she's taught it to a few children in the area who were born blind."

Pearl reached Jane Gardner late that afternoon.

"Can you come by this evening?" she asked Pearl.

"I usually stay with Nathan until eight. But tomorrow is Saturday and I'm off duty. Could I come by in the morning?"

The Gardner home was a small bungalow on Floweree Street north of Mount Helena. Jane Gardner was outside waiting as Pearl's taxi pulled up. She was a tall woman in a flower-print dress, her grey hair pulled back into a bun. Pearl guessed she was in her mid-fifties.

"Hello, Pearl," she said warmly, as if they were old friends. "Come in." She held the door open for her, then introduced her husband, Ben, a heavy-set, balding man.

"I'm just leaving," he said. "Got to see that sick foal at the Carters."

"Ben's a veterinarian," Jane said, showing Pearl into the kitchen. "Do you mind talking in here? I think it's cozier. Would you like some coffee?"

She placed their cups and saucers on the embroidered tablecloth. "Here's cream and sugar," she said. "Well, Clara Jennings told you something about me. Now tell me about yourself."

Pearl felt very much at ease and in a matter of minutes she covered her childhood in Saint Joseph's and the nursing she had done in Missoula before returning to Helena to work at the veterans' hospital. Then she talked about Nathan.

"You're planning to marry this young man?"

"I'm trying to convince him. He thinks I want to because I feel sorry for him."

"Do you?"

Pearl hesitated. It was a question she had asked herself numerous times, but she wasn't used to hearing it from someone else. "I don't think so. I mean, I am sorry this happened to Nathan, but I don't think I want to marry him out of pity. We'd always talked about getting married. Nathan wanted to even before he left for the Navy."

"But Nathan wasn't blind then."

I don't understand, Pearl told herself. I thought this woman was going to help me.

Jane smiled. "I'm not telling you not to marry Nathan. I'm only trying to make sure you're going into this with your eyes wide open." She paused. "And that's a good way to put it since your eyes will be the only ones that can see. It won't be easy, I assure you. And I do speak from experience.

"Clara told you my mother went blind when I was a child. I was only nine at the time and my older brother was eleven. Retinitis pigmentosa was a disease none of us had heard of. It's hereditary, but no one in my mother's family or my father's family had ever had it. No one we knew of, anyway. Two years later my mother's younger brother also went blind from the same disease. My mother fortunately was a strong woman. She had been teaching school for almost ten years when it happened to her. She immediately learned Braille and insisted upon continuing as a teacher. The school was reluctant but because she was popular with the students, and probably because the principal felt sorry for her, he offered to give it a try. The students went out of their way to be helpful in the classroom and my brother and I helped her to grade papers and prepare assignments. In fact, we helped her with everything. We had to. My father had to work. He was devastated, of course, but he acted as if nothing had happened.

"He'd drop my mother at the school and go to his hardware store. Even though she couldn't see my mother insisted on doing the cooking and cleaning. She had us arrange everything in the kitchen so that she'd know what she was picking up without anyone telling her. Even though my mother was special, it still wasn't easy for any of us. Her brother's life was far different. He couldn't accept the fact that he was blind. When he was fired from his job it was the end of the world. His wife had to support them and she had never worked before. They had a child, my cousin Vicki. She was a few years younger than I. Her childhood was terrible. Every hour outside of school was spent with her father, trying to help him. When she was fourteen, my uncle killed himself by turning on the gas stove. It was Vicki who found him when she came home from school. She's been in and out of mental hospitals since."

Pearl sat with her head lowered as she listened. She did not want Jane to see the tears welling in her eyes. Until that moment she had tried not to think of Nathan's blindness as a burden. Now, for the first time, she felt it as an unbearable weight on her shoulders.

"Pearl, I'm telling you all this just so you'll know what you're getting into. That said, let's talk about Nathan. Has he mentioned wanting to learn Braille?"

Pearl shook her head. "It's only recently that the skin grafting on his face was completed. He still doesn't talk about his blindness."

"You have no idea how much longer he'll be in the hospital?"

"No, the doctor hasn't said anything."

"Where will Nathan live after he's discharged?"

"His mother wants him to move in with her, but he refuses. I think he should live with me."

"You haven't told him that yet?"

"No, I thought it was too soon to bring it up. I'm trying to take things a step at a time with Nathan."

"I'd be happy to visit Nathan at Fort Harrison one or two afternoons a week after school."

"Thank you," Pearl said. "How much do you charge?"

"Nathan gave his eyes for his country. There'll be no charge."

"That's so generous . . ."

Jane made a dismissive gesture. "I want you to understand that there are far fewer books in Braille than in regular print. I suggest you also begin reading to Nathan when you visit him. That will help him. And he should have a radio."

She scheduled Nathan's first lesson for the beginning of the following week. That afternoon, Pearl told Nathan about her visit with Mrs. Gardner. "I think you'll like her. There's nothing superficial about her."

"What if I do learn Braille?" Nathan said sourly. "How's that going to help me? I still can't work."

"Jane Gardner's mother was blind and she worked as a teacher."

"Yeah, but she was a teacher before she lost her sight. What was I? A stock clerk? A lab assistant? Even for lousy jobs like that you have to be able to see."

"I don't have all the answers yet. Why don't we start with something you can do? Like learning Braille."

■■■

"Did you tell your parents you'd be learning Braille?" Pearl asked that evening.

"No. I don't like telling my mother anything. I get the feeling she likes me helpless. She's making noises again about my moving in with them when I get out of here."

"Do you want to?"

"Of course not. But where the hell can I go on my own?"

He was agitated, clawing at the sheet with his fingers.

"I was going to talk to you about that. You'll move in with me."

"But we're not married. What about your neighbors?"

"There's no law that says we have to be married. If it bothers you that much we can get married the day you leave the hospital. And for your information, I don't even know my neighbors. Furthermore, it's none of their business."

"You haven't thought this out."

"Who would you rather live with, me or your mother?"

"Pearl, that's not fair."

"My offer stands even if you don't want to marry. You may feel comfortable enough after a while to live on your own, but living with me will at least give you the chance to adjust. I'm at work during the day so you don't have to worry about me pampering you. Your mother on the other hand . . ."

"Let's not talk about her."

"Think about what I've said. Just remember that you lost your sight, not your ability to think. Now, I stopped at the library and took out two books I've never read. We can read them together. Do you want me to start with *For Whom the Bell Tolls* by Ernest Hemingway or *Two Years Before the Mast?*"

"Can I say one thing?"

"Yes."

"You're really something."

"Are you just finding that out? I thought that's why you once proposed to me."

Nathan raised his arms in surrender.

30

In the middle of October Doctor Wheeler told Nathan that his discharge was coming up. "Do you want us to arrange a transfer to a facility that cares for blind people?" he asked.

That was an option Pearl hadn't thought of, but it was one Nathan had no intention of considering. "That won't be necessary. I already have an offer to stay with a friend."

"Pearl tells me you've been studying Braille. How are you doing?"

"Fine. I can read it."

"That's good. Have you thought about what you might like to do when you're out of here?"

Nathan shrugged. "Blind people don't have many options."

"You're not feeling sorry for yourself, are you?"

"No, I'm happy to be blind. It's a lot of fun. Why does everyone worry about my feeling sorry for myself?"

"You might be surprised at all the possibilities out there. Anyway, let your friend know that you'll be discharged soon."

The following morning, after making his rounds, Doctor Wheeler motioned to Pearl.

"Did Nathan tell you I'm planning to discharge him?"

"No, he hasn't said anything."

"He told me he'll be living with a friend. That's you, I assume?"

"I've asked him but he hasn't given me a definite answer."

"He's very angry about what happened to him. It'll take time for him to come to terms with it. I don't want to frighten you, but some people never get reconciled to something like this."

"I'd like to believe that Nathan will. I'll do my best to make it happen."

"He'll be in good hands then. I'll let you know a day or two in advance."

For the next few days Nathan kept his conversation with Doctor Wheeler to himself. He'll have to tell me at some point, Pearl thought.

The Rubins were not aware of the upcoming discharge for their son. Mrs. Rubin chatted with him at each visit as if it was the most normal thing in the world for Nathan to be in the hospital. I want to like her, Pearl told herself, but somehow everything she does makes it more difficult. Why, Pearl wondered, does she act as if he belongs here? Does she think they'll keep him here until one day he miraculously regains his sight?

When Nathan finally mentioned his discharge, Mrs. Rubin was monopolizing the conversation as she always did. Pearl, out of sight behind a curtain surrounding the bed of another patient, stole glances in their direction.

Her patient, a young Marine from Idaho, had suffered a penetrating wound to his bladder when a grenade exploded near him. "Can you believe it?" he had told her more than once. "Every piece of that damned grenade missed me except one. And look where the hell it ended up." The surgeons had repaired his bladder and it was just a matter of time until they would remove his urinary catheter. Pearl was now replacing the full bag of urine with an empty one. "A sweet young thing like you shouldn't have to do things like this," the Marine said. "I really appreciate it though. Can I buy you dinner when I get out of here?"

"Corporal," smiled Pearl, "you sound too healthy to be in the hospital. Now behave yourself or next time your mother comes to visit you I'll tell her you've been getting fresh with the nurses."

She then drew the curtain and carried the catheter bag to the lavatory.

Mr. Rubin motioned to her as she returned. "Pearl, Nathan wants to tell us all something."

"The doctor says I'll be going home before long," he said.

"Oh, that's wonderful," said Mrs. Rubin. "I'll have your bedroom all ready for you."

"I said I'll be going home."

"I don't understand," Mrs. Rubin said, looking from Nathan to her husband.

"I'll be staying with Pearl."

"But that's impossible."

"Why is it impossible?"

Mrs. Rubin sputtered. "You and Pearl aren't married. It wouldn't be right. Besides, she has to work. I'd be home all day. I can take care of you."

"I'm going to Pearl's."

"Did you put him up to this?" his mother snapped, glaring at Pearl.

"Roberta . . ." said Mr. Rubin, placing his hand on her arm.

She jerked away and stood up. "How can you do this to him? Who'll take care of him when you're not there?"

"Nathan is capable of taking care of himself when I'm not around. He does it here on the ward when I'm busy with patients." Pearl met the woman's stare head-on.

"But he's my son."

"He's also twenty-four years old and has a mind of his own."

Without saying another word, Nathan's mother stormed out of the ward.

"Don't mind her," said Mr. Rubin.

"Is she gone?" Nathan asked.

His father patted his leg. "She left, but she'll be back. You know how she likes to get her own way." He gave Pearl a sad smile. "I just want to say thank you."

"You'll have the address," Pearl said. "You know you're welcome any time you want to visit."

"Well," he said, standing up, "I'd better be going, too. I'll have to calm your mother down. Oh, Nathan, I did want to mention something else. I'm glad Pearl is here to hear this. I'm not getting any younger, you know, and I could use some help in the store. The way it is now I'm stuck there all day, every day. Any time I have to get out, even to come here, I have to close up. Until you decide what you'd like to do, I wish you'd consider working with me. It would make my life a lot easier."

"I'm blind, dad,"

'You don't need eyes to learn where all the cigars and stationary are. And you'll find my customers are honest. You don't have to tell me now. Just think about it." He hesitated, groping for the right words. "I sometimes think we haven't spent much time together. I'd sure like you there with me.

"Anyway, that said, you and Pearl can talk about it. You're a lucky guy to have found someone like this young lady here. I'll see you both tomorrow."

"Is he gone?" Nathan asked after a few moments.

"Yes."

"I don't know how he puts up with my mother."

"Some day our children may say that to you."

"What do you think about his offer?"

"I think it's up to you."

"I have to do something."

"If nothing else, it will give you the confidence you need. And I do believe your father was sincere when he said he could use the help."

"From potential doctor to clerk in a cigar store—quite a comedown."

"No self-pity allowed here."

"You'll have to keep reminding me."

31

Pearl felt a sense of triumph as she guided Nathan up the stairs to her apartment. She had been surprised that the day after her confrontation with Roberta Rubin, the woman had returned with her husband during regular visiting hours, acting as if nothing had happened.

"Your mother didn't try to persuade you to change your mind?" Pearl had asked when they left.

"She was on her best behavior today. I think she concedes defeat."

She's not that gracious a loser, thought Pearl.

"And I told my father I'd work in the store. At least for a while."

"He must have been pleased."

Three days later Doctor Wheeler had discharged Nathan, presenting him with a walking stick and dark glasses as parting gifts. "The stick will come in handy," he said, "and the glasses will make you look more dashing than that patch you're wearing."

That same walking stick now tapped on the stairs to Pearl's apartment.

"Are we there?" he asked when they reached the first landing.

"The apartment just down the hall to the left is ours. I'll have a key made for you in case you want to go out while I'm working."

"Where would I go?"

"After a while you'll learn your way around outside. There are benches so you can sit in the sun."

Pearl took his hand and led him into the apartment, closing the door quietly behind them. She cupped his face in her hands and brought his lips down to hers. "Welcome home."

Nathan took her in his arms, pressing against her. "Oh, Pearl, it's so good to hold you again."

"Plenty of time for that. Let me show you around." She put her arm around his waist. "There are four rooms. We came directly into the living room, which has a sofa, a chair, a radio, and a coffee table, all of which you'll recognize since they're yours from Missoula." Pearl guided him to the sofa. "Now, if you walk about eight or nine steps from the end of the sofa you'll find the door to the bedroom. There's our bed. A dresser is against this wall. And finally, the clothes closet.

"Now let me show you the kitchen and bathroom. Later I'll go over everything on the shelves with you."

"Not a day went by on the ship when I didn't dream of being with you like this," Nathan said after they completed their tour.

"And what else did you dream?" she asked, turning to kiss him and placing his hands on her breasts. "What are we waiting for?" she said, taking his hand and leading him back to the bedroom.

"Is it safe?"

"I bought something for you to use."

"Weren't you embarrassed to ask for them?"

"I'm a nurse. Nothing embarrasses me."

■■■

"I hope this is better than hospital food," Pearl said later as they sat having dinner.

"I'm sure glad I was able to talk you into letting me stay here," Nathan said, laughing.

"Your parents didn't stay long yesterday afternoon."

"My father had to get back to the store. He had a delivery coming in."

"Did you tell him when you'd start working?"

"He'll be picking me up eight-fifteen on Monday. I'm nervous about it."

"You'll learn very quickly where everything is."

"It's not just that. I don't know how people will feel about a blind man waiting on them."

"Just show them who's in charge. You must be used to that."

"Can I dry?" he asked when Pearl got up to wash the dishes.

"Sure." She handed him a dishtowel.

"Do you still want to marry me?"

"Are you proposing?"

"I suppose I am."

"Then rephrase the question."

"Will you marry me?"

"Yes. If you're sure that's what you want."

"I know it's what I want. Whether it's fair to you is another question."

"If you're going to think like that, I'll have to say no."

"You know what I mean."

Pearl handed him a plate to dry. "Here's what I propose," she said. "Ask me again in the spring. Maybe by then you won't be thinking about what's fair and what's not. Then we can get married in June. Isn't that what all brides want?"

"I'd like to marry you tomorrow."

"If you feel the same way in six months, I'll agree."

"Do you know what will really make me feel sorry for you when we're married?"

"What?"

"Your having my mother as an in-law."

Pearl smiled. "What did she say to you yesterday?"

"She said 'remember, if you change your mind we'll come get you and bring you home.'"

"What are you thinking?" Pearl asked later that evening as they sat on the sofa. A large book written in Braille rested on Nathan's lap.

"I was thinking about your work at the hospital. It takes courage to do what you do."

"What do you mean?"

"I used to talk to the men on the ward so I know about their wounds. I don't know if I'd have the stomach for it."

"You make it sound like nurses are a different breed. We're not. It's just that after a while we get used to what we have to do. I like my work. It makes me feel good to know that these men need me and that I can help them. I have you to thank for that."

"Me?"

"You're the one who gave me the idea, remember?"

Nathan sat quietly for a moment. "Am I included among those men who need you?"

Pearl thought for a moment. "I don't think you are. I've never thought about your needing me. I was always more concerned with your wanting me." She rested her head on his shoulder. "Besides, I'm not your nurse, I'm your lover."

32

There were times now when Pearl completely forgot about Nathan being blind. He moved easily around their apartment, his walking stick resting near the door. The only time he depended on the stick was when he went out for a walk alone. Nathan's father had commented to Pearl about his son's dexterity at the store.

"I forget he can't see. So do the customers. I've seen them look at him with surprise when he asks them what denomination the bill is before he makes change.

"There are times now when I feel like a man of leisure. To be able to leave the store whenever I want is wonderful. And it's nice for me when we're there together and can talk. I was always too busy when Nathan was growing up." He laughed. "Even when I wasn't, my wife did all the talking."

"How is Roberta?"

He hesitated. "She's fine. Well, you know . . . women her age go through changes. You know all that. Sometimes I think she needs more to do."

"We can always use volunteers at the hospital."

"I'll mention it to her, but I already know what she'll say. Roberta has never liked being around sick people."

"Who took care of Nathan when he was growing up and got sick?"

237

"She did, of course. But she was always such a nervous wreck. Ready to call a doctor whenever he had a sniffle. Well, who can blame her for worrying? Both of her parents died in the influenza epidemic in 1918."

That evening as Pearl was preparing dinner, still thinking about her mother-in-law, Nathan came in and gave her a hug. "How did your day go?" she asked.

"Pretty busy. How are things at the hospital?"

"We had to pull extra beds out of the basement and move them into the ward. Ten new admissions today. None of us got a minute to sit down."

"Some customers were talking today about our bombing raids in Europe and wondering when the Allies would invade France. When that happens I don't know what the hospitals here will do with all the wounded."

"It's frightening to think about. We're not getting the acute cases but the hospitals that are will have to transfer more and more patients out to make room. I don't mean to bring these things up at dinner time," Pearl said, as they sat down at the table.

"Mmm, the hamburgers and mashed potatoes are great. Where did you learn how to cook?"

"Whenever we get a break at the hospital, we all seem to talk about recipes."

"My father told me a nice little house on Eleventh Avenue just came on the market. He asked me to tell you about it."

"We can't afford a house."

"He seems to think it won't cost too much. We do have the money I was saving before I enlisted. The house is only a few blocks from the store."

"That means it's close to your parents, too. I wonder if your mother put him up to this."

He laughed. "I wouldn't put it past her, but if she had I think my father would have mentioned it. Besides, if we did anything like that you'd have a problem getting to the hospital."

"It would be a problem."

"Anyway, I'll tell him I told you."

On Sunday morning, Nathan's father surprised them with a visit. "I hope I'm not disturbing you," he said.

"Not at all," said Pearl, pleased to see him.

"I just wanted to chat for a few minutes." He rubbed his hands as he came into the apartment. "It's getting chilly out there. Before you know it we'll have snow."

"Come sit down. I was just about to start breakfast. Would you like toast and eggs?"

"I've already eaten but if it's not too much trouble, I can always eat a little more."

"Mother didn't want to come with you?" Nathan asked.

"She was tired. She's not sleeping well." He took a deep breath. "You two know that I try not to interfere and would never tell you what to do, but it would be nice if once in a while you'd drop by on a Sunday just to say hello. I know Roberta would appreciate it and I'd be happy to pick you up."

"We'd be glad to," said Pearl. "The only reason we haven't come by is that we hate to make you drive here on a Sunday. You do it six days a week."

"How would you like to learn to drive?" he asked.

Pearl laughed. "There's no reason. We don't have a car."

"A cousin of mine wants to sell his car. He had a stroke recently and can't drive now. It's a Chevy, six years old and in good condition."

"I'm not sure we can afford it," Pearl said. "Nathan was telling me about a house and now you bring up a car. Nathan and I just make enough for us to live on."

"I would like to buy the car for you."

"We couldn't let you do that. I know it's a chore for you to come out here twice a day but—"

"It's not that, Pearl. Look, I've always been honest with you and I'll tell you exactly what I'm thinking. That house Nathan told you about? I've been in this town for a long time and I know the value of property. It's a good buy and it won't stay on the market for long. Some day that house will be worth a lot more money. I came today because I wanted to take you out to see it. Wouldn't it be nicer for you to be in town rather than isolated out here? And I understand about the problem of your getting to work. That's why I wanted to give you your first driving lesson today. What do you say?"

"I don't know what to say. Nathan?"

"It's up to you, Pearl."

"All you have to do is look at the house," said Mr. Rubin. "And then we can head out onto Custer. There's very little traffic there. It's a good place to learn to drive."

"Well, let's finish breakfast and we'll go look."

■■■

"So, Pearl, what do you think?" Mr. Rubin asked after they finished their tour. Nathan was still running his hands along the walls to gauge the size of the rooms while the owner waited outside to give them privacy.

"It's a lovely house and the neighborhood is very nice. But we really can't afford it."

"Do you have any money saved?"

"Eleven hundred dollars," said Nathan.

"How does this sound—you put half of it toward the down payment, I'll put the rest, and I'll co-sign the loan for you at the bank? Ted Johnson, the bank president, is a friend of mine. There'll be no problem getting the loan. Instead of paying rent to a landlord, you'll be paying the bank."

"This is all going so fast," said Pearl.

"You like it, Pearl?" Nathan asked.

"I'd be lying if I said I didn't. There's even room for a little garden out back. But can we afford the payments?"

"I think we can work that out tomorrow at the bank," said Mr. Rubin. "But for now, I'd like to give the owner a deposit to hold it for us. It's only been on the market a few days and we're the fourth ones to look at it. I just think it's a wonderful opportunity for you."

"It can't hurt to give a deposit until we find out what the bank has to say, right, Pearl?"

"I'll agree on one condition," Pearl said, surprising them both. "The house will be in Nathan's name only."

"Why, Pearl?" Nathan asked. "I don't understand."

Pearl turned to Mr. Rubin. "We have an agreement that if he still wants me we'll be married in June. But until that time I'd feel better about it if—"

Mr. Rubin placed his hand on Pearl's arm. "I can only say this, Pearl. If Nathan says he doesn't want you, I would have to question his sanity."

"Do you think we should talk this over with Roberta?" Pearl asked.

"I know she can be a little headstrong, but I assure you she would want this for you both. So let's take care of business and then we can put you behind the wheel."

Two hours later Pearl was driving Mr. Rubin's Ford along the unpaved roads surrounding the western end of Custer Avenue.

"I don't know which scares me more," Pearl said, "getting that house or driving this car."

"Just be patient, you're doing fine," said Mr. Rubin. "It takes time to learn the shifting. Just let your clutch pedal up slowly."

After another hour of practice, Pearl's shifting was smoother, the car stalling only once.

"I think you're getting it," said Nathan from the back seat.

"I think she is, too. A few more lessons and you'll have it. Do you want to drive us into town, Pearl?"

"I'm not ready for that."

"Can I ask one favor? Why don't you and Nathan come home with me to say hello to Roberta? It would make her happy and we can tell her what we did today."

"Won't she mind if we just barge in on her?" Nathan asked.

"No, Nathan, she won't mind," he said, smiling.

■■■

"Are you losing weight?" Roberta Rubin said, embracing her son.

"No, Pearl takes good care of me." He put his arm around Pearl.

Mr. Rubin, standing behind his wife, winked at Pearl. "Well, we had a busy day today."

"Come sit down and be comfortable," said Mrs. Rubin. "I'll make some coffee. I baked a cake this morning, too. Would you like to stay for supper?"

"Let's do that another day, mother," said Nathan. "It's already been a long day for us."

"Nathan and Pearl are going to be homeowners," said Mr. Rubin as they sat drinking their coffee. "They're buying that house on Eleventh I was telling you about."

"Did you like it, Pearl?"

"Nathan and I liked it very much. We have to see though if we can afford it."

"Nathan and I will stop at the bank tomorrow to see Ted," Mr. Rubin said. "He'll let us know how much it will cost. And Pearl had her first driving lesson today. She did very well."

Mrs. Rubin gave her husband a frown. Pearl wasn't sure if she was joking when she said, "he never taught me to drive."

Mrs. Rubin sipped her coffee, staring over the cup's rim at Pearl.

"Is everything all right at home, Pearl?"

"Yes, everything is fine."

"And at work?"

"Busy. I hope this war ends soon."

"We all wish that."

"Excuse me for a minute," said Nathan, standing up. Headed for the bathroom, he collided with a chair near the living room archway. "Ouch!"

Mrs. Rubin sprang to her feet and rushed to him. "Are you all right? Let me help."

Nathan pushed her hand away. "I know my way."

Pearl and Mr. Rubin exchanged glances and he sighed.

Mrs. Rubin sat down on the edge of her chair, picking nervously at her finger nails. "He's all right, isn't he, Pearl?"

"Yes, he's fine. He gets around very well. He even goes out for walks by himself."

"Isn't that dangerous?"

"Not when he knows the route. Nathan likes to be as independent as he can."

"I told you," said Mr. Rubin, "a lot of my customers don't know he can't see. That's how good he gets around."

"But that's in the store. And you're there with him in case anything happens."

"You don't have to worry," Pearl said.

"Let's see if you say that when you're a mother," Mrs. Rubin said, her lips trembling.

Nathan's mother had aged since Pearl had first seen her. Although she was not yet fifty, her hair was grayer, her face more lined, and she had dark shadows beneath her eyes. The prominent wrinkling around her lips and at the corners of her eyes made her look angry more often than not.

In a short while Nathan's father drove them home. "Another lesson next Sunday, Pearl? I won't come quite so early."

"Thank you for everything," Pearl said.

"Thank you for visiting today. Tomorrow, Nathan, we'll stop at the bank before going to the store."

"What a day," said Nathan when they got back to their apartment.

"I hope we're not getting in over our heads," Pearl said.

"It's a nice house. And it'll be a nice place to raise kids."

"Oh? Is that what you're thinking?"

"Well . . ."

"Do you want me to be a worrier like your mother?"

"I think you'll be different. And do we really have to wait until June?"

"I may not know what I'm getting into with a house and a car, but I want you to know what you're getting into with me. The years can be very long if you're with the wrong person. And it might bother you more and more that your mother and I don't seem to get along."

"My mother wouldn't get along with anyone. And I'm marrying you, not my mother. Are you worried that you might be with the wrong person?"

"I've never thought that."

Pearl threw her arms around him, covering his face with kisses. "I love you," she said loudly, but not loud enough to drown out the doubts that nagged at her.

33

All in all, we made the right decision, Pearl thought. She was lying in bed on a Sunday morning in April, Nathan asleep beside her. She thought back on the many changes in their life during the past six months. She had come to love their new home and would always be grateful to Nathan's father for making it possible for them. Living in the downtown area made it possible for them to take walks after dinner, even stop at the Parrot for an ice cream soda. For the first time in twenty-four years, Pearl felt a part of the town she had lived in for most of her life.

Mr. Rubin had also been right about the car. Driving between their home and Fort Harrison was sometimes tricky in the winter, especially when packed snow and ice made the streets slippery, but Pearl had become a good driver. The vehicle had made it possible for them to live in town, and living in town gave Nathan more independence. No matter how bad the weather, he walked unguided to and from the store each day.

At first, Pearl worried, especially after a few falls when he had skinned his hands and bruised his knees. There was also the concern about cars, but the drivers in their neighborhood were aware of Nathan's blindness.

One Saturday morning a week after they had moved into the house, Pearl had followed Nathan as he walked to work. She felt a mixture of amazement and pride as she watched how confidently he walked, the striped stick in his hand swinging from side to side in front of him. It was hard to believe that this was the same man who less than a year before had lain in a hospital bed believing his life was over.

Nathan rolled over and put his arm around her. She snuggled against him, kissing his face, feeling the differences in the texture of his skin with her lips. The left side, which had skin grafts, was taut like coarse, stretched fabric, while the right was soft and yielded to her kisses. It had taken a while for her to become accustomed to the loss of his eye. Except when he was in bed, Nathan always wore his dark glasses. As time went by Pearl didn't even give it a second thought.

"I'll make us some breakfast," she said, sliding out from under the covers.

"It's April," Nathan said, as they ate.

"What's special about April?"

"You don't remember?"

"No."

He surprised her by standing up and coming around the table. Kneeling in front of her he placed one hand on her thigh and the other over his heart. "Pearl Schneider, would you do me the honor of becoming my wife?"

Pearl laughed. "Yes, gallant sir. Now stand up and stop being so silly."

"When?" he asked, sitting back down.

"You're sure?"

"Never been more sure of anything.

Pearl got up and walked over to the wall calendar. "How about June sixth?"

"June sixth it is."

"That was easy. Where?"

"No religious ceremony of any kind, right?"

"Right."

"We can have a justice of the peace perform it."

"Sounds perfect. I'll arrange it."

"Now for the hard part. Who should we invite?"

Pearl sat down and placed her chin in her hand. "That is the hard part. Your parents, of course."

"I'd just as soon leave it at that, unless there's someone from work you'd like to ask."

"You mean no one else in your family? No uncles, aunts, cousins, friends . . . ?"

"Do you want a repeat of what happened at that terrible birthday party? The thought of it makes me shudder. I wouldn't mind having some friends, but if we ask them, we'd have to have relatives."

"Your parents won't like it."

"You mean my mother won't."

"You'll have a battle on your hands."

"It's our wedding, not hers."

"Well, just so you don't have to listen to it for the next two months, don't mention anything until a week or two before."

"Good idea. Do you have any plans for today?"

"No. It's nice and sunny." She walked to the window. "A lot of snow has melted. We can walk to the park."

"Sounds good. But first there's something else we should do."

"What's that?"

Nathan pushed his chair back and patted his lap. "Come sit here."

"You have a one-track mind," she said, easing herself into his lap and kissing him.

■■■

"No surprises when it comes to Roberta," Nathan said six weeks later as he came through the door.

"Since when do you call your mother by her first name?" Pearl asked, noticing that he was upset.

"She's lucky that's all I call her."

"Nathan!"

"I told my father today we'd be getting married in two weeks and that he and my mother would be the only people we wanted to be present."

"What did he say?"

"He was pleased, of course. He said we might miss out on some presents but he seemed to understand. He even offered to go with me to the jeweler's to buy your ring. I told him we were going to do that."

"He's the most generous person I've ever known. If I wasn't marrying you, I'd want to marry your father."

"He's spoken for, poor fellow."

"Nathan, be nice."

"Anyway, I girded my loins as they say and telephoned my mother. Her response was predictable."

"She wasn't happy, I take it."

"To put it mildly. I hung up on her."

"Nathan, you didn't!"

"It didn't do much good. She walked down to the store. My father and I kept hoping a customer wouldn't come in while she was ranting and raving."

"How did you resolve it?"

"We didn't. She said if her brothers and sisters and their children couldn't come, she wouldn't come."

"That's terrible."

"I won't back down."

"Maybe we should . . ."

"No."

"Nathan, this is supposed to be a happy occasion. Wouldn't it be better . . ."

"No. You know better than anyone how she is."

"Why don't we compromise?"

"How?"

"Have your parents as the only ones at the wedding and let your mother give a reception for her immediate family afterwards."

"You should have been a diplomat."

"Don't forget, they've seen me before so it won't come as a surprise. My face won't shock them."

"Mine might."

Pearl laughed in spite of herself. "You are something. Let it be a happy time. Call her tomorrow."

■■■

"Shall I carry you across the threshhold?" Nathan asked as they stood outside their door.

"Don't you dare. Let's go in."

"So how does it feel to be married?"

"No different than it felt this morning. But I like it."

They embraced and kissed before taking off their coats.

"I thought things went very well today."

"You mean my mother didn't make a scene? Whenever I heard her say anything she sounded like she was at a funeral instead of a wedding."

"Your mother is an unhappy woman. I think she's still mad at your Uncle Harvey, too. Every time he tried to talk to her, she walked away."

"She's not the forgiving type."

"He told me any time I get tired of nursing I can have my job back at Gans.'" She laughed at the thought.

"Funny, isn't it, that the invasion occurs on the day we get married?"

"Now you'll never have an excuse to forget our anniversary."

"Did you hear my uncles? Asking me all those questions about the war, like I'm an expert or something? Just because I was on a destroyer and was wounded they think I've got a direct line to Roosevelt and Churchill."

"To them—and to me—you're heroic."

"I'm not heroic. I wish I could have exchanged my medals for eyes so I could have seen how you looked when I slipped the ring on your finger."

"Nathan, don't . . ."

"I'm sorry. My family upsets me."

"At least you have a family."

"Okay, okay. I said I was sorry." He laughed. "Did you hear what I told Aunt Ethel? She asked where we'll be going for our honeymoon. I told her we'd already had it."

"You didn't say that, did you?"

"No. I actually told her Eleventh Avenue."

"That's better. Your father made a nice toast. Welcoming me as his daughter."

"He's crazy about you."

"I think the first thing we should do with the gift money is pay your father back for his part of the down payment on the house."

"He'll be insulted."

"It's the right thing to do."

...

"Are you asleep?" Nathan asked, as they lay in the darkness holding hands.

"No."

"I've been thinking."

"About what?"

"Having children."

Pearl tensed.

"What's the matter?"

"I have to work. I know you're working, too, Nathan. I didn't mean for it to sound like that. It's just that with the war still on, it's not the right time. They need me at the hospital."

"And when the war is over?"

"Then we can talk about it."

34

We shouldn't have done it without a condom, Pearl thought to herself during the early morning hours. Maybe this one time we'll be lucky and nothing will happen.

But by the Fourth of July Pearl knew she was pregnant. Her period was two weeks late and her breasts were swollen. She'd been late before, but only by a few days. Without telling Nathan, she took a urine sample to a gynecologist's office in town later that week for a pregnancy test.

On Monday of the following week Pearl received a call at the hospital.

"Congratulations. You're test is positive," the doctor said. "You can make your appointment for prenatal care with the secretary."

"I can make that appointment for you now, Mrs. Rubin," said the secretary, coming on the line.

Pearl quickly hung up. Her stomach was twisted in a knot. She told the clerk she'd be in the bathroom and locked the door behind her. Pearl sat on the toilet seat, her fists pressed into her eyes. She was furious with Nathan. Why hadn't he listened? she said to herself. And you, you fool, why did you let him? She calculated how far along she was and came up with March second as a due date. What are we going to do? she thought, tears streaming down her face. Knowing Nathan would be ecstatic only made her angrier.

■■■

Nathan was greeted by silence when he came home. There was nothing cooking in the kitchen. She must have been detained at the hospital, he thought. Or maybe she stopped on the way home to do some shopping. He sat down on the sofa, a nagging disquiet gnawing at him. He stood up and made his way to their bedroom. Standing in the doorway, he heard the sound of breathing. Groping along the bed, his hands touched Pearl.

"What's wrong? Are you sick?"

She pulled away and sat up abruptly.

"Pearl, what's the matter?"

"I'm pregnant," she said, squeezing the words out.

"Oh, God, that's wonderful."

"Wonderful," she repeated sarcastically. "And how are we going to live after the baby comes? How will we be able to make our home payments? We'll never manage on your salary," she snapped out at him, surprising herself at how hostile her voice sounded.

"Pearl, honey, it's wonderful news. We'll manage."

"How, Nathan, how? We'll never be able to afford it. And if I go back to work who'll take care of the baby? And how much will that cost us?" She covered her eyes and burst into tears.

Nathan sat down beside her. "I'm sorry, Pearl. I didn't realize how—"

"I said we'd think about it when the war is over. Well, the war isn't over and I'm pregnant."

"Even if we'd waited another year or two, would it really have made a difference?"

Pearl knew he was right but she would not admit it. She also knew that if it was up to her, she would have delayed indefinitely. That realization made her question her own character. Why was she so opposed to becoming a mother?"

"I'm sure my mother would be glad to help us with the baby," he said softly. "I think that would give meaning to her life."

251

"I'm not worried about giving meaning to your mother's life. I'm concerned about us."

"I've always thought children bring people closer."

"Having a child didn't do anything for my parents, did it?"

Pearl was surprised at her words. Was that what all this was about? she wondered. Was this the real reason for her anger?

A silence hung there between them.

"I'm sorry, Nathan," she said finally, placing her hands on his. "I don't know what got into me. Do you forgive me?"

"There's nothing to forgive. Besides, I'm the one who's responsible."

The very air in the room now seemed oppressive. Pearl knew by the cold limpness of Nathan's hand that he, too, was now afraid of what the future held for them.

35

Nathan's father had noticed a change in his son.

"Pearl, is Nathan having some kind of problem?" he asked, calling her one morning at the hospital.

"What do you mean?"

"He's just not himself. It's hard to explain. He seems preoccupied, as if he's worried about something."

It's all my fault, Pearl thought.

"Pearl, are you there?"

"Yes. I was just thinking about what you said."

"Am I imagining it?"

"Could Nathan and I drop by your house this evening after dinner?"

"Of course. Is anything wrong?"

"Would seven-thirty be all right?"

"Yes. Nathan's just coming through the door. Shall I tell him?"

"You can put him on. I'll tell him I called you and suggested we visit."

"Pearl, is anything the matter?" Nathan asked with worry in his voice.

"I was thinking it's time we told your parents about the baby. I asked your father if we could drop by this evening. Don't spoil the surprise."

"I won't," he said.

"And Nathan?"

"Yes?"

"Please stop worrying. Everything will be fine after the baby is born. We'll manage."

"I know," he said half-heartedly.

At dinner that evening Pearl decided to clear the air. "Nathan, please forget all those things I said when I found out I was pregnant. We will manage just fine. I'm really glad we're going to have a child."

Nathan nodded. He wants to believe it, Pearl thought, but he can't.

"Do you remember how happy you were when I told you? That's how I feel now. I feel so guilty about the mean things I—"

"There's nothing to feel guilty about. I'm the one who wasn't fair."

"But you were right. If you had left the decision up to me, God knows when I would have felt ready. It's better this way, Nathan. I mean it."

"You really aren't angry at me any more?"

"Not at all."

He reached across the table and Pearl took his hand, kissing it. "Well," she said, "let's go drop our little surprise on your parents."

"Nathan and I have a surprise for you," Pearl said when they were all seated in the Rubins' living room.

Nathan cleared his throat. "Well," he said slowly, "you're going to be grand-parents."

Nathan's father leaped to his feet and pumped his son's hand, then planted a kiss on Pearl's cheek.

"That is wonderful news," Roberta Rubin said, laughing. "We thought there was some crisis."

Pearl was surprised at how pleased she seemed.

"Jerry said you were so serious on the phone, Pearl, he couldn't imagine what you were going to tell us. I'm so happy. When is the baby due?"

"Early March, some time around the second."

"Isn't that something?" said Mr. Rubin, sitting down again and putting his arm around his wife. "How does that make you feel, grandma?"

It's like watching a movie, Pearl thought. Whenever someone says she's expecting a baby, everybody gets excited.

"Are you planning to keep working?" Mrs. Rubin asked.

"That's something we'll have to figure out."

"I'd be happy to take care of the baby when you're at work."

Nathan turned in Pearl's direction. A smile played on his lips.

"That's very kind, but I don't want to impose."

"Impose? You don't know how happy it will make me."

"Better take her up on the offer, Pearl," said Mr. Rubin, "before she changes her mind. I'd like to spend time with my grandchild, too." He scratched his head. "Nathan, how would you like to switch roles with me? I'll put the business in your name and I'll work for you."

"Whoa," said Nathan. "It's fine the way it is."

"But I really would like more time off. You're a young fella and you can run that store as well as I can. Why not a partnership?"

"It's too generous. You've spent years building up the business."

"And now it's time for me to rest on my laurels. Fifty-fifty then."

"Quite an evening," Pearl said, as she and Nathan walked home from the Rubins. "I told you everything would be fine."

"I thought that was my line." Nathan swung his stick jauntily in front of him as Pearl held his arm.

Pearl looked up at the waning moon and the stars of Orion's belt. She was about to call Nathan's attention to the night sky when she caught herself. For a moment she had forgotten he was blind.

36

"It's good to be home," said Pearl, standing in the living room with their baby still bundled in blankets in her arms.

"Here, let me hold her so you can take your coat off," said Roberta. "Jerry, stop gawking at your granddaughter and help Pearl with her coat."

"You're so beautiful, little Sarah," Roberta said.

Nathan stood next to his mother, moving his hand gingerly along the blanket to the baby's face. He touched her lightly with his fingertips, then placed his face next to hers. "She smells so good."

"That won't last long," said Pearl. "I hope you remembered to arrange the diaper service, Roberta."

"It's all taken care of," she said, rocking the baby in her arms.

"Better take those blankets off," said Pearl. "It's warm in here."

Nathan slipped out of the room and returned moments later with a bottle in his hands. "Look what I have for the occasion," he said.

"Wonderful," said his father. "I'll get the glasses."

"Champagne at ten in the morning?" said Pearl.

"Champagne any time, right, Sarah?" said Roberta, nuzzling the baby's cheek.

"I don't think my mother is going to let anyone else hold her," said Nathan.

"Thank you again, Pearl, for naming her after my mother," said Roberta.

"Sarah is a beautiful name. Nathan and I both agreed on it."

Jerry Rubin poured champagne for everyone. "We'll toast to the beautiful baby Pearl brought us. Sarah looks just like you, Pearl."

"I still can't understand why they keep you in the hospital for a week," said Pearl. "It was an easy delivery. Two days after she was born I asked the doctor to discharge me and he wouldn't hear of it."

"They want you to get your rest," said Roberta. "They know you won't get any when you're home."

"I'd better prepare some formula. She'll be getting hungry soon."

"She's wet, too. I'll change her, Pearl."

"You'll spoil me, Roberta."

"She doesn't know what a pleasure it is, does she, Sarah?" said Roberta, heading for the bedroom.

'I haven't seen your mother this happy in a long time," Jerry Rubin whispered to Nathan.

"Maybe you should have had more children."

"Well, I guess that's my fault. I thought we couldn't afford more and then when we could, well . . ."

"You did very well with the one you got," said Pearl, coming into the room with the bottle. She kissed Nathan on the cheek and headed for the bedroom. Moments later she returned. "Roberta wants to give her her bottle. Since there's nothing for me to do, I might as well go back to work tomorrow," she said, laughing.

"I guess we'll know Sarah is in good hands when you do go back to work," said Nathan.

"She's fast asleep in her crib," said Roberta, joining them. "I knew I was saving your crib for a reason, Nathan."

"Your mother saves everything," said Jerry. "Well, Roberta, we'd better let these folks get some rest."

"Thanks for picking Pearl up at the hospital," said Nathan. "I'll see you bright and early tomorrow."

"Don't rush to get in if Pearl needs help with the baby."

"I'll be fine. Thanks for everything."

"Give Sarah lots of kisses for me," said Roberta as they left.

Nathan laughed when they had gone. "Can you believe my mother? She's a changed woman thanks to you."

"I guess babies have that effect on some people. Come hold me. I've missed you."

Nathan held her in his arms, gave her a kiss, and pressed his body against her.

"Uh uh. Doctor said no hanky-panky for six weeks."

"Six weeks! How will I survive?"

"Can you believe Sarah was born only one day after her due date? We calculated very well."

"March third, 1945, the third happiest day of my life," said Nathan.

"What were the first two?"

"The first was the day I met you. The second was the day we got married."

■■■

Three weeks later, on the day Pearl was to return to work, Roberta arrived promptly at six-twenty in the morning.

"I'm sorry to make you come so early," said Pearl.

"I'm up anyway and it's never too early to see my precious Sarah. Is she still asleep?"

"Yes. I gave her a bottle at four so that should hold her until seven or eight. I've made up enough formula to get you through the day. You know where the diapers are. If there's anything you need just call me at work."

"Everything will be fine. I've done this before."

Pearl dashed into the bedroom for a final look at the baby, then gave Nathan and Roberta a kiss. "See you by four," she called to Roberta as she left.

Driving to the hospital in the pre-dawn darkness, Pearl felt a sense of exhiliration about returning to work. She had never expected so much help from her mother-in-law. For some people, caring for babies is enough, she told herself, trying to dispel the nagging guilt she felt about leaving her infant with someone else. Pearl had been home with Sarah for three weeks and much as she loved her daughter, she found her maternal duties unfulfilling. Each day as she fed and diapered the baby, her thoughts turned to the ward at Fort Harrison. How many new admissions had they had in the past month? What types of cases? Had she been missed?

Her ego received a boost when she was welcomed back with open arms. The ward now held twice the number of patients it should have.

"We're having to turn away new transfers," Mrs. Jennings said.

Pearl and the other nurses were deluged with work. "We just have to do the best we can," said Mrs. Jennings. "As the fighting gets heavier in the Pacific, things will only get worse. Our operating room is busy most of the time now. We've been told that all our chronic care patients are going to be sent out to make room for more acute cases."

The war can't go on much longer, Pearl thought hopefully. The Allies were making headway in Germany and there was talk of the Russians making the final push against Berlin. But even if Germany surrenders, she thought, what about Japan? How many Americans would die or be wounded in trying to take those islands?

Pearl came home from work each day exhausted but with a feeling of accomplishment. Her skills were so desperately needed. And Sarah seemed content in Roberta's care. Pearl invariably found Nathan's mother walking around with the baby in her arms or sitting on the sofa with a magazine, the baby nestled in the crook of her arm.

"She's an angel," said Roberta.

"Is grandma spoiling you?" Pearl asked, nuzzling the baby.

"Of couse I am. Isn't that what grandmas are for?"

37

In early August, the war in the Pacific ended abruptly. The Americans had unleashed a terrible new weapon, the atomic bomb, and two Japanese cities had been obliterated.

As the excitement over the news swirled about her, Pearl looked around the ward. It was wonderful that the war was finally over, but for these men the ending had come too late. Their bodies would never be whole again, she thought. Her eyes fell on a young man who had just been admitted. A grenade blast had blinded him and destroyed his mandible. "I just want to die," he repeated over and over again, his speech barely intelligible without his lower jaw.

The war might be over but for the nursing staff there was no respite. Transfer patients, the overflow from military hospitals, continued to arrive. Wards that had held chronically ill patients were filled to double their capacity with more acute cases.

Pearl found she had inexhaustible energy while at work and it was only at the end of her shift that she became aware of how tired she was. Slumped in a chair in the nurses' lounge, she tried to gather the energy to take off her uniform and change into street clothes. "You look like I feel," said Lori. "If I got into bed now I'd sleep for a week." She slowly unbuttoned her uniform and smiled at Pearl. "Too bad we didn't marry millionaires, huh?"

"We'd probably be doing just what we're doing now, even if we had," said Pearl.

"You're probably right. Well, now comes the hardest job of all. Bringing my son home from the neighbor's. Wait until you have to cope with a four-year-old."

"Let's not rush things," said Pearl.

As the months passed, Pearl had to agree with her mother-in-law. Sarah was an easy baby. She seldom cried and almost always slept through the night. Nathan doted on her and Pearl watched admiringly as Nathan changed her diapers as if he had eyes to see what he was doing. He had also taken over her morning and evening feedings, holding the baby in his arms while she had her bottle or sitting in front of her high chair to feed her pureed vegetables and pablum. it was amazing, Pearl thought, how his hand knew how to carry the spoon directly to Sarah's mouth. Just as Nathan's hearing and sense of smell surpassed Pearl's, his blindness had led to a more acute spatial awareness.

But the baby was most excited when her grandmother arrived. Sarah kicked her legs and babbled excitedly. Pearl began to realize that her daughter showed little or no reaction when she got home from work. Even Nathan's arrival in the evening elicited a smile and a waving of Sarah's arms. Don't be foolish, Pearl told herself, but it rankled just the same.

The baby's first words were "da da." "Did you hear her? Did you hear that?" Nathan said, laughing loudly.

"She's daddy's girl all right," said Pearl, unfazed. But one thing bothered her a lot. "Ma ma," Sarah called when Roberta arrived. "That's na na," said Pearl. The baby, sitting in her high chair, looked at her and repeated "na na," then held out her arms to her grandmother. "Ma ma," she said.

Roberta, seeing Pearl's frown, laughed. "She'll get it straightened out."

"I've got to go," Pearl said as pleasantly as she could, trying to mask her irritation. "Be good with grandma."

A Chinook had blown through the previous day raising the temperature more than thirty degrees in a matter of hours. Now, the below freezing temperatures of early morning had turned the runoff from melting snowbanks into ice slicks on the roads. Pearl drove slowly, hunched forward on her seat, gripping the wheel tightly. You're an idiot, she told herself. How can you get upset because a baby not yet a year old doesn't know the difference between ma ma and na na? Isn't it natural for Sarah to respond more to her grandmother? She spends the entire day with her. Roberta was right. The baby would get it straightened out. Still, it upset her. It was as if her daughter were being lured away from her. Pearl's old feelings about her mother-in-law threatened to surface even though she knew she was being unfair. What would she have done without Roberta's help? She vowed to spend every moment of every evening with Sarah. And on weekends, she thought, Sarah is going to be my first priority.

Pearl's determination only succeeded in making her more frustrated. By the time she did the shopping on the way home from work, then prepared dinner and cleaned up, it was Sarah's bedtime. Nathan was the one who always seemed to find time to play with their daughter.

Weekends were only a little better. It was impossible for Pearl to ignore the cleaning, laundry, ironing and cooking. Except for amusing Sarah, any help Nathan gave her was limited by his blindness. Standing at the sink and watching him bounce Sarah on his knee, the baby gleefully squealing, Pearl felt an overwhelming sadness. I'm losing her, she thought. She tossed the dishtowel onto the counter and picked up a book.

"She may be too young for this" said Pearl, sitting down next to her husband, "but I'll read her some nursery rhymes. Lori gave me this book as a gift."

"You hear that, Sarah. Ma ma will read to you. Here, you sit on ma ma's lap."

Sarah craned her head back to look at Pearl. For a moment Pearl thought she was going to cry, but a picture Pearl pointed to caught her attention.

"Little Miss Muffet sat on a . . ." Sarah's eyes were glued to the pages as Pearl read. Poem followed poem and Sarah was fascinated. After more than a dozen rhymes, Sarah twisted in Pearl's lap and looked into her face. "Book," she said.

"Yes, it's a book," said Pearl excitedly, kissing the top of Sarah's head. "Did you hear, Nathan?"

Pearl had found a way to communicate with her daughter. Not a day went by without the cry of "book" ringing through the house. But Sarah still called

Pearl "na na" except when Pearl read to her. "Ma ma," she said then, leading Pearl to wonder what kind of strange being she had brought into the world. And she never asked her grandmother to read to her. "Even when I offer," Roberta told Pearl, "she says no."

"It looks like I'm the designated bookreader," said Pearl, wondering why.

By the time Sarah was a year and a half she was tiring of the same rhymes every evening. Pearl then brought home simple children's stories from the library and Sarah was again mesmerized by her reading. By the time her daughter was two, Pearl had introduced her to *Aesop's Fables*. "At this rate," she told Nathan, "I'll be reading Charles Dickens to her in another year."

"Maybe you should teach her to read."

"I think she's too young," Pearl said, wondering if she was right.

Pearl enjoyed reaching out to Sarah through books, but she was still troubled by her daughter's lack of emotional connection. Sarah dutifully kissed her goodnight when she and Nathan tucked her in, but displays of joy were reserved for Roberta.

At three, Sarah knew the alphabet and could count to a hundred. "I think we've got a little genius on our hands," Nathan said.

One evening Pearl asked Sarah to bring her crayons into the kitchen. They both sat down at the table and Pearl spread out some sheets of paper. "Do you want to learn how to read?" she asked. Sarah nodded. "First you have to learn to print the alphabet. I'll write each letter and then you do it."

Sarah gripped her crayon the way Pearl showed her and set herself to copying Pearl's letters. Each time they completed five letters, Pearl pointed to one to see if Sarah remembered what it was. To Pearl's astonishment, Sarah never made a mistake.

When Sarah had mastered recognition of the letters, Pearl then introduced her to easy words so she could learn the sounds. Again, her daughter amazed her.

Only two weeks after having learned the sounds of letters, Sarah surprised her mother. One evening while Pearl held Sarah on her lap she opened *Aesop's Fables* to *Androcles and the Lion,* one of Sarah's favorites. She had just begun reading when Sarah suddenly turned and put her hand over Pearl's mouth. She then turned back to the book, placed her index finger on the first word in the story, and began to read. Pearl looked over at Nathan to see if he realized what was happening. He placed his hand on Pearl's shoulder and gave it a slight squeeze. Sarah insisted on reading the entire tale, stumbling over very few words.

"That was very well done," said Pearl. "Now you can read stories to daddy."

Sarah shook her head.

"Why not?"

"If there are words I don't know, daddy won't be able to help me with them. Daddy only reads with his fingers."

"Sure I will," said Nathan, "if you'll spell them for me."

"Okay," she said, "then I'll read to you."

"It's scary," Pearl whispered to Nathan when they were in bed that night. "I can't believe how precocious she is."

"I told you she's a genius."

It's not funny, Pearl thought. If Sarah was able to read by herself, she would no longer need her mother to do it for her. The one activity she seemed willing to share with Pearl would come to an end.

If only Sarah could tell me what she's thinking, thought Pearl, not able to sleep. But then again, maybe she herself doesn't know. Perhaps it's just something she feels between us, but why? Pearl tossed and turned for what seemed like hours before she fell into a troubled sleep.

As time passed, Pearl's discontent increased. She wasn't able to have the relationship she had hoped for with Sarah, and her work at the hospital no longer provided the stimulation it had in the past. In the years since the war's end, there had been a gradual change in the kinds of patients on the ward, the more acute cases now having been discharged or transferred to specialized hospitals. Pearl was again taking care of chronically ill patients, those with emphysema or heart failure or after-effects of a stroke. She found little challenge in her tasks and missed the closeness that had developed between her and the young, badly wounded men. She was no longer the ministering angel, just another faceless nurse.

Even her relationship with Nathan had changed. The passion and the challenges of the early years of their marriage had been replaced by a monotonous sameness. She knew she should consider herself fortunate in many ways. Nathan had made a life for himself. He ran a business, virtually by himself now that his father took more time off. She loved him and things were comfortable between them. They had a nice home, a car, and lacked for nothing. What was it that was troubling her then?

■ ■ ■

Sarah had just turned five when Pearl surprised herself with a gesture so spontaneous and out-of-character she was sure it had lain just beneath the surface for a long time. On a mild spring evening with Sarah asleep, Pearl reached for her husband's hand.

"Come with me," she said softly.

In the bedroom, she pressed against him and slowly began unbuttoning his shirt.

Nathan, aroused by Pearl's desire, quickly slipped out of his pants and underwear.

"Come on top of me," she said, guiding him into her.

"Is it safe?" he asked.

Pearl responded by pulling him even tighter against her.

38

"What's she doing now?" Nathan asked as they sat in the park on a Sunday afternoon in mid-summer.

"It looks like she's made friends with another little girl. They're taking turns on the slide."

Nathan listened intently, the sounds of the children shaping images in his mind.

"And, Nathan, it won't be long before she'll have a little playmate all her own," Pearl said softly.

"What?" he said, not understanding what she had said.

"Sarah is going to have a little brother."

"That night in May . . . ?"

"That wonderful night in May." She laughed.

"You don't mind then?"

"Not one bit."

He slipped his arm around her shoulders and kissed her cheek. "That's wonderful, Pearl. But you said Sarah was going to have a brother? How do you know?"

"I just know."

"Did you have a pregnancy test?"

"A test would only tell me what I already know. Besides, I'm smarter than a frog."

"When will you see the doctor?"

"In September. I figure I'm about three months."

"So the baby will be born in . . . ?"

"End of February or early March."

"You mean it might come on Sarah's birthday?"

"It could happen."

"That would be something."

"People might think we only have sex once a year on the same date."

Nathan put his head back and laughed. "When should we tell Sarah?"

"Let's wait until I see the doctor. Just to make sure everything is okay."

"Shall I say anything to my parents?"

"Not yet. I don't know if your mother will be up to taking care of two of them."

"Pearl will be starting kindergarten in September. That will make it easier. But you know, you don't have to go back to work if you don't want to. I'm doing well enough with the business."

"Let's see how I feel about it when the baby comes. In the meantime, we can concentrate on more important things, like what we'll call him."

"You are convinced it's a boy, aren't you?"

"There's not a doubt in my mind."

In September, Doctor Hagler assured her that the pregnancy appeared to be perfectly normal. That same month, Pearl enrolled Sarah in kindergarten. She seemed happy at the idea and on her first day, her usually serious demeanor was replaced by a light-hearted chattering, especially with her grandmother, come to accompany Sarah and her mother to the schoolbus stop.

"Don't be sad, grandma," said Sarah, as Roberta wiped away a tear.

"I'm not sad, sweetheart. It's just that you've become such a big girl, going to school already. It happened so fast."

"Now grandma will have no one to play with," Nathan teased.

"She might have someone to play with sooner than she thinks," Pearl said, a smile on her face.

"Oh, Pearl," said Roberta. "Is it true?"

"And Pearl is convinced it's a boy," Nathan said.

"When? Oh, wait until Jerry hears this."

"About the same time as Sarah's birthday."

"I can't believe it," Roberta said. "I'm so happy."

"Now then, we'd better get Sarah to the bus stop. It wouldn't do to miss your bus on the first day of school."

Nathan kissed his daughter goodbye and started for the store while Pearl and Roberta, each holding one of Sarah's hands, took her to the bus stop in the middle of the block. Sarah trotted up the steps into the bus, as if she had been riding it all her life. She quickly found a window seat and waved to them as the bus pulled away.

"You were right," Pearl said to her mother-in-law. "It happened so fast."

"Do you want me to come by for a few days to take Sarah to the bus stop?"

"Knowing Sarah, she'll insist she's big enough to do it herself. I've got to run. Give my love to Jerry."

At dinner that evening, Sarah told her parents about the other students in her class. "Some children know the alphabet," she said, "but they don't know how to read."

"Did the teacher ask you if you could?"

"Mrs. Olson asked all of us."

"And did you read for her?"

"She gave me a baby book but I told her I read books for big children."

Pearl suppressed a smile.

"She had *Grimm's Fairy Tales*. I read the story of Rumpelstiltskin to the class."

"My goodness, what did Mrs. Olson say?"

"She said she wants you to come to see her after school."

"Well," said Pearl, surprised, "I'll call the school tomorrow and set up a time."

That night, after Sarah had gone to bed, Pearl thought of Sister Margaret for the first time in a long while. She had written to the nun after her marriage and when Sarah was born, but except for Christmas cards there had been no contact since. Pearl knew that the schools at the orphanage had closed. The children were now bussed into Helena. Her own years at Saint Joseph's seemed like a lifetime ago. Any time Pearl thought of stopping at the orphanage for a visit, something in her recoiled at the thought. Now that she had her own family, she found it even harder to come to terms with the fact that her parents hadn't wanted her. Stepping through the doors of Saint Joseph's and confronting the only childhood past she had ever known would only intensify the pain of that abandonment for her.

Nevertheless, Sister Margaret had been kind to her and Pearl felt obligated to maintain a correspondence. She must be well into her fifties by now, Pearl thought. While Nathan sat on the sofa, his fingers skimming over his book, Pearl wrote her letter, apologizing for writing so infrequently, then going on to tell the nun about the upcoming birth of her second child, Sarah's entering kindergarten, her own work at Fort Harrison, and Nathan's partnership with his father at the store. She closed with the hope that Sister Margaret would write to her and promised to try to be a better correspondent. She'll think it odd that I don't come by for a visit, Pearl thought, but so be it.

The next day Pearl headed directly for Sarah's school after work. Mrs. Olson, a tall woman with graying blond hair, met her in the assistant principal's office.

"Sarah is a remarkable little girl," she said. "You've certainly done a fine job in teaching her to read so well."

"It didn't take much effort on my part," Pearl said. "She learns so quickly."

"The reason I asked you in is because Sarah is so far ahead of the other kindergarteners, I don't think it would be fair to keep her in the class. How would you feel about our placing her into first grade? She'd be a little younger than the other children, of course, but I don't think that would pose a problem." She smiled. "But the only thing that concerns me about that is the possibility of first grade boring her. I'm not sure what we would do then."

She's only been in the school for two days, Pearl thought, and already they don't know what to make of her. Given her own difficulty in understanding Sarah, the teacher's remarks made Pearl feel better. "I think moving her up to first grade would be a good idea at any rate. Sarah can be a challenge."

"But a pleasant challenge. It's more common for us to encounter the opposite. Those children tend to fall further and further behind."

Roberta, who had come to the house each day a little before three in order to be there when Sarah's schoolbus arrived, was peeling vegetables at the sink when Pearl arrived. Sarah knelt on a chair watching her grandmother.

"Since you were going to be late today, I thought I'd help you get a start on dinner," Roberta said.

"Thanks, Roberta. I just met with Mrs. Olson, Sarah's teacher," Pearl said looking at her daughter. "And you're not in kindergarten anymore, Sarah."

"What did I do?" she said, looking worried.

"You didn't do anything wrong. Because you read so well, Mrs. Olson thinks you should be in first grade. Beginning tomorrow, you'll be in Miss Clark's class."

"That's wonderful," said Roberta.

"But I like Mrs. Olson," Sarah said.

"I'm sure you'll like Miss Clark, too."

"We're very proud of you, sweetheart. Wait until your daddy and grandpa hear this."

"Nathan teased her the other evening about being ready for college," Pearl said after Sarah left the room. "I'm beginning to wonder if he might have been right."

"Are there any little girls in the neighborhood Sarah can play with?"

"No one on this block. I think it would be good for her to be with other children more. I'll have to ask her new teacher if anyone in the class lives near us."

In spite of Pearl's efforts to put her daughter in touch with other children, Sarah resisted. Whenever another parent dropped her child off to play with Sarah, it proved to be the first and last time.

"I don't understand it," Pearl said to Nathan. "She avoids being with other children. I don't think it's good for her to be around adults all the time."

"Maybe that will change when she gets a little older. Did you talk to her teacher about how she's doing?"

"She says even though Sarah reads better than the other children she doesn't seem to be bored. She participates in class, plays with the other kids at recess."

"Then why worry?" Nathan gently placed his hand on Pearl's abdomen. "She'll have another child in the house soon enough. Ooh, did you feel that kick?"

"Sometimes when I'm at work he kicks so hard I have to stop what I'm doing."

"Maybe he'll be a football player."

"How do you like Charles for a name? Charles Rubin."

"Charlie Rubin," repeated Nathan. "Not bad."

Pearl had her first contractions at Sarah's birthday party. Nathan's parents were there but Sarah didn't want to invite any children from her class.

"Don't tell me," said Roberta.

"I'll start timing them."

"What's the matter?" Sarah asked.

"Mommy has a belly ache," said Nathan. "She must have eaten too much cake."

"She hasn't had any yet, daddy."

"It's a delicious cake," said Jerry, licking his lips. "And I like the way you blew out all six candles with one blow."

"Seven, grandpa. There was one for good luck."

"You're right. There were seven."

"Can I look at my new books now?"

Pearl waited until her daughter was out of earshot. "She can't wait to start reading them," Pearl said softly. "Have you ever seen a six-year-old so excited about books?"

"You don't think they're too hard for her?" Roberta asked.

"Hard? The last time we went to the library I found her sitting in a chair reading *Les Miserables*."

"I don't believe it," said her grandfather.

"What did I tell you?" Nathan laughed. "She'll be in college by next year."

"What's Sarah going to think if her brother has the same birthday?" Roberta asked.

"I don't know what she'll think," said Nathan, "but I think you both should plan on sticking around for a while in case this is the real thing."

An hour later Pearl's contractions were coming every ten minutes.

"We should go to the hospital," said Roberta.

"I agree," said Nathan. "Come say goodbye to everyone, Sarah," he called.

"Where are you going?" Sarah asked her mother.

"To the hospital to get your little brother."

"How do you know he wants to come now?"

"Believe me, Sarah, mama knows," Roberta laughed.

"Be a good girl with daddy," Pearl said. "Give me a kiss goodnight, too." She bent down for Sarah's kiss, then embraced Nathan. "It will be nice to have this watermelon out of the way, won't it?"

"You'll call?" he asked.

"Don't worry," said Roberta, "I'll call. Pearl will be busy."

A few minutes past midnight the phone rang, waking Nathan from his nap on the sofa.

"It's a boy," his mother said excitedly. "A big, healthy boy. Eight pounds."

"Eight pounds! That's great. And Pearl?"

"She's fine. She said to send you her love. We're going to head home now. We'll be over bright and early in the morning so your father can drive you to the hospital."

■ ■ ■

Pearl's eyes were closed, the baby nestled in her arm, when Nathan and his father arrived.

"Good morning," said Jerry. "I brought someone to see you."

Pearl opened her eyes and smiled.

"Come meet your son," she said to Nathan, placing his hand on the baby's head.

"He doesn't have as much hair as Sarah did."

"I still can't believe this eight pound bruiser came out of me."

"That's a pound and a half more than Sarah weighed."

"I've decided to breastfeed him," Pearl said.

"How will you do that and work?"

"I'm going to put in for a leave of absence."

"Your mother-in-law will be crushed," Jerry said, "but I think that's great."

"It is great," said Nathan, a hint of uncertainty in his voice.

Pearl couldn't be sure if Nathan really meant what he said. In spite of his having told her the past summer that she didn't have to work, that the store could support them, she now wondered if that was true. Well, it doesn't matter, she quickly decided. She turned her head to look at her son and placed her lips against his soft skin. No one would stop her from spending time with this one. This baby was hers.

39

Mornings with her son were the best part of each day for Pearl. After Nathan left for work and Sarah for school, a soothing peace settled over the house.

Pearl never tired of gazing at Charlie as she cuddled him in her arms or as he slept in his crib. Touched by his vulnerability, she scooped him up immediately when he cried. He always rooted hungrily for her breast, latching on with a tenacity surprising for such a small creature. Poor Sarah, Pearl thought, she missed out on this when she was an infant.

But with Sarah, who knew if it would have mattered? She was such a strange, self-possessed child. Her appearance at the front door when she returned from class brought with it an alteration in the house's tranquility, a reflection really of the change in Pearl's mood. Disturbing images from her own childhood often came to her when Sarah came home. A sand castle she had painstakingly built destroyed in an instant by another child's inadvertent clumsiness. A cold wind that cut like a knife through the warmth of the orphanage chapel when someone opened the outside door during the winter.

Aware that she had come to look upon her daughter's presence as an intrusion on her private time with the baby, Pearl tried to make up for it by chatting about school. She encouraged Sarah to help with the baby's care, allowed her to push the carriage when they went out for a walk, and gave her kitchen tasks when she prepared dinner. Sarah obediently did what her mother asked, but there was no enthusiasm. Hasn't it always been this way? Pearl thought.

"What do you think of your brother?" Pearl asked more than once, eliciting only "he's cute" or a shoulder shrug.

Once, while watching her mother diaper the baby, Sarah saw an arc of urine from Charlie's erect penis land on the front of Pearl's blouse. Instead of laughing, Sarah simply looked from the baby to her mother, as if she were curious how Pearl would handle the situation.

It was Pearl who laughed. "Your brother has bad manners."

Sarah smiled, then ran off to continue reading.

Now that her grandmother was no longer around every day, Sarah lavished most of her attention on her father. She greeted him enthusiastically each evening when he came through the door, running into his open arms. Nathan often lifted her into the air. "Be an airplane," he would say, and Sarah would hold out her arms and mimic a plane's drone as her father turned in a circle.

Sarah idolized Nathan, leaping from her chair if he asked for something or couldn't find where something was. She never tired of sitting next to him as he read. If his fingers paused and he seemed distracted, Sarah usually asked if he'd like her to read to him. And when he shaved in the morning, Sarah hovered at the sink and watched. "You missed some whiskers on your chin," she'd say, or "there's still some shaving cream on your cheek."

"I wonder why Sarah doesn't like me," Pearl said one evening after she and Nathan had gone to bed.

"Are you serious?" he said, rolling onto his side and propping his head on his hand.

"Can't you sense what's going on—or not going on—between us? We don't relate to one another. Look how different she is with you. I'm with her a good part of the day and I never hear her laugh. We barely talk."

"Maybe you're just being too sensitive. It could be a phase, you know, a little girl having a crush on her daddy."

"I just don't know what to do. You don't have to see to realize what's going on in this house, Nathan. Listen to how she is with you, with your mother. But not with me."

"Perhaps she sees how busy you are with the baby and—"

"It has nothing to do with Charlie. This is the way she's always been. I know now I should have taken more time off when she was a baby. The only mother she knew was Roberta. That's why I have no intention of returning to work until Charlie knows who I am."

"I like your being home with the baby. We're managing."

"It still makes me feel guilty sometimes. I feel like I'm not contributing my share. I know most women stay at home with their children, but I've always worked."

Nathan's fingers moved absentmindedly up and down her arm. "What are you thinking?" Pearl said.

"I'm wondering what to do about Sarah."

"I don't mean to upset you with this. I keep hoping things between us will change as she gets older, but I don't know. Haven't you noticed, too, that she never brings a friend home? I don't think she has any friends."

"I don't know what's normal for a kid Sarah's age. I'm trying to remember what I was like at her age."

"And?"

"I don't think I was all that different. I played by myself mostly. I don't think I had any friends until I was eight or nine."

"Well, maybe I'm worrying for nothing about that. How did you get on with your mother?"

Nathan moved over onto his back. "I don't know. She was my mother and she was just—there."

"Well," said Pearl, "that describes me all right."

■■■

When Charlie was six months old, the hospital told Pearl they could no longer hold her nursing spot. If she didn't wish to return to work, they would fill the vacancy and Pearl would have to take her chances for an opening should she decide to return. Pearl asked for a few days to think about it.

By this time there was no doubt in Charlie's mind who his mother was. He was willing to spend a few minutes in Roberta's arms, but then he would fuss and reach for Pearl. So much for that concern, Pearl thought. But if she returned to work she'd have to introduce Charlie to a bottle. In the end that was the deciding factor. She told Fort Harrison to go ahead and fill her position.

As the months passed and Charlie became a toddler, Sarah began to take more interest in him. She let him hold her fingers as he walked unsteadily across the room and she also tried reading to him. Charlie, however, did not have the attention span Sarah had as an infant. He would squirm out of his sister's lap and crawl across the floor, more curious than literary.

Soon Charlie began losing interest in breastfeeding and Pearl started him on baby food. By the time he was two, Pearl gave up on trying to get him to nurse. And it was now often exhausting for her to keep up with her son. She had never thought of all the potential hazards in the house—electrical outlets, stove knobs, water boiling on a burner, hot radiators. As a baby, Sarah had avoided these things as if she instinctively knew she might be hurt by them. But Charlie knew no such thing. Anything that represented a danger lured him like a magnet. It was only when she heard his sudden cry that Pearl knew she hadn't been vigilant enough. Although she now felt ready to return to work—eager, in fact—she was unsure if Nathan's mother could cope with Charlie. The baby liked his grandmother, but wouldn't obey her any more than he would Pearl. To make matters worse, Nathan had insisted on buying him a small tricycle and Charlie rode through the house like a hellion, colliding with people and furniture.

One day Pearl called the hospital and was told that one of the nurses was moving to Seattle with her husband at the end of the month. Putting aside her misgivings, especially after Roberta reassured her, Pearl decided to go back to work.

Sarah was now eight, capable of amusing herself and helping her grandmother with the baby when she came home from school.

"Now listen, young man," Pearl said, holding a squirming Charlie in her arms on the morning she was to start. "You be good with grandma while mommy is at work."

Roberta laughed. "He'll be good, won't you, Charlie?"

"Only when he sleeps," said Nathan, as he ate his breakfast.

■■■

It was a miracle, Pearl thought, but everything appeared to be under control. Roberta was handling her rambunctious grandson well and she herself was glad to be back at work. The hospital was receiving wounded from the Korean War and she found herself as busy as she had been in the forties. "The bloodshed never stops, does it?" she said to Lori, who was glad to have her old friend on the ward again.

"I don't know if any of us will live long enough to see that," Lori replied.

When she got home each day, Pearl would find the house a shambles with Charlie's toys strewn everywhere. Even Sarah, home only for an hour, seemed worn out by her little brother. Another miracle, Pearl thought, when her daughter actually seemed glad to see her.

In late March of 1954, only a few weeks after Charlie had turned three and Sarah nine, Roberta called Pearl at the hospital.

"I'm a little concerned about Charlie," she said. "He's feverish and threw up the little bit he ate for lunch. I noticed red stains on his diaper, too."

"Give him baby aspirin and try to get him to drink. He's probably coming down with a cold. I'll give Doctor Davis a call."

Pearl had noticed that Charlie hadn't had much appetite for the past week and had seemed lethargic. But his weight was good. If anything, he seemed to be putting on weight. But what would cause blood on his diaper?

40

Pearl stood at the side of the examining table while Doctor Davis, a white-haired, thin-faced man in his fifties, examined Charlie. He placed his hands on Charlie's swollen abdomen and looked at Pearl. "You just noticed this today?"

"No, for the last couple of weeks actually. I thought he was putting on weight. He has a good appetite—or did until about a week ago."

He slipped out the rectal thermometer and held it up. "One hundred one."

Pearl carefully watched the doctor's face as he listened to Charlie's chest and back with his sthethoscope. He concentrated on one area in particular, listening intently, which only increased Pearl's apprehension.

Doctor Davis helped Charlie to sit up on the table. "Charlie, if I give you a cup can you make a pee pee in it for me?"

Charlie shook his head.

"I haven't been able to get him urine trained yet," said Pearl.

Doctor Davis tied a cup on him and moments later frowned as blood-tinged urine slowly filled the cup. The doctor removed it and excused himself.

"I think you can get Charlie dressed," he said when he returned. "Then we'll talk in my office."

A feeling of sudden dread settled over Pearl. Something from her pediatric training in nursing school kept trying to insinuate itself in her memory. It's nothing, she told herself. He's a healthy little boy.

"Sit down, Pearl. Charlie, you can sit on the floor and play with these toy soldiers."

"You're a nurse, right?" Doctor Davis asked.

"Yes, at Fort Harrison."

A few moments of silence hung between them. "What is it? Tell me," Pearl said, finally.

"I can't be sure yet until we do more tests. Charlie needs some X-rays and we'll do those in the hospital. Do you know what a nephroblastoma is?"

Pearl silently repeated the word to herself. "It's a Wilms' tumor?" she asked, barely able to get the words out.

"As I said, I don't know for sure, but given his age and the mass in his abdomen, that would be my preliminary diagnosis. The blood in his urine makes it even more likely."

"What are you going to do?"

"We'll have to admit Charlie to the hospital. You can bring him in the morning. I'll order X-rays of his chest and abdomen and have Doctor Stoddard, the pediatrician, see him in consultation."

Pearl drove home slowly, her teeth digging into her lower lip as she tried not to cry. When she opened the door, Roberta looked at Pearl's face and knew everything.

41

The slate grey sky was in keeping with Sarah's mood. From her thirtieth-floor office window she looked down at the East River, cutting its swathe like a muddy green highway between Manhattan and Queens. The first frigid day of November had arrived, a portent of the looming winter. Somewhere in Queens a white cloud of smoke hung suspended over three tall chimneys. Only several blocks away from where she now stood, on exclusive Sutton Place, was the apartment in which she and Roger lived.

To the west, within walking distance of work, were the Museum of Modern Art and the posh shopping emporia of Fifth Avenue. Thirteen years ago it had been a fairy tale world, a fantasy on the verge of being fulfilled. It had taken her all that time to learn that getting what she wanted had made her just as unhappy as she had been before coming to New York.

"The golden girl," that's what the local newspaper in Helena, Montana had called her. Straight A average in high school, valedictorian of her class, winner of a full scholarship to Columbia University at the age of sixteen. And so beautiful many well-meaning people had tried to encourage her to enter the Miss Junior Montana contest. Anyone else might have basked in all that attention.

But pride had no place in a world where tragedy lurked behind every corner, where happiness was as ephemeral as the bitterroot flowers that appeared in Montana's brief spring, only to be gone overnight. She remembered her childhood as a time of darkness, as black as the glasses her father always wore. It was not that she was unloved, just the opposite in fact. Her father and grandparents doted on her, but somehow that had not been enough. The missing part had been her mother, an enigmatic figure whose mysterious, unknown past had left her in this world as a person bereft. The link that was missing between Sarah and her mother was the same as the absent link between Pearl and her own mother. Love. Trite and misused as the word might be, what it represented was everything, Sarah thought. Goddamn everything.

If her mother had known who she was, and if Sarah had known who her mother was, everything could have been different. Love might have had a chance to take root. As fragile and illusory as happiness was, love would have sustained the family in its suffering. All the tragedies—her father's blindness, her brother's death when he was only three, and the deaths of her grandparents within a few weeks of each other—would have been more bearable, would have drawn Sarah and her parents even closer, had there been enough love. So simple.

And now her mother herself lay dying. Only weeks earlier her father had called to tell her breast cancer had been diagnosed and was already in its terminal stages. For almost six months Pearl had ignored the back pain that practically incapacitated her, insisting on working when it was obvious that she was not well.

"Shall I come home?" Sarah had asked her father.

"The doctor has her on morphine and most of the time she just sleeps. When she does wake up she's confused."

Too late, thought Sarah, too late to cross the divide between them. Her going back now, she knew, would change nothing. Her mother would always be a solitary creature, even in death. Nathan loved her, of course, but perhaps it was his blindness that made that possible. Blind love was something Sarah could not offer. Perhaps if Charlie had lived, Pearl would have been able to break free from the bonds of her anonymity, to love someone enough so that the void of her own past would no longer matter. But Charlie, the little brother Sarah, too, had come to adore, had died. Even if he hadn't, would Pearl have been able to excavate enough love from the rubble of her orphaned childhood to share with Sarah? Who knows? Sarah thought bitterly. Who the hell knows?

Instead of love, books had sustained Sarah and imbued her with a desire to write, to compose stories that might offer solace to others, in the same way that those she pored over in her youth had helped her to survive.

"Someday," her high school English teachers told her, "you will be a great writer. We'll be proud to say we had you as a student."

How proud would they be if they knew the great writer spent her days working on television commercials? They might be kind and tell her she had pursued a successful career. After all, she was a highly paid account executive at Grayson Advertising. I've sold my soul and I know it, Sarah thought.

But it was her writing ability that had led her to where she was now. While still a student at Columbia, Sarah had sold short stories to publications like *Paris Review* and *The Atlantic Monthly*. One story was a parody of the advertising industry. A month after its appearance, her English professor handed her an envelope. "Roger Delaney, a visiting lecturer in the Department of Economics, asked me to give you this," he said.

"*I enjoyed your recent story in The Atlantic Monthly,*" the enclosed letter said. "*May I take you to dinner one day next week? There's something I'd like to discuss with you. You can reach me any evening at . . .*"

They had dinner at Fiorello's across from Lincoln Center. The waiter showed her to a table in a quiet corner in the back. Roger Delaney, already waiting for her, was much younger than she had imagined, thirty-five at most. If anyone had asked Sarah later that evening to describe him she would have said slender, medium height, sandy blond hair, reasonably good-looking, a great smile. It was that great smile that greeted her as she approached. He stood up and held out his hand.

"Thank you for coming," he said.

"How could I not be curious?" she said. "An economist who reads the short stories in *The Atlantic Monthly?*"

"I have to be honest. *Forbes* is more in line with what I read. But a friend brought me your story and I really liked it. And actually, I'm not an economist. I'm in advertising. Columbia invites me to lecture so I can tell their economics majors how to get rich."

"Is there some magic formula?"

"One part hard work, two parts good ideas, and three parts luck."

A smile flitted around his lips. Sarah knew he was appraising her.

"Something to drink?" asked the waiter.

"Shall I order wine?" Delaney asked.

"That would be nice."

"I really enjoyed your story, *Brand Names*. You seemed so knowledgeable about the advertising industry I wondered if you had ever worked for an agency."

"It all came from my imagination."

"Well, that's remarkable. It was such marvellous parody, I found myself thinking you might be a natural fit for us. I'm a vice president at Grayson Advertising. We're one of the larger advertising agencies in the city. Lots of big-name clients willing to spend millions to convince consumers to buy their products."

"Mr. Delaney, are you offering me a job?"

"To be honest, yes. And please call me Roger."

"But I made fun of the industry."

"What I'm looking for is talent and wit and a sense of humor. I think you have all three."

"I'm flattered, but I'm a writer."

"I know writing advertising copy doesn't sound as glamorous, but it pays very well. And you could still write on your own time. What were you planning to do after graduation?"

"I thought I'd try to find something with a publishing house."

"I don't think they pay their editors very well."

"It's not just about money."

"Do you have independent means?"

Sarah laughed. "I'm on full scholarship. Otherwise, I could never have afforded to go to college."

"Full scholarship at Columbia? Now that is something."

It proved to be an unexpectedly enjoyable evening for Sarah. She found herself opening up to a perfect stranger, very out of character for her. Not even her roommates in the dorm, girls who had known her since freshman year, were aware that Sarah's father was blind, her mother an orphan, and that she had a sibling who died young. And yet, she had shared all this with Roger Delaney.

He, too, spoke about his family and childhood. "I grew up in Rochester," he told her. "My father was an executive with Eastman Kodak. One younger brother, one older sister. A very upper middle-class household, one with few surprises, which is the way my parents liked it. That all changed when my sister eloped with a musician when she was nineteen. My parents were fit to be tied. He now works for Capitol Records, they have two kids, and live a very bourgeois life in Long Island. Next it was my turn. I put off going to college and sailed on a freighter to Europe. I hooked up with a wealthy Spanish couple in Algeciras and went to work for them on their yacht. I did a lot of travelling but two years of being a servant was enough, so I came back to the States and went to . . ." He paused. "Columbia University."

"So we have that in common."

"Yes, but I'm sure you're a better student than I was."

"You're just being modest."

"Not entirely," he laughed. "Anyway, while trying to figure out what I wanted to do with my life, I went to work for Grayson. I must have had natural huckster ability. They liked my work and I enjoyed what I was doing."

"How many years have you worked for them?"

"Eight."

"And you're a vice-president? Now that is impressive."

"Have you always wanted to write?"

"As far back as I can remember. I think I was reading by the time I was three. That's what my parents tell me. I've always loved books."

Three days after that first evening together, Roger called and invited her to the opera. "*Tosca*," he said. "Should be great."

"Before I say yes, I should ask you something."

"Fire away."

"You're not married, are you?"

He laughed. "Not married. Not divorced. And no kids. Now will you go?"

Two months after her graduation, Sarah went to work for Grayson Advertising. Delaney had been right. Salaries for neophyte editors were barely enough to live on. Sarah rationalized her decision by telling herself she would always have been so worried about money, she'd never have been able to concentrate on her writing.

Delaney had also been perceptive. Sarah turned out copy that was used in major campaigns. In less than eighteen months she had been promoted to account executive and given full responsibility for a major women's wear account. She earned more money than she had ever dreamed of, rented an efficiency apartment on Lexington Avenue, and had a wardrobe of fashionable clothes.

What she didn't have was the time to write. Her work was demanding, the hours long. She seldom left work before seven, too exhausted to even think about sitting at a typewriter. Several attempts at short stories were disasters.

Sarah and Delaney dated regularly, each committed to the relationship without actually putting it into words. In 1968, after she had been with Grayson for two years, Delaney proposed. The rest of the country might be descending into madness with its antiwar riots, civil disobedience, and assassinations, Sarah thought, but we'll make our lives ones of affirmation.

Their wedding took place in Rochester, New York in a Unitarian Chapel. The Delaneys would have preferred a Catholic ceremony but Roger refused. "I left that Church when I was fourteen," he told Sarah, "and I'll be damned if I have anything more to do with it." Afterward, Sarah had wondered if Roger's parents blamed her. They were nice enough to her, but would have liked her better, she thought, if she were a Catholic.

Sarah's parents flew to Rochester for the wedding. Nathan had aged well. His hair was graying but his bearing was still erect and his movements self-assured. "It's hard to believe he's blind," Roger whispered to her.

Pearl, on the other hand, had undergone a transformation that shocked Sarah. She had last seen her parents at her graduation from Columbia. In the two years since then, Pearl appeared to have aged ten. After Charlie's death, Sarah could not remember a single time when she had seen her mother smile. As if in solidarity with death, the last vestiges of Pearl's beauty had been consumed by the ravages of premature aging. Her face was pale, the large, almond-shaped eyes perched like dead stones on her high cheekbones. Always slender, she was now skeletal.

Excusing herself from the guests, Sarah had managed to get her mother to one side. "Are you all right?" she asked.

"Your father and I are fine."

Nathan was no more forthcoming than her mother. "Don't worry about us.

We're doing very well. I try to talk your mother into leaving her job and taking her pension but she won't hear of it. And everything is fine at the store. I've got a nice young fellow working for me."

"Dad, mother looks awful."

"Just overworked. And since Charlie . . . well, you know."

■■■

Six years since the wedding, Sarah thought, and she hadn't seen her parents once. She had called them, but could not find the time—nor the inclination—to visit. She shuddered at the thought of what her mother must look like now.

A few snowflakes drifted past the window and Sarah's mood grew darker. In Montana Sarah had loved the snow, delighting in its gradual descent to the lower slopes of the Elkhorns and Big Belts. The ponderosa pines and Douglas firs wore their white coats like royalty adorned in ermine. In New York it was different. Snow was a nuisance, a filthy one at that, a brief precursor to the rivers of mud and slush that followed.

Six years, she repeated to herself. What had six years brought to the golden girl?

42

As a student at Columbia, Sarah had never found the time to get to know New York. Even at Grayson her days before she was married were consumed by work. Weekends, on the other hand, were reserved for Roger. And it was Roger who opened up the city for her. The Village, Chinatown, the Lower East Side, Inwood, Park Slope in Brooklyn—images washed over her.

She had studied the faces around her and imagined their lives—Arabs, Hassidic Jews, Puerto Ricans, blacks wearing dashikis—it was an entire world in microcosm.

On Friday and Saturday evenings she and Roger went to shows, operas, symphonies. And afterward they went to Roger's apartment in Kips Bay.

One early autumn evening they had stood, wine glasses in hand, on his small terrace twelve stories above the city. Sarah was mesmerized by the play of lights—blinking traffic signals, car headlights, windows lit up one moment, dark the next, flashing neon signs. She had been in the city for so many years that the noise of car horns, sirens, shattering glass, and drunken shouts, only slightly muted at this height, were like white noise.

As a child in Helena a car parking half a block away or the distant drone of a plane would have awakened her, a jarring intrusion into the silence. But Helena was so long ago it was no longer real. Sarah's only reality now was this wonderful, terrible city and the man she stood next to.

Then she felt his lips on her neck and moments later he had led her into the bedroom.

Afterward they lay in silence, her head on his shoulder. "I love you, Sarah," he said.

That same week Sarah had gone to Planned Parenthood and began taking birth control pills. Sex with Roger now became part of their weekend.

"Now that we've had our honeymoon," he had joked, "will you marry me?"

Two months before their wedding they bought an apartment on Sutton Place. "Aren't we being too extravagant?" she had asked.

"We can afford it," he had said.

The shopping spree that followed was, as Sarah thought later, more of a shopping frenzy. They got rid of all their old furnishings and bought everything new. "I've got a surprise," Roger said after a Saturday lunch at Minetta's in the Village. He had a big smile on his face as he pulled in at a midtown Mercedes dealership.

"Isn't this fun?" he said, his face glowing with pleasure, as they left in their new car.

"What was wrong with the old car?" Sarah asked.

"We deserve better," Roger told her, reaching for her hand.

During the first years of their marriage Sarah had tried to convince herself that she was happy. They had a luxury apartment, a luxury car, ate in fine restaurants, and had an active social life, even though there was no one Sarah considered a close friend. Their guests were business associates and clients, and Roger left nothing, not even the dinner menu, to chance. "Why should you have to preoccupy yourself with that?" he'd say, hiring a chef for the evening. Sarah also took her first trips outside the country—cruises in the Mediterranean, the Caribbean, the Aegean. Their port calls were always too brief and Sarah found herself looking longingly from the deck at the places they were leaving. It was not the way she wanted to travel. "What's wrong with being pampered?" Roger would say.

When Sarah grew restive she'd blame herself: you have everything—a man who's solicitous and loves you; all the things money can buy; you have a maid to do the cleaning, a chef to do the cooking. What more do you want?

No sooner had she asked herself that question, she pushed it from her thoughts. And then tears would suddenly flow without warning.

The first time it happened, Sarah was frightened. She was in her office, studying charts on markets and product sales, rapidly scribbling notes for a new campaign, when the numbers blurred and hot tears rolled down her cheeks. Sarah buried her face in her hands, then groped for a Kleenex. What's wrong with you? she kept asking herself. It must be the birth control pills, she decided, and immediately placed a call to Planned Parenthood.

The nurse practitioner, after listening to Sarah's complaint about mood swings, agreed to change her pill. A month later, while standing in front of a Barnes and Noble store window, her tears again took her by surprise. I must be going mad, she thought, walking quickly away.

Her secretary didn't expect her back for almost an hour so Sarah headed up toward Central Park. She settled herself on a bench near the entrance and struggled to regain her composure. You're too strong a person to let whatever's causing this get the best of you, she told herself.

A week later Roger had invited her to have lunch with him and a client, but she had turned him down. "I'm too busy," she said. "I'll just grab a sandwich."

Sitting in the Olympus Diner, two blocks from her office, Sarah had stared at her uneaten sandwich and sipped her tea. Fragments of conversation from the two women in the booth behind her caught her attention.

"You're not going to do it then?"

"My analyst doesn't think I'm ready to make that kind of commitment."

"What if Ted doesn't want to wait any longer?"

"I've known Doctor Markham longer than I've known Ted. I trust him."

Sarah quickly paid her bill and stopped at the payphone. She opened the yellow pages and found Doctor Royce Markham listed under psychiatrists. She picked up the phone, hesitated, then deposited her coins and dialed. Doctor Markham himself answered the phone. "I've had a cancellation for four this afternoon," he said.

At three-thirty, Sarah left her office. "If Roger looks for me," she told her secretary, "tell him I had an appointment and I'll see him at home."

Doctor Markham, an exceedingly tall, bald man of about fifty, sat in a chair facing her. He looked at her questioningly.

"You can begin by telling me why you think you're here."

Sarah told him about the crying. "It scared me. Both times it was without warning."

"What were you doing when it happened?"

"I was studying sheets of figures the first time and writing up a proposal for a new ad campaign. The next time I was standing in front of a bookstore window."

Her lip began to tremble.

"Do you like your work?"

"Yes, I—" She felt a constriction in her throat. "I hate it," she cried, "I hate it." Turning her face away, she started crying. "I'm sorry," she said.

He stood up to hand her a box of tissues.

"Tell me a little about yourself, your childhood, your background."

He listened intently, jotting notes on a yellow legal pad.

"Have you told your husband what you're feeling?"

"He'd never understand. Roger thinks we've got it all, a life to die for."

"To die for?"

She stared at him. "For him it's to die for."

"Do you think your husband has changed since you married him?"

"When I first met Roger, I thought here's a man I can talk to. He seemed interested in me, in my life. I thought he believed in me."

Sarah paused, thinking he would ask her something, but he sat quietly, waiting.

"I know now that he's controlling. That's it, controlling." The word came to her as a revelation. "Everything has to be his way, everything in place. We live in the apartment he wants, we see the people he wants, we travel the way he wants, we do every goddamn thing that he wants!"

"And it makes you angry?"

"It makes me furious!" she almost shouted, surprising herself. "I don't know who I am anymore."

43

Three weeks after her first appointment with Doctor Markham, Sarah hailed a taxi for his 73rd Street office. She had arranged to see him on Mondays and Thursdays at eleven.

Soon, sitting in the small waiting room, its walls decorated with Japanese prints, she felt a sense of relief.

"I'm a little embarrassed to be here today," she said as Doctor Markham showed her in.

"Why is that?"

"Because I made such a spectacle of myself last time."

"Do you think of yourself as a spectacle?"

"I don't like losing control."

"I thought your husband was the one who was controlling."

"I mean losing control over myself."

"Have you told him you're seeing me?"

"No."

"Why not?"

"He'd think I was crazy." She laughed and Doctor Markham rewarded her with a smile.

"I want you to know," he said, "that most patients, once they feel comfortable enough, recline on the sofa during our sessions. It frees the mind and they find it easier to talk. Analysis depends on stream of consciousness, saying the first thing that comes into your mind. It involves doing away with your internal censor. You can say anything you like in here. And I'd like to hear your dreams."

"Do you want me on the sofa now?"

"Only if it makes you comfortable."

Lying there and staring at the ceiling, she found her gaze drawn to a small brass plate where a light fixture had once been.

"What are you thinking?" The voice seemed far away.

"I'm thinking of my father. That brass plate reminded me of him. It's opaque, just like his world. He was blinded during the Second World War."

"Tell me about him."

"I always felt close to him when I was a child, but . . . ."

"But?"

"But his dark glasses were like a wall between us. It sounds silly, I know. I knew he was blind and I knew he wore the glasses because of his appearance. One eye was completely gone and his face was scarred."

"You knew that but still you felt his dark glasses were a wall. Why?"

Tears formed in Sarah's eyes. "Because I wanted him to be able to see me."

"Did you feel more sorry for him or for yourself?"

Sarah thought for a moment. "Both. No one talked about his blindness and he didn't act like he was. He and my grandfather were partners in a store and some customers didn't know he was blind. He even walked to work by himself. When he came home in the evening I'd jump into his arms and he'd swing me over his head. Sometimes, when I sat next to him on the sofa while he was reading Braille, he'd rest his hand on my head and slide it over my face, as if I was one of the pages in his book."

"What about your mother?"

"More walls."

"What do you mean?"

"My mother was an orphan. She was raised by nuns."

"She knew nothing at all about her family?"

"No. It must have been interesting though."

"Why do you say that?"

"Her eyes. She has Asian eyes and her maiden name was Schneider. My eyes are shaped a little like hers."

"Did your mother express any curiosity about her family?"

"Not that I ever heard. But I was always angry at them even though I didn't know who they were."

"Why was that?"

"Because they gave my mother away and she never knew love as a child. How can a person who was never loved give love?"

"Give love? To whom?"

"To me."

"You felt she didn't love you?"

"I don't know. It's complicated. She never beat me or yelled at me. She just couldn't—couldn't free up her emotions. I never felt loved by her. The love I got was from my grandmother, my father's mother. She took care of me when my mother worked."

"Do you think your mother loved your father?"

"I guess so. They had originally planned to get married when the war was over. My mother was a nurse and he wanted to go to medical school. When he came back—blind, disfigured—my mother married him anyway. So she must have loved him."

"Are you sure it was love?"

"What's the difference? She married him."

"But did she love him? You said your mother couldn't give love."

"I don't know. Maybe I'm wrong about her not being able to give love. I know she loved Charlie. Losing him almost drove her mad."

"Who was Charlie?"

"My little brother. He died of cancer when he was three. My mother was crazy about him."

"Who are you more like? Your mother or your father?"

"God, what a question. You mean pathetic like my father or a cold bitch like my mother?"

"Those weren't my words."

Sarah couldn't believe what she had just said.

"Our time is up," said Doctor Markham.

Sarah was angry. She wanted to explain herself before she left the office. I didn't mean it, she wanted to scream. I don't know why I said that.

■■■

From that moment on, Roger seldom came up in her sessions with Doctor Markham. Sarah surprised herself by talking mainly about her parents and her childhood, dredging up incidents and remarks and feelings that had been buried under the silt of years. Why do I keep going back to childhood?" she asked during one session. "I feel like I'm in a rut and can't get out it."

"It took almost thirty years for you to become the person you are today. The most formative of those years were the ones in childhood."

"Well, I hope it doesn't take another thirty for me to understand myself better."

He chuckled. "I think you'll be able to do it a little faster than that."

As the months passed, Sarah was surprised that Roger hadn't commented on her absences two mornings a week. Several times Mandy, her secretary, mentioned Roger's coming by. "I told him you'd be back at twelve and he said you could call him later."

When she called him, he never asked what she was doing or where she'd been. "Want to have lunch today?" he'd say, or else he'd remind her about an executive meeting coming up.

■■■

"What do you enjoy doing?" Doctor Markham asked one day, surprising her with his question.

She thought for a few moments and heard him clear his throat. "I know," she said, "the first thing that comes to mind. Well, it was sex."

"And Roger is the person you enjoy sex with?"

"Yes. Even with all my bitching about him."

"What else do you like?"

"Books. Reading. Do you know, I used to read a few books a week, even as a kid? Now I'm lucky if I read a few in a year."

"You mentioned once that you wanted to be a writer. What changed that?"

Sarah didn't respond.

"What are you thinking?"

Tears were rolling down her cheeks. "I don't know."

"How did you get into advertising?"

"By the time I graduated from college I'd had a few short stories published and planned on being a writer. I looked for a job with a publisher but editing doesn't pay much. I had met Roger by then and he offered me a job at the agency he worked for. He said I could write in my spare time." She paused, listening to the sound of his pen on paper. "But there was no spare time," she said. "There was only work, turning out the drivel that I write. I can't blame Roger. He didn't force me to take the job."

"But you're well off now, aren't you?"

"Yes. Well off enough for my husband to buy the things that seem to give him so much pleasure. A fancy car we hardly ever use. An expensive watch to replace the expensive one he got tired of. A set of Waterford crystal that just gathers dust."

"So you no longer have to work if you don't want to."

"You don't understand."

"What don't I understand?"

"If I stop working then I lose the last bit of my self-respect. What am I then? A kept woman."

"But you could write if you left the ad agency. Don't you consider that work?"

"It's work all right. But there's no guarantee of success."

"Life doesn't offer guarantees."

"I never thought I'd have to accuse you of cliches."

"Cliche or not, it's the truth. If you stay where you are, there'll never be any chance of success in a way that's meaningful to you."

"I don't want to discuss it any more."

Sarah stormed out, refusing to even look at Doctor. Markham. It's no good, she thought, as she took the elevator down to the lobby. Why am I wasting my time and money?

Three days later she was back on his sofa.

44

Sarah had been seeing her analyst for a year when Roger stuck his head into her office one morning.

"Are you free for lunch today?" he asked.

"If you promise to get me back by two. Jim Randall is coming to see me about a new product they want to introduce."

"I promise. Incidentally," he said, stepping into the office and closing the door behind him, "I love you."

She smiled. "You came down here to tell me that?"

"That and the fact that I've set up a meeting of account executives for tomorrow at eleven. We're doing well in some areas, poor in others. Phillips is concerned and he wants me to develop a better comprehensive plan. He's serious this time. I think some heads are about to roll."

"Is mine one of them?"

"Are you kidding? If everyone was as successful as you there'd be no need for a meeting. Your input will really be helpful. It might light a fire under some laggards."

"I'm sorry, I can't make it."

"Why not?"

"I have an appointment."

"Can't you cancel it? This is important."

"So's my appointment."

"Do you mind telling me what's so important."

"I have an appointment with my analyst."

"Someone in accounting?"

Sarah laughed. "Not that kind of analyst. My shrink."

"You're kidding."

"No, I'm not."

Roger sat down at the side of her desk. "Is something wrong?"

"I have some issues I have to resolve."

"Am I one of those?"

"It's not just one thing. I have to—" She sighed in exasperation. "Look, this isn't the time to discuss it. It's just something I have to do for myself."

"How long have you been seeing this—shrink?"

"About a year."

"A year! And you haven't said a word to me about it?"

She shrugged. "I wasn't sure how you'd react."

"You don't think I'm supportive?"

"I don't know what I think. That's why I'm seeing an analyst."

He studied her in silence. "If I've done something wrong, I wish you'd—"

"Anyway, I can't make it tomorrow. If you'd like to reschedule for any morning but Monday or Thursday, I'll gladly be there."

He stood up and turned toward the door.

"Are we still on for lunch?"

"I've lost my appetite," he said, closing the door behind him.

■■■

"What happened after that?" asked Doctor Markham.

"He brought me flowers that evening and we went out for dinner. Then we came home, read for a while, made love, and went to sleep. It was a night not much different from other nights. Except for the flowers."

"He didn't mention your analysis?"

"No."

"How did that make you feel?"

"I thought, maybe he does think I'm unstable. A human minefield ready to blow up any minute. My father can't see because he's blind. Roger's not blind but he still can't see."

"What can't he see?"

"Me."

"That's the same thing you said about your father, that you wished he could see you."

"My father had an excuse. He didn't think the world was created in his image."

"And Roger does?"

"All I know is that he pampers himself and I don't care much for his values."

"But you go along with them."

"Maybe I'm more like my mother than I know. I take on an obligation and then feel I'm committed to it forever."

"What attracted you to Roger?"

"He was charming, personable, handsome, seemed bright."

"You once told me Roger seemed interested in you, that you thought he believed in you."

"I was deluding myself."

"You said he can't see. When did you become aware of that?"

"I think I always knew that. From the very beginning. But if I did, why would I have married him?"

"The unconscious chooses, Sarah. It chose what you had known in your childhood."

"If that's the case, I've ruined my life."

"You make it sound so permanent. Is it really?"

"Are you suggesting I divorce him?"

"I'm suggesting nothing. You're the one who has to make decisions. I'm here to help you understand yourself."

"But if what you say is true, then he's not what I want."

"Do you know what you want?"

"I think I do."

"But you haven't talked to him about it."

The minutes ticked by, Sarah saying nothing.

■■■

In the following weeks, Sarah talked only about what she wanted for herself. "I want an intellectual companion, someone who can talk to me about literature and history and different cultures, not someone who knows what's hot on Broadway or which tenor's performances always sell out. I'm not interested in pop culture. I want to travel, to explore countries and know the people, not look at them from the deck of a cruise ship. I want to free myself from the grip of money. I want to find the courage to be poor again if that's what it takes. I want to rediscover what I felt when I was in school, that everything was possible, that someday I'd succeed as a writer."

She talked until the sound of her own voice bored her. But it seemed she could not bridge the gap that would carry her to Roger's side.

"You still haven't tried to talk to him?" Doctor Markham asked.

"I can't."

"And why is that?"

"He wouldn't understand."

"Are you so sure that he doesn't know that there's something not entirely right with the relationship?"

"I can't say what he knows. He doesn't act like anything is wrong."

Month followed month and Sarah seemed to have hit a wall. She continued to insist that talking to Roger would be a waste of time.

"I tell you he won't understand," she shouted angrily at her analyst during one session as he prodded her.

"Are you afraid of his response?" Doctor Markham said.

"Why should I be afraid of what he might say?"

"You tell me."

"Words can't hurt me."

"What if he rejects you?"

"What do you mean by that?"

Doctor Markham focused on his notes and didn't answer. She wondered if he was growing tired of listening to her. Maybe he doesn't care, she told herself. But she knew that wasn't true. It was she who was was being obtuse, refusing to take the next step. After more than two years in therapy nothing had really changed.

How long things might have gone on like that, Sarah didn't know. Ultimately, it wasn't she who effected a change, it was the physiology of her own body.

Sarah's periods had been light since she began taking the pill. On some occasions she had seen little more than spotting. There had also been times when she forgot to take her pill, doubling up on her next dose. She never experienced a problem, at least not until late in August when she forgot her pill for two consecutive days. She doubled up for two days, but had no bleeding in September before it was time to start her next pack. It'll come next month, she thought. In October she again had no bleeding. It's impossible, she thought, but she made an appointment at the Planned Parenthood Clinic. Her pregnancy test came back positive.

■■■

Thinking back on everything that had happened over the last few years, Sarah's thoughts were as bleak as this November day as she stared out her office window. How could she have been so stupid? After being on the pill for years, how could she forget for two days in a row? Unless she wanted to forget. Ridiculous, she thought, but it continued to nag at her.

"It's your father on line one," Mandy said, buzzing her.

"Dad, are you all right?"

"I'm fine. But your mother isn't doing well. The doctor just left. He thinks it's a matter of a day or two at the most."

Sarah eased back in her chair and closed her eyes. Everything converging at once, she thought. How can I cope with this pregnancy and my mother's death at the same time?

"Sarah, are you there?"

"I'm here, dad. I'll try to get on a flight this afternoon or tomorrow morning."

45

Sleet lashed the windows as Sarah's plane landed in Minneapolis. From here she would connect to Billings, and then on to Helena. By the time her connection to Billings left two hours later, it was snowing. Sarah settled into her seat, closed her eyes, and thought about her father. It had been six years since she had seen him. What would happen to him after Pearl was gone? How could he possibly manage alone? Walking to his store was one thing, but what about shopping? Cooking? Reading the mail? Paying the bills? She could afford to pay someone to stay at the house and attend to his needs, but she knew he would resist that. Just as he would probably resist coming to live with her. Still, she had to try.

The small plane she boarded in Billings banked low over the Helena Valley. There was only a light dusting of snow on the wheat fields. On the city's northern outskirts they flew over a demolition site. The shattered remnants of brick buildings were surrounded by rubble and machinery. It took her a moment to recognize Saint Joseph's—or what was left of it. Her father had told her long ago it was where Pearl had spent her childhood.

What must that have been like? Sarah always wondered. She remembered asking her mother to take her there for a visit when she was twelve.

Pearl, who was at the stove cooking, had turned to face her. There was a look on her face that let Sarah know she had brought up a forbidden topic.

"I don't want to go there," Pearl said simply. "Not even for a visit."

Sarah, who had read *David Copperfield*, visualized a gloomy, prison-like atmosphere where orphans were beaten and starved. She had berated herself for asking.

As the plane landed, Sarah looked out the window at the Elkhorn Mountains to the south. They already had snow on their higher elevations. Then she leaned forward and glanced across the aisle, catching a glimpse of the Big Belts through the opposite window. She got a brief look at the flat hump of Hogback Mountain, its surface covered with only a light dusting.

As she entered the small terminal and looked around at the mounted heads of Montana's fauna on its walls, Sarah felt she had taken a step back in time. The entire complex would fit into one corner of New York's LaGuardia Airport. Nothing has changed, she thought. Helena remained as it was.

She took the single taxi parked at the curb to her parents' home on Eleventh Avenue, the stucco-covered house appearing smaller than she remembered. Dried-out leaves from the green ash tree at the side of the house littered the lawn, an indication of how ill her mother was. Pearl was as fastidious outside the house as in. Normally, at this time of year, the leaves would already have been raked into piles and packed into trash bags.

Nathan opened the door just as she was about to knock.

"Hi, dad." She kissed his cheek, covered in white stubble.

"It's been so long," he said, his voice breaking.

"Too long, I know," Sarah said, swallowing the lump that had formed in her throat. "Is mother . . . ?"

"She's still with us. Come on in."

She had expected her father to look older after six years, but his once erect bearing had given way to a round-shouldered sagging, as if the weight of his problems had grown too heavy for him. His walk, as he led her into the living room, was more of a shuffle. She placed her suitcase on a chair and slipped out of her coat. She took a look around the room. It was exactly as she remembered it, only smaller, more confining.

"I doubt Pearl will realize you're here," he said, apologetically. "She's been in so much pain the doctor had to increase her dose of morphine. I sometimes wish . . ." He cleared his throat. "Come, let's go see her."

Sarah followed him into the bedroom, noticing that the double bed had been replaced by twins. She was unprepared for what she saw. The emaciated figure bore little resemblance to her mother.

"Pearl," Nathan said, leaning over her. "Sarah is here." He waited a few moments. "I can't rouse her, Sarah. I'm sorry."

"That's all right. It's best that she sleep."

Pearl gave a soft moan. Sarah stepped hesitantly toward the bed. "Is she waking up?"

"No," said Nathan. "Sometimes the pain is so bad, she cries and moans in her sleep."

Tears welled in Sarah's eyes as her gaze moved from the cadaverous face in the bed to her father's face, its expression hidden as always by his dark glasses. Death's hand rested not only on her parents, but on what remained of her youth. Soon new people would inhabit this house and no vestige of her parents or of her childhood would remain.

"You must be hungry," her father said, distracting her from her morbid thoughts. "Let me make you something."

She followed him into the kitchen, noticing the coffee stains on the counter and the drain board. Dust had accumulated in the corners of the room. She knew Nathan tried his best to keep the house clean. Her mother had known that, too. Whenever Nathan had prepared anything in the kitchen, Pearl always came in after he left it, looked around with a frown, then silently tidied up after him.

"How is work going?" Nathan asked as he grilled cheese sandwiches.

"Same old thing. What about the store?"

"Same old thing," he smiled. Placing the sandwiches on plates, he poured coffee. "I just made it. Say when."

"That's fine."

"Bud Holliman, the fellow who's working for me, made an offer for the business last week."

"Are you going to take it?"

"I don't think so. I'm only fifty-five. What would I do with myself? Especially without your mother."

"You could move to New York and live with Roger and me. We have more than enough room."

"Me move to New York?" He laughed. "I'm a small town boy, Sarah. I know my way around, know my neighbors. I'd be lost in a big city."

She knew he was right.

"Still," she said, "how will you manage after . . .?"

"I'll have to, that's all. Same as I do now."

"But who will take you shopping? Who will write checks for you? How about finding someone to live here with you? Roger and I would pay—"

"I don't want a stranger living here. My neighbors will take me to the market when they go. And Bud down at the store can read me the mail and write my checks for me. Which reminds me. The mail's been piling up here for the past few weeks. You better take a look through it, make sure there are no bills that need to be paid." He stood up.

"Finish eating, dad. We can do it after."

"No, it'll only take a minute."

He left the room, reappearing moments later with a stack of mail.

Sarah sipped her coffee as she flipped through the envelopes, a manila-colored one catching her attention. It bore the return address of the Sisters of Charity in Leavenworth, Kansas, and was addressed to her mother.

Sarah quickly tore it open and removed a letter and another sealed envelope addressed to Pearl Schneider at Saint Joseph's orphanage, bearing the postmark: Butte, Montana, 1968. The letter read:

> *Dear Mrs. Rubin,*
>
> *My name is Sister Agatha and I'm with the Sisters of Charity. The oldest member of our order, Sister Margaret, died recently. While going through her things I came across this letter. I can only assume that Pearl Schneider was your maiden name and that you are the same person as Mrs. Pearl Rubin, to whom the manila envelope was addressed. I don't know how the letter came into Sister Margaret's hands nor why she never mailed it, whether she simply forgot or had misplaced it. The poor thing hadn't been well for many years, but I'm sure the good Lord is now taking care of His faithful servant.*

I can only apologize for the delay and hope that this letter finds its way to you.

"Any bills?" Nathan asked.

"Still looking. There's quite a little stack here," said Sarah, tearing open the envelope addressed to Pearl Schneider. The letter was written on expensive stationary and dated October 14th, 1968.

> *Dear Pearl,*
>
> *You don't know who I am but your mother, Hannah Schneider, was a dear friend. I'm now eighty-three and my arthritis has gotten so bad I've decided it's time I enter a home, much as I hate to. I was the person who took you to the nuns at Saint Joseph's. It's troubled me all through the years that you had no idea who your mother was. Since I don't know how much longer I have to live, I've decided to contact you. I'm enclosing a card with the address of the home I'll be going into. I can only hope that this letter will reach you and that you will come to see me.*
>
> > *Claire Stewart.*

"Find anything else?" Nathan asked.

"No. Nothing. Dad, would you like to go to the store with me to do some shopping?"

"I don't want to leave your mother alone. The car keys are on the counter."

"Well, let's see what you need and I'll pick it up for you."

Sarah's mind was in turmoil. She needed to get out of the house just to collect her thoughts. Hannah Schneider. So that was her grandmother. Right now it was just a name, but Pearl, she thought, hadn't even known that much about her mother. And if Claire Stewart, whoever she was, had died that was all Sarah would ever know. How ironic life was. If the nun, Sister Margaret, had mailed that letter in 1968, Pearl would have been able to solve the mystery herself. For Pearl it was too late. She would carry the mystery to her grave. Sarah could only hope that by some miracle it was not too late for her. If the Stewart woman was still alive, she would be eighty-nine.

Sarah stopped at the Edwards store on Montana Avenue. Even though it was getting dark and had grown cold, it was impossible for her to wait until tomorrow. She paused at the payphone outside the store, reached into her coat pocket and pulled out the card Claire Stewart had enclosed with her letter. Sarah dialed the number of the Evergreen Home in Butte.

"Do you have a resident named Claire Stewart?" she asked when a female voice came on the line.

"Yes, we do."

Sarah's heart raced.

"I'd like to visit tomorrow. Is there any special time I should come?"

"Any time you'd like. I can't recall anyone ever visiting Claire. You'll make her day."

"Is she still . . .?"

"Sharp as a tack. Well, most of the time."

"Thank you, I'll be there tomorrow."

Sarah then purchased the groceries and drove back to the house, fantasizing about what she would find out the next day. She visualized herself telling her mother who her parents were, why they had given her up. She would make it possible for Pearl to die at peace with herself. It was the greatest gift Sarah could give her, a gift that would bring them together.

While putting the groceries away, Sarah suddenly realized that the house was very still. She turned on the light in the hallway and tiptoed to the bedroom. Nathan was sitting next to the bed, holding Pearl's hand.

"I didn't hear you come in," he said, smiling.

Sarah then noticed a gold locket on a chain around her mother's neck.

"I'd forgotten mother's locket," she said.

"Pearl told me it belonged to her mother."

"I thought she didn't know who her mother was."

"The name Hannah is engraved on it. She assumed that was her mother's name. I can't remember exactly how the locket came to be in Pearl's possession."

So Pearl knew her mother's name. Another mystery, Sarah thought, looking closely at her mother.

"Your mother's hand is so cold," Nathan said.

"I think she's gone," Sarah said haltingly, as she reached for her father's hand.

Nathan sighed and removed his dark glasses. Sobbing, he pressed his face into the quilt.

"I'm sorry, dad," she murmured.

"You'd better call the doctor," he said as he regained his composure. "His number is next to the phone. Doctor Malkin. He took over Doctor Davis' practice when Davis retired."

"Dad," Sarah asked quietly. "Do you think it would be all right if I wore mother's locket?"

"I think she would have liked that," he replied.

Sarah reached down and gently unlatched the fine gold chain. The locket rested in her hand as lightly as if it were a piece of fluff.

■■■

Nathan was sitting at the kitchen table with his coffee as the first dawn light filtered through the window. Sarah joined him, patting his shoulder before she sat down.

She had been awake most of the night, wondering how her father was faring. More than once she found herself fingering the locket, which she now wore, trying to chase the image of her mother in death from her mind and replace it with the way she remembered her.

"The coffee is hot, Sarah. Shall I make you some toast?"

"I'll just take some coffee. Were you able to sleep?"

"Not really."

"I guess it wasn't a good night for either of us."

"Well, at least her suffering is over. But I'll miss her."

"What will you do today?" Sarah asked.

"I'll probably head over to the store. Make sure Bud hasn't driven the business into the ground."

"Would you like me to shave you?"

He ran his hand across his face. "No, I'll do it."

"If you're going to the store maybe I'll take the car today. I'll be back by dinnertime."

"That's fine. Just do whatever you have to do."

"I should give Roger a call, too, and let him know what's happened."

While Nathan was in the bathroom, Sarah first called her office.

"It's Mrs. Rubin, Mandy. How is everything?"

"Nothing that can't wait for you to get back. How is your mother doing?"

"She passed away last night."

"Oh, I'm so sorry."

"Thank you, Mandy. I'll let you know when I'll be back. Can you transfer me to Mr. Rubin's line?"

Moments later, she heard Roger's voice. "Hi, it's me," she said.

"It's good to hear you. I was getting worried."

"Mother died last night."

He paused for a few moments. "I'm sorry, Sarah. At least you were there. How's your father taking it?"

"It's hard to tell. As well as can be expected."

"And the funeral?"

"She'll be cremated tomorrow. It's what she wanted."

"Do you have any idea when you'll be back?"

"I'm not sure. I'll have to see how things go."

"And how are you?"

"I'm okay."

"Don't worry about anything at work. It can all wait. I miss you, Sarah."

46

It was shortly after noon when Sarah stopped at a service station after taking the Butte turnoff. She remembered that Nathan hadn't asked her where she was going. He hasn't changed, she thought. Even when she was a teenager, he'd never ask. Back then she thought he didn't care, but now she wondered if that was the case. It was always her mother who asked and Sarah had resented her for it. Poor Pearl, she thought, she couldn't win.

After getting gas, Sarah asked the attendant for directions to the Evergreen Home. Ten minutes later, she pulled up in front of a three-storey, beige-colored building that took up much of its block. She shivered when she got out of the car, surprised at how much colder it was in Butte.

"Can I help you? said an officious woman sitting at a desk in a corner of the lobby.

"I'm here to see Claire Stewart."

The woman checked a register. "She's in room 207. Everyone has already had lunch so she's probably in the solarium. That's on the third floor. There's an elevator over there."

Light streamed in through large glass panes as Sarah got off the elevator.

There were about a dozen men and women in the room, some dozing in their chairs, one or two reading, and a few playing board games.

"Who are you looking for?" asked a young, black-haired woman in a white skirt and blue-striped blouse.

"Claire Stewart."

The woman looked surprised. "The duchess? Really? I'll take you over to her."

"Did you say the duchess?"

"Well, that's what we call her. Like she's royalty."

Claire Stewart was sitting in a leather chair facing a window, her snow-white hair fashionably coiffed. Bifocals were perched on her nose. Sarah noticed that she was reading *Mademoiselle*. The old woman's face was a mass of wrinkles but her blue eyes were clear and alert, appraising in their look as she turned to face Sarah.

"I've brought you a visitor, Claire," said the black-haired woman.

"I wasn't expecting anyone," she said, her voice surprisingly youthful.

"I'm Sarah Rubin," Sarah said. "Pearl's daughter."

There was a moment of incomprehension on her face, then a flash of awareness.

"Pearl Schneider was my mother's maiden name. Her married name was Rubin."

"Baby Pearl has a daughter your age? I can't believe it. That makes you Hannah's granddaughter." She studied Sarah's face and nodded. "You have Hannah's mouth, I can see that now. I wrote to your mother years ago and asked her to come see me, but she never did."

"She died yesterday, Miss Stewart," Sarah said. "I'm afraid she never received your letter."

After Sarah's explanation, Claire Stewart shook her head. "Nuns," she said. "I knew they weren't to be trusted. Why don't we go back to my room to talk. These old fogies here will be falling out of their chairs trying to eavesdrop on us. I'd be all right if it wasn't for this arthritis," she complained. As she reached for her cane, Sarah noticed the deformed joints of her hands for the first time.

"I can bring a wheelchair for you," said the aide, coming over.

"If I want a wheelchair I'll ask for it, thank you."

"Do you enjoy reading *Mademoiselle?*" Sarah asked as they walked slowly toward the elevator, Claire leaning heavily on her arm.

"I like keeping up with fashions. I may be old but I'm not planted yet."

Sarah laughed. "Far from it, I'd say."

"Make yourself comfortable," said Claire when they got to her room. "Should I have them bring us some tea?"

"I think I'd just like to talk."

"I want you to know how badly I feel," she said, "that I didn't make contact with your mother sooner. I should have."

"I'm not sure I understand why you didn't."

"Your mother wasn't conceived in a way that's easy to talk about. Let me start at the beginning and tell you how I first came to know your grandmother, Hannah. Claire took a deep breath.

Her eyes misted over during the telling. When she had finished, she removed her glasses. "Pass me a Kleenex from the table, would you, dear?" She dabbed at her eyes and smiled self-consciously. "I always loved her, right up until the end."

Sarah could only stare with amazement. I can't believe it, she thought.

"That locket you're wearing," Claire said, leaning forward. "Where did you get it?"

"It was my mother's. My father said he didn't know where she got it."

"Well, I gave it to Hannah as a Christmas gift and when I took Pearl to the orphanage in Helena, I told the nuns to keep it for her."

Claire leaned back in her chair, her eyes suddenly lustreless. She now looked as old as her years.

"I'm sorry if I've tired you," Sarah said, reaching across the space between them and placing her hand on Claire's arm. She glanced at her watch, surprised to see it was past four o'clock. "I'm sorry, but I promised my father I'd be back for dinner."

"When are you going back to New York?"

"I haven't decided yet."

Sarah stood up and kissed Claire's cheek. "I'll be back," she said.

47

Nathan was sitting in the dark when Sarah walked in.

"Sorry I'm a little late," she said, turning on the light. "I hope you haven't eaten."

"No, I only got in about a half-hour ago. I was just waiting for you. Did you have a nice day?"

"I visited an old friend," she said. "How was everything at the store?"

"Bud seems to have a handle on it. Still, it was good to be back. Takes my mind off things."

"Well, let me get some dinner going," Sarah said, remembering how much Nathan liked fried chicken.

In the kitchen she thought about all that Claire Stewart had told her, trying to remember every detail. It's like a Greek tragedy, she thought. So much suffering and all undeserved.

"I spoke to the funeral home this afternoon," Nathan said at dinner. "The service will be at ten tomorrow morning."

"Will anyone else be there?"

"A few of the neighbors perhaps. Some of your mother's co-workers. We have no other family."

No family, Sarah thought. It was true. She remembered being unhappy about that when she was a child. The children at school had talked of uncles, aunts and cousins. Sarah had swallowed her envy and made books her family.

"The chicken's delicious," said Nathan, interrupting her thoughts.

"Let me know if there's anything else you'd like. I never get the chance to cook at home. It seems like we're always eating out."

"You know I'll eat most anything. Are you planning to head back home right after the funeral?"

"Roger and my job can get along without me for a while."

■■■

The next day after the funeral, the thought of returning to New York made her uncomfortable. She did not want to confront Roger, her job, her analyst, and she didn't want to have to decide what to do about the pregnancy. Leaving all that behind, even temporarily, had given her a sense of relief. It's bizarre, she thought, but coping with Pearl's death and Nathan's mourning was much easier than facing what awaited her.

"It feels like snow coming," said Nathan, as they left the funeral home.

Sarah looked up at the steely grey sky. "I can't tell. Would you like to go home or to the store?"

"You might as well drive me to the store."

Nathan broke the silence between them in the car.

"I don't know if you realize how strong a woman your mother was," he said. "She had to cope with so much, but she never complained. I only hope I made her half as happy as she made me."

"Come meet Bud," he said, as they parked in front of the store.

Bud, a pleasant young man with sandy hair and wire-rimmed glasses, greeted them warmly and shook hands with Sarah. She liked him immediately. I'll have to have a talk with him about my father before I go back to New York, she thought. "You know, dad," she said, looking in Bud's direction, "I think it would be a good idea for me to have Bud's address and phone number, too."

"My daughter is a worrier," said Nathan.

"I'll be home for dinner," she said. "Nice to have met you, Bud."

48

It was midafternoon when Sarah, carrying two bottles of sherry in her bag, and a handful of magazines, entered the solarium.

"Are you looking for Claire?" asked the dark-haired aide. "She's not feeling well today. Didn't even want her lunch."

Sarah quickly headed down to the second floor. She knocked on Claire's door but there was no reply. "Claire?" she called softly, pushing the door open.

Claire was sitting in bed, pillows propped behind her.

"I didn't mean to wake you," said Sarah.

"I wasn't asleep. I just didn't want the aides bothering me."

"I hear you're not feeling well."

"All that talking about the past must have worn me out."

"I brought you something that might make you feel better." Sarah held up the bottles of sherry.

"Oh, you are a dear. I feel better already. There are paper cups in the bathroom."

"I brought you these, too," she said, placing the magazines on a table near the bed.

"You're very kind. Pull a chair here next to me." She raised her cup to Sarah. "To your health."

"And yours," said Sarah, smiling.

"You had Pearl's funeral this morning?"

"Yes."

Claire sipped her sherry for a few moments. "I have a question for you. You told me yesterday you'd been married for six years. Did you never think of having children?"

"No, I never did. But you've been so forthcoming with me, I'll let you in on a secret. I'm pregnant."

"That's wonderful. But you don't look happy about it."

Sarah shook her head. "My husband doesn't even know. I'm still not sure if I'm going to keep it."

The old woman's smile faded.

"It's difficult to explain," Sarah said. "I'm not sure I understand it myself. I'm beginning to wonder if I'm capable of happiness."

Claire slowly placed her cup on the night table. "I'm very tired all of a sudden, Sarah. You don't mind? I can't tell you how much I appreciate your coming."

"I'll let you nap. And I'll talk to you again before I go back to New York."

■■■

"Whatever you're making smells delicious," Sarah said as she arrived home.

"I only made the soup," her father replied. "But this platter on the stove with the cover on it?" He tapped it with his finger. "Bud just brought these steaks over. He grilled them and they're still warm."

"That was sweet of him."

"Well, he went hunting last weekend and didn't want you to leave Montana without having an elk steak."

"Good soup," Sarah said, tasting a spoonful.

"In that case, let's eat. Did you visit your friend today?"

"I did." Wouldn't he be surprised, she thought, to know that my friend, as he calls her, is eight-nine years old? "And I decided, too, that much as I hate to leave you, it's time I get back home."

"And much as I hate to see you go, I agree. You have a lot of responsibilities back there."

"Tell Bud the steaks are delicious," she said.

"Speaking of Bud, I wanted to ask you something. He and his wife live in a double-wide in the scratchgravels. It's all they can afford. And they have a new baby. He's not exactly getting rich working for me. Drives an old clunker that's always in need of repairs. What would you say to my giving Bud your mother's car?"

"That's very generous, dad."

"Well, he's been a big help to me. Taking care of the store by himself all those weeks when Pearl was sick. I just feel I should do something for him."

"If that's what you want to do, that's great."

He laughed. "I wish I could see his face when I tell him."

Sarah thought of the Mercedes languishing in a Manhattan garage. Their monthly rental for the space was probably more than Bud's salary. And for what? The old anger toward her husband returned.

Sarah managed to reserve the last seat on the following morning's first flight out of Helena and she also arranged to have a taxi pick her up.

The next morning, after a quick breakfast, Sarah embraced her father as the cab waited at the curb, the vapor of its exhaust curling up into the frigid morning air.

"You take good care of yourself and call me if there's anything you need."

"Let's not let another six years go by without seeing one another," he said. "Maybe I'll surprise you and visit you in the big city."

She waved to him from the taxi window, forgetting for a moment that he couldn't see her. Feeling the urge to cry, she quickly removed her sunglasses from her pocketbook and put them on.

After she had checked in, Sarah had enough time to make a phone call. When Evergreen's receptionist answered, Sarah asked for Claire.

"I'm sorry," she said. "Miss Stewart passed away last night."

49

It was after eight in the evening when Sarah quietly opened the door to their apartment. Roger was asleep on the sofa, a magazine on his lap and a glass with melting ice cubes on the table next to him. Sarah hung her coat in the closet and tip-toed into the bedroom. Returning to the living room, she stood motionless in the doorway observing her husband. She then walked slowly past him into the kitchen and opened the refrigerator. As usual, very little. Annoyed, Sarah filled a glass with water at the sink.

"Sarah?"

She whirled around to find Roger standing behind her, blinking in the bright light.

"Why didn't you let me know you were coming?"

"I didn't know myself until last night."

He put his arms around her, but Sarah turned her cheek as he tried to kiss her.

"It's good to have you home. You must be exhausted."

"I'm pretty tired."

"How's your father doing?"

"Doing better than I thought."

"You think he'll be okay by himself?"

She shrugged. "I think he'll manage. He gets around pretty well."

"And how are you doing? You seem—strange."

"I'm all right. How are things here?"

"Very good actually. Listen, you must be starved. There's not much in the house, but we can head over to Romano's. Or I can send for Chinese."

"I'm not very hungry. Do we have any sherry?"

"Let me take a look." He went to the living room and opened the liquor cabinet. "Here's a bottle. I didn't know you liked sherry."

"Me either."

He poured her a glass and they sat down, Roger on the sofa and Sarah in a chair facing him.

"So you say everything is going well?"

"Better than well. I have a surprise." He dashed off to the study, returning with a small packet. "Two tickets to Hawaii."

"What?"

"Remember before you left I mentioned we were wooing Kreutzer, the big brewing company? I got the account. Phillips was so pleased he gave me a fat bonus and told me to take you to Hawaii for a week when you got back. It'll do us both good, Sarah. Sunshine, beaches, the Pacific."

"I'm not going to Hawaii with you, Roger."

"What do you mean?"

"There's a lot we have to talk about."

"Well, I'm all ears."

"Being away gave me the chance to do a lot of thinking. I've made some decisions."

"Maybe I'd better get a drink," he said, eyeing her nervously. He picked up his glass, added ice cubes, and poured two fingers of scotch from the bottle of Chivas sitting on the bar.

"I'm giving notice as soon as I return to the office," Sarah said.

"You've been so successful, you're heading for—"

"I don't care. I'm quitting. I only joined Grayson out of fear."

"I don't understand what you mean when you say you went to work for the agency out of fear. Fear of what?"

"Fear of failure," she snapped. "Fear of not being able to make it as a writer. Fear of living poor. Well, after eight years at Grayson, I'd rather try and fail, and I'd rather live poor, than go on the way I have."

"I thought you were happy with the way you were living."

"You're the one who's happy. I'm not saying you shouldn't be happy with your work. I'm glad you are. And I'm not blaming you for my being at Grayson. You didn't twist my arm. If I wasn't such a coward I would have been gone a long time ago."

"If leaving Grayson will make you happy, I say by all means, do it. If I had known all this I would have encouraged you to leave."

"It wasn't so simple. I had to know I was pulling my weight, doing my share, whatever you want to call it. I asked myself, how can I go off and do what I want to do if there's as much chance of my failing as succeeding? Is that fair to Roger? To put all the responsibility for supporting us on his shoulders?"

"You know it's not necessary for you to work."

"You're talking about reality. I'm talking about what I was feeling."

"Is that it then? Is that all that's troubling you? My God, Sarah, the solution is easy. You'll just go in and give your notice. Then you can write. There'll be nothing to stop you."

She took a sip of sherry and looked over at him. "That's not all. I'm not sure we're right for each other."

"How can you say that?" Roger said, looking as if she had slapped him. "We've been happy together for six years. At least I thought we were happy. I love you. During the day I dream of being next to you in bed at night. When I wake up in the morning and you're lying there with your head on my chest I think of how lucky I am. And now, all of a sudden, we're not right for one another! Did you find someone else? An old beau I didn't know about? Did he give you that locket?"

"My mother was wearing this locket when she died."

"Goddammit, Sarah, I don't know what to think."

"Roger, when I first met you you told me you'd sailed to Europe on a freighter and crewed on a yacht for two years. I thought, wow, here's an interesting guy. Was I so off the mark? Did you only see the inside of a boat's galley? I never hear you talk about anything you learned. Buying toys that suit your fancy, like that Mercedes we never use, seems to be the only thing that gives you plea-sure. Have you read a book in the past year? Any book? Do you ever consider travelling to places that aren't swarming with tourists? Or are you so spoiled you can only go on luxury cruises where people take care of you?"

"Why are so angry? What have I done except try to be a good husband? I was under the impression this apartment, our car, and everything else we own is for us. Just because you're frustrated, don't take it out on me. And don't forget, we went together for two years before we married. Are you going to tell me now you didn't know who you were marrying?"

She shook her head. "No, you didn't deceive me. I deceived me."

"Maybe you should have hung around Columbia for a few more years. You might have met the aesthete you seem to be craving." He stood up, clenching his fists.

He stalked out of the room without another word. She heard the hall closet door open and close and a moment later the apartment door slammed behind him.

50

Sarah slept fitfully, waking at every sound, thinking it might be Roger returning. She found herself worrying about him, hoping she hadn't pushed him to do something foolish. But Roger wasn't the type to do anything stupid, she tried to reassure herself. In six years of marriage, this was the first real discord between them.

Finally, her time sense distorted by jet lag, Sarah crawled out of bed at five. She showered and sat in front of her mirror, trying to disguise the deep shadows under her eyes as she applied makeup. She then dressed for work, the only place she could think of where Roger might be.

Shivering in the bitterly cold morning air, Sarah realized she hadn't eaten in almost twenty-four hours. She stopped at a Greek diner for breakfast and, warmed by the food and hot coffee, she walked to work. Her fatigue, for the moment at least, had dissipated.

She arrived at Grayson's before eight. Mandy, her secretary, would not arrive for another hour. Debating with herself, she took the elevator up to Roger's office. No one was there, so she quietly opened his door. He was lying on the sofa, one arm across his face. Sarah closed the door behind her and sat down on the edge of the sofa. He opened his eyes, which were as bloodshot as hers had been.

"I'm sorry," Sarah said softly. "I started out meaning to tell you what was troubling me, not to attack you the way I did."

He took her hand and sat up. "Let's get out of here," he said. "Take the day off."

"Have you had breakfast?" he asked, as they left the building.

"Yes, but I could use some more coffee."

They soon found a quiet booth at the rear of a coffee shop on Second Avenue.

"It's strange to see you unshaven on a work day. I like it. Makes you look roguish."

"I'll have to do it more often then. I did a lot of thinking last night about everything you said."

"A lot of it was unfair. You were right when you said I was taking my frustration out on you."

"Yeah, but a lot of what you said was pretty accurate. I've been too preoccupied with work, not enough with our life together. Twenty years from now who'll care about an advertising campaign for beer? I've been corrupted by money."

"I'm not blameless on that score."

"But you've been aware it's not what you wanted. I remember telling you that you could still write even though you worked at Grayson. I knew better. I knew how little time the job left me, how all-consuming it was. Fear of losing an account to a rival agency always hangs over you. So why did I lie? I know now it was pure selfishness on my part. I wanted you near me because I was falling in love with you."

"You didn't twist my arm. I barely earned enough to support myself until I came to Grayson."

"But who knows if that would always have been the case? You were having your work published even while you were a student. Success may have been waiting for you. It was wrong of me to lure you away."

His toast and coffee grew cold as he talked. Sarah couldn't remember a time when he had opened up like this. Maybe this is a new experience for both of us, she thought.

"And believe it or not, Sarah, I used to read. I'm not a total ignoramus. Somehow that fell by the wayside, too."

"Just because I'm not happy being at Grayson doesn't mean you have to dislike your work. We both know how good you are at what you do."

"You're good at it, too. But you still don't want it."

"That's right. But you're not me. Maybe you need more of a balance in your life, but who the hell am I to give advice? I'm only just beginning to learn all this."

"Did your shrink help you come to these realizations?"

"To some extent, I think. That, and being back home. In Montana, I mean. My childhood home. Talking to people there, my father and an old woman named Claire. I'll tell you about her some day." She sipped her coffee, then placed the cup on the table. "Doctor Markham is probably wondering what happened to me."

"Are you going to continue seeing him?"

"I don't know."

"So what comes now, Sarah?"

"I'm going to see Phillips tomorrow and give my notice."

Roger nodded. "I wasn't expecting you to change your mind."

"Maybe I'm deluding myself. Maybe whatever spark of writing talent I had got extinguished."

"You'll find it again."

"If I'm going to make a serious effort, there can't be any distractions."

"Including me?"

"Including you. I have to find a place where I can get away. I don't want a phone ringing or errands that need doing."

Roger rubbed the bristles on his chin. "My sister, Marjorie, you remember her? You met her once years ago."

"The one married to the record company guy?"

"Right. I haven't spoken to her in almost a year. They have a house on Martha's Vineyard that they use on weekends during the summer. Otherwise it just sits there. Want me to ask her about it?"

"You don't mind?"

"I'll give her a call tomorrow. But what about us?"

"I want some time to myself."

"I don't know where that leaves me."

"We'll have to wait and see. I'm not trying to be difficult, just honest. And there's something else I have to talk to you about. Let's go back to the apartment."

"I'm pregnant," she said quietly, as they relaxed on the sofa. "I found out just before I left for Montana. I'm a little more than two months along."

"That's great," he said, sitting up with a broad smile on his face.

"Is it?"

"I think it is. Isn't it?" he said, suddenly wary.

"The timing isn't the best. Not with everything that's happening."

"You're not thinking of doing anything, are you?"

"When I first found out, I thought about it. But now . . ."

"Doesn't it matter that I want a child with you?"

"Since when? I can't remember you ever bringing the subject up."

"I thought you didn't want children. That's why I never said anything."

She shook her head. "And I thought it was you. God, we're no good at communication."

"I guess you're right. But, Sarah, please—I want you to have it."

"It isn't just your Catholicism talking, is it, Roger?"

"You know what I think about religion."

"Sometimes things get rooted so deeply in us, we're not even aware they're influencing us."

"All I know is that I love you and I want this child. I can't make it any clearer than that."

"I just wanted to be sure how you felt."

She stood up and stretched. "I'm going to take a nap. I don't think I slept at all last night."

"That makes two of us."

"Are you going to join me?"

She held out her hand. Moments later they were in each other's arms.

51

Sarah's heart was pounding and her hands shaking as she stepped into the hallway after giving Jordan Phillips her notice. Why is it always so hard for me to say what I want? she wondered. Well, at least she had done it without torturing herself for weeks or months. It's an improvement, she thought.

She stopped at the water cooler, trying to control her shaking hand as she drank. When she got to her office she asked Mandy to come in. Her pencil poised over a pad, her secretary looked expectantly at Sarah.

"I just came from Jordan Phillips' office," said Sarah. "There's no easy way for me to tell you this, Mandy. I've given my notice."

"No," Mandy said, her arms dropping to her sides. "Why?"

"There are other things I want to do. Phillips will be sending someone over to take charge of the Bernini account. I'm sure whoever it is will be as happy with your work as I am."

"I wish you weren't leaving," Mandy said, her voice breaking. She turned and left, closing the door quietly behind her.

The flashing light on her phone indicated a call coming in. Sarah quickly picked it up.

"You sure took the wind out of Phillips' sails," Roger said. "He wanted to know if things were okay between us. You should have heard his questions. Did I put you up to it because I didn't want you to work anymore? Were you ill? Were you pregnant? I didn't answer that one. Was I planning to leave, too? Did we have better offers from a competitor? On and on."

"I just told Mandy. She was pretty upset. It seems like whenever I want to do something for myself everyone gets upset."

"So how do you feel now that you've taken the bull by the horns?"

"It hasn't sunk in yet, but I feel better about myself."

"I called Marjorie about the Vineyard house and she was pleased. She said they'd feel much better knowing someone was living there. We'll have to get the water turned on and the phone hooked up, but otherwise it's fit for habitation. She gave me the driving directions. Oh, and we have to cover the utilities."

"That was generous."

"And one final piece of news. No more Mercedes."

"What do you mean?"

"I sold it to John Muller this morning. You know John. Art Department."

"You didn't have to do that on my account."

"John's always wanted one. It was a perfect fit."

"Maybe you should have waited. Now we'll have to rent a car to get to Martha's Vineyard."

"I wanted to talk to you about that. Why don't we take the Mercedes money and get two inexpensive cars? Then you'll have one to get around in on the island and I'll keep the other down here."

"That might make sense."

"When would you like to go?"

"My last day at Grayson is the twenty-third. Any time after that."

"Why don't we spend Thanksgiving there? We'll take both cars and then I'll drive back and you can start working."

"That sounds like a good plan."

52

After four months on the island, Sarah was enough of a regular to the people working the cash registers at the Oak Bluffs Supermarket for them to inquire how she was doing out in the wilds of West Tisbury. "Better load up today," one said as he stocked the shelves with bread and muffins. "That nor'easter should hit by this evening."

Out in the parking lot, Sarah stowed her groceries in the trunk of her Chevy Caprice. It still amused her when she thought of their 'his' and 'hers' Caprices.

Marjorie's house was on a dirt road, twelve miles from the Vineyard Haven and Oak Bluffs stores. Sarah had fallen in love with the cottage the moment she saw it. Encased in a shell of grey, weathered shingles, it seemed to grow directly out of the brush-covered sandy soil. Sarah had set up her typewriter on a desk in one of the three bedrooms.

The window to the side of the desk looked out on a thicket of stunted trees and thorn bushes. There were three other houses scattered over the half-mile of road beyond her house, the last one perched on a low-lying knoll at the point where the road dead-ended. None of the houses were occupied in the off-season. Sarah never saw another car or person until she get onto the paved road that led to Vineyard Haven.

She had become enamored of the island even before setting foot on it. From the moment the Islander shattered the winter silence of Woods Hole with a horn blast as it pulled away from the dock, she felt a thrill of anticipation. Sarah had stood shivering on the ferry's rear deck and watched the shoreline receding as the boat's wake stretched out like a frothy ribbon. Gulls hovered overhead, swooping low over the sea in search of food.

The wind had picked up as the boat made its way out into the Sound. "I'm freezing," Roger said, "let's go inside."

They found a booth and sat drinking coffee as they stared out at the water. "I can't believe we're doing this," Roger had said.

They had been out on the water for only a half-hour when a spit of land appeared off their starboard side. Sarah's excitement grew as the first houses appeared.

"Look," she said, pointing to a lighthouse. "Isn't this wonderful?"

As the ferry entered the slip at Vineyard Haven, Sarah and Roger had followed the other passengers down metal stairs to the car storage deck. Roger had left his Caprice in the Woods Hole lot for his return the next day and they had driven Sarah's onto the ferry.

A half-dozen shivering people, hands thrust deeply into their jacket pockets, waited on the dock to greet foot passengers. Sarah drove off the ferry to an intersection where signs indicated the road to Chilmark and West Tisbury. Following the directions Marjorie had given them, they had found the dirt road to the house.

"It's so isolated," Roger had said.

"Oh, Roger, it's lovely." She had rolled her window down and breathed in the salt air. "In fact, it's heaven."

Roger rolled his eyes and she laughed.

■■■

During the months on the island Sarah had given little if any thought to her relationship with Roger. Her book had taken over her life and little else mattered. There had to be resolution in the world she had created before she could deal with anything else. She had been distracted every time he called and she knew he picked up on it. She tried to be polite when he spoke of his work, but the world of writing copy for media commercials and planning campaigns for influencing consumers was so far removed from her present reality she could scarcely believe she had once been a part of it. Even when he told her he loved her and missed her, she couldn't bring herself to reply in kind.

■■■

The nor'easter hit that evening with a fury. It was a perfect accompaniment to the point she had reached in her story, a time when characters' lives were shattered due to forces beyond their control. During the night the windows rattled in their frames and Sarah left her bed more than once to peer into the blackness, wondering how the house could withstand the wind. Sleet slashed like saber cuts across the window panes.

It wasn't until almost four that the wind began to subside and Sarah fell into a deep sleep. When she awoke, an hour later than her customary seven o'clock, she discovered a white world outside the cottage. Almost a foot of wet snow had come down, burying scrub pines and thorn bushes. She stood at the window with her coffee cup, her thoughts gradually turning inward. The snow was forgotten as she hurried to her typewriter.

53

Spring came slowly to the island. Flowers appeared to cower under the stiff breezes sweeping in from the ocean. But that all changed by mid-May. Temperatures moderated, skies were clear more often than not, and bright sunshine acted as a beacon to islanders and tourists as they flocked to the beach at Oak Bluffs and the secluded coves of the Vineyard.

Sarah, however, paid little attention to the world outside her cottage. The end of her book was in sight, but the road which until now had led her unfailingly toward the finish had suddenly become obscured. Get away from it for a while, she told herself. She decided to take a walk, following the dirt road running past her house.

Sarah felt fatigued after she had gone about a mile. Her pregnancy was now difficult to ignore. Not only did the added weight make her tire more easily, but the baby was moving more. There were times when a sudden kick took her breath away.

She turned back to the house, and as she opened the door she realized that Roger hadn't called her that weekend. Every Sunday, like clockwork, the phone rang in the early evening. But distance between them was now more than geographical. It was as if they no longer knew what to say to one another. Even

Roger's customary terms of endearment had fallen by the wayside. "Take care," they each said when their brief conversation was over.

Not once in her six months on the island had Sarah placed a call to New York. She had, in fact, never made a call to anyone. But at nine o'clock on a Tuesday evening she picked up the phone and dialed. She let the phone ring seven or eight times but there was no answer. At eleven, just before going to sleep, she tried again. Still no answer.

A nagging thought came to her as she tried to get comfortable. What if Roger had tired of their arrangement? It was, after all, not his idea and he was a man used to getting what he wanted. They hadn't seen one another in six months. Roger was young, handsome, and successful, attributes that would make him irresistible to any number of attractive women in Manhattan. For the first time she had to face the fact that Roger might have met someone. If that were the case, what would she do? She had taken him for granted, counting on his devotion even while making it clear that she did not want to see him, at least not until the first draft of her book was completed.

The following morning she got ready for her trip to Doctor Carmody in Falmouth, the doctor who was looking after her. She'd have to catch the eight o'clock ferry to get there in time. She hesitated at the door, debating whether to try Roger again. She would try him at work in the afternoon, she decided.

It was mild enough for Sarah to sit out on the deck. Even with the weather's change for the better, she spent so little time outdoors that this brief interlude was a treat. She watched as seagulls swooped down to take crackers from the out-stretched hand of a young girl. The child squealed with delight each time, and Sarah's thoughts turned to the child she carried.

Her obstetrician confirmed that everything was fine and said she'd have to see him weekly now. "I know it's a hassle," he said, cutting off her protest, "but it's really important."

Sarah decided to do her shopping in Falmouth before heading back. Stores she'd never been in and lunch in a restaurant near the harbor made it seem as if she was on vacation. As she sat on the Islander's deck on the return to Vineyard Haven, the elusive ending of her novel suddenly came in a flash. She could hardly wait to get home.

Quickly putting away her groceries, Sarah sat down at her typewriter and worked steadily for the rest of the day. When she finally looked up, it was past eight o'clock. She had been in her chair for four hours. The baby gave several sharp kicks, which brought Sarah to her feet.

Because it was so late, Sarah opted for only a sandwich and salad. As she ate, she stole glances at the clock on the kitchen wall. It was now past nine. She put the sandwich down and headed for the phone. Leaning against the counter, she dialed and waited. Roger answered on the fifth ring.

"Oh, it's you," he said, surprised.

"Are you all right?"

"You're not in labor, are you?"

"No, the doctor says there's still a month to go."

Silence hung between them.

"You didn't call last weekend. I tried to reach you last night but you weren't in."

"I should have called to let you know I was going fishing."

"Fishing?"

He laughed. "Hey, the weather has been so good that even Phillips couldn't stand being in the office. He asked me to join him in Block Island and we spent almost a week on his boat. Caught more fish than we could eat."

Sarah was relieved. "That's great. I'm glad you had a good time."

"To be honest, I think the only reason he asked me along was to talk about you. He knows about the pregnancy, of course, but he wanted to sound me out about your coming back to Grayson's after the baby is born. He's tried two replacements on the accounts you handled and isn't pleased. I told him there was no possibility, which didn't make him happy.

"I just got back today. You caught me getting out of the shower. It's nice to know you're thinking about me."

"Well, I'm close to finishing the first draft and I'll even have time to begin my revising while waiting for the baby."

"Listen, I'm pleased that your work is going well, but I'm mostly pleased that you'll be coming home soon. You know, asphalt streets, marble floors in the lobby, parquet floors in your apartment—no dirt roads, wood floors, seagulls. I don't know how happy—or unhappy—that makes you."

"I'm looking forward to coming home," Sarah replied, surprising herself.

54

Sarah woke up early the next morning with the final paragraphs flowing through her mind. Switching on the bedside lamp, she picked up her pad and pen and wrote quickly, trying to get the words down before they disappeared. She read them aloud, decided she liked the sound of what she had written, and slipped out of bed. It was a little past five and dawn was just breaking.

She opened the front door and breathed deeply. Before the morning was out the first draft of her novel would be complete.

Then comes the hard part, she thought, as she fixed coffee. The art of writing is rewriting, she had once read. Art it might be, but she remembered that it was also damn hard work. She sat down at her typewriter and picked up the stack of papers from the desk, unable to believe that so many words filling so many pages had poured out of her imagination. She pounded away for ten minutes, weighing each word as it appeared on paper. "The end," she said aloud, sitting back in her chair. She felt a sudden emptiness, as if all her vitality had drained away, but a sharp kick from within served as a reminder that another birth was imminent.

■■■

"Sounds like your membranes have ruptured," Doctor Carmody said on the phone. "Labor will probably begin sometime today or tomorrow, but you'd better come in today. Just go to the hospital and ask them to call me. I'll meet you there."

Sarah debated calling Roger, then decided to call him from the hospital. By the time she got there, she was having contractions every ten minutes.

"It's a good thing you came in," the obstetrician said. "You're four centimeters dilated."

Sarah called Roger from the labor room.

"I'm leaving right now," he said nervously.

"Don't rush. I'm not going anywhere."

At nine that evening, the nurses wheeled Sarah into the delivery room.

"You're speedy," one said. "It's a fast labor for a first baby."

Trying to prepare for her next contraction, Sarah gripped the handles on the table. "Speedy? It feels like it's taking forever."

"Doctor Carmody just arrived," one of the nurses said. "He's got to change into scrubs. Try not to push."

"How are you doing?" the doctor asked as he appeared at the foot of the table. "Just take a deep breath, push hard, and hold it as long as you can."

Sarah gasped for breath as she followed his instructions.

"Here's your daughter," said Doctor Carmody, only moments later as he held the squalling infant up for Sarah to see.

"That's some headful of hair," said a nurse. "I'll clean her up and then you can hold her."

Sarah stared in puzzlement at the bundle resting in the crook of her arm, amazed that this living creature had actually emerged from her womb. At that moment, Roger, dressed in blue scrubs, cap and mask, followed a nurse into the delivery room. He stroked her forehead as Sarah looked up into familiar blue eyes.

"Say hello to your daughter."

"You knew it was a girl all along, didn't you?"

"I'd like to call her Hannah," said Sarah.

"It's a nice name. I like it."

"I can't keep my eyes open," Sarah said, feeling suddenly sleepy.

"I'll see you in the morning."

"I love you" seemed to come from far away, as if she was dreaming the words.

■ ■ ■

The cottage looked very different from the way Roger remembered the previous November. Perennials around the house were blooming and the hum of bees drowned out the distant cries of gulls.

He had spent the previous two nights in a motel in Falmouth to be near Sarah. This morning he had taken the ferry to the island to gather up her belongings. Then he would head back to Falmouth to pick up his wife and daughter at the hospital for the drive back to the city. Stepping into the quiet house, empty for two days, he was aware of Sarah's presence everywhere. An uneaten sandwich sat in its plate on the kitchen table. He smelled the faint aroma of her cologne as he stripped the sheets and pillowcase from the bed. Roger gathered up the linens and towels, stuffed them into the washer and started the cycle. He removed Sarah's clothes from the closet and drawers and packed them. He'd wait until the washer and dryer had completed their tasks, then load Sarah's suitcase and typewriter in the car.

Wandering through the rooms, he spotted the manuscript on the desk, next to the typewriter. He picked it up hesitantly, feeling like an intruder, then carried it into the living room, sat down, and began to read.

Isaac Schneider's long fingers deftly fed a swathe of silk fabric over the steel plate of his sewing machine, the needle rising and falling so rapidly its movement was a blur.